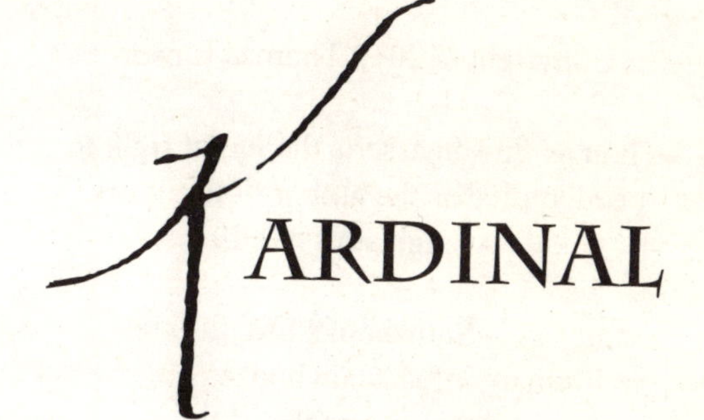

THOMAS EMSON

snowbooks

Proudly Published by Snowbooks in 2012

Snowbooks Ltd
email: info@snowbooks.com
www.snowbooks.com

British Library Cataloguing in Publication Data
A catalogue record for this book is available from the British Library.

Paperback:978-1-906727-32-1
Hardcover: 978-1-906727-24-6

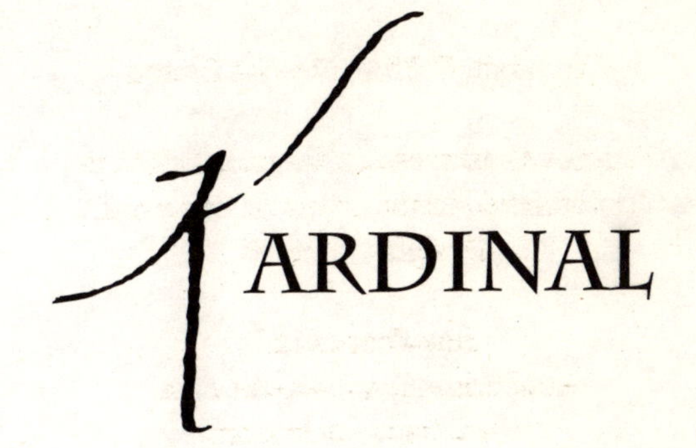

THOMAS EMSON

PART ONE.

AFTERMATH.

CHAPTER 1.
THE SHEPHERD AND THE CROFTER.

OUTER HEBRIDES, SCOTLAND – 5.01PM (GMT), NOVEMBER 28, 2016

"IF you would have asked me seven years ago," said the shepherd, "I would not have believed that vampires existed. Who would?"

The crofter shook his head. He had a shaven scalp and a heavy, black beard. It was a winter's evening, cold and gloomy, but he wore aviator-style sunglasses.

Scars criss-crossed the crofter's skull. Blood spattered his face. Although the temperature was barely above 4°C, he wore only a T-shirt. The material clung to his lean, powerful body, and muscles corded on his strong arms. His flesh was stained with gore. The smell of raw meat hung in the air.

"They said it was drugs that started it all," said the shepherd. He leaned on his crook. He scanned the landscape. It was barren. The crofter's cottage was the only building for miles. The shepherd's flock dotted the fields. He'd come out to check on them before nightfall. He was new to shepherding. Only a few months of experience, despite being in his sixties. He continued. "Some red pill at a nightclub in London. It is always London, isn't it, sir?"

"Always London," said the crofter.

He had a deep, quiet voice. The kind of voice you'd listen to. The kind that was laced with authority.

"You're a Londoner, sir?" said the shepherd. He plucked the red cloth from the breast pocket of his tweed jacket, and touched his forehead with it. His skin still itched after all these years. The fire had melted the flesh on the left side of his face. He'd suffered a great deal of pain. The anguish had caused him to lose a lot of weight over the past four years – he'd gone from eighteen stone to nine stone. "From the big city?"

The crofter nodded. He leaned against the doorway of his cottage. It was made of stone, a single-storey structure with a thatched roof. A fence enclosed the crofter's land. He had only a couple of acres. But on it he kept chickens, goats and a vegetable garden.

"You're far from home," the shepherd said.

"So are you," the crofter said.

The shepherd silently cursed himself – he'd been found out, he was sure of it. He tried to hide his discomfort. He was a disciplined man, so it was relatively easy to keep his feelings under wraps.

The Atlantic Ocean whispered in the distance. The shepherd's dog barked from his 4x4, parked outside the cottage gate. The crofter picked up a cane that was propped against the wall. It had a gold ferrule. He tapped it against his shoe in a menacing way.

"Safer here than in England," the shepherd said after a while. "But the plague reached these parts, too, you know."

Again the crofter nodded. The moonlight splintered off his sunglasses.

The shepherd had been watching him for a few weeks. The villagers had said he'd moved here four or five years ago. No one knew who he was. They'd not asked his name, and he'd not given it. They said he was a refugee from the wars between humans and vampires. Some said he *was* a vampire. Others said he was a villain. One of those Nebuchadnezzars who supported the undead.

As he was surveying his flock, the shepherd had seen the crofter skinning the animal in front of the cottage. He'd stopped the 4x4 and shouted, "Hello," from the gate, before entering the crofter's territory.

At first, the shepherd thought that either the crofter would go inside the cottage and shut the door, or he'd use the knife he wielded.

He'd done neither. He stood there, staring at the shepherd through those dark glasses.

Now the shepherd said, "They said that soldier chap was the hero."

"They said lots of things."

"One thing's for sure: London was in ruins. That war, five years ago. Fighting in the streets between humans and vampires. The government falling. Terrible business."

"Terrible… "

"And that soldier – hero one day, villain the next."

The crofter dipped his knife in a barrel of water.

"And they damn well poisoned the water in London, didn't they?" said the shepherd. "Awful thing to do. Making all those people dead and then alive again. Making them hunger for blood. Spreading the plague. What do you say to that, fellow?"

"I say nothing," said the crofter. He was wiping his hands on a cloth. The shepherd couldn't tell if the man was looking at him or not, the dark glasses hiding his eyes.

"Best to say nothing sometimes," said the shepherd. "There was a time you couldn't say a thing. Vampires everywhere. A dictatorship of the undead, someone called it, I think. And those Nebuchadnezzars listening at every door. Human scumbags, don't you think? Would you say? Quislings, eh? Looking for rebels or traitors. Like that soldier chap."

"I have to go now," said the crofter.

"Oh yes, very nice to meet you. I'm Ronan, by the way, Jim Ronan. What's your name?"

"Nice to meet you, Ronan," said the crofter, and he went into his cottage and closed the door.

CHAPTER 2.
THE VISITOR.

THE man using the name Jim Ronan drove home. He was sweating. The collie in the back seat whimpered. The dog sensed evil.

Night had fallen fully. Ronan had never minded the dark. Not before she came. But three days ago she had arrived.

He should have gone straight home from Meg's house in the village on that night. But they'd had an argument. He was fuming and needed a drink.

So he had dropped into The Sheep and Anchor and drank two pints of Guinness and four scotches.

He had staggered the two miles home. By the time he got back to the smallholding, it was after midnight. Cold and pitch black.

Staring towards the front door of his home, he felt queasy. His vision blurred. He blinked, trying to clear away the haziness. And trying to get rid of the two, tiny red spots glittering at head level near the door.

He swayed, feeling sick.

The red points blinked.

Like eyes, he thought. *Just like* –

Her voice was a blade, slicing through his bowels.

"He's here?" she said.

The shepherd whined. He dropped to his knees. Nausea swept over him. He bent his head and retched, his vomit splashing across his knees. It smelled like acid. He moaned and slowly looked up.

She stood over him. He quaked. She was beautiful and terrifying.

The surviving Nebuchadnezzars had spoken about her.

"One lives," they'd whispered in all the secret places where they were forced to meet. "One lives, and she'll bring us victory. She'll bring us Babylon."

And when the rumours of her existence proved to be true, he was sent north to Scotland on an errand. He was just a foot soldier these days. A grunt in the new army. Not so long ago, he was important, and he often pined for the days when he had wielded power.

Terror had clutched his heart. He dropped his gaze. His eyes fell on her bare foot. He didn't want to look at her face, but he couldn't help it. She was alluring. His gaze started up her leg. Her skin was smooth and dark. At her knee, the hem of a white gown fluttered. If he just dipped his head slightly, he would be able to see up her dress. Up, up…

He moaned, his groin aching.

"Is he here?" she said. "Look at me, shepherd."

He was scared but aroused. A terrible concoction. A dangerous one.

He looked up at her face. Her beauty chilled his blood. Crow-black hair cascaded down her shoulders, over her breasts. The tresses framed a picture-perfect face – high cheek bones, full lips, almond-shaped eyes.

The eyes, he thought. *Those awful eyes*.

Red like blood. Red in the blackness. Like two warning lights, alerting him to danger ahead.

She drew back her lips, and he saw her fangs.

His bladder nearly emptied there and then, but he managed to control himself.

"Stand," she told him.

He struggled to his feet. His legs felt weak and shaky. He instinctively reached out to stop himself from falling. But there was only her to hold on to. She hissed and swatted his arm away. His knees buckled, and he nearly fell flat on his face. But he managed to stay upright.

She tore the red cloth from the breast pocket of his jacket. She sniffed it, rubbing it against her face. He gawped. Every fable he'd heard told him she shouldn't be able to do that. She shouldn't be able to be near that ancient, scarlet flesh. She tossed the cloth aside.

"This is no protection from me," she said. "I didn't come from that flesh. I am new. I am young. I am strong. And you… you are weak. I don't need you. The new breed won't need humans at all. This time we won't be sharing power with you. All of you will be our slaves."

He whimpered.

"Is he here?" she had hissed.

Ronan tried to speak but just couldn't, so he nodded instead.

"Where?" she said.

He managed to tell her where he lived before adding, "But no one has seen him for weeks."

"Go to his house," she had told him. "Speak to him. Make sure it's him. I'll be back in three nights. If you do well, I'll give you a reward. You won't have to fuck sheep and old women again."

He groaned and came, without her laying a hand on him. He collapsed, and she swept away, sailing through the night until her white gown faded into darkness.

He parked the 4x4 in the farm yard.

I'll be back in three nights, she'd said.

Tonight was that night. She had promised him pleasure.

She might be dead, he thought, *but she was more alive than Meg and her stinking house and her smelly skin.*

He stepped out of the vehicle. His legs were weak. His throat was dry. The collie barked and whined, but Ronan didn't let him out. He didn't want the dog to die.

He stared towards the house, and she emerged out of the darkness like a ghost, her red eyes glittering, her white gown floating.

As she approached, he again felt dread and lust. He fell to his knees.

"You've found him?" she asked.

He nodded.

"It's him, you're sure?"

He nodded again.

"Good. I'll kiss you."

He nodded once more.

"Stand," she said.

He struggled to his feet.

She smelled of death – a beautiful odour. She raised her hand and held it in front of his face. It was supple and soft, the fingers long and lithe. The inch-long nails were sharp and painted red. Red like her eyes. Red like his blood. Her hand moved swiftly across his throat. He felt the nails rake his flesh. The hot blood gushed from his open vein. He became cold and weak very quickly. His blood sprayed across her dress, staining it. She laughed and massaged the blood into her gown. And the man who'd named himself Ronan died slowly and coldly.

PART TWO.

DREAMS.

CHAPTER 3.
BLOOD DEATH.

SOUTHERN CARPATHIANS, ROMANIA – 8.35PM (GMT + 2 HOURS), 16 MAY, 2011

SORIN and Ionuţ were hungry. They had not eaten in two nights. One more night without blood and they would die. This would be their last chance to find prey.

They had been huddling on the old railway station for a day and a night. The rain had poured. A fierce wind lashed the platform. Not even a lone guard supervised the station.

"I'm dying," Ionuţ said.

Sorin ignored him. His younger brother had been a pain in life, and now he was a pain in death.

"I've got to feed," said Ionuţ. "We've both got to feed, Sorin, or we'll die – we'll die at dawn."

Sorin was cold and shaky. His stomach ached.

Blood death was near.

They had to kill and drink blood in the next few hours, or they'd be dead at sunrise.

Sorin sniffed the air. Not a human scent anywhere. He thought of London and the food stocks there. It made him salivate.

The brothers had moved to England in 2005. They had always dreamed of coming to London. They supported Arsenal. They liked to speak English and particularly liked to swear. They wanted to go on *X-Factor* and become pop stars.

When they got there, they'd lived in Edmonton. It was rough and poor, and crime plagued the estates.

But the brothers did OK, starting a mobile disco service and making their way in the world. Not a long way. But enough to get by. Enough to rent a flat. Enough to buy food and beer.

But then the vampires came. And in February of that year, war broke out between humans and nosferatu. The brothers were killed by the undead and became alive again.

Soon after becoming vampires, they did what all vampires did – they started to home. They left England and followed their instincts, heading west across Europe, heading home to the Southern Carpathians.

"My chest is hurting," said Ionuţ as he cowered on the platform. "I'm going to die any minute, Sorin."

"No you're not. We've got plenty of time. We've got until dawn."

"I don't think I can make it."

"You will make it."

"Why isn't there any food?"

Sorin stayed quiet. His red eyes scanned the darkness. He could see in the night. The landscape was clear to him. The grey fields. The empty buildings. Geographically, he wasn't sure where they were. Instinctively, he knew – they were going home.

He heard a noise.

Ionuţ started to speak.

"Be quiet," Sorin told him. "Listen."

The rumble grew louder. Sorin felt the platform trembling.

He leapt to his feet and looked down the track.

"A train," he said.

"Will it stop?"

"How do I know?"

"It has to stop."

The train blared out a warning of its approach. Suddenly from the darkness, a powerful light appeared, momentarily blinding Sorin.

The train roared. It wasn't stopping. The station must have been abandoned years ago, Sorin realized. But that didn't matter. Only one thing mattered.

"Jump," he shouted at his brother.

They sailed off the platform and clamped themselves to the side of the speeding train.

Ionuţ whooped with glee.

Sorin felt the same exhilaration. There would be blood here. There would be food.

Holding on to the side of the carriage, he noticed that it was a freight train. No passengers, but still a driver and crew.

Still food.

Sorin crawled along the side of the train.

Being a vampire had changed him from a clumsy idiot into a lethal killing machine. It had given him the ability to leap and bound. The ability to hold on to the sides of buildings – and trains.

He'd never had so much fun in his life.

His human existence had been dull and boring. He was a geek. He never got girls. He was never one of the lads. But now, he was a powerful creature. He had planned to return to his home town and terrorize the bullies who had made his childhood miserable.

The thought of blood made his jaw ache. He clattered his teeth together, his instincts rehearsing the killing bite that would drive his fangs into a victim's jugular.

Ionuţ crawled after him along the side of the train as it hurtled through the night. Sorin slid open the trailer's door. He leapt inside, followed by his brother, who shut the door.

They were cast into darkness.

"Can you smell it?" said Ionuţ

Sorin said he could.

Ionuţ said, "Blood," and then louder, "There's a little human in here. A stowaway. Hey, you know what happens to stowaways?"

Ionuţ moved forward.

Sorin grabbed his arm.

"What, Sorin? There's blood here."

"Something's not right."

He scanned the darkness. The carriage was crammed with crates. It was electrical equipment. DVDs, TVs, Hi-Fis. Stuff that would have interested Sorin a few months ago. Stuff he didn't care about any more.

His belly stirred with fear. Something in the trailer made him cautious, uncomfortable – and there was nothing a vampire should really be scared of apart from the sun and…

It couldn't be, he thought.

Ionuţ was growing impatient, but Sorin said, "Can't you feel it?"

"Feel the hunger, that's what I feel."

"Just sense the atmosphere, Ionuţ."

The crates cast shadows. The train jerked and rattled.

Sorin smelled the air and surveyed the gloom.

There was a human here. He smelled it. Smelled the blood gushing through its veins. But there was something else. Something you couldn't smell or see or hear. Just something you could sense. Something a vampire could sense.

A warning. A threat. A red flag.

A red –

Sorin stiffened. Fear gripped him.

"He's one of them," he said.

"Them?" said his brother.

"He wears the mark. The red of the Nebuchadnezzars."

"No," said Ionuţ.

"He wears the flesh of our fathers."

"No, no… "

"Can't you sense it?"

"Yes, yes, but… "

Of course Ionuţ could sense it. Every vampire sensed it. It was part of their DNA. It was the source code. A fragment of flesh worn as a mark by their human allies. A fragment that came from Kea, Kakash, and Kasdeja, the vampire trinity that had given birth to all the undead that now prowled the earth.

Nebuchadnezzars, he thought. *If I could, I would kill them too.*

But that red mark protected them. That red mark told a vampire, *You die before laying a hand on this human, because this human is chosen.*

And he knew he couldn't attack a Nebuchadnezzar even if he wanted to – everything in his nature stopped him.

"Come out," Sorin called into the gloom. He could see everything in the darkness, his predator's eyes making it easy for him.

A figure reared up in the darkness. It was like a shadow creeping up the wall. The man stood in silhouette. He stood still. He was waiting.

Ionuţ hissed and cowered, probably sensing the mark on the human at last.

"We're hungry," said Sorin. "Will you give us a little of your blood, to tide us over?"

Some Nebuchadnezzars were willing to do that – give a few drops from their veins if a vampire was suffering. If blood death was near. The vampire would only take what it needed, leaving the Nebuchadnezzar still human.

The man said nothing.

Sorin grew angry. "Help us, you're a Neb."

The man stepped closer.

Sorin's belly cramped.

He saw the man more clearly now. Saw that he was armed. Armed with a weapon in each hand. Short swords made of ivory. Short swords made from the horns of –

Sorin lurched backwards, terrified.

The man glared at them. And in the darkness, one of his eyes glowed red.

CHAPTER 4.
SAVING BRITAIN.

WESTMINSTER, LONDON – 8.45PM (GMT), 16 MAY, 2011

ELIZABETH Wilson said, "It's Lawton who's responsible for this."

Christine Murray bristled but kept quiet

Wilson continued. "We can only assume he escaped because he's guilty."

"He didn't escape, Prime Minster – "

"Only interim Prime Minister. I haven't earned that title yet. Call me Liz, for God's sake."

Murray stared out of the window of the Millbank office building where Britain's interim government had its headquarters. The streets below were quiet. Only a few locals scurried through the darkness, eager to get indoors. Traffic was at a minimum. It was desolate.

Murray fought back the tears, biting her lip.

Across the street stood Victoria Tower Gardens. Dozens of refugees cowered under the trees. Refugees from the war between vampires and humans three months ago. A war that destroyed much of Westminster, including the Houses of Parliament.

Liz Wilson put her head in her hands. She had been Chancellor in the previous government, which had collapsed when the Prime Minister, Graeme Strand, was murdered.

His assassin was Jacqueline Burrows. Her method was vampires. She was a Nebuchadnezzar, a descendant of the Babylonian king of the same name who ruled alongside the undead.

Burrows was a minister in Strand's government, and after his death she'd taken over the party and the country. She'd imprisoned Strand's supporters, including Wilson. She'd installed her allies in positions of power and unleashed vampires on the streets of Britain.

But fortunately the humans had fought back. They drove the vampires into the shadows. Burrows and many of her cohorts had been killed. The other Nebs had disappeared.

Until now.

George Fuad was back. He was challenging Wilson in Thursday's General Election.

Her head still in her hands, Wilson said, "I don't know who to trust, Christine."

Wilson was forty-eight. She had once been regarded as a political high-flier. Any hopes she'd had of power were gone. Now she was a shell of a woman, trying to hold together a shell of a country. Her hair was prematurely grey, and on her face lines mapped the journey she had taken from bright, new MP in 1987, to stressed leader in 2011.

Wilson said, "I'd have him arrested if I knew where he was hiding."

Murray couldn't stay quiet any more.

"He's the only one who's been fighting this from the start. He was there three years ago when that pill made the first vampires. He has sacrificed so much. He doesn't have to do this. He has no family. He owes Britain nothing. The country drummed him out of the army and turned him into a villain – "

"With your considerable help, Christine."

Murray felt ashamed. It was true. In 2004, she had been an ambitious freelance journalist who'd neglected her husband and two sons. She had heard about a soldier being kicked out the British Army after allegedly killing an innocent civilian in Iraq. It was when the Iraq War had been hugely unpopular. Papers and politicians were looking for scapegoats. Every day the press was publishing photos and stories of prisoner abuse. One stupid editor in the UK had even printed fake images of a soldier pissing on an Iraqi prisoner. He'd been so desperate to jump on the bandwagon. Everyone was desperate.

Even Murray.

She'd pursued Jake Lawton relentlessly, demanding he be charged with murder.

Then two things had happened. First, she realized Lawton was innocent. His victim had been a suicide bomber targeting a busy mosque packed with worshippers. Second, with the unleashing of the vampire plague in 2008, Lawton was the only one who supported Murray and helped her fight the undead and their human allies.

During the past three years, Murray had lost her husband and eldest son, and her youngest boy, David, was missing. He was angry and resentful towards his mother and apparently unleashing his rage on vampires.

"I know," she told Wilson. "I know, but I was wrong, and you are wrong too."

"Where is he?"

"I don't know. Somewhere in Europe."

After the battle in Westminster in February, Murray, David, Lawton, and Kwan Mei, the Chinese girl who'd led an army of migrants against the vampires, fled Britain by boat. They were going to Iraq. To Ancient Babylon. They were going to kill a myth. They were going to kill Nimrod, the Great Hunter, creator of all vampires.

Kill him, and all vampires die.

That was their incentive.

But Lawton had been badly injured in the battle. He'd lost an eye. He was a determined man, however. He already had five bullets in his body. Losing an eye wouldn't stop him.

When they arrived at Rotterdam, they had been stopped by Dutch police. The rest of Europe was nervous about the plague blighting Britain. After the government fell and Burrows took over, the UK's European Union allies had closed their borders. Many British citizens had tried to escape, mostly by boat. But when they reached mainland Europe, they were turned back. The Dutch sent David, Kwan Mei and Murray back to Britain. But Lawton escaped. Murray could only hope that he'd got away, that he was still alive.

"Heading to Iraq to kill Nimrod," she said. "That's where I hope he is."

Wilson sneered. "Nimrod, indeed. Just a fairy story."

"Like vampires were three years ago, Liz."

Wilson glared at her. "Maybe we should listen to Fuad."

"Absolutely not."

"Maybe we can live side by side with the vampires, like he says."

"We can't do that, Liz. They hunt us. They kill us. It's what they do."

"Fuad says not."

"Fuad lies. Tell him to walk into a room of vampires without that red rag he carries."

"You have one, too," said Wilson, indicating the scrap of red material clipped to Murray's lapel. It protected her from vampire attacks. Lawton had given it to her three years ago, after stealing it from a Nebuchadnezzar he'd killed.

"We should speak to Fuad."

"Are they your kids?" said Murray, gesturing to the photos on the wall behind Wilson's desk. The other woman nodded. Murray went on. "Fuad wants power. He wants vampires on the streets of London. He wants to be king. He's not going to share anything with anyone, and he won't want vampires to live side by side with the rest of us. How can you live side by side with something that wants to kill you, that wants to destroy your way of life?"

"We don't know that they want to."

"Have you not been in Britain for the past three years?"

"I have, and it's your fault – "

"My – "

"Lawton. His fault." She was lashing out. Trying to find someone to blame. "If he hadn't been so aggressive, Christine, if he hadn't attacked the vampires, they might not have felt the need to defend themselves. It's humans who have instigated this war."

"This is Fuad talking."

"Yes it is. I'm desperate. I don't know what to do. There are organizations now advocating the protection of vampires. Do you know that? Would you believe it? All the time. It's the same lot. The same bunch supporting every lunatic cause. Any chance to attack authority and… and Western liberal democracy, if such a thing exists any more. Conspiracy theorists and extremists."

Murray was dumbstruck. *Protecting vampires?* she thought.

"Britain lies in ruins," said Wilson. "The evil is spreading. I want to curb it. If that means aligning with Fuad, I'll do it. I'll do it to save Britain."

"The only thing," said Murray, "that can save Britain is Jake Lawton. He's out there somewhere fighting for us, for no reason at all other than his humanity. We've given him nothing. We've abandoned him and treated him like a criminal. But still he stands on the frontline. Still he takes blows for us. He bleeds for us. If you can't stand behind him, Prime Minster, why don't you stand in front of him?"

CHAPTER 5.
LORD OF HELL.

SOUTHERN CARPATHIANS, ROMANIA – 8.49PM (GMT + 2 HOURS), 16 MAY, 2011

JAKE Lawton stood in the shadows. A few feet away, the vampires cowered. The train hurtled along the track. Moonlight speared into the trailer from the gap above the door.

Lawton gripped the Spear of Abraham. Legend said the weapon had been forged thousands of years before by Abraham, from the horns of Nimrod, god of the undead. Lawton didn't know if the legend was true or not. What he did know was that the artefact was effective in killing vampires.

He'd pulled the two horns that formed the double-pointed spear apart, so now he held a short, bone-bladed sword in each hand. One blade for each vampire in the trailer.

Lawton had been trying to sleep. He'd been trying to sleep for eight years. It had become virtually impossible, so for many years he'd not even bothered trying.

But in the past couple of months he'd started to nod off briefly. And during those moments of slumber, he'd been dreaming.

Dreams that made him wake up sweating. Dreams he wanted to dream again.

One of the vampires whispered, "It's him… "

The other said, "Is… is it you?"

"Might be," said Lawton.

"You are not him. You have the red mark," said one of the vampires. "You're a Nebuchadnezzar. Help us."

"I'll help you – by putting you out of your misery."

The vampires hissed.

Lawton steeled himself. He had to be careful. The vampires were strong and quick – stronger and quicker than him. But they were afraid of him. Afraid because they thought he was Jake Lawton.

Lord of Hell they called him. He turned vampires into ashes.

But they were also wary of him because he carried the mark. The skin of the vampire trinity.

But Lawton did not wear the red mark around his wrist or clipped to his shirt. It was part of his body. It was *in* his body.

Three months earlier, he'd lost his left eye while fighting a monster forged from Kakash, Kasdeja and a vampire called Nadia Radu.

He destroyed the creature as the Houses of Parliament burned.

Lawton and his companions had fled across the English Channel.

Murray, David, Kwan Mei, and the yacht's owner were sent home to Britain after they'd been captured. Lawton escaped.

Trying to keep a low profile, he lived as a beggar on the streets of Rotterdam for a week. Every day he washed his wounded eye to prevent it from becoming infected. It was a terrible injury, one that needed hospital treatment. But he couldn't turn up at a hospital. Everyone was looking for him. He'd be returned to the UK immediately. And then he'd have to start again in his quest to reach Iraq. On the streets of Rotterdam, he listened, he watched, and although he couldn't understand Dutch, it soon became clear that Holland and its European neighbours had shut their borders. They were battling to keep out the vampire plague blighting Britain. But viruses crept through the tiniest pores. And inevitably, vampire attacks were being reported on the continent.

The news roused dread in Lawton's heart. There was no escaping the undead. Soon they would vanquish Europe. And what then? Clutching the red mark tightly to protect himself from vampires, Lawton had visited a glassmaker.

They made him an ocular prosthesis. A glass eye. It contained the skin of the vampires. He paid with the last of his money. He'd fixed the eye in its socket. The eye settled. Lawton blinked. Then he'd suffered a strange sensation – he felt the eye shift, as if it were alive. The glass fixture was not completely sealed. There was a pinprick of a hole at the back of the globe, to ensure the material was oxygenated. Lawton thought if it shrivelled, it would no longer protect him.

But viruses crept through the tiniest pores.

That night, with his prosthesis in place, he surprisingly fell asleep – and he dreamed.

He dreamed in red.

He dreamed of red tentacles spewing from a black heart.

He dreamed of the tentacles coiling around him.

He dreamed of them penetrating him, sliding into his mouth and down his throat.

He dreamed of them pushing up his nose, snaking into his ears.

He dreamed of them looping around his bones.

He dreamed of them slithering over his brain.

He dreamed of them poisoning him and changing him.

And he'd woken up sweating, his head throbbing.

"Don't kill us," said one of the vampires now.

Lawton ignored the creature's plea.

He was quick.

The vampires shrieked.

They tried to claw at the door.

Lawton got the first one through the back, piercing its black heart with the tusk.

The other creature turned. Horror etched its face. It hissed, its fangs reflecting the fire spraying off its disintegrating companion.

Lawton drove his sword deep into the second vampire's chest. Arteries of fire raced along its body. Smoke puffed from its hair. Its face started to melt. Flesh burned away. Bone went to cinders.

And the vampire became dust.

Lawton stood in the shadows, and he felt something he'd never felt before when he stood over the remains of the undead – he felt grief.

CHAPTER 6.
BRANDED A TRAITOR.

LAWTON had sneaked on the freight train in Rotterdam. He didn't know its destination, but he knew it passed through Romania. And that was all the information he needed.

Romania.

Tălmaciu.

Where the Sadu and the Cibin rivers meet.

For some reason, he knew he had to go there.

Someone was waiting for him.

Someone who would help him in his quest.

Someone who had spoken to him in his dreams.

He kicked at the remains of the vampires and retreated to his corner again. He curled up under a blanket and tried to go back to sleep, tried to go back to his dreams.

Three months ago, when he'd arrived in Rotterdam, there was only one thing on Lawton's mind.

Kill Nimrod.

He'd planned to travel to Hillah, in Iraq, near where the ancient ruins of Babylon lay, find out if the god of vampires was real – and then kill him.

It would end the war.

It would wipe out the plague.

When Nimrod died, so would the undead borne of his unholy children, Kea, Kakash, and Kasdeja.

Waiting for sleep, Lawton realized that three years ago, he would never have believed in vampires or gods.

But now he'd believe anything just to bring an end to this hell.

When it was all finished, he and Aaliyah could be together. They would find somewhere quiet. They would live simply. They might make a family. If so, they would bring them up in a world without fear, a world where monsters didn't lurk in the shadows, where predators didn't hunt you for your blood.

Aaliyah, he thought. His heart wrenched. He missed her desperately. She was so much more than a lover – she was his ally, his comrade. She was fearless in the face of the undead. If he thought prayer would work, he would have said a few words and asked God to keep her safe.

Aaliyah had left for Iraq with Apostol Goga. They had gone to find and kill Nimrod. But Lawton had argued they should first make sure Britain was safe. He and Aaliyah had fallen out. She wanted to destroy the vampire god.

"Destroy him, and every vampire will die," Goga had said.

"Destroy him, and we can be together," said Aaliyah.

But Lawton couldn't abandon his country.

He'd chosen to stay and fight monsters.

Now, he couldn't sleep, so he rolled himself a cigarette.

His body ached. Years of fighting had taken their toll. Five bullets were lodged in his body from his days as a soldier. Scars covered his body. Broken bones had healed badly and ached permanently. And now he had lost his eye.

Every bullet, every scar, had been taken for his country.

But how had his country repaid him?

By branding him a traitor.

So what? he thought. *I've always been blamed.*

When he was in the army, he'd fought for his mates – not for Queen or country. And that's what he would do now. Fight for his friends. Fight for Aaliyah.

He shut his eyes and wished he could dream of them together in a cottage in the middle of nowhere.

But that dream would not come.

Another came in its place.

A dream of a derelict church. Fire burned in the fields surrounding it. A forest of stakes was silhouetted against the flame-red skyline. Thousands of figures writhed on the poles. Screams filled the night. But through the baying came another voice. A sound like honey. A velvet voice.

"*Voivode... voivode... voivode...*"

The voice came from the ruins of the church. Deep in the bowels of the dilapidated building. It called to Lawton. It wanted him to come. And although his head told him that it was only a dream, and meant nothing, his heart said differently. And it was his heart that won the day.

Lawton got to his feet. He dropped the cigarette and crushed it underfoot. He gathered his things quickly. It was time to get off the train and follow his dream to Tălmaciu.

CHAPTER 7.
BROTHERLY LOVE.

HILLAH, IRAQ – 12.01AM (GMT + 3 HOURS), 17 MAY, 2011

ALFRED Fuad wore a black-and-white chequered shemagh, which covered his head, his mouth, and his nose. He shivered against the chill. Nights got cold here. And the pre-fabricated units they had used to construct their camp on the outskirts of the town didn't really protect against plummeting temperatures.

Alfred was sitting behind the desk in his unit. He yawned and looked at his watch. Just gone 3.00am. In Britain, it was midnight. *Vampire time*, he thought.

He fired up his laptop and logged on to Skype.

He pulled the shemagh away from his mouth so he could speak, but it was his brother who spoke first.

"Who do you think you are, Lawrence of Arabia?" said George Fuad, his image slightly distorted on the computer's screen.

Alfred baulked. He loved his brother but hated him just as much. Sometimes he wished him dead. Sometimes he dreamed of being the only Fuad.

They were twins, born in 1946 to a half-Arab father and an English mother.

“Take that thing off,” said George. “You look like a fucking Arab.”

“I am a fucking Arab.”

“You’re a quarter Arab, Alfred. You’re not Sheikh Abdul Abulbul, you know. Remember that? Carry On Camel? What a laugh.” His smile faded, and he was suddenly serious. “You found Nimrod yet?”

Peeling the shemagh from his head, Alfred said, “Not yet. Still digging. It’s deep, George. How’s it going at home?”

“Election on Thursday. Should romp it. Got a rally in Hyde Park later on. Thousands of idiots bound to turn out to lick my arse. People are so stupid. They hate their own country. They’re so easy to manipulate.”

“I’d love to hear your speeches, George.”

“They’re cracking, I’m telling you. Full of Lawton-bashing. Blaming the bastard for everything. I’m saying, ‘Vampires want to live peacefully, side-by-side with us humans.’ Nice, eh? The message is *each to his own*, that kind of thing.”

“They fall for it?”

“Hook, line and sinker, son,” said George. “I say to them, ‘The enemy within is your own government and the people who attack vampires without reason.’ And they say, ‘Good for you, George, we’ll vote vampire,’ or words to that effect.”

“You think we’ll win the election?”

“We’ll storm it, mate. Our dream of Babylon is coming true. How far are you from Nimrod?”

“I don’t know, George.”

“You didn’t know last week, neither, Alfred.”

“And I might not know next week.”

“Know quickly. We need him.”

Alfred stared at his brother’s hard, cruel face. Unlike his twin, George was clean shaven and wore his hair much shorter. Alfred now ruffled his own long tresses, which were dusty and greasy.

He said, "How do we know he won't just kill us all?"

"You got the red mark, ain't you?" said George.

Alfred studied the scarlet-coloured strip of skin before using it to tie his hair into a ponytail.

Alfred said, "But Nimrod's supposed to be the creator of all vampires. He made the Trinity. He made Kea, Kakash, and Kasdeja. Maybe this mark means nothing to him."

"Maybe, maybe, maybe, Alfie. Just get going with your dig. You got the government on board?"

"The Iraqi State Organization for Heritage and Antiquities is now officially sanctioning us."

"Good fella, Alfred."

"They think we're looking for artefacts."

"You are. How's it looking at the site?"

"We're sixty-two miles south of Baghdad. A few miles outside Hillah, in the desert. And we've built a town, basically. These ex-Royal Engineers Howard Vince hired are incredible. We're corralling the dig area. We've got security fencing, armed guards. We've got our industrial drill going down deeper into the desert every day. If this is the site of Babylon, and if the stories are true, then we will find Nimrod, George, I promise you, mate. But we're not finding anything at the moment. And it makes me think there is nothing to find."

"You were always impatient, son," said George.

That was a lie. George was the impatient one. The one who wanted things yesterday. Alfred could wait. He was the cat. Stealthy and patient. George was the dog. *I want it now*. But Alfred didn't say anything. No use arguing with George. He was on a high.

Alfred's cover in Iraq was that of a British archaeologist. His team were students and researchers, fellow archaeologists – "and a few security personnel, of course."

But apart from the security team and the labour, everyone was a Nebuchadnezzar.

It was exciting for them to be where Babylon had stood. It was where their ancestor Nebuchadnezzar had built a golden empire. He had forged an alliance with the undead. They were his army. He was their provider. They gave him victories over his enemies. He gave them slaves to feed on.

"We're getting close," said George, breaking Alfred's train of thought. George's eyes were glazed over. He looked like he was on drugs. He said, "Our grandfather came to Britain in 1900, escaping the Ottomans. He brought our history with him and handed it down to us, Alfie. Our heritage is in that earth under your feet. The bones of our people. The blood of our ancestors. The cardinal of our church. Find him. Find him so he can lead us in worship, Alfie. He can lead us to glory. He can anoint me king and you prince. We can rule the world with this new religion, Alfred. Don't you want to rule the world?"

Before he could answer, someone knocked on the door of his unit, and, without waiting for an answer, two men entered.

Alfred signed off from his brother, pledging to contact him later in the day.

And then he turned to greet his visitors.

CHAPTER 8. THE GENERAL AND THE MERCENARY.

THE two men who entered Alfred's office uninvited were JJ Laxman and Howard Vince.

Laxman was in his fifties. He was a bear of a man. His coal-black hair was peppered with sand. He had a thick, black beard. A scar ran across his bronzed forehead, the result of a domestic. His wife had thrown an iron at him.

He ran White Light Ops, a private security firm. He was an ex-Royal Marine who'd seen action during the first Gulf War in the early 1990s and in the Falklands and Northern Ireland.

The other man was General Howard Vince, the former Chief of the General Staff in the UK. Vince was fat. To Alfred, he looked a little bit like Tony Soprano but lacked the Mafioso's menace. For someone who had been a soldier, Vince didn't look like he could fight his way out of a nursery school, let alone a hostile country – but apparently that's what he had done in the Lebanon in the 1980s. He was part of a special forces team who'd gone into Beirut to find and rescue British hostages. The mission failed. The troops had to flee. Although it was never made public, the story Alfred heard said Vince and two colleagues had fought off fifty armed men.

As Laxman gave his daily security report, one thing was certain about Vince – he had grown to hate the mercenary, despite hiring him in the first place. Tensions between them had grown in the few months they had worked together on Alfred's project.

White Light Ops, Laxman's organization, came highly recommended. Vince and the mercenary fought together in the 1991 Gulf War.

Alfred had told Vince, "I need a man who would kill his own grandmother and not feel bad about it afterwards."

Vince had said, "I know just the fellow."

Alfred had said, "Whoever you hire, Howard, will be killed when this is done. If we find Nimrod, he'll demand a sacrifice – and Laxman and his mugs are the perfect meat and potatoes for a hungry god."

Laxman, sounding bored, was giving his security update: "No new security threats in Hillah or the surrounding area. All quiet in the region since the car bomb that killed 45 here in May last year. That's your lot."

Alfred grunted. Laxman left.

Vince said, "How close are we?"

Alfred scanned an Excel spreadsheet on his desktop. It was a report from his site supervisor detailing the depth they had reached. After studying the document for a few seconds he said, "Let's go over to the site, take a look."

Outside, the temperature had dropped. It was the middle of the night. It seemed to be the time when they worked best. Nebs liked the night, it was said, because they enjoyed seeing the vampires going about their killing.

The Euphrates streamed past the camp, and her tumbling waters filled the air with a great whooshing sound. Her roar dominated the pre-dawn silence. She made Alfred think about Eden. The Euphrates ran from the first garden. She had been there at the beginning, her waters quenching the thirst of the earliest civilizations – and now a new civilization would drink from her waters. Alfred felt excited.

They made their way along a terrace of pre-fab units. Floodlights illuminated the whole site. A pair of Laxman's mercenaries strolled by.

They looked mean. Gorilla big. Faces creased with contempt. But they made him feel safe. They were the best comfort blanket he'd ever known.

They came to a high wire fence gate. A warning written in English, French, and Arabic said trespassers would be shot. An armed guard stood at the gate. Alfred and Vince flashed their IDs. Even though the guards recognized them, Laxman had ordered everyone to carry and show ID at all times.

Alfred's excitement grew as he walked through the gate. Up ahead in the earth was a large hole, which had the circumference of a circus ring. The great drill towered above it. The machine was silent now. But in a few hours it would churn into the ground again.

Alfred and Vince reached the tape that marked the edge of the hole. They stared down. Alfred was tempted to scale the metal ladders attached to the side of the pit, and descend. He would tear through the earth with his hands to find Nimrod.

It was as if Vince had read his thoughts.

"Do you think he exists, Alfred?"

"Did you think vampires existed?"

"Always. Since my father told me."

"And you believed what your father told you?"

"Why wouldn't I believe I'm descended from a king? What a dream to have, to be regal. We have royal blood in our veins."

"That's one thing, but to believe in the undead is another."

"Which you do – and I think you believe in Nimrod, too. Otherwise, you wouldn't be here."

Alfred gazed into the abyss where a god lurked. He did believe it. And he believed that the god would bend to his will.

"There are creatures in this world that we know nothing about," his father had told him and George once. "And those creatures are ours to control. They are vampires, boys. Night creatures. Immortal beings that live on human blood."

As a nine year old, the story had filled him with dread. But his dad had told him and his brother they had nothing to fear from vampires. They were the masters of the undead, he'd said, "and one day, lads, you will be kings."

"I hope you can control this thing if he's down there," said Vince.

"Of course we can. We need each other."

Alfred listened to his own words but suddenly wasn't convinced by them.

Why would a god need him?

He stared into the chasm. His belly heaved. He had the feeling that something was watching him.

CHAPTER 9.
SPIES.

"WHAT can you see?" said Aaliyah Sinclair.

Apostol Goga trained the powerful binoculars on the camp in the distance. The former Romanian security officer said nothing. Aaliyah shivered and pulled the cloak tighter around her shoulder. It was getting really cold. The temperature dropped to about nine degrees centigrade at night, sometimes lower. She was tired and wanted to sleep. But Goga insisted on holding a round-the-clock watch on Alfred Fuad's camp.

They were crouching on the flat roof of a house on the outskirts of the town called Hillah. They had rented the property. It was built of compressed mud bricks, which had been whitewashed. The landscape around them was mostly green. It was nourished by the Euphrates.

About three miles away, Fuad had started to dig. His makeshift camp stood out in the darkness. Huge floodlights pointed quite clearly to the site. Fuad wasn't worried about people knowing where he was. He had the authorities on his side. *He had duped them, probably*, thought Aaliyah.

She nudged Goga. "Did you hear me?"

"I am watching," he said, eyes still fixed to the binoculars perched on a tripod. Goga had attached a night-vision lens on the equipment, so he could spy on Fuad after dark.

"All right," said Aaliyah. "Let me look."

She elbowed the Romanian out of the way. He grunted. Aaliyah pressed her eyes to the lens. She recoiled. The magnification was powerful. She could see the camp clearly. The single-storey structures covered a considerable area. Above them, the floodlights towered, spilling down their powerful beams. Vehicles were parked to the west of the site. Aaliyah clocked gleaming 4x4s and an Army truck.

The whole site had been constructed in less than a day by a team of military personnel. The equipment had been shipped from Dubai, and Aaliyah and Goga had tracked it after they'd arrived in the region. Soon after their arrival in Iraq, countries started to close their borders to anyone travelling from Britain. Governments were worried about the vampire plague. But what Fuad planned to dig out of the earth near Hillah sounded much worse than vampires.

Perhaps Goga had been right

"Forget Britain," he'd told them all. "Britain is doomed now. You have to save the rest of the world. Find and destroy the god of vampires. Kill Nimrod, and every vampires dies."

Aaliyah fell for Goga's pitch. She had a future planned with Jake. A future without death and blood. Dreams of Jake and her living an idyllic life. And Goga's promise of a world without vampires made that future possible. So she'd abandoned Jake. She'd turned her back on him so they could be together. So she could live her dream.

But Jake had wanted to stay and fight for Britain, not fight for them – for her and him. Her heart ached. Maybe he didn't love her like she loved him. Maybe he didn't see the same future she did.

And now, to make matters worse, there were rumours that he was dead.

The idea made her sick. Life without Lawton would be meaningless.

But they were only rumours, she kept telling herself. She would remain hopeful until someone showed her his dead body. Because until you knew for sure that Jake Lawton was dead, you couldn't believe it. She'd seen him go through hell. She'd seen him fight monsters. She'd seen him survive impossible odds. He was alive, she was sure of it. Alive and coming for her.

"What are we going to do?" she asked Goga. "Let's tell the authorities."

"They are aligned with Fuad. He has tricked them. We have to do this ourselves."

"Just you and me?"

"Who else is there?"

"If we wait, Jake will come."

"We cannot wait for him," said Goga. "Fuad will not wait. Nimrod will not wait."

"We can't on our own – "

"It is not only Jake Lawton who can kill monsters."

He put on a pair of aviator-style sunglasses and strode towards the stairs running down the side of the house. He slung his black cane over his shoulder as he descended. His footsteps were heavy and angry.

CHAPTER 10.
THE RALLY.

HYDE PARK, LONDON – 6PM (GMT), 17 MAY, 2011

GEORGE Fuad put his feet up on the table in his trailer.

He gazed up at the flat-screen TV bracketed to the wall, and he smiled.

The smile became a chuckle. The chuckle became a laugh. The laugh nearly threw him off his couch.

The TV screen showed 10,000 people crammed into Hyde Park. They had come to the rally to hear him speak.

Members of George's United Party mingled with the crowds. You could spot them. They carried large white banners, emblazoned with a red U. The flag bearers were mostly Nebuchadnezzars. But other citizens were joining the campaign. *People are picking the winning side*, thought George. They could see what was going to happen, and they didn't want to be on the wrong side come the revolution.

George got up and poured himself a drink. He gazed out of the trailer window. It was a bright day over London. Hyde Park wasn't what it used to be. The grass was overgrown. There was litter everywhere. The gates and fences were rusted and broken. The buildings were boarded up. But at least today it offered glimpses of its former glory – it was packed with people. People who had come to hear him lie to them.

He laughed.

The locals loved a good lie.

He rubbed his chest proudly. He felt strong and powerful. The world was within his grasp. Three months ago, he had been convinced his dream was over. Vampires and humans had battled in the streets of London.

And humans, it seemed, had won the day.

They had fought back as vampires over-ran the streets.

They had fought back as poisoned water turned more of them into the undead.

They had fought back as the Nebuchadnezzars had Britain in their clutches.

They had driven the vampires back into the shadows. They forced the Nebuchadnezzars into hiding. They reclaimed Britain.

But the country was ruined.

And the excitement of victory over the vampires quickly faded. The interim government's honeymoon period hadn't lasted long. Soon, the people were in revolt again. They were fed up of having no jobs, no food, no water.

And George stepped into the breach.

He saw how desperate people were. He saw their anger. They were looking for someone to blame for the vampire plague and for their miserable lives.

So George gave them someone.

"It is people like Jake Lawton," he'd said in an early broadcast, "who have brought this misery upon us. Many say he's the hero. But that's a lie. He is the villain. He is the aggressor. He angered vampires who had innocently appeared in Britain. He attacked them. And what do you do when you are attacked? You fight back. What would you do?"

Thinking back to that speech, he smiled. He took a sip of his drink and swilled it in his mouth. A speaker had taken the podium. Her voice echoed through the sound system. Checking the programme on his desk, George saw that she was called Leeza Dervish. She used to be an anti-war campaigner. She was an anti-*anything* campaigner, as long as it meant opposing America or Britain, or Western principles such as capitalism and democracy.

Just my kind of girl, thought George.

"Jake Lawton's a killer," Dervish was saying. "He was part of the occupying forces in Iraq, who killed thousands of innocent Iraqis" – she was really shrieking into the microphone – "and now that he's killed enough humans, he's turning on another species – a rare, beautiful species. A species that is related to us, that is almost us. An ancient species that has the same rights to this earth as we do. This man Lawton is not a hero. Support the United Party. Bring vampires and humans together."

The crowd roared its approval.

George laughed and thought what idiots they were.

This was going like a dream.

It was so easy to dupe people. When they were desperate, they would believe anything. When their hate burned strongly, all you had to do was stoke it gently.

Dervish continued to speak: "What if Lawton's victims were gay or black or women? Then we would be up in arms. Then we would join forces against his fascism. I say vampires are the new oppressed. They are the new victims of Western imperialism. I say stand up for the vampire. Stand up against the Jake Lawtons of this world. Stand with the U.P. and George Fuad."

The crowd was in a frenzy. Their cheers washed across Hyde Park.

Someone knocked on the door, and a pretty blonde head appeared. "Five minutes, Mr Fuad."

"Thank you, Jade," said George. "You want to come in here and speak to me for a few minutes?"

"I'm actually quite busy, Mr – "

"I said, come in here and speak to me for a few minutes, Jade."

She was a slim, pretty thing, aged about twenty. She had pale skin and bright blue eyes and was delicate. George liked them delicate. They snapped more easily.

He smiled at her. "Now then," he said, starting to undo his chinos. "I want to go over a few things with you before I wow the crowds."

Jade quailed. "No, please don't make me – "

"You know what'll happen to you, Jade." He grabbed her arm, and with his other hand plucked at the protective red mark on her collar. "I'll throw you to the vampires, darling. And without this, you know what'll happen to your pretty little veins, don't you? There, now. Seeing sense. Down you go, darling." George put his hand on her head and pushed her down.

After he was finished with Jade, her lips were bleeding, and blood and semen were smeared across her mouth. He gripped her chin and looked at her pretty, soiled face. He liked the mess he'd made of her. He slapped her gently across the cheek and said, "Go fuck someone else – make yourself useful."

After he'd dismissed her, George pulled on his jacket and adjusted his tie. Outside, a voice boomed from the sound system: "And our next speaker needs no introduction… "

Nerves suddenly gripped him. It always happened moments before he had to speak publicly. He wasn't used to it. George had preferred to be in the background, planning and conspiring. But over the past few years, a real hunger for power had burned in him. Still, speaking to thousands of people made his balls shrivel.

His old mate Bernard Lithgow would have been good at this. Lithgow was smarmy and sly. He was a barrister, skilled at lying in front of an audience. But that bastard Lawton had killed him while Lithgow was trying to poison the London water system with vampire DNA produced by Dr Afdal Haddad. It was the old doctor who had gathered all the Nebuchadnezzars together in the first place. He'd produced Skarlet, the pill that created the first London vampires in 2008. But Haddad showed a lack of vision. He only wanted to rule Britain. George wanted to rule the world. And no one was going to stand in his way. His plan was to control a vampire army, and leading them would be Nimrod.

He mentally urged his brother to get a move on and excavate the Great Hunter.

Make our dreams come true, *Alfred*, he thought.

In Hyde Park, the crowd cheered when the announcer said George's name. He left his trailer and strolled along the wooden walkway towards the stage area. The noise of the crowd grew. It made George shudder with excitement. By the time he walked on to the stage, the noise was like thunder, and it seemed to shake the whole earth.

George lifted his hands to greet the crowd.

They cheered even louder.

He loved politics.

CHAPTER 11.
THE SPEECH.

GEORGE lapped up the welcome. The crowd cheered. Banners flapped. There was one depicting George as Christ, with long hair and a beard, a serene expression on his face, a halo crowning his head, and awed kids at his feet.

He nearly burst out laughing.

Fools, he thought.

He came to the microphone and quieted the crowd, thanking them for the welcome. The day grew darker. Night was coming. The time of vampires.

He scanned the area.

Outside the park perimeter, police loitered. They mingled uncomfortably with the black-clad Nebuchadnezzar militia George had formed "to protect humans and vampires". The militia sported the red flesh of the vampire trinity on their uniforms to protect them from the undead.

Police and government had opposed the militia when it was formed. But George argued they were necessary to keep the peace.

The police, he claimed, had been infiltrated by supporters of the "Lawtonites". They were sympathetic, he said, to Jake Lawton and the foreign gangs that had led the war against the vampires in February.

As soon as George started to speak, the crowd was in awe. These people were looking for a saviour. They were desperate. You could spin them any old yarn, and if you told them you were going to transform their lives, they'd believe it. George merely told the people what they wanted to hear, and a few things they needed to hear. He started now on the "vampires are our friends" speech.

"We destroyed their country. How would you feel if someone destroyed ours? Remember, the vampires are only defending themselves. We are the aggressors. Not them. They are defenders. But the truth, the truth that has been hidden from you by the authorities, is that we can live side by side with vampires. This is what the vampires want. They don't want to harm us. It is true, some people have tried to manipulate the species for their own ends. There were malign forces who distributed drugs some years ago, creating a violent sub-species of vampire. And only this year, as you all know, London's water network was poisoned. It has caused much illness, many deaths, and terrible suffering. But the men who committed these criminal acts, the men who poisoned your children's drinking water, are allied with the likes of the murderer Jake Lawton and the illegal immigrant Kwan Mei and her army of foreign invaders."

The crowd cheered.

George nodded and looked mournful. But inside he was laughing – at his own lies and how the crowd fell for them. He could almost taste the power. He salivated. His heart thundered and his loins simmered. He'd have to pay that Jade girl a visit when he got off the stage. He felt violently excited and wanted to run riot on her body.

"On Thursday, in just two days, Britain votes for a new government. The country is in ruins, brought to its knees by aggressors like Jake Lawton – who has now abandoned these shores – and cowards like Elizabeth Wilson, who has allowed this violence to spread. They have fed you lies. They have led you into an illegal war against a unique species. I say it again: we can live side by side with vampires. Human and vampires are biological cousins. Only a little DNA separates us. They, like every other living thing, have a right to share this earth with us. We protect pandas and polar bears, and today I say: let's protect the vampire."

More cheers came from the crowd. The night approached. Vampires stirred in their hiding places.

"I dream of a Britain," continued Fuad, "where vampire and human live side by side. They don't want to kill us. They don't want to feed on us. They are our friends. They have emotions like we do. They love. They feel fear. They feel anger. They want to protect their kind, like we do. So, on Thursday, I urge you to vote United. Vote United for a Great Britain. Vote United for peace, for water, for food, for jobs, for education – vote United!"

After his speech, they applauded for ten minutes. They chanted his name – "George! George! George!" – and they waved their banners. He left the stage, waving at the horde. And when he turned his back, he winked at a Nebuchadnezzar in the wings.

"Went well," George told him.

The man scowled.

"What is it?" said George.

"You've got some guests in your dressing room."

"Who?"

"Unhappy ones."

CHAPTER 12.
KILLING FUAD.

DAVID Murray, nearly fourteen but older than his years, barged through the Hyde Park crowd as it started to disperse.

The people were excited. They jabbered and gossiped. They were full of love for George Fuad. They were full of hate for Jake Lawton.

David's fury grew. He was already angry. He'd been angry for years. He had been ten when all this started – a ten-year-old boy whose childhood was stolen, whose family was destroyed.

He'd lost his father and his brother to the vampire plague. His mother, who was hardly a mum before all this had started, had disappeared. He'd not seen her in months.

And now his friend, Jake Lawton, who was like a father and brother to David, was also missing – and worse than that, Jake was hated by the people he'd saved.

David kept moving. He was heading towards the stage. He elbowed his way through the crowds. He kept a tight grip on the strap of his rucksack, which contained stakes and a hammer. Under his jacket, tucked into his belt, he had a gun. He was planning to shoot George Fuad with it.

Someone touched his arm.

He wheeled in panic, ready to lash out.

It was Kwan Mei. He'd forgotten that she'd been with him in the park. Forgotten that she'd had to listen to Fuad insulting her in public, calling her an enemy of Britain.

Mei was eighteen. She was from China. She'd arrived in Britain earlier that year. She'd come hoping for a better life. But she had no idea that she, and the other migrants, were being trafficked into the country as food for vampires. Jake Lawton and Aaliyah Sinclair saved Mei's life on Ramsgate harbour. Since then, the Chinese girl had been committed to helping Jake defeat the vampires.

She had built an army of migrants in the north of England and marched them to London, where they had battled the vampires a few months previously.

Mei was brave. She wanted to save Britain. It was her home now, whatever people like Fuad said.

Now she said, "Vampires here."

"Yeah, so?"

"We kill them, David."

"I'm killing George Fuad."

"Waste time. Kill the vampires."

David looked around nervously. He didn't want the dwindling crowd to hear them talk. They were among enemies.

He leaned in to Mei and said, "It's not a waste of time. Not for me. It'll make me feel better."

"But not country."

"It might make the country feel better. At least he won't win the election."

"They choose someone else like him. Make no difference. Without George Fuad, vampires will still be strong. Without vampires, George Fuad will be weak. We kill vampires."

"You kill the vampires, Mei. I will kill Fuad."

He started to walk towards the stage.

Mei grabbed his arm again.

"What?" he said.

"You are good vampire killer," she told him. "Like Jake was. You are like young Jake."

He looked at her face. She was really pretty. She stared right at him, her brown eyes shining.

Mei had been a good friend to him. He liked her. A lot. But he was embarrassed. He always blushed when he thought about her in *that* way. He was too young to be her boyfriend. Just a kid to her. And she was friendly with a young Turkish guy named Ediz Ün. He was part of her army. A nice bloke. He was about twenty and a brave fighter.

"But not always like Jake," said Mei.

He stepped away from her, turning his back. He knew what she was going to say. She said it anyway, loudly: "He never put people in danger. He never use human as bait."

David whirled to face her, trying to make her shut up. Some of the crowd remained, despite the advancing darkness. They looked up as Mei shouted.

"Be quiet," he said.

"You have bad in you, David."

"I have anger in me."

"Why?"

"You know how much I've suffered." He was nearly in tears.

"You know how much *I* suffer."

He stomped towards the stage.

"I wait for you here," said Mei.

He raised his hand to acknowledge her and kept walking.

He slipped his hand inside his jacket and felt for the comforting butt of the handgun. It would be of no use against vampires, but its bullets would finish off George Fuad and any other Neb who tried to stop David.

He wasn't worried about vampires. He was protected. He wore the red mark of the Nebuchadnezzars, set in a ring. Jake had stolen it from a Neb years ago.

David cried as he walked, thinking of his dad, his brother, his mum, everyone who had died during the plague.

He slipped behind the stage area. It was dark. A maze of passageways weaved around the compound. There were trailers and mobile TV studios. There were trucks and cars. The smell of piss came from a row of portable toilets. The murmur of voices could be heard. A generator hummed.

David wiped his eyes.

If any of his enemies saw him crying, they'd laugh at him.

He sneaked along the side of a truck. He came to a dogleg and peeked around the corner. There were gazebos on either side of the walkway. Tables and chairs had been stacked up in the gazebo on the left. The smell of food lingered. *The canteen*, David thought. He walked around the corner and made his way down the walkway, trying to be light on his feet over the wooden planks laid on the ground.

He saw figures in the gazebos, and they were clearing away furniture. They ignored him. Must have thought he was just another worker going about his business.

He turned another corner, and before him stood a clearing. At the far end was parked an impressive trailer, gleaming silver and red in the moonlight. It had eight wheels and a cab for a driver. Something jerked in David's belly. He knew instinctively that George Fuad was inside the trailer.

He stepped forward.

A hand fell on his shoulder and dragged him back.

He spun round.

A big man in a black bomber jacket scowled at him.

Pinned to the man's lapel was a scrap of red material.

"You got ID?" said the big man.

David showed his ring. "I'm one of you. I'm a fan of Mr Fuad's. I'd like to see him."

The big man creased his brow.

"Can I see him?" said David.

"What've you got in the ruck sack, son?"

"Sandwiches."

"Sandwiches?"

"Yes, lunch. For the rally today."

"Oh yeah? Show me."

David hesitated. He was cold inside. He tried to maintain his smile, but his face was starting to quiver. What would Jake do in this situation? He knew what Jake would do. David reached inside his jacket. But the big man was too quick. He slapped David around the head. The boy fell, his scalp stinging.

"Right, you little shit," said the big man, drawing out a billy club from inside his bomber jacket. "You're going to get a hiding before I grant you your wish to see Mr Fuad. But I don't think he's going to sign any autographs."

The big man lurched forward, as if he were toppling.

He would fall right on top of David and crush him.

David covered his head and waited for the impact.

CHAPTER 13.
POP-STAR VAMPIRE.

THE vampire said, "Without that red mark you'd be food, Georgie. Nothing but food."

"Don't call me *Georgie*, sunshine, or I'll have you crucified in Hyde Park, and you can wait for dawn."

The vampire baulked. It hissed, bearing its fangs.

George recognized the bloodsucker. It used to be a pop singer when it had been human. It might have been called Ben, and his band, George remembered, was The Eclipse. They once had a No.1 record and were second or third on one of those TV talent shows. Ben had been in his early twenties when he became a vampire. He still looked a little like a pop star. Just a little. His T-shirt, which might have been trendy once, was ripped and soiled by his victims' blood.

George surveyed the room. Ten vampires had been waiting for him when he got back to the trailer.

He warned them, "I'll have you *all* crucified. Or better, impaled. Just like old Vlad used to do, eh."

They hissed at him in unison, some backing away.

He turned his back and started to fork the Chinese takeaway on a plate. The odour of sweet and sour sauce saturated the room. As he salivated over the meal, he heard the vampires shuffle closer. But they would not dare attack him, because he wore the mark.

George stuffed a chicken ball and some fried rice into his mouth and, as he chewed, said to the vampires, "You have to be patient. I know you *want* to kill. I know you *need* to kill. But if you don't do it reasonably for a while, there will be a war again."

"We don't care about war," said the pop-star vampire. "We care about blood."

"You'll have plenty of it. We'll harvest it for you. But you can't just kill randomly just now. Eventually, you will run out of humans. You know how this works – we run the country, you keep us in power. We control the population, provide you with food. In return, the stocks never run out and you never, ever die." He went back to his takeaway. He was so hungry. He scooped another fork-full into his mouth and again spoke as he chewed. "Just take what you need. No mass killings. Not like before. It will piss people off."

"We're still being hunted," said the vampire. "Remnants of Kwan Mei's army are stalking us every day while we sleep. Why can't we fight back?"

"You will be allowed to fight – and hunt," said George. "But you have to wait. We ain't powerful enough just yet. But we will be. Your dream of blood will come true, brothers. You will fucking swim in it. If you behave for now, people will be more willing to accept my little fib that you mean them no harm, that your brutality stems from the need to defend yourselves against the likes of Lawton."

The vampires hissed at the mention of Lawton's name. He scared them. Fuad envied Lawton's power over the undead.

"Appease us, then," said the pop-star vampire. "Give us something while we wait. It's not easy to be patient, you know. Not as easy as it is for humans."

George walked through the cluster of vampires. They stank of rivers and of flesh. It made him want to puke and put him off the idea of eating his sweet-and-sour chicken. He opened the door and called for Jade. The blonde girl appeared from a nearby tent. She looked scared.

"P-please, Mr Fuad, don't – "

"I won't. Honest. I won't hurt you, Jade. I want to apologize, that's all."

She was thinking about it. But then she approached. George quickly stepped out of the trailer. He grabbed the girl and tore the red mark from her pullover. Before she could respond, he shoved her into the trailer and slammed the door shut.

From inside, she shrieked.

"Don't say I never give you anything," said George quietly and walked away.

CHAPTER 14. WAKIZASHI.

THE big man hit the ground next to David, who winced and waited for the thug to attack. But he didn't. He just stayed on the ground. Stayed very still, with two swords sticking out of his back.

"I came to help," said a voice, and David looked up to see Mei standing there.

She bent down and plucked the swords out of the thug's back. Blood ran along the steel. She sheathed the weapons. They were wakizashi swords. Fourteen-inch long samurai blades. Not that Mei was a samurai. She wasn't even Japanese. But she was deadly with those weapons. As the big man in the bomber jacket proved.

"I kill Fuad with you," she said.

"OK," he said. "Uh, thanks for… for saving me."

She nodded.

They looked at each other.

Someone screeched and broke the moment.

David's nape prickled. The cry came from the red and silver trailer in the clearing. And whoever it was in distress shrieked again.

Mei reacted first. She shot out into the clearing. David raced after her. He was reaching into his jacket for the gun.

"Fuad's in there," he said to Mei.

"Someone in trouble in there," she said.

Another scream came from within.

David's heart thundered. He was so close to Fuad. He had been determined to kill the man. He dreamt about cutting the bastard's throat, shooting him in the head. And now, with his nemesis within reach, he was hesitating. He was a coward.

What would Jake do? What would Jake say?

"Please, no… no… " came a voice from inside the trailer, a desperate, terrified voice.

Mei whipped her swords out. She kicked down the door. She bolted inside, baying like a banshee.

David followed her.

He quickly scanned the room. Ten vampires at least. A blonde girl lying on the floor. Mei screaming, slashing with her swords.

She'd already killed two vampires by the time David made a move.

Their burnt bodies left an odour of seared flesh in the air.

The vampires had recognized the red marks both David and Mei wore. The creatures bristled and panicked. They threw themselves at windows. They clawed at the walls.

David drove his stake through the back of one creature, and it turned to ash in seconds.

Screams filled the trailer. The smell of fiery flesh was strong. Everything went by so quickly. David didn't think, he just killed. And he thought he'd killed four or five by the time it was over. Mei might have killed four or five, too. But some of the vampires had escaped. Now only David and Mei, and the blonde girl lying on the floor, remained.

"She dead?" said David.

"Will be soon," said Mei. "Look… neck."

The girl had bite marks on her throat. Wounds also peppered her arms. Her clothes had been torn by teeth trying to get at her skin. She had bloody holes in her legs and back, where fangs had torn into her flesh. She was breathing rapidly.

"Let's get her out of here," said David.

Then the blonde girl looked up. Her face was smeared with blood and tears. She looked pale.

"Please… " she said. "Please… " Then she coughed. Blood spurted from her mouth. She arched her back and a terrible noise came from her throat. An animal noise. A noise of anguish. Her body became rigid. And then she sagged and lay still.

"She's… she's dead now," said David.

"And we have to kill her again," said Mei.

David swallowed. A chill ran through his blood. His mother had been forced to burn his father's body after he was attacked by vampires. David knew she'd had no choice, but at the time he had hated her. And the anger had never gone away, despite the fact he knew what she did was right.

"We have to kill her," said Mei. "We have to."

He shook his head. He wasn't sure if he could. He was hesitating, staring at the girl.

He slowly turned away, tears rolling down his face.

Mei tutted.

And then David heard the swish of her wakizashi and the thump of its blade striking the floor after penetrating the girl's body.

He smelled flesh on fire. He shut his eyes and tried to think of a time when all this would be over. But he couldn't.

CHAPTER 15.
A RUIN.

TĂLMACIU, NEAR THE TRANSYLVANIAN-WALLACHIAN BORDER, ROMANIA – 10.30PM (GMT + 2 HOURS), 17 MAY, 2011

"WHY do you wear a patch over your eye?" asked the old man.

"Easier to aim when I'm shooting," Lawton answered.

"What do you shoot?"

"Anything that moves."

Lawton dropped the backpack on the floor of the pub. The backpack contained the Spear of Abraham. It contained water, bread, some forged papers.

He'd hitchhiked to Tălmaciu after getting off the train when it stopped at a rural station, soon after he'd killed the vampires.

By the time he'd arrived in Tălmaciu, the heavens had opened. The rain fell heavily. Lawton was drenched.

It was a small town, set in a rural landscape. The Făgăraş and Cibin mountain ranges loomed over the settlement. Ploughed fields indicated the agricultural nature of the region.

Why here? thought Lawton. *Why have my dreams brought me here?*

He was soaked when he got to the pub. Only two customers frequented the drinking hole. He asked the old man behind the counter if he spoke English.

"*Cateva cuvinte*," came the reply.

"What?" said Lawton.

"A few words," said the old man.

He knew more than a few. His English was good. He'd learnt it for the tourists, he said.

He made Lawton a very strong coffee. The odour was pungent and the taste bitter, but it made Lawton alert. He rolled a cigarette and offered one to the old man, who shook his head.

"You are from England?" the old man said.

Lawton nodded. He lit the fag.

"We hear terrible things from England," said the old man.

Lawton shrugged. He smoked.

"*Vampir*," said the old man. "*Demoni*, yes? Our government warn us not to travel to UK. The news tells us it is war in your country. War against the dead. Is it war?"

Lawton asked for another coffee.

The old man, preparing it, said, "We have legends here in Romania."

"I know."

"Vlad Tepes?"

"I've heard."

"Mr Bram Stoker bases Dracula on our Vlad Tepes."

Yes, thought Lawton, *but according to Apostol Goga, Stoker got it wrong*. Vlad Tepes was not a vampire, he had been a vampire killer. He'd spent years preventing the Nebuchadnezzars from resurrecting the vampire trinity in Europe. But fighting the undead had taken its toll on Tepes. It corrupted him. It drove him mad. During his last few years, he could barely tell the difference between human and vampire, and innocent people suffered in his purges.

The old man served Lawton the coffee.

"You stay here long?" said the proprietor.

"I'm looking for… for something." He furrowed his brow. The truth was, he had no idea why he was here. He had been led here by his dreams. Years ago he would have dismissed what he'd seen in his sleep. But not now. Not in the days when the dead drank your blood.

His eye suddenly ached, and he put his hand over the patch.

"Are you all right, friend?" said the old man.

Lawton nodded.

"So, what are you looking for, Englishman?"

Lawton gave himself a moment, allowing the ache to dissipate. Then he said, "Is there an old church or an old castle in the area? A ruin?"

"Many ruins."

"Something isolated, surrounded by – " He nearly said, "surrounded by a forest of stakes", but stopped himself. Instead, he said, "Surrounded by fields, trees."

"There is the ruin of an old church to the north, about three miles. They say a ghost lingers there, a witch."

A knot tightened in Lawton's stomach.

A voice echoed in his mind:

"*Voivode... voivode...* "

The old man said, "They say she is *străine*… foreign."

Lawton felt cold. The pain in his head had returned. His glass eye throbbed, the strand of skin in the globe writhing.

"It was abandoned maybe five hundred years ago," said the old man. "Burned by the Dracul, some say."

"The Dracul?"

"Tepes."

"Who's the ghost?"

"No one knows for sure. Foreign, as I say. But no one speaks of her. When we were children, we were warned never to visit the ruin. Children who did never came back."

"Is that true or just a scary story?"

"It is true."

"How do you know?" said Lawton.

"Because one night my brother, who was nine, went there with his friends. He never came back. Men searched the fields and the forests, but no one went too close to the church. I wanted to. I said to my father, 'He has gone to the ruin, father, he has gone to the ruin.' But my father said, 'No, Viktor, no… he is lost in the forest, that is all, he is lost... ' and my father was crying, crying all the time."

"What do you think happened?"

The old man shrugged. "Romania has many legends. But we are a modern country. No one is superstitious any more. It is backward to be supertitious. I don't know, and I will never know – that is how it is."

"Which way to this ruin?" said Lawton.

The old man gave him directions before adding, "But not in the dark, Englishman. Wait until the dawn."

Lawton left.

CHAPTER 16.
AS PALE AS DEATH.

11.57PM (GMT + 2 HOURS), 17 MAY, 2011

IT was like in his dream.

A barren landscape. Scorched fields. A dark forest. Black mountains tearing at the horizon. The moon full and glowing. Rain lashing down.

And the ruin. An old church, battered by time and the elements. Vines coiled around the bell tower. Weeds clawed at the foundations. The stonework was charred by fire. The windows were like empty eyes, its doorway like the mouth of some monster, permanently open and waiting for prey.

The old man had told him no one came out here. He realized why. Firstly, it was quite a way out of town. Why would anyone make the effort? Secondly, the ruin could well have triggered irrational thoughts. It was difficult to weed out superstition, even among the most educated and rational of populations. As Lawton had witnessed during his time in Romania, the idea that rural parts of the country were still mired in legends and folklore was way off the mark. This was a modern country. This was a successful country. A small, European nation, marching forward, and seemingly overtaking the traditional big nations. It was certainly now in a better way than Britain. But peel away the veneer, and you could still find those traditional beliefs, those ancient fears. People crossed themselves. They prayed. Why was that any different to hanging garlic on your porch or putting a pumpkin in your windowsill?

All of it is superstition, thought Lawton as he approached the abandoned church's entrance.

He gripped the strap of his backpack. The spear was in there. He'd arm himself if he sensed any danger. And he was very good at picking up on any threats. His military training had honed his instincts. Fighting vampires had sharpened them further.

At the moment he felt no dread. Only cold. Only wet.

But once he stepped through the entrance and into the ruin, the atmosphere changed. His skin crawled, and he gasped for breath. He quickly got the spear out, grasping it tightly. A cold sweat broke out on his back. His nerves tightened. His heart pounded. Blood thundered through his veins, and his dead eye pulsed, sending a jolt of pain into his skull. He gritted his teeth. Something was here. Something that had been inside his head over the past few weeks. The thing that had been calling to him in his dreams. The dreams that were impossible a few years ago because he didn't sleep.

An image flashed in his head, staggering him.

It was of a woman in white, her skin pale like the moon, her eyes red like blood, her hair a crow-black waterfall.

His chest tightened.

He held the spear in his sweaty palm, fearing he would drop it, fearing he would be vulnerable without a weapon.

He'd never sensed anything like it.

He could almost taste the fear, and he tried to lick it off his lips. Lawton scolded himself. Told himself to take control. Tried to master his alarm and his body's reaction to it. Slowly, he grappled himself out of dread's tight grip and focused on where he was.

He looked around. The rain came in because there was no roof. The wind howled through the relic because the windows and most of the walls were gone. The altar had been destroyed. The pews were rotted away. No icons remained, no images of faith. But one thing still stood. Lawton fixed on it. He narrowed his eyes, wondering how it was possible, after all these years, that the structure remained.

It was the confessional. A wooden cupboard, its door ajar as if inviting someone to step inside and unload their sins.

Lawton strode towards the confessional. He ignored the rats that spilled through the door. They squealed as if they'd been scared by something. Lawton walked through the vermin, scattering them. Without fear, he ripped open the confessional's door.

The smell hit him.

Death.

Sweet and rotten.

He reeled away.

He coughed.

He retched.

Hot water filled his throat.

He nearly threw up but managed to stop himself.

He grabbed some water from his backpack and drank. It was tepid, but it washed away the sour taste in his throat.

He steeled himself and entered the confessional.

There was a door at the back, hanging off its hinges. Cold air came through it. Lawton nudged the door aside. His sense of smell was adjusting to the rancid odour, and he was getting used to it.

"Christ," he said, staring at some stone steps that were covered in moss and damp. The steps spiralled downwards. He felt he had to go down them. He had no choice. Whatever he was looking for, whatever had been calling him, was at the bottom of those steps.

He shook his head.

Was he going mad?

Was he losing his mind?

Four years ago, he would never have believed dreams were anything more than emissions from the sub-conscious. They had no meaning. They had no message. But things had changed. He now believed in vampires. He now believed the undead lived. He now believed everything, because if you didn't, you could die.

Scepticism in this new world could kill you.

Belief could save your life.

If you doubted that vampires existed, you'd stroll out after dark without a care in the world. Accept they were real, and you'd stay indoors after sunset – and that, in 21st-century Britain at least, would ensure your survival.

The steps were narrow and dark. The walls dripped with water. Thick cobwebs draped from the ceiling. Large insects Lawton could not identify scuttled over his shoes as he walked down. It was slippery, and he had to be careful. He used his torch to guide him, but the beam was weak in the deep darkness.

He kept descending.

Water dripped. Rats skittered. Lawton braced himself. He was ready for an attack. Human or vampire, he would deal with it. He feared no one. Vampires baulked at the sight of him, armed with the spear, marked by the red skin of the trinity – he was their nemesis. And no human worried Lawton. He had faced the strongest and the deadliest as a soldier, and, during the past three years, as an illegal bareknuckle fighter. He'd retired undefeated. But he'd come out of retirement if anyone fancied their chances. *Right now*, he was thinking. *Right now. Bring it on*.

Down he went, spiralling deeper into the bowels of the ancient church. Finally, he reached the bottom of the stairs. Ahead of him, another door, hanging off its hinges. It led into a dark room. Lawton threw a beam of light into the darkness. Images flashed in the illumination. He saw two rats eating raw flesh. He saw another rat cocooned in cobwebs. He didn't want to imagine the spider that had trapped the animal in its silk.

Entering the room, the air grew colder. The sound of water dripping became louder. He scanned the room with the torch.

Something hissed. Lawton stiffened. It sounded like a voice, a whisper. He shook his head, dismissing his initial judgment.

It couldn't have been, he thought.

He traced the beam around the room. The light fell on a pile of bones. Lawton froze, holding the remains in the torchlight. Even before he started to approach, he knew what animal the bones belonged to.

They belonged to a human animal.

He cursed as he surveyed the skeletons. There were dozens. Children among them.

Something scraped along the wall. Lawton jerked the flashlight towards the noise. He staggered in horror at what the beam showed.

Pinned to the far wall, there were more skeletons. They had been crucified. Their jaws hung open as if in eternal agony. He moved the torchlight along the remains and counted fifteen before the wall turned a corner. Shining his torch around the bend, he caught glimpses of more human bones, either piled on the floor or nailed to the walls.

"Jesus," he said.

It was a charnel house.

These people had been murdered.

They'd been tortured.

But why?

"... *voivode...* " came a whisper.

Lawton wheeled. The torchlight sliced the darkness. In its beam, Lawton was sure he saw a figure. But in that split second he decided it was his mind playing tricks. He had to keep calm. He had to stay in control of his body.

He kneeled, gripping the spear tightly, and raised the torch slowly towards the area where he thought he'd seen the figure. A cell was tucked into the far corner of the cellar. The bars were rusty. They were bent outwards. He lifted the flashlight slowly, and the beam settled on the hem of a white dress.

Lawton's bowels turned to ice.

He stood.

He aimed the light at the figure in the cell.

He clenched his teeth, trying not to pass out.

The woman sat calmly. She had coal-black hair, and her skin was snow-white. Her red eyes burned in the gloom, and the dress she wore seemed to float around her.

Lawton's throat locked.

It was the woman from his dream.

The one who had been calling him.

She was incredibly beautiful. He could not take his eyes off her. He was transfixed, and his body suddenly ached for hers. But there was something abominable about her. Something that made him sick. He was desperate to touch her skin, but knew if he did it would be cold and dead.

Then the woman smiled, revealing her fangs.

She said, "*Am asteptat 500 ani pentru tine, voivode.*"

Lawton tried to say he didn't understand. The woman rose and floated through the buckled bars of the cell. Lawton tried to move away. But he was frozen to the spot. He was terrified. He'd never known such terror. His hand tightened on the spear. But he felt weak, his body sapped of energy.

She came to him, and he smelled her – roses and death.

With one hand, she held his wrist, preventing him from lifting the spear. He had been right: her touch felt cold and ancient.

She said, "*Vorbi cu mine.*"

"What… what did you say?"

"*Vorbi cu mine.*"

“What are you saying… saying to me?”

“I say to you, ‘Speak to me,’ and you do, and I have your language. I know it. I have waited 500 years for you, prince.”

PART THREE.

POWER.

CHAPTER 17.
BEAUTIFUL MONSTER

POIENARI CASTLE, WALLACHIA, ROMANIA – DECEMBER 1476

SIMEON of Tălmaciu nervously opened the door to Vlad's bedchamber.

He peeked inside, and what he saw almost made him faint. He had to sit on the trunk he'd only moments before dragged out of the room.

He had been told to take the trunk to Bucharest, seventy-five miles away, where his Nebuchadnezzar brother, Prince Mehmed, waited for him with the Ottoman army. Mehmed would return the chest's contents to the East, to Constantinople. The prince was not really an Ottoman. No more than Simeon was truly Christian and European. They were both descended from King Nebuchadnezzar. They both strove to bring Babylon back. Babylon and her vampires. Mehmed had once told him, "We are not Christian, we are not Jews, we are not Mussulmen."

They weren't. They were none of those religions. They were of an older religion. A religion born in the bowels of Babylon thousands of years before Christ. The most powerful faith in history.

"Go," Simeon's mistress had told him. "Go and find Mehmed, and keep the chest safe."

And then his mistress had faced Vlad the Impaler, enemy of all vampires, killer of the living and the dead. The *voivode* had murdered Simeon's father months earlier. Impaled him as he'd impaled the vampires. Left him alive with a post driven into his bowels. Left him alive to rot and have his eyes plucked out by the crows. It took days for his father to die, and every second was agony. Simeon craved revenge, and his mistress would be his sword.

His mistress Ereshkigal.

The ancient witch.

One of Nimrod's hundred brides.

The oldest vampire in the world.

Five thousand years old.

A beautiful monster.

Simeon's father, whose cover was as priest of Tălmaciu, had been so close to resurrecting the trinity.

But Vlad, the Wallachian prince, had been at war with the Nebuchadnezzars and their vampires allies for decades. He had harried them and murdered them. He was a dangerous man who showed very little fear and no mercy.

Forests of stakes had dotted Wallachia.

Screams filled the mountains.

Death saturated the air.

Vlad would impale the vampires, but not through the heart. They would be alive and pinned to the tall, wooden poles through their bellies. They could not escape. They writhed in agony and terror, waiting for dawn to come. Waiting for the sun to fry them alive. The Wallachian mass murderer had done the same to Simeon's father. Driven a sharpened post up into him. Simeon could still hear his father's dreadful shriek as the stake pierced him.

After a moment sitting on the trunk, he now stepped into Vlad's bedchamber.

The *voivode* lay dead, an arrow wound in his chest.

Ereshkigal's remains were scattered on the stone floor.

She was dust.

Simeon cried out.

He raced to the window and stared out. Down in the valley near the River Arges, Vlad's army was camped.

A man with a longbow strapped across his back trudged down the gorge towards the camp.

Simeon looked at Vlad's body.

The archer walking down to the valley must have fired, aiming to kill Ereshkigal. But he'd also struck his own master.

Simeon wanted to laugh at the archer, wanted to mock him.

But he needed to stay alive and not draw attention to himself.

He needed to gather his mistress's remains.

Hurriedly, he found a clay jar. He tossed out the contents. They were trinkets – rings, bracelets, necklaces.

Simeon carefully swept up Ereshkigal's ashes. She was dirt now. But he knew she could be resurrected. The trinity had only been fragments. However, the right conditions allowed you to bring such immortals back to life.

And he would bring Ereshkigal back to life.

He found a donkey and cart in the stables.

He loaded up the trunk, which carried the Spear of Abraham, on the cart. He kept the jar containing his mistress's remains under his cloak.

Simeon rode out and began the dangerous journey to Bucharest.

CHAPTER 18.
DEATH'S KISS.

TĂLMACIU – MARCH 1497

SIMEON enjoyed torturing people. He found he was good at it. It made him feel powerful. That was important for such a weak man. He spent half a day on inflicting pain, and that was after telling his victim what his or her fate would be. That always made their suffering much worse. That made his joy greater. It filled him with strength, as if he were feeding off the sufferer's dread.

The man suspended above the cellar floor screamed.

"Please," he begged. "I have gold – I have silver – I have a daughter – you can have her – she is ten – please don't do this to me – I shall burn in hell – "

Simeon dragged the coffin across the stone floor and placed it directly beneath the man, who screamed and bellowed when he saw its content. The noises he made did not sound human. His struggles increased. Simeon had tied him to a scaffold. Leather straps bound the man's wrists and ankles. He was stretched in a star fashion, facing down. He was about five feet above the coffin.

He was shrieking now: “Please – No! – In the name of God – In the name of Jesus and his Holy Mother – ”

Simeon had found him at the inn down in the village. He was drunk and clearly a sodomite. He made lewd suggestions to Simeon, who had used the man’s lust to tempt him outside.

Once in the dark street, Simeon had clubbed him across the back of the head. He had hefted the man’s body onto the cart, and hen whipped the donkey along the narrow road that led from town, through the forest, to the ruins of the church where Simeon’s father had been captured and murdered by Vlad Tepes.

For months, he had lived in the bowels of the church. It had been where his father had tried to resurrect the vampire trinity. It was where he would resurrect Ereshkigal.

After he left Vlad’s fortress, he had travelled to Bucharest. He made it to Mehmed’s camp and gave him the spear.

Mehmed had promised to return it to Constantinople. He had offered to take Simeon with him. But he’d declined the offer, saying he had duties in Romania. And when he had told Mehmed what they were, the prince had baulked.

“Do not bring her back,” he had warned Simeon, his eyes wide with fear. “She is death.”

“She is beautiful, and she killed The Impaler.”

“Good,” said Mehmed. “She has been useful. But the brides of Nimrod, like Nimrod himself, cannot be controlled by men. They are *not* the trinity. Our duties, as Nebuchadnezzars, lie with Kea, Kakash, and Kasdeja. That is our pledge, Brother Simeon. Nimrod and his witch wives are better off dead. They are not beholden to us. Do not give this creature life again.”

Simeon promised he would heed Mehmed’s warning.

But he hadn’t. He wanted to see Ereshkigal again. He wanted to worship her. And he wanted, as Vlad had done, to make love to her undead flesh.

"What is that creature?" cried the man on the scaffold now. "What are you doing to me?"

Simeon looked into the casket and gazed at what had terrified the fellow.

Ereshkigal was coming to life.

She looked haggard and ancient. A cadaver. Her skin was like leather, wrinkled and thin. Her body was emaciated, her face gaunt. You would not say by looking at her that she was a beauty. But she would be when she had been nourished. And Simeon was sure that the blood of this man would be enough to give her life.

During the past few weeks, he had brought six victims here and bled them into Ereshkigal's ashes – and with each sacrifice, she became more formed. Simeon felt like God, making life out of clay.

He was so excited. He was erect beneath his cowl – erect for her, his dead queen.

He took the knife, and the man on the scaffold squealed.

Simeon gutted him.

The man howled. His innards spooled out of his belly.

Blood and slime gushed out.

The gore splashed over Ereshkigal's remains.

The opened man bellowed and twitched.

Simeon then sliced him from throat to sternum, sawing through bone, which splintered and cracked.

The man jerked.

Blood rained.

The man died with a terrible noise coming from his throat.

Simeon snapped open his ribcage.

He clawed out the man's heart and lungs, slopping them into the coffin.

Ereshkigal's remains hissed.

Smoke rose from her cadaver.

Simeon stepped back.

The smell was terrible.

Steam filled the cellar.

Simeon retched.

And then he froze.

She reared up out of the smoke.

More beautiful than she had ever been.

She was naked and pale. Her black hair streamed over her shoulders. Her eyes burned red.

She opened her mouth. Her fangs were sharp.

Simeon fell to his knees, jabbering.

He was shaking with awe.

Ereshkigal floated up out of the coffin and slowly hovered down towards Simeon.

She clutched the red rag around his throat, the mark of the Nebuchadnezzars, protection against vampires.

Her voice was like a snake's.

"Do you think this protects you from me?"

"I am your servant, Simeon," he cried. "Do you remember me, my queen?"

He stared at her naked body. He was shaking with desire.

She tipped his chin back with her finger.

"Oh my queen," he gasped.

She grinned at him, showing her deadly teeth.

"Shall I kiss you, Simeon?"

"Oh… kiss me, my queen."

"If I do, you shall die. Shall I kiss you? Or will you live and be the eunuch in my court?"

He groaned.

"Choose, or I shall kill you," she said.

He chose.

And he shrieked when she gelded him.

CHAPTER 19.
SHE IS THORNS.

TĂLMACIU – 12.15AM (GMT + 2 HOURS), 18 MAY, 2011

LAWTON reeled, his head spinning. Every drop of strength he had seemed to leach out of his body. He suddenly felt weak in the woman's presence.

"Five hundred years," she said. Her eyes flashed. She hissed out a breath and it was putrid.

"Who are you?" he asked.

The woman didn't answer. She was staring goggle eyed at the Spear of Abraham.

"How did you come by this?" she asked.

"I asked you who you were."

She looked him in the eye. "Ereshkigal. *Mireasă de Nimrod.*"

Lawton furrowed his brow. "What?"

She shook her head as if she'd forgotten herself by speaking Romanian instead of English. "Bride of Nimrod."

Lawton's nerves fizzed.

"Where did you come by the spear?" she said again.

He didn't answer. He was trying to regain control of his senses, trying to find his strength again. Slowly, it was returning.

The woman's hand shot out, and she laid it flat against Lawton's chest.

He stiffened. It felt as if pulses of electricity were passing from her palm into his body. He could have easily retreated, but he stayed put, not wanting to show any weakness. He had a feeling such a revelation would put him in danger.

"I can feel your heart," she said. She panted, her lips partly open. Her tongue slithered across her lips.

Lawton's defences were crumbling again. He had faced this temptation before. Three years ago, he had been forced to kill his ex-girlfriend Jenna McCall after she became a vampire. When she'd first appeared to him as an undead, Jenna had demanded he give her blood – or she would go out and kill. Lawton had given in, and she'd fed from him, taking enough blood to survive, but not too much so as to kill Jake. She had mocked him, and he'd felt weak after she'd fed. But days later, he'd killed her. And he'd not hesitated. He did not shirk either when it came to crafting the death of another woman he loved when she'd returned from the dead. Sassie Rae had died at the Religion nightclub when Lawton and his companions prevented the Nebuchadnezzars from unleashing the vampire god, Kea, on London. After coming back to life, Sassie had hunted him down, and he'd watched as Aaliyah drove a stake through her heart.

He had the measure of vampires, even if he had loved them when they were human.

Or he thought he did.

This one was different.

She had power. Real power.

Vampires might be dangerous. They might be terrifying to most people. But they never conjured feelings of awe. Certainly not in Lawton.

But for some reason, that was exactly what he felt standing in front of Ereshkigal.

He sensed she was the most dangerous thing he'd ever met.

Her hand became a claw on his chest, and her long nails dug into his skin.

He gritted his teeth.

He gripped the spear.

He could have rammed it up into her chest.

She might have been quick enough to avoid his attack.

But he decided not to test her.

"You like pain," she said.

"I try to avoid it."

"You reek of it."

"I should get a better deodorant."

"Or let me heal it."

She stepped towards him, her face turned upwards to stare into his. Her breath was on his skin. Her teeth flashed white and sharp, inches from his throat. Heat rose from her body. It warmed Lawton. Her hair smelled of roses. Her flesh smelled of death.

Thorns, thought Lawton. *She is thorns*.

"Your eye," she said. "What is behind your patch?"

"Why are you close to me? If you are what you are, then you should be scared of this," and he removed the patch to reveal the red skin of the ancient vampires encased in the glass eye.

Ereshkigal did not flinch.

"The mark of the Nebuchadnezzars," she said. "You are one of them. A servant of my Lord's offspring?"

He said nothing.

"Another Simeon for me," she said.

"This doesn't make you flinch? You're not throwing a hissy fit."

"A what?"

"Forget it. It doesn't frighten you?"

"I am Ereshkigal. I am of Nimrod, not of his offspring. I watched him tear them from his chest. I saw him birth them, his children. I was there when they began. I gave them freedom when the prophet of Yahweh stole into Irkalla, killed my sisters – and buried my Lord."

Her anger was mounting.

"And these," she said, gripping both ends of the Spear of Abraham, "these the prophet of God tore from my husband's head."

Lawton finally shoved her away. She hissed. He quickly pulled the spear apart to make two swords.

"How did you come by it?" demanded Ereshkigal again, crouching like a panther. "I sent it back to the east. I sent it with Nebuchadnezzars returning home after a war with Vlad Tepes. How did you come by it?"

"I won it in a raffle," he said.

She cocked her head. "Who are you? Are you a *voivode*? I sense pain in you, but I also sense… power. Are you a Nebuchadnezzar?"

He paused before saying, "I kill Nebuchadnezzars – and I kill your kind. And I'm going to kill your husband, too, if I ever find him."

She straightened. "You are going to find Nimrod?"

"If I can."

"Take me with you."

He creased his brow. "What?"

"Take me home to Babylon."

"I'm going to kill him, and you want to come with me?"

"I can gain you entry – I can protect you."

"Why would you protect me?"

"Because you are taking me home."

"Why should I trust you?"

"You shouldn't."

"But," said Lawton, realizing that she wasn't as powerful as she seemed, "without me, you are trapped here – for eternity."

She shuddered.

"Give me blood," she said.

Lawton raised his eyebrows.

"A few drops. I won't kill you. I need you if I am going home. I've not fed in 500 years."

"Five hundred years?" he said. "I thought you could only live three days without it."

"Your experience of my kind has been limited to lower creatures. I am not a lower creature."

She moved closer again and touched his brow with her cold hand. "Your blood, here, where your eye is red – there is something inside that is different. There is something alive in you that isn't of you."

He gently eased her hand away. "Can you take me to Nimrod?"

"After blood."

When he'd given Jenna his blood, he'd felt weak. Now he couldn't afford to be vulnerable. He faced a long journey. He faced a dangerous one. Enemies hunted him. He was becoming paranoid, and needed to be alert.

"Blood," she said, throwing herself against him. "Blood, now."

He dropped the swords and gripped her arms. He wanted her, this undead thing. This witch. She was the most beautiful thing he'd ever seen. He twisted her around, aiming to toss her on the floor and mount her.

But he managed to control himself again and shoved her away.

"No," he said. "No."

But she flung herself back at him, sailing through the air as if on wings, and crashed into him, sending him staggering backwards.

CHAPTER 20.
DESCENDENTS OF KINGS.

HILLAH, IRAQ – 12.30AM (GMT + 3 HOURS), 18 MAY, 2011

ALFRED Fuad knew he was being watched. He was aware of it even before the scouts from Hillah came that morning to say a man and a woman had rented a house on the outskirts of the city. They were foreign, said the scout. The man was tall with dark hair and a thick moustache. He carried a cane decorated with a gold ferrule. The woman was tall and beautiful, her skin dark, her eyes fiery. The scout said she looked like an African princess.

Aaliyah Sinclair, thought Alfred.

Did that mean the man could be Jake Lawton?

The name made Alfred shudder.

He got up from his desk, where he'd been reading the scout's report and viewing some photographs.

He got a bottle of whisky from the cupboard and poured himself a tumbler.

Lawton? Was that possible?

The description did not fit the ex-soldier, but who knew with Lawton? He might have changed his appearance. He might have miraculously made it to Iraq.

"No," Alfred told himself. "It's impossible. You are being paranoid."

He drank again. The liquid was fiery. It gave him confidence to believe the man wasn't Lawton. It just couldn't be. Nebuchadnezzar agents had been tracking the bastard across Europe. They'd lost him a few times. Found him again. Lost him again. He was devious and slippery. He was clever and dangerous. Very dangerous.

They knew he'd left Britain after the battle in February. He and his companions had been picked up in Rotterdam. Christine Murray, her son, David, and the Chinese troublemaker, Kwan Mei, had been sent back to the UK. The Chinese woman was due to be deported back to her own country, because she was an illegal immigrant, but once in London, she'd slipped away with David Murray.

But Christine Murray, that interfering hack, was apprehended by George's men in Folkestone.

He downed another whisky. His head was swimming. He needed a nap. But he didn't have time. George would not be happy if he slept on the job.

Alfred loved his brother. He always wanted to please him. Perhaps if Lawton had a brother like George, he wouldn't be so much trouble. He would have had guidance. He would have had a sibling to smack him around when he did something wrong. Burn his back with their dad's cigarettes. Force his hand into a jarful of wasps. Rub his face in dog shit.

Bloody Lawton. The man was impossible. Five bullets lodged in his body from various conflicts. Two from Afghanistan, they said. One from Iraq. The other two, who knew. But he was still alive. None of his enemies had managed to kill him.

But I will, thought Alfred. *If he is the man in the house, if he ever comes here, I will kill him. I will kill Jake Lawton, and George will love me even more.*

He drank again, brimming with confidence now.

He surveyed the maps and the plans pinned to the wall of his office at the dig. He buzzed with excitement. He felt so powerful. He was making history. He was creating a new future. He would excavate a god and give it to his brother.

He thought about travelling home with Nimrod in tow. *We will go by road*, he thought. Every nation would kneel before Nimrod as Alfred's convoy passed through its territories. Prime ministers and presidents, kings and emperors, would bow and offer homage to the new world order of vampires and humans.

George would be master of the earth. Alfred would be his dutiful deputy.

He wondered if George would take a queen. He'd been married twice. But Alfred had sent them packing. Driven them mad. Made up stories about them and whispered nasty rumours in George's ear.

Alfred didn't want his brother to have anyone else. Why did he need anyone else? George could take his pleasure from whores as Alfred took his from young men.

They needed no one else. They had each other.

Mum had always said, "Family's the most important thing in the world, darlings. You stick together. You're blood. You're brothers." Mum was an East End girl. London born and bred. In his drunken state, he pictured the capital as a golden city.

He pictured a throne.

On the throne sat George – King George.

George VII.

And next to the throne would be Alfred, the faithful advisor, the loving brother.

And behind the throne, the real power. The religion. The faith. The fear. It was always superstition that gave kings their might. The new church the Nebuchadnezzars planned to build in England would be the most powerful in history. It would make the Catholic Church, and all its authority, look like a scout hut meeting. Its atrocities would pale beside those the Nebuchadnezzars would commit. As in the Christian faith, the threat of suffering would hang over worshippers, and for non-believers it would be the same as the message conveyed by Yahweh – follow me or die. But unlike Christianity, the Nebuchadnezzars would carry out their threats. That was the only way to maintain control – terror.

Alfred drank another whisky and felt blurry. He wanted to grip the world in his fist and crush it. He was sure he would be doing that in the next few months. He was quaking with excitement, and he grew hard. He would have that young student brought to the office. He picked up the phone, but he was seeing double by now, and he fumbled with the receiver. It crashed to the floor. Alfred dropped his drink. It spilled everywhere. He fell to his knees. He was on all fours, scrabbling about, feeling dizzy, wanting to puke.

Not looking much like ruler of the world, he thought.

Something crackled. Static exploding in his head. He thought he might have broken his skull, because he had a terrible headache.

But then he realized the noise came from the walkie-talkie on his desk.

He got to his knees and reached for the transmitter.

A voice came through the interference, "Mr Fuad, Mr Fuad… "

He answered, slurring, "What is it, Malik?"

"You need to come down. Something very big. Very big."

The excitement in the dig supervisor's voice sent pulses of adrenaline coursing through Alfred's veins.

CHAPTER 21. VAMPIREOPHOBIA.

LONDON – 12.45AM, 18 MAY, 2011

GEORGE Fuad felt bloated with power. And he was hungry for more.

He grinned at Elizabeth Wilson and thought, *You're fucked*.

Fucked leader of a fucked country. In thirty hours or so, the polls would open, the election would be under way, and Wilson and her country would be on the road to hell.

Near the door stood Christine Murray. She bristled with hatred, her eyes burning. She looked a bit of a mess.

He'd had the women woken up and hauled out of bed, so no wonder they looked bedraggled.

It wasn't the first time he had called a meeting with Wilson in the run-up to the election. And to keep her on her toes, he had been dropping by at all hours. He could do that. He was in the ascendancy. She knew it, and he knew it. He wanted her to throw in the towel. He wanted to humiliate her. Force her to quit even before voting began. But she was holding on. "Liz, sweetheart," he said. "This is your last chance to drop out. You don't want to make a fool of yourself, do you?"

She baulked, obviously hating the way he was speaking to her.

"Liz," he continued. "You're fucked, see. This time very early on Friday morning, I'm going to be pissing in your mouth – "

"You're a murderer and a liar," said Murray.

"I am going to win the election – "

"By murdering and lying," said Murray.

"People will believe what they want to believe," he said. "You got your truth, I got mine. We offer our respective truths to the voters, and they choose the version they like best."

"Your truth is blood and death," said Murray.

"Don't be fucking melodramatic, darling."

"Don't darling me, you murderous – "

"That's enough, Christine," said Liz Wilson.

"Yes, that's enough, Christine," said George.

"Mr Fuad," said Wilson, "I won't stand down, but can't we come to some sort of accommodation after the election?"

He leaned back in the leather chair and scanned Liz Wilson's office in the Millbank building. It was a paltry little hovel. Once he was master of the world, he'd live in golden palaces. He'd surround himself with beautiful things. He would empty the mansions, the castles, and the churches, and fill his coffers with their treasures.

He'd be rich and powerful.

"Yeah," he said, "if you're not willing to step aside, we can certainly come to an accommodation, like, erm, Wandsworth Prison maybe. And you can rot there in a cell while I sort out this fucking country."

Wilson paled.

At one stage he had considered the type of accommodation Wilson had in mind – a coalition.

She would have been a good partner because she was easily manipulated and reasonably presentable. It would have been one of those old-fashioned coalitions forged by marriage. He would have taken her as his queen. Then he would have locked her away in a castle somewhere while he romped his way through the British female population.

He'd not bedded enough birds recently. There had been a dry spell in the past few years. After his second marriage broke down, and he had started to focus fully on acquiring power, his desire for flesh dwindled while his hunger for power grew.

But now the cravings were back.

Kings should always spread their seed, he thought. It was their responsibility. They had to keep the gene pool as potent as possible. They had to make sure there was an heir in place.

And Wilson was too old to produce a successor.

He'd lock her up in a castle as a traitor. Marry a young thing. Make a baby or two. Breed a boy. He'd make it a law that only males could inherit the empire. Then he'd produce some bastards. Distribute the Fuad DNA fairly.

"You'd be a fool," said Wilson. "You can't lock me up for no reason."

"There would be a reason, Liz," he said. "I don't like you."

"Have the bastard arrested, now, Prime Minister," crowed Murray.

George laughed. "I'd like to see you try, Christine. Oh yes, that would be fun." His face darkened. He was going for his serious look. He said, "The people are worried and distressed and scared."

"You've caused that with your monsters," said Murray.

George tutted. "You see, that's *your* truth, not mine. Mine is that this catastrophe was brought about by people like you, Christine. You and your hired thug, Jake Lawton – "

"Jake Lawton is the only one who cares and – "

"Shut it," he told Murray. She flinched. "Shut it and listen up, both you bitches."

The women gawped.

He leapt to his feet.

He started to prowl the office.

He spoke.

"The water supply in London was poisoned by a disaffected member of my party, Bernard Lithgow, and now the people don't know whether to drink it or not. Bernard has been punished."

The women's faces were a picture. Their jaws dropped. Their eyes widened. They were taking in George's fable, his truth. And they were finding it difficult to stomach.

He didn't care. He went on spinning his yarn.

"A deadly drug was distributed by another bad man, Afdal Haddad, who has also been dealt with – "

"Dealt with out of a fifth floor window," said Murray.

George ignored her.

"See, girls," he said, "my message is clear – vampireophobia won't be tolerated. It stokes the fires of hatred. It brings about more violence. We should respect the undead and how they live. And if they need to kill and feed now and again to survive, let them. We'll use criminals and enemies of the state as a food supply. We'll have public slayings. Traitors, murderers, rapists, thieves, perverts, they'll be executed by vampires. Keep the jails empty, won't it? For people like you. Until it's your turn."

Murray leaned against the wall. She looked as white as a sheet. Her mouth was opening and closing, trying to get words out. But none came.

Wilson managed to say something: "No one will allow that."

"Who'll stop me?" said George. "No one in Britain will stand in my way. And what'll Europe do? They've already shut the borders. No Brits allowed into any EU country, now. And they've never been up for a fight, Europe, apart from Germany, when good old Adolf was in charge. Now they're all fucking surrender monkeys."

"America," said Wilson, desperately.

"America, bollocks. Just like in World War Two, the Yanks'll stay out of it –

until they're attacked, of course. And *when* they're attacked, it'll be too late. They can fight back against the Japs, they can fight back against Al Qaeda. But they can't fight back against my vampire armies."

"You're a fool," said Murray. "Nothing more than a pantomime villain."

"Boo, hiss," said George. "Look at this country. It's a mess. And the world's not much better off. Everyone's panicking. First, the economies teeter. Now, there's a plague that can wipe out humanity. And you can't produce an antibiotic to fight it. You can't give people a jab. There's no cure for it. There's only submission. There's only slavery. The world will fall, girls, and someone's got to be on the ball, ready to pick up the pieces. And that's me, my darlings."

He grinned at them. Their hopes were dashed. Any tiny fleck of optimism they had was now gone.

But then Murray said, "There is a cure, you know."

George creased his brow.

"Jake Lawton," she said.

He bristled. A little bit of his strength ebbed away. Not enough to weaken him, but enough to irritate him.

"Lawton is the subject of countless contracts – humans and vampires are on his tail. I doubt he made it to Amsterdam."

"I doubt you're right, George," said Murray, a smile forming on her lips.

For the first time in a while, George felt a little uneasy.

CHAPTER 22.
A SACRIFICE.

TĂLMACIU – 12.48AM (GMT + 2 HOURS), 18 MAY, 2011

LAWTON pushed her face away from his throat, but she was strong. They had been tussling for a while. She had raked his skin and drew blood, then rolled away and licked at her fingers. Spots of blood were peppered around her mouth. She snarled at him, her eyes blazing red.

The wound smarted. His T-shirt was ripped at his shoulder. He touched the scored flesh, and he screwed up his face.

"You taste of lead," said Ereshkigal.

"That'll teach you."

"Let me drink. You won't die."

"I know, it's been done before."

"A vampire has taken blood from you?"

He said nothing. He checked his wound. He should have killed her. He knew he'd have to do it at some stage – kill or be killed. But he felt he could use her. If he could somehow make an alliance with this creature. It would make finding Nimrod easier. But first he had to survive.

"You know," she said, "that if a vampire draws blood from you three times, without killing you, you will become a vampire yourself."

"That won't happen. I'll never be like you."

"But you already are."

She moved towards him again, head cocked. She was terrifyingly beautiful. She could mesmerize you, make you forget everything – and that's when she'd pounce.

"Your eye," she said. "The eye of skin made from Nimrod's offspring. It is alive in you. It is merging itself with you. It is giving you its traits."

He felt sick and dizzy again, the wound in his shoulder burning. He was about to faint, but fought back against the nausea. If he were out cold, this creature would take his blood – and maybe just kill him and make him undead.

"You are more than human, *voivode*," she said. "More than vampire. The weapons of men will soon barely graze you. Your name. Tell me."

He told her.

"Jake Lawton," she said. "You are like my Lord in so many ways. And you are like Haran."

"Haran?"

There was longing suddenly in those lethal red eyes.

"My betrothed. I was to marry him. I remember, but… but I have no pain. I have no… no desire for him now."

"You're lying," said Lawton. "I can see it in your eyes."

Her face darkened.

"What happened?" he asked.

"The night of my wedding, before I was to be married, an old woman brought me red flowers. Beautiful red flowers. *Red flowers for the bride-to-be*, she said. Poisonous red flowers. I fell into a deep sleep. And after dark, soldiers came to take me away. I was stolen from Haran and our future together. Stolen because of a pact between a god and mortals. The Great Hunter also wanted a wife. And what the Great Hunter wanted, he got. Or Babylon would fall. The king sent his men for me after the witch had drugged me with her flowers. I was taken to Irkalla, where I was wedded to my lord. Wedded by the drinking of my blood and the eating of my flesh. I became one of his brides."

"Why you?"

"I was young, a virgin, a bride-to-be. I was a sacrifice to nourish Babylon. My blood maintained the city. Now let your blood maintain me."

She shot forward.

Lawton raised the spear.

"No," he said.

"I could kill you."

"Kill me, then."

It was a dare. To see how much she wanted to get out of here. For a moment he thought she would outsmart him, cut him down. He didn't know how long he could fight her off. He'd gambled that if she was trapped here and was desperate to leave, he'd be more valuable to her alive than dead.

"Give me blood so I can escape these walls," she said.

"Then lead me safely to your husband so I can kill him."

CHAPTER 23.
EXCAVATED.

HILLAH, IRAQ – 1.10AM (GMT + 3 HOURS), 18 MAY, 2011

ALFRED was drunk. He stared down into the pit. It made him feel queasy. He suffered a sudden bout of vertigo and reeled backwards. He looked skywards. Looming overhead was the huge industrial drill. The enormous bit was encased in a circular frame, which sliced at the ground while the awl bored into the earth.

A guard asked Alfred if he was OK, and he nodded that he was.

He went back to the safety fence that encircled the hole.

Alfred stared into the deep.

Strip lights had been attached and wired to the sides of the chasm, and they showed him how far his team had been able to drill.

It just kept going down and down.

He shivered.

The guard said, "Need a hand, sir?"

"I'm going down. The dig supervisor wants to see me."

The guard nodded. Alfred followed the mercenary towards the gatehouse and thought, *You are going to be dead soon, mate, and you don't know anything about it.*

That gave him a thrill. To have the power of life and death over someone he didn't know was very exciting.

He stepped into the lift at the gatehouse, and it was soon descending, ferrying Alfred down into the abyss.

His heart thundered, and he was sweating. The booze was having an effect.

It became hotter as he descended.

He grew dizzier the deeper he went.

The lift hummed. He scanned his surroundings. The walls of soil and rock didn't look solid. He imagined them crumbling in and collapsing, burying him alive. Panic clutched his chest, and he panted, grabbing the metal grid that surrounded him. It rattled. It clanked. Alfred's legs buckled. His stomach rolled. The elevator was going to break and plummet, and he would be crushed, and then the walls would crumple, and –

The lift reached the bottom. It jerked to a halt. Alfred blew air out of his cheeks and relaxed. He was safe. He hadn't fallen. The walls still stood.

The lift door slid open, and Malik, the dig supervisor, stood there, a smile on his face. Behind Malik stood Laxman, his face blotchy. They led Alfred into a tunnel in the wall. It was about fifteen feet high and ten feet wide. Strip lights hummed, and they showed Alfred what lay up ahead.

The tunnel forked into two passageways, and people were digging in the soil with trowels. They were students hired cheaply to do the grafting. They were the kids who, like Laxman and his men, would be thrown to the monster that lurked in this abyss.

"What have you found?" said Alfred as they approached the forks.

"Something remarkable," said Malik.

They entered the right-hand passageway.

Malik spoke in Arabic to the students, and they scuttled away.

Alfred froze. He stared at the skeleton in the tunnel. It was complete and looked liked the remains of a dinosaur. It was the size of an elephant, but Alfred could not identify what kind of creature it had been.

"A three-horned creature that we cannot name," said Malik excitedly. "A tail like a cedar tree, like is described in The Book of Job. Ribs like armour. Many regarded that as a hippo, and some have said it describes a bull – but it may be this."

"That's not a bull," said Laxman.

"It ain't no hippo, either," said Alfred.

What had they found? Was it a dinosaur? How could it be? This strata was not millions of years old. It was merely thousands. Dinosaurs had died out 65 million years ago, Alfred knew that. But then, some people didn't believe vampires existed.

Alfred looked at Malik. "Does this mean we're close to finding Nimrod?"

"Perhaps."

"Perhaps?"

"Please, Mr Fuad. There is something else."

Malik led Laxman and Alfred into the other passageway. Nailed to the wall was a skeleton.

Alfred said, "Who's that?"

Malik said they didn't know. "But look here," he added.

Painted on the wall was an image showing the two forks in the tunnel. The skeleton of the unidentified beast had been drawn in the right-hand passageway. The left tunnel, the one in which they were now stood, was crammed with figures of women. They were ethereal creatures, like angels, and they were all wearing white.

"A hundred of them," said Malik. "The hundred brides of Nimrod."

Alfred felt a surge of excitement run through him.

"And this figure here," said Laxman, pointing to a bearded man standing at the head of the fork, "who's that?"

"That," said Malik, "we believe, is Abraham. Said by legend to have destroyed Nimrod."

"How do you reckon it's him?" said Alfred.

"He has signed his painting, Mr Fuad. Here."

Malik showed him a scribble on the wall.

"He has named himself in the cuneiform language of Akkadia, of Babylon – it says 'Avram'."

"What does this mean?" said Alfred, knowing it meant something – and something big.

"These are the brides of Nimrod. They are supposedly legend. And Abraham came this way. He, too, is regarded as only a legend by mainstream historians and theologians. But this appears to be his signature, his work. He saw the brides of Nimrod, here in this tunnel. He saw the beast we excavated in the opposite tunnel and drew it. That means Nimrod is almost certainly real, too, Mr Fuad. We are very close, I am sure. Very close to unearthing the greatest archaeological find in history."

CHAPTER 24. DESTINY.

ŞANLIURFA, TURKEY – 7AM (GMT + 2HOURS), 18 MAY, 2011

LAWTON had let her drink his blood. Only a little. Only enough so she could leave the ruins. Only enough that she had the strength to step out into the night. Only so he could use her to get to Nimrod.

It had been like watching something being born. She had screamed and writhed after stumbling out of the old church.

Lawton had also been weak. And he felt emotionally drained. Because her lips had touched his flesh. Her teeth had broken his skin. She had been cold and ancient, but also warm and young. She was a witch and an angel.

He glanced in the rear-view mirror and thought about her sleeping in the back of the truck.

He could easily stop, leap out, fling open the back doors, and let the sun scorch her.

Make her dust.

Make her dead.

But Ereshkigal had got into his head. She'd been in his dreams, and that had to mean something. It had to be some kind of sign or message. And when he'd finally found her, there *had* been a message – she would lead him to Nimrod.

To his objective.

He looked at the clock in the truck. Just after seven in the morning. He was driving along the E99 road, Necmettin Central Avenue, in Şanliurfa. They were nearing the end of their 2500km journey from Romania. Lawton was stunned that the truck was still going. He'd stolen it from a council depot in Tălmaciu. Ereshkigal had come with him on the raid and killed the night security guard, drinking his blood. Lawton had been furious. There was no need to kill an innocent man. But Ereshkigal didn't understand the concept of innocent. To her, humans were food – or servants.

"Better get a new category for me," he'd told her.

Lawton had driven a stake through the security guard's heart to stop him becoming a vampire.

"Every time you feed, I'll have to do this to your victim," he'd said.

"Bring plenty of stakes," she'd said.

"You can't kill – "

"Then *you'll* have to feed me," she snapped. "From your own veins. Again."

The journey to Turkey had taken more than 24 hours. He'd driven without rest. He didn't feel he could sleep. He didn't feel he needed sleep. It was like the old days, before the dreams.

But now the dreams were gone.

Their subject was sleeping in the back of the truck.

They'd led Lawton to her.

It was as if all this was meant to be.

As if fate had him by the throat, controlling his every move. He would have never believed such a thing a few months ago. He thought life was random. That it had no meaning. But his dreams and where they had taken him had made him think twice. Now he started to think that there might be a pattern to life, a meaning, a plan. He wondered if someone, or something, somewhere, knew his destiny.

Who, or what, had that kind of power?

He felt anger that someone, or something, could be pulling his strings and had supremacy over his future.

My fate is in my hands, he thought. *No one will take that power away from me.*

He drove along a busy road. Apartment blocks lined the avenue. Traffic was heavy. He hoped the local police wouldn't notice he was driving a truck with Romanian number plates. He'd left the main routes to cross from Bulgaria into Turkey, just in case the authorities decided to stop him and check the back of the lorry.

He wondered what might have happened had they found a 5,000-year-old vampire huddled under piles of tarpaulin.

He still wasn't sure why he was doing this. *You're Jake Lawton*, he told himself, *vampire killer*. But they had a deal. She would get him to Nimrod. He would get her home.

What would his friends say if they knew he'd made a pact with a vampire?

Maybe Nimrod didn't exist, and this was a plot against him by the Nebuchadnezzars. He stirred in his seat, feeling wary, feeling nervous again. He didn't know what to believe anymore. He didn't know what was genuine or what was a scam.

The unreal was real.

The fake was fact.

Myth was truth.

But one thing was the same. One thing had not changed.

His instinct to survive.

And to him, survival meant fighting.

He recalled what Ereshkigal had told him about his false eye and how the skin of the trinity was a living thing. How it sought to fuse with other organisms – his genes.

Again he tried to pry the eye out of its socket. But it hurt so much when he tried to pluck it out. It felt as if he were pulling out the insides of his own head. The pain flashed and momentarily blinded him in his good eye. The truck veered. Car horns blared. Lawton felt the steering wheel spin out of his hands. He gasped. He grabbed the wheel and gritted his teeth and wrestled the truck back into the middle of the road. His heart pounded. He looked in the side mirror, looking for cops. No cops. Just angry drivers. Waving their fists and cursing. He steadied himself, got the truck under control again. He blew air out of his cheeks. His nerves loosened, and he was calm once more. Calm and in control.

He was on the E90 now, İpekyol Avenue, the road leading out of Şanliurfa.

A steady anger simmered in his chest.

He thought about his mother dying of booze and drugs.

He thought about tracking down his dad to Birkenhead, only to be told to fuck off.

He thought about finding somewhere to belong, the Armed Forces.

He thought about being rejected by all of them.

Then he thought about Aaliyah. About being with her. That was what made him fight. The hope that one day he and Aaliyah would have peace, that they would live together quietly in a world without death and blood and fear.

That's why he kept fighting.

It doesn't matter if they tell lies about me, he thought. *It doesn't matter if they hate me. I know I'm in the right. I know I have a cause.*

That's what gave him power.

He accelerated.

CHAPTER 25. TV STAR.

LONDON – 8AM (GMT), 18 MAY, 2011

"BRITAIN'S weak," said George Fuad. While the make-up girl touched foundation on his cheeks, he spoke to the producer. "There's no leadership, and at a time like this, you need leadership. You know what I'm saying, Kaz?"

Kaz, blonde hair cut like a boy, overweight, too much lipstick, said, "You don't need to tell me that, Mr Fuad. You can tell Jeffrey – "

"What questions is he going to ask me, love?"

"Questions?" said Kaz.

He glared at her. "Yeah, things that require answers."

"Questions. He – we won't be giving you the questions beforehand, Mr Fuad."

He eased the make-up girl aside and whipped the towel from his collar. "You don't seem to understand, Kaz, how things work now."

"You, Mr Fuad, don't seem to understand how things work."

George flushed. He got into Kaz's face.

"You know who I am?"

"I… I do, Mr Fuad."

"You know what's going to happen to the BB-fucking-C when I win tomorrow?"

"Are you threatening me, Mr Fuad?"

"Yes, Kaz, of course I'm fucking threatening you."

"If you threaten me again, I will call security."

George laughed in her face. He snapped his fingers. His two heavies opened up their blazers to show the handguns strapped into holsters under their armpits.

Kaz gawped. "You… they… they can't bring weapons – "

"This is not the world you used to live in, Kaz," said George. "This is a different world. My world. You better start seeing that. The Beeb might be gloating that it's now the only TV channel on air, that you've beaten off your competition. But you didn't do that 'cause you're better. You did that 'cause you're richer. Soon you won't be. No freedom. No balance. When I'm in charge, I'll be telling *you* what to broadcast, you hear me?"

"This is outrageous – "

"Where's this Jeffrey cunt?" he said.

George stormed out of the make-up room. He strode down the corridor. Kaz followed. His two heavies followed. His advisors followed.

Kaz was speaking to someone, saying, "He said the C-word, he called Jeffrey a… C-word. Who does he think he is? This is the BBC."

He barged on to the set during a live broadcast.

The presenter, Jeffrey Mathers, greeted him.

Mathers was slick. Oil in his hair. Oil on his skin. Oil in his veins.

"What a nice surprise," he told the camera, the confident grin never leaving his face, "Mr Fuad has joined us early. We'll get you miked up, sir, and we can have our chat, but first – "

"No 'first', Jeff." George sat down in the empty chair opposite Mathers. A sound guy scuttled forward with a radio mike. "Me first. I have a few things to – "

"If you could wait for the microphone, Mr Fuad. Then the audience can hear you."

"Sure, Jeff, sure," said George as the sound guy fixed the microphone to his tie.

"Right, the country can now hear you, Mr Fuad," said Mathers. "Welcome to Election Special, this morning."

"The country has been hearing me for a long time, Jeff, it's just the powers-that-be, and the establishment, who have been deaf."

"I'm sure you would say that – "

"I'm sure I… " George nearly said "fucking" but managed to stop himself " …would, Jeff."

"But if you'd allow me – "

"I will allow you, Jeff."

" – to ask why, why you think vampires are not a threat to human life?"

"I don't think, I *know*. I *know* they are not a threat. They have been sullied. They have been disparaged. They feel threatened, Jeff. And if someone feels threatened, they will, naturally, defend themselves."

"It doesn't seem they defended themselves, it seems they attacked first – "

George raised a hand. "Jake Lawton, a disgraced soldier and criminal, triggered a war against this species. An ancient, lost species. If he did the same against the panda, there would be outrage."

"But pandas don't kill humans."

"All right, tigers then. Tigers kill people."

"I don't think we need to be discussing pandas or tigers. I think we should stick to vampires."

"Let's do that," said George.

"It is true that vampires require blood to survive. If they are not killing innocent people, like you claim, how will they feed?"

"Criminals."

"Criminals?"

"They will be fed criminals."

A gasp went around the TV studio, and Jeffrey Mathers's eyes widened. But he kept going: "So… so you don't believe in rehabilitation then, Mr Fuad?"

"Not for murderers, rapists, and perverts I don't. And no one else outside the liberal, lefty, criminal-loving corridors of the BBC does, either, Jeffrey."

"Maybe not, but do you think those people believe in feeding criminals to vampires? That would seem like an outrageous solution."

George leaned forward, put on a concerned frown. "Let me tell you what is outrageous, Jeffrey. What is outrageous is to attack the heart of democracy, as Jake Lawton did, and burn it to the ground. He did what Guy Fawkes attempted to do – destroy parliament. He also encouraged an army of *foreign* criminals to invade the streets of London and cause mayhem."

"They were said to have saved a lot of lives, Mr Fuad. They carried the Union flag and represented Britain."

"Another lie. These immigrants attacked first. Britain is a great country, Jeffrey. She will fight back against the enemy within, be they foreign or local insurgents. We should accommodate all species here. One day, vampire and human will live side by side, and Britain will again be great. But there must be pain, Jeff. There must be suffering to achieve this greatness. Don't let anyone tell you it will be easy. Greatness is never easy, Jeff. Greatness comes from sweat and blood and difficult decisions. The government – or interim government, should I say – does not have the stomach to make these decisions. Elizabeth Wilson leads an impotent executive. It is weak and fragile, and corrupted by haters and colluders. When the United Party win tomorrow's election, the rescue mission will start. We will make Britain great again. We will not put up with foreign troublemakers, or home-grown ones. We'll make London a golden city. We'll make England a great nation. We'll make Britain a world-respected empire again."

Applause burst out in the studio.

George had never felt so powerful.

CHAPTER 26.
FRONTIER.

TURKISH-IRAQI BORDER – 9PM (GMT + 3 HOURS), 18 MAY, 2011

THEY crossed the Tigris into Iraq a few miles northwest of where the country's borders met the frontiers of Turkey and Syria.

It was dark, so she was awake and sitting in the cab next to Lawton. Her presence unnerved him. He kept glancing at her from the corner of his eye, making sure she wasn't about to attack him. But she didn't. She stared ahead, fascinated by the world she was seeing for the first time. Ereshkigal had never seen cars or trucks or planes or roads like these, or towns like these.

The landscape was barren. A mist hung over the mountains. A town lurked in the distance.

"I followed Alexander the Great's army across this border and fed on his men," she said. "He was going to conquer Babylon."

And destroy the trinity, thought Lawton.

He drove, sweat pouring off him, fear chilling his blood. His knuckles were white, so tightly did he grip the steering wheel. His head ached, and his injured eye pulsed. He had to stop, or he felt like he would explode. He slowed the vehicle and switched off the engine. He leapt out of the truck.

The chill hit him.

He looked up. No stars, no moon. Just deep, dense blackness. Surrounding him, the mountains looked threatening. He felt sick. He felt lost. He had turned his back on her, and he was almost waiting for her to attack. But she didn't. She stayed in the cab.

His shoulders sagged, and he turned, ready to get back into the truck.

Headlights blinded him. The vehicle came storming along the road. Its horn blared. The shape of a man holding a gun poked out of the passenger-side window.

Lawton reacted.

He raced back towards the truck.

Gunfire raked the road.

He threw himself to the ground.

He threw his hands up.

The Land Rover came to a halt, kicking up dirt.

Three men leapt out.

They shouted at him in a language that wasn't Arabic.

Kurds, he thought.

They pointed guns at him.

He scowled and cursed his stupidity.

Glancing towards the truck, he was about to warn Ereshkigal.

But the cab was empty.

She was gone.

He focused on the men and quickly formulated a plan to disarm and kill them.

It would be difficult and dangerous.

A gun appeared in his face. Its owner shouted at him again. The bloke was a middle-aged lump with a beard and a scar on his cheek.

Lawton studied him.

Warlords, he thought.

The other two men were checking the truck.

They babbled.

The lump held the gun to Lawton's head and kept jabbering. Had he yakked in Arabic, Lawton might have understood. He knew a little of the language. But not enough to save his skin. The only way he knew to save his skin was to fight back.

The other two came back from the truck. They had his rucksack. They emptied it, and the Spear of Abraham fell out, along with a handgun, bullets, water, stale bread, his wallet containing some cash, maps, notebook, and pens.

One of the men picked up the spear and studied it, his brow furrowed.

They chattered, obviously discussing the weapon.

"Careful with that," he said.

The three men gawped, as if they'd never heard anyone speak before.

"English?" said the bearded lump.

Lawton nodded.

The other two started laughing. They took the money out of his wallet and shared it between them.

Lawton licked his lips. They were dry.

He was being robbed.

And he was going to get shot.

The bearded lump nodded at him and smiled, showing toothless gums.

He cocked his rifle.

Lawton thought, *I'm going to die.*

He felt powerless.

But then a figure reared up against the darkness on the roof of the truck. A slight, slim frame, her dress fluttering in the night air. Her scent carried on the breeze.

It was death.

CHAPTER 27. DIGGING DEEPER.

HILLAH, IRAQ – 10PM (GMT + 3 HOURS), 18 MAY, 2011

ALFRED fanned the smoke and coughed. Laxman took the hint and stubbed out the cigarette on the ground.

The tunnel was gloomy. It sloped downwards.

Deeper, deeper, thought Alfred.

As they walked, electricians were wiring neon strip lights to the walls. Every step Alfred took was a step into the light. It was as if he were illuminating the darkness. He allowed himself to think that. It filled him with a sense of power he'd rarely felt.

The mining team had dug through both the left-hand and right-hand tunnels in the fork. The bones of the un-named creature and the skeleton of the nailed man had been packaged and stored. They'd be returned to Britain. Perhaps they'd be artefacts at a museum opened in Alfred's name. The cave painting thought to be by Abraham had been photographed and encased in glass to protect it from deterioration. Malik had requested that his team have some time off after their remarkable discovery. Alfred said no. He told them to get back to work – and to do 24-hour shifts, if need be. There could be no delay in the search for Nimrod. George was waiting for news.

"I wish my brother could see this," said Alfred.

"What's to see?" Laxman said.

Alfred stared ahead. The tunnel was about twenty feet high. A drill purred up ahead in the gloom. They were going deeper and deeper into the earth.

"An underground city on a greater scale than any city on earth," said Alfred. "Irkalla, home of Nimrod."

"You scared of what you might find down there?"

"I'm excited, Laxman. My brother will be delighted."

"You're a bit obsessed with your brother."

Alfred glared at the soldier.

"You're always going on about him," Laxman added.

"You have siblings?" said Alfred.

"Sister."

"You see her often?"

"I see her never."

"She dead?"

"Might as well be."

"Why's that?"

"I beat her husband up on their wedding day."

"Did he deserve it?"

"Anyone gets beaten up deserves it, Fuad. If you ask for it, you deserve it. If you're in the wrong place at the wrong time, that's stupid, so you deserve it."

"What did he do, your brother in law?"

"He got too smart. He was a banker. Said I was scum."

"Maybe he was drunk."

"He was. Makes no difference."

"Maybe you were looking for a fight."

"I'm always looking for a fight, Alfie."

"You might have one here," he said, gesturing down the tunnel.

"You think?"

"Nimrod might wake up angry."

"I'll have my SA80 trained on him."

"Think that'll make a difference, a gun?"

"Soon find out."

"You'll know he'll want a sacrifice."

Laxman furrowed his brow.

"He'll want blood," said Alfred.

Laxman shrugged.

"What if he wants yours, Laxman?"

"He'll have to fight me for it – and he'll regret waking up, I tell you. I'll put him to sleep for good."

"You can't kill Nimrod."

"Everything can be killed."

"He can only be killed in one way."

"How's that?"

Alfred told him.

Laxman looked confused. "Make him one again? Make him whole? Don't get it. Just have to rely on my gun."

They kept walking.

"You queer, Alfred?"

"Does it matter?"

Laxman shrugged. "Your brother queer?"

Alfred glared at him.

"He ain't married, neither," said Laxman.

"He has been. Twice."

"What happened?"

"They betrayed him, like women do."

"You don't like birds, do you?"

"I don't like anyone, Laxman – except my brother."

"Think he'll make a good Prime Minister, then?"

"The best ever. Him and me, we'll rule together. Him, first among equals."

"You're a bit sick, I think."

"I'm paying you not to think."

"Oh, don't get me wrong – I don't give a shit. You be as sick as you like. I'm just commenting."

"Don't comment, either. Just do your job."

"Seems there's not much of a job left to do."

"You'll have more than enough on your plate in the next few days, Laxman."

The mercenary lit another cigarette.

Alfred fumed and was about to berate him when a voice boomed from the darkness.

"We are through, we are through… "

CHAPTER 28. WHAT DO YOU WANT?

THE way she'd killed the three tribesman shocked Lawton.

She'd moved so quickly. A white blur against the night. Sliced each man's throat with her razor-sharp nails. Before one hit the ground, the second was dead, and then the third.

And as rapidly as she'd killed them, Ereshkigal returned to each body and feasted on the blood gushing from their open throats.

Once she had drained them of blood, they were embryonic vampires, waiting to be born again within 24 hours. So Lawton waited for the bodies to stop twitching before driving a stake into each man's heart, and their bodies combusted.

Mutilating corpses wasn't his idea of fun. But he had no choice. He didn't have much choice in anything he did these days. He wondered again about fate and how powerless he'd become and determined once more to fight for his own future.

As he stood over the tribesmen's remains, he asked Ereshkigal, "What do you care about?"

She said nothing. She wiped blood from her mouth.

"Do you want a vampire world, like the Nebuchadnezzars?" he said.

"These are human things – dreams, power, destiny. They are drained out of us when we become vampire."

"Then what do you care about?"

"Survival," she said.

"But you love your husband. You want to go back to him."

She furrowed her brow. "Love? I don't remember."

"I think you lie. You remember the love you felt for Haran, you told me."

She scowled. "I don't remember love. I want to go home because it is where I belong. I have lived in dread for 5,000 years, wandering the earth. Now, I want to sleep in my husband's darkness, in my city of bones. What do you want, Lawton?"

"I want to die an old man, wrecked and broken by life."

"What a miserable wretch you are. You have a woman?"

He said nothing. He thought of Aaliyah. His heart ached. Was she still alive? Would this journey end in a broken heart for him?

"I see you do," said Ereshkigal. "Where is she?"

"Here in this country. Hunting your Nimrod."

"Then I shall I have to kill her after I kill you."

He said nothing. There was nothing to say. This was an irrational alliance for him. He wasn't sure if he was still dreaming or not. How could he have aligned himself with a vampire? How could they both be headed towards the same destiny? A face-to-face with the god of the undead. And how could they work together when their end goals were poles apart?

"If I left you here," she said, "would you survive?"

"If I left you here, would you? Kill me now, you're alone out here. No hiding place. The sun'll get you. You need me to get home. But if I kill you, what's the worse that'll happen to me?"

"Killing me is not so easy."

"I'm good at doing stuff that's not easy."

"You are not like other humans."

He didn't want to know that he was different. He didn't want to think about what the skin in his eye was doing to him. If he could, he would rip it out of his head. But he knew it would take all the nerves out with it, and much of his brain. It was attached to him. And it was living inside him, poisoning him. He rejected the notion that he was becoming something different, that he would not be Jake Lawton anymore. But in truth he had been changing every day. And he had changed more during these past few years than at any time in his life.

CHAPTER 29. THREE SECONDS.

7AM (GMT + 3 HOURS), 19 MAY, 2011

HER company was strangely comforting.

They lay in the rear of the truck. It was pitch black. Outside, the sun scorched down. It was nearly 10am in Iraq. Mid-morning. Blistering heat. Deadly to the creature lying next to him.

They had driven through the night, covering more than 100km on off-road routes. They had left behind the regions of Iraqi Kurdistan, and they were now in Iraq itself. They had stopped a few kilometres outside Tel Isqof, an Assyrian town of around 7,000 people. Lawton had driven the truck into some trees on the side of the road. As long as no one made their way through the woods, they should be safe enough. But you couldn't be sure. And that fear prevented Lawton from resting.

Ereshkigal, though, slept like the dead thing she was, curled up into a ball next to him under the tarpaulin.

His mind drifted. He felt relaxed. He looked at her pale face. Her flesh was like porcelain. She was completely still, not breathing. But she was dead, after all. She didn't need air. Only blood. He touched his neck where she'd bitten him. He felt queasy, the thought of her cold lips on his throat, the blood pulsing out of his vein, into her mouth.

He sat bolt upright.

He didn't want to feel any sympathy towards this creature. You had to be merciless with them. You couldn't have them as allies. They were made to hunt and kill – to hunt and kill humans.

But maybe, if you looked hard enough, you could find some humanity in them.

He stared at the sleeping vampire.

Maybe there was a hint of what they'd been before.

And Ereshkigal had been a young woman in love. A bride-to-be, excited at the prospect of her wedding day.

There had to be something of that left in her.

He shook his head, rejecting the notion.

There had been nothing of the human Jenna left in the vampire Jenna.

There had been nothing of the human Sassie left in the vampire Sassie.

Or if there had been, he'd not seen it – or maybe not looked hard enough.

He put his head in his hands. His skull ached all the time. His eye burned. Again he tried to pluck the glass sphere from the socket, again it felt as if he were yanking out all the nerves and muscle.

He didn't know what was happening to him. He thought he might be changing as Ereshkigal had suggested. And that change meant death to him. He didn't want any vampire blood in his body. He would kill himself if that were true. He had decided – after ensuring that Aaliyah was safe and killing Nimrod, Lawton would end his life. It wasn't worth living anymore.

He got up, planning to get going again.

He covered Ereshkigal in the tarpaulin before opening the rear door narrowly and peering out.

He stepped outside. It was hot. He blew air out of his cheeks. He started sweating straight away.

He was making his way round to the front of the truck when he saw them.

Four men in military fatigues loitering near a jeep, just twenty yards away.

They straightened when they saw Lawton.

His immediate reaction was to protect Ereshkigal. He didn't question his instinct. If he'd considered it, protecting a vampire would seem bizarre. But that's what every sinew in his being told him to do.

He waved at the soldiers and said in Arabic, "*Sabah al-khair.*"

Good morning.

Then he bolted. Away from the truck. Away from Ereshkigal. Away from the men.

He heard shouts of, "*Qif! Qif!*"

Stop! Stop!

He heard the jeep's engine roar.

He looked behind him.

Three of the troops were chasing on foot.

The fourth drove the jeep.

It crashed through the trees after him.

Lawton sprinted. His heart pounded. He was tired and weak, his legs ready to buckle. But he had to get them as far away from her as he could. She had no chance of protecting herself in daylight.

A glance over his shoulder showed they were gaining.

He opted for some delaying tactics.

He put his hand up and slowed down.

They came up to him, shouting, and shoved him on the ground.

He got a mouthful of dirt. He spat it out. They were yelling at him. They prodded him with their weapons.

"*Qif,*" said a voice. A fat man in his fifties who looked suspiciously like Saddam Hussein stepped out of the jeep.

He huffed and puffed. The drive had obviously taken a lot out of him.

Lawton tried to identify the man's stripes. He was certainly the senior officer. But he couldn't make out the Iraqi insignia.

Lawton sat up, his hands still over his head. His arms and his back hurt where they'd jabbed him with their rifles.

The fat man pulled out a packet of Marlboro and put one in his mouth. Lit it with a Zippo. Offered a cigarette to Jake. He took one.

The fat officer gestured, and two of the soldiers picked Lawton up, roughly.

The fag hung in his mouth. The officer lit it. The smoke was strong, and he coughed. Much stronger than the rollies he usually smoked. He'd not smoked a proper ciggie in years. *It was here in Iraq*, he thought. When he was fighting Saddam. And here he was now face-to-face with a Saddam look-alike.

"You are American? British? Français?" asked the officer in English. Then he said something in French, a question.

Lawton smoked.

"You talk to me," the fat man said. "*Vous me parler. Sie reden mit mir*. English? French? German? No matter, you will talk to me." He nodded.

Lawton got a rifle butt in his belly. It knocked the wind out of him, and he bent double. The fag went flying. The fat man stamped on it.

He felt himself being picked up again and his pockets rummaged. He had nothing on him. The only thing of value he had was the Spear of Abraham, and that was in the truck.

"No ID," said the fat soldier. He gestured towards the truck. Two of the men started to trot towards it.

Lawton said, "All right, you win," as calmly as he could, not wanting to draw attention to the fact that there was something in the truck. "I'm British. On a mission."

The fat man scowled. "I know nothing of this. I command this post. I know nothing."

"Your government would know."

"They say nothing to me."

"Your English is very good, sir."

The fat soldier smiled. "Sandhurst."

Bollocks, thought Lawton. *American TV, more like.*

"I'm sure you learnt how to treat allied troops," he said.

"I know how to treat friends – and enemies."

Lawton was getting ready to fight. He'd worked out he could take all of them, even though they were armed. It was high risk. But they looked slow and soft. The fat bloke, easy. Stub a cigarette in his eye. Guy number two, next to him, would lose his gun before fatso started to scream. And that weapon would kill guys three and four before the butt slammed into guy number two's jaw.

Four down. Less than three seconds.

He was ready to make those three seconds count when something hard whacked him across the back of the head, and stars burst before his eyes before he passed out.

PART FOUR.

DESTINY.

CHAPTER 30.
ELECTION DAY.

LONDON – 7.22AM (GMT), 19 MAY, 2011

IT was looking good for George Fuad and the United Party. The polls showed they were going to win. Or *he* was going to win. And it was a good victory. Not a landslide. But a solid majority.

It was early days so far, but the turnout had been low. Below ten per cent in some areas. But they'd expected poor figures. People were either too scared or had given up hope.

George longed for it to be the latter.

Apathy was a gift to tyrants. And he was a tyrant. He made no bones about it. Tyranny was his weapon. Terror would be his modus operandi.

He'd known this day was coming since he was a child. Since his dad had told him the Fuad family was special.

The sun was shining, and George felt happy. He was standing outside a polling booth near Leicester Square Tube Station. The streets were still relatively quiet, considering this was London soon after rush hour. But there hadn't been much rushing in the city over the past few years. And life had dwindled to a crawl recently.

George was being interviewed by a radio reporter, and he said, "Britons will vote in their thousands for a change. They feel abandoned. They have been left high and dry, caught in the middle of a war between weak government and dangerous foreign gangs. The people have been misled into thinking that vampires are our enemies. Today, the British people will tell the government, the corrupt, dirty government, what they think of them. This will be a vote for unity – unity between human and vampire."

"Mr Fuad," said the reporter, "what do you say to those who claim you have lied about the dangers posed by vampires."

"What do I say? I say it's them are the liars. Look at what they've done to Britain. Look at what Elizabeth Wilson, who has brazenly accused me of lying, has done to Britain. She let it die. I'm going to bring it to life again. I'm going to make this country great. And London will be a great capital, just like Babylon was."

"Like Babylon?"

"A golden city," he said.

"We can barely run our schools and hospitals. Rubbish is strewn on the streets. People are homeless. There are no jobs. The capital's water supply is poisoned. How can you justify spending so much money on making, as you say, a golden city?"

"We won't spend any cash," said George. "We'll take it back. We'll take it back from Europe. We'll take it back from everyone who has ferreted cash away illegally in our vaults. And we'll send an army to take it back."

"But our Armed Forces are in tatters."

"No, our new allies, the vampires. They will be our army. They will work with us to build a golden city. We'll work together, humans and vampires, for the benefit of Britain. This is what people want. This is what they will vote for."

Yes, he thought, *they will foolishly vote for panic and fear*.

But that would come. For now, let them see just a little bit of hope on the horizon. A day or two of hope.

Cheers came from across the street. George waved at his supporters. They waved white flags emblazoned with a red U, symbol of his party.

The radio reporter said, “I’m here with George Fuad, leader of the United Party, the man who appears to be headed into government. You must be happy with what the opinion polls suggest, Mr Fuad?”

“Today is the most important poll.”

“If you win, what will be your first act as prime minster?”

Declare myself emperor for life, he thought. *Turn the screw on you lot at the BBC. Unleash vampires on the pathetic population.*

He smiled. “If I win, I will have a cup of tea, the most English thing a man can do.”

She thanked him.

He walked towards his car. One of his bodyguards opened the door for him. George got in the back seat. He let out a sigh of relief. An advisor sat in the back. She held out a satellite phone.

“More interviews?” said George.

“Your brother,” said the advisor.

He grabbed the phone excitedly.

“Hello, Alfred?”

The line crackled.

“It’s good to hear your voice,” said Alfred, his love for George coming through the bad line.

“You too,” said George, not meaning it so much.

“We – you’re going to win.”

“Looks like it. What’ve you got to say to me, Alfie?”

“We’re through to Irkalla. We are at the outskirts of this incredible underground city, mate. There are buildings here. Pillars stretching miles into the darkness above me. It seems impossible, because… because we’re only a thousand feet under ground. It’s like a mirage. It doesn’t make sense, but it’s – ”

“Have you found Nimrod?”

"Not yet, no, but we're... we're – "

"Hurry up, Alfie."

"I will, I will. But I have even better news for you."

"There can't be better news than finding Nimrod."

"Might be," said Alfred. "Jake Lawton has been arrested. He's being held by Iraqi security forces."

It *was* good news. It made George feel even happier. Fate was smiling down on him.

"Make sure he never leaves Iraq, Alfie. If the Iraqis don't do him, send some of those hired killers you've got there. Send anyone. Don't let Jake Lawton see the light of day ever again."

"He won't," said Alfred.

CHAPTER 31. DESPERATE DAYS.

ELIZABETH Wilson ran a hand through her hair. She looked demoralised. She looked old and broken. She sat behind her desk in her office at Millbank, elbows on the desk, head in her hands.

"I should have done as Fuad asked and stepped aside," she said.

"No," said Christine Murray. "He wanted to humiliate you."

"And this isn't humiliating?"

"Liz, we haven't lost yet. The polls only opened three hours ago."

Wilson snorted. *She was right*, thought Murray. It was a disaster.

She glanced out of the office window. It was a sunny day. But few people wandered the streets. Those that did looked downtrodden as usual. A beaten population. A crushed electorate.

"It would have made no difference had you thrown in the towel," Murray finally said.

"What do you mean?"

"He would have imprisoned us, killed us, all the same."

In the main office, party workers were gloomily packing boxes with files and stationery. Men in blue overalls were folding desks and chairs and piling them up against the walls.

"We could have struck a deal," said Wilson. "This is politics. I'm good at politics. I could have made a deal."

But she didn't sound convinced.

"With the devil?" said Murray.

"Better deal with the devil than lose a bet to him."

"Lawton will – "

"Lawton caused this," Wilson snapped.

"Caused it?"

"He pissed them off, didn't he. Attacked them without cause. Picked on them. Murdered them."

"You can't murder something that's already dead. And Jake Lawton has saved this country time after time."

"And where has that got us? The waters are still poisoned. The people are starving, they're jobless, they're homeless. And we've still got vampires. Lots of them."

Murray stayed quiet. There was no getting through to Wilson. The politician was desperate. And who could blame her? She'd never guessed when she became an MP in 1987 that this would be her fate. She'd had an affair with another newly elected MP at the time. He was called Graeme Strand. He, too, had become Prime Minister. And he, too, suffered at the hands of the Nebuchadnezzars.

Strand had been murdered in office.

At least Wilson was alive – for now.

"Perhaps Lawton did kill that man in Iraq," said Wilson.

"He did kill a man."

"An innocent man, then."

"A suicide bomber targeting men and boys at a mosque."

"That's not what you believed at the time."

"I was wrong."

"You were a hundred percent convinced; I saw what you wrote."

"Liz, I was wrong. I was very wrong. A hundred percent wrong. And I'm ashamed of it to this day that I accused him of murder. I accused him before I knew the truth. Before I knew him."

Wilson was quiet for a few seconds before she said, "I never thought it would come to this. I wanted to be Prime Minister, you know, but not like this. And I didn't want it to end in this way. What are we going to do, Christine?"

"Jake's out there – "

"But where?"

"And… and my son."

"How does that help?"

"He won't give up. My child is an angry young man. He… he had spoken before of killing Fuad. He thought it was his destiny. Fuad and the Nebuchadnezzars have destroyed out family. My husband is dead, my eldest. There's only David now, and he sees it as his mission to kill Fuad."

"Your thirteen year old is planning an assassination, and you allow it?"

"I don't believe you said that."

Wilson put her head in her hands. "Neither do I. My democratic instinct. My moral compass."

"Our moral compasses point in different directions, now. Needs must."

"I don't know if I approve."

"You're not in a position to approve or disapprove, Liz. The time for fair play is over. It's war, now. And sometimes war is unpleasant, and it means not talking to your enemies, but killing them."

"Did Jake Lawton teach you that?"

"He did, and he was right."

CHAPTER 32.
A COUNTRY OF GHOSTS.

DAVID Murray had seen photographs of elections like this. But they weren't held in Britain. They were in poor countries where democracy had only just been introduced.

Here in the UK, democracy was dying – but the images were the same. Long queues of wretches waiting to go into a polling station. Waiting to vote. Waiting to change their destiny.

But unlike those voters in poor countries who were celebrating the birth of freedom, these London voters weren't smiling. They looked sad and scared. They looked grey and doomed. Their fates were sealed, whichever way they voted.

And they seemed to know that, David thought.

The polls suggested that the Nebuchadnezzars were going to win the election.

He'd heard on the radio that morning that not many people were likely to vote. But it was different here. More people were turning up.

David, Kwan Mei, and her Turkish friend Ediz Ün watched dozens of voters filing into the polling station in Brixton.

David would have voted himself, but he was not even fourteen, yet. Mei was eighteen but an illegal immigrant. Ediz was twenty and had a UK passport. He'd voted earlier, although he'd said it was pointless.

"The Nebs are going to win," he'd said. "But I have to make my voice heard. That's why I'm going in there and voting."

Now, sitting on the wall outside the polling station, Ediz said, "Look at them guys."

David looked. Three Nebuchadnezzar thugs stood like bouncers at the door of the polling station. They were big guys dressed in black. The sun glinted menacingly off their sunglasses. Sweat glossed their shaven heads. Muscles bulged under their jackets – or maybe those were their weapons. They were certainly armed. Every Neb thug carried guns, despite it being illegal in Britain. But they ignored the law. They made up their own. And no one tried to stop them. They had already taken over – even before the election result was known.

"They're checking out the voters," said David.

One of the Neb thugs put his arm out to stop a woman entering the polling station. She seemed to argue with the men in black. But it made no difference. One of the thugs just shoved her out of the way. She staggered away and crashed to the floor, crying.

David started to leap off the wall and rush to her aid. But Mei grabbed his arm. He looked at her. She shook her head.

Now, the thug stomped towards the woman.

He towered over her.

"You ain't coming in if you're wearing a Tory badge, darling."

"I'm... I'm voting," said the woman. "I've a right to wear any badge I want. It's a free country."

The thug laughed. "You think so?" He kicked her. She cried out. The other voters, filing into the polling station, looked away. The Neb kicked the woman again. She cursed him. He said, "Fuck off before I put a bullet in your brain, bitch."

The woman staggered to her feet. She was crying. She limped, holding her side where she'd been kicked.

"I have a right to vote," she screamed.

"Not here you don't," said the Neb thug.

The woman stumbled away.

The thug turned to face those waiting in line. "Anyone else planning to vote the wrong way? Tell you now, you ain't going in there if you're wearing badges or anything supporting the Opposition parties. You want to vote, take them off right now."

Mei said, "We have to leave London."

"Leave?" said David.

"Yeah, leave," said Ediz. "Go north. Start killing vampires. Start killing them up there, then travel south, killing them as we go. Wipe them out, yeah?"

"You two go," David said.

"Why you not come?" Mei said.

"I'm going to kill George Fuad."

"You never get to him if he wins," Mei said.

"Mei's right," said Ediz. "He'll be protected. Best to kill the vampires."

David folded his arms. "Screw the vampires. Fuad's the head. Cut off the head, the body will die."

Mei rolled her eyes. "He is not head. He is man. I come from country not democratic. Like Britain will be. You can't get to leaders. They are like ghosts."

David watched the people. They were like ghosts, too. A country of ghosts.

He said, "I've lost nearly everything in the past few years. I was ten when all this started. Going to school. Looking up to my big brother. Playing football with my dad. Wishing I could see more of my mum. Now, my dad and my brother are dead. My mum is virtually held prisoner by the government. And when Fuad gets into power, she might not even survive."

"Vampires killed your father and brother?" said Ediz.

"No, the Nebuchadnezzars did. George Fuad and all of them. The vampires are just weapons they use."

"Then take away weapons," said Mei.

David shook his head. "This is all about the Fuads. They started all this. When that old man Afdal Haddad was six years old all those years ago, he came to Britain to live with the Fuad family. They looked after him. They helped him become clever, and when he became clever he made those pills that started all this. He made the first vampires because the Fuads looked after him and helped him."

"But the vampires are more of a problem," said Ediz.

David leapt off the wall. "You go and kill vampires. Jake will kill Nimrod. Me… I'll kill Fuad."

"You're just after revenge," said Ediz.

"Too right," David said.

"That's OK, but you've got to be cool about this," said the Turkish youth. "This is a war, and you can't think of war as revenge. You've got to plan. You've got to think about strategies and all that kind of stuff."

"Fine, you think of all that stuff," said David.

"I lose people too," said Mei, her eyes full of tears.

David felt himself blush. "I know."

"I lose my mother when I come to Britain. I lose friends in war against vampires. I never go home, now."

"I know," he said again. "I know."

"But I not go crazy," said the girl.

"I know you don't go crazy."

She jumped down to join him, her eyes red with tears. She reached out to touch his face.

Gunfire barked.

Mei and David instinctively threw themselves to the pavement. Ediz dived off the wall and joined them.

Screams filled the air.

David glanced up.

The people filing into the polling station were also on the ground.

The Nebuchadnezzar thugs had their pistols out and were firing.

A young man dressed in a messy grey suit was running down the street.

The Nebs chased him. They kept shooting in his direction. There was panic.

David got up and grabbed Mei. Ediz leapt to his feet. The three of them ducked away behind the wall and peered over it.

They saw the young man buckle. Hit in the leg. He staggered and fell. The Neb's caught up with him. One of them was dragging another black-shirt away and saying, "No, be careful." But another thug reached the fallen man and stood over him. The Neb aimed his weapon at the bloke. He was going to shoot him in cold blood. Shoot a wounded man.

The second Neb shouted, "Get away from him, Tony."

But it was too late.

The young man pulled open his jacket.

David gasped.

He had explosives strapped to his body.

"Down," said David.

He, Mei, and Ediz ducked behind the wall.

"Humans first!" shouted the young man.

And then the explosion came. It shook the wall. It rocked the pavement. It made David's ears ring. Lumps of meat rained down. A scrap of grey material floated around in the debris. The smell of flesh and cordite filled the air. Then the sounds became muffled. David couldn't hear. Mei was shouting at him, but he couldn't hear what she was saying. She was pulling at his arm, hauling him to his feet. He got up. He was dizzy. His head hurt. He was virtually deaf. Mei's face was grey with dust. Ediz was slapping the side of his head with his hand, as if he were trying to dislodge something from his ear.

David scanned the street. Smoke and blood everywhere. People running. People screaming. Nebs shooting. Killing indiscriminately.

Mei dragged David away. Along with Ediz, they fled.

CHAPTER 33. HUMANITY.

"IT was a guy from Humans First," said David. "He sacrificed himself. I couldn't do that, I just couldn't. But maybe I'm not meant to be a hero. I'm just meant to be a scared little boy who wants all this to be over, who misses his dad and his brother and his – his mum."

His companion said nothing. He was an old man. Sixty or maybe seventy. It was hard to tell. His face was covered in a wiry, grey beard. His skin was creased and tinged yellow. But his eyes, they shone like diamonds. His name was Bill, and a long time ago he'd been a soldier. Now he was homeless. He spent his time near Leicester Square. David sat with him on a bench, watching the people scuttle by, watching the litter blow around. It was about 1.00pm. In the past, Leicester Square would have been teeming with people at that time. Not anymore.

The square was desolate. The cinemas were shut now. The shops selling trinkets to tourists were gone. Most of the restaurants were boarded up. And no Starbucks, no Costa Coffee. A few sad-looking cases loitered around, some eating burgers they'd bought from a van on the square. They would all try to disappear after dark. The vampires would come, so humans had to find hiding places – if they could.

But David wasn't scared of vampires. He wore the Nebuchadnezzars' mark. Bill did too. David had stolen him one. Clipped it to the old man's hat. "Since you never take that off," he'd told Bill, "it'll be safe there on the brim. Don't lose it."

David had met Bill the previous year. The boy had been looking for Jake Lawton. He had been looking for him because he wanted to kill him. A Nebuchadnezzar called Bernard Lithgow had told David that if he killed Lawton, it would bring his brother Michael back to life.

In his heart, David knew it was a lie. But he was desperate. Desperate to see his brother again. But his brother was a vampire. You couldn't make vampires human again. And why should David have believed a man like Bernard Lithgow?

He was Fraser Lithgow's dad. Fraser was how this all started. He had been a low-life drug dealer. He got hoodwinked into distributing the pills called Skarlet that produced the first batch of vampires in 2008.

At the beginning, Fraser had been an idiot. Jake had been out to get him. But soon they became friends, and they fought the vampires together.

But Fraser's dad tried to tempt his son to the dark side. Like Darth Vadar did with Luke Skywalker. Unlike Luke Skywalker, Fraser had crossed over.

David didn't know why, but Fraser went to the Nebuchadnezzars. He went and was used as a weapon. Used like a terrorist organization would use a suicide bomber. They sent him to poison London's water supply, telling him the drug he put into the system would cure people of vampirism.

Why had he believed such a stupid thing? Why had David believed such a stupid thing?

They were desperate, that's why. Desperate for all this to come to an end. Desperate for a normal life.

But normal life wasn't going to be that easy. There would have to be suffering and war and death before Britain could be normal again.

David had found Bill last year because the old man knew where to find Lawton. Bill knew where to find a lot of former soldiers. He lived on the streets, and he heard all the rumours and the whispers that buzzed around. With some suspicion, he'd led David to Jake.

He was never going to kill the man who was like a brother and a father to him. Although he made a half-hearted attempt, and nearly got himself killed by Aaliyah, he'd never really mean to hurt Jake Lawton. Not that he had much chance of doing that in the first place.

"I didn't mean to kill him, you know," said David now. "Jake. I never meant to. I couldn't have, anyway. You know that, don't you?"

Bill waved his protests away.

"You understand why I did it, Bill?"

Bill drank some cider from a plastic bottle. David smelled it. The drink made him thirsty.

"I feel so scared, Bill."

"We're all scared."

"I feel like I haven't been a kid, like it's my destiny never to be one."

"There's war for you. Kids grow up quickly. You should be proud. You're a hero."

"No I'm not."

"No you're not, then. What do I know? Old soldier."

"I want to kill George Fuad."

Old Bill nodded.

"But my friend Mei – "

"She's a brave one, that little Chinese lass."

"Yes. Mei wants to go after vampires. Not after Fuad. But if you cut off the head, the body dies, doesn't it, Bill?"

"Yes, but you also want him dead 'cause he's got your mum."

David flushed.

"And," Bill went on, "because you reckon he killed your dad and your brother."

"I have seen some shitty things in the past few years, Bill. Things if you'd told me about when I was ten, I'd say they were cool. But they weren't cool. I've seen kids die. I've seen boys my age being shot these past few days because they stole bread to feed their families. I saw that guy today sacrifice himself. Is this our fate, to suffer and die?"

"'Fraid it might be. Everything ends up in death."

"Unless you're a vampire. They go on. They never end."

"They do, David. They do when they face you or Jake or that Chinese lass and her friends. This is a bad war. Worse than war between men. I know some people think it's time we lived alongside these vampires."

David grunted.

"I know," said Bill, "I know it's a crazy idea, but some people think it's time to talk to them, make peace."

"You can't make peace with an enemy that just wants to kill you. Not just defeat you, but kill you."

"You know, maybe we don't like them because they are our predator. Humans ain't had a real predator since we left the Savannah. Maybe they are nature's way of culling us. We've had our way too long."

"Doesn't mean we shouldn't fight back."

"That's true, we should fight back. And it don't mean it's wrong. Me, I think it's crazy. We can't live side by side with vampires. We have got to fight them and beat them, or we are fucked, son – seriously fucked."

The old man drank again. His breath smelled. His beard was stained.

He said, "Humans are odd, you know. We hate anything different. It scares us. I was a racist when I was younger. Not kick a Paki to death or nothing like that. Just, you know, what the fuck are you doing in my country? Fuck off."

David listened.

"Then I met and fell in love with this gorgeous West Indian girl," said Bill. "Flora was her name."

The old man's eyes watered. Memories making him cry.

He said, "She was wonderful and taught me to see that people are just people. Some good, some bad. Colour's not a bar to goodness. But it ain't a bar to badness, either. I served with some Indian fellows in the Army. Great they were. Hell of a laugh. Seriously brave. You learn as you go on. What I'm saying is, humans don't like anything that isn't like them."

"So you're saying we should give vampires a chance?"

"No. Ain't you listening? I said we should fight them. Because, son, vampires don't have the thing that made those Indian troops special, that made Flora gorgeous, that makes you a brave lad who's scared, but knows he has to stand up and be counted and do the right thing."

"What?" said David.

"Humanity."

CHAPTER 34.
THE BEGINNING OF A LONG NIGHT.

MOTHERHOOD, marriage, journalism, and now politics – fate had decided that Christine Murray would fail at them all.

Is there nothing I can do right? she thought.

Murray, Elizabeth Wilson, and a few supporters were watching the end of Britain play out on television at party's Millbank HQ.

It was 10.00pm. The ballot had just closed. The first exit poll predicted a landslide. Fuad was going to romp to victory, according to the survey.

Commentators sounded the death knell of democracy. Analysts suggested cautious optimism in any dealings with the vampires.

"Fuad's Union Party has won sixty-two per cent of the vote," said a BBC reporter on the portable television.

Murray's heart felt heavy. She thought of what she'd sacrificed over the past few years. She thought of what others had sacrificed. And for what?

She looked around the office. Most of the furnishings had been removed during the day. Soon the place would be abandoned. Murray wondered if it would become a relic of democracy.

In a thousand years' time, would children be shown round the building and told that this was where human Britain died, and where the handing over of power to the undead took place?

Would there be humans left in a thousand years?

There will have to be, she thought. Humans were necessary for vampires to survive. No predator lived long without its prey – even an immortal predator. Three nights without blood meant death to a vampire. Murray glanced around the office. *Maybe that's what we should do*, she thought. Maybe it was the only way to defeat the vampires.

Deny them food.

Kill ourselves, she thought.

Mass suicide.

What was there left to live for?

She felt dizzy and sick, thoughts of her family filling her mind. David was out there somewhere. Her young son lost to her, desperately trying to survive. She looked towards the windows. It was dark outside. She hoped David was safe, wherever he was.

She wondered where she would go after that night. They had to stay in the building for now. The streets were probably crawling with vampires. When dawn came, it would be safe to leave. But what was there for them in New Britain?

Families gone. Homes gone. Jobs gone. Country gone.

Tomorrow was the beginning of a long night for the British people.

George Fuad and the Nebuchadnezzars would be in charge. Other humans, non-Nebuchadnezzars who refused to collaborate, would be second class citizens. Slaves. Criminals. Food.

But maybe we deserve it, she thought.

Humans had thought for so long that they were masters of the world. But that was a false belief. It was a myth. Now the species was in danger of becoming extinct, just like millions of other life forms.

We are nothing, Murray thought to herself. *Nothing.*

Nothing without him.

Without Jake Lawton.

She closed her eyes and prayed to any god listening to protect Jake and help him destroy Nimrod.

The phone in Wilson's office rang. It made Murray jump.

Wilson looked around nervously, as if she were surprised that anyone would call. Journalists had been contacting her all day on her mobile, but she'd had advisors and members of her party answer their questions. Wilson didn't look in any state. She headed for her office saying, "Only my family has that number."

Something cold went through Murray's veins.

"Put it on speaker," she said.

Murray and some of the others gathered around Wilson's office door as the politician pressed the speaker button on the phone and answered the call.

"Hello?"

"On speaker phone, darling?" said George Fuad's greasy voice.

"How did you get this number?" said Wilson.

"Your very nice husband gave it to me."

Wilson paled. Some of the other party members gawped in horror.

"We had a nice chat," said Fuad, "about your affair with Graeme Strand all those years ago. He was very hurt, your husband. You should talk to him about it. See, Liz, you lack a caring side, which is why you have failed as a politician and a wife."

Now Wilson was turning red.

"Get out of my house, Fuad," she said.

"I am not at your house, Liz. We are all at my headquarters in Soho. A lovely old building with a deep dark cellar. Murray there with you? Hello Christine. You remember the cellar, don't you?"

The basement at Religion, the nightclub owned by the Fuad brothers. The place where the vampires were first born in

Britain. Beneath the club lay the basement where three years previously Murray nearly lost her life. Others had died there as the Nebuchadnezzars tried to resurrect the vampire god, Kea.

"I shouldn't imagine that place holds good memories for you, George, since Jake Lawton killed that ugly red monster of yours," said Murray, trying not to let her voice shake.

Fuad hissed out a breath. She'd landed a blow. But he recovered quickly.

"You won the battle," he said, "but you've lost the war."

"Not yet," said Murray.

"Where's my family?" said Wilson. "This is outrageous. I will have you – "

"Have me what, Liz?" said Fuad, and he laughed.

The laugh chilled Murray. She'd heard it so often. She had gone undercover at the Fuads' villa in Spain the previous year. They'd found her out and kidnapped her. She'd been tied up in the back of a truck with the remains of the Nebuchadnezzars' other monsters. And while the truck travelled to the UK, Murray had to witness young runaways and immigrants being murdered to feed the creature.

"Are you going to concede defeat, Liz?" said Fuad.

"Let my family go."

"You can see them soon enough, but concede defeat."

"I concede, of course I do. Don't lay a finger on my family, Fuad."

"They'll be treated fairly," he said.

The look on Wilson's face said she didn't believe him. And Murray didn't believe him, either.

Fuad said, "And all your staff and party members will also get a fair hearing."

"A fair hearing? They've done nothing wrong."

"I'm sure we can think of something," said Fuad. "My team will be over to Millbank in the next hour and we'll sort the transition. Since there's no Queen here anymore, we don't need to go through all that palaver. I'll just take the reins, and get to work sorting out the mess you've made."

"It's not necessary that your people come here, Fuad," said Wilson. "We're packed up and we'll be heading home, soon. We are all returning to private life, so we'll be – "

"No, no, no," he said. "You're being taken into custody."

A gasp of dread went through the office. The men and women looked at each other, fear in their eyes. Some of them started to leave. Wilson urged them to go. Murray wanted to stop them. There would be vampires outside. The streets were dangerous. But so was everywhere else, it seemed. The Nebuchadnezzars were coming for their enemies.

"And one more thing," Fuad said, "I'm going to – "

Murray lifted the receiver and slammed it down on its cradle, cutting off the call.

"We need to get out of here," she said.

"What does he mean 'custody'?" said Wilson.

"Elizabeth," said Murray. "Wake up. This is not a democracy now. Your rights are gone. We are not citizens. We are fugitives. Enemies of the state."

"He can't do this."

The doors suddenly burst open. Black-shirted Neb militia men swarmed in. Screams erupted around the office.

Murray felt a cold sweat break on her back. She touched her red mark, the protection all Nebs wore. It had kept her safe, too. Safe from vampires. But not anymore. She knew they'd rip it off her shirt. They'd throw her to the beasts.

"Oh, my God," said Wilson.

Murray thought she was reacting to the Nebuchadnezzar thugs. But she wasn't. She was looking at the windows. Murray turned slowly. Seven vampires appeared glued to the window pane, just like giant insects. They snarled and hissed. Their hands and feet seemed to grip the glass. As Murray watched in horror, more of them crawled up the side of the building, hundreds of feet above the streets.

CHAPTER 35. GOGA BRICKS HIMSELF.

HILLAH, IRAQ – 10.27PM (GMT + 3 HOURS), 19 MAY, 2011

AALIYAH turned and saw that Goga had stopped in the shadows. For the first time since she'd known him, there was fear in his eyes. They glittered in the moonlight, and his face was pale.

She said, "What's the matter with you?"

He shook his head. He put on the aviators to hide his eyes, to hide his fear.

Aaliyah had initially persuaded Goga not to launch a one-man attack on Fuad's compound. The Romanian had been reluctant. He wanted to go ahead. They couldn't wait for help, he'd said. They couldn't depend on Lawton to turn up. He would not put off the raid on Fuad's compound.

"You look scared, Goga," said Aaliyah.

"Fear is good."

"Not for me it's not. I don't want to fight alongside someone who's bricking himself."

"I will not," he said, shoving past her, "*brick* myself. This has been my life, the hunt for this creature. I shall not waver."

"I saw wavering."

He wheeled to face her. He was gripping his stick, the gold ferrule catching the moonlight.

"I do not waver," said Goga. "I remember. I remember my grandfather and my father, that is what I do. I remember. And that makes me shudder."

He looked around quickly, checking to see if they were safe. They were a hundred yards from the compound.

Goga and Aaliyah were in the shadows between a row of trucks. She didn't know what his plan was, other than to sneak into the site and do whatever needed to be done. It wasn't a new way of working. That's how she'd always done things with Jake. You clock the enemy. You hit them fast. You hit them hard. You make sure they stay down. Not too much planning. But at least with Jake she felt safe. He made you feel confident that if the shit hit the fan, he'd be able to clean it up quick and get you to safety.

She didn't feel that way about Goga.

"You're scared of facing that creature?" she said.

"It is not a human thing."

"Neither are the vampires, but they've never scared you."

"This is different."

"You've been looking for Nimrod all your life, and now you get cold feet?"

"Cold feet?" he said, not getting the idiom.

"You get scared," she clarified.

He slumped against the truck and looked deflated.

Christ, she thought. *This is the last thing I need.*

For a second she wanted to be back in Britain. Yes, it was dangerous, but it was a danger she could cope with. Here, she also had to cope with Goga. You just didn't want to be looking after your buddy in a dangerous situation. You'd get them out if you had to, and you always had their back. But you hoped that they had your back, too. It didn't seem to be the case with Goga.

"I know why you're scared," she said. "Once you kill this thing, it's over – everything is finished."

He shrugged. The moonlight glittered on the lenses of his Aviators.

"You're scared of seeing him, sure," she said. "He's supposed to be some terrifying god, and you don't really know how to kill him. Is that right?"

Goga nodded.

"But once you do kill him," said Aaliyah, "you're just scared of what happens next."

"What happens to my life?" he asked.

"You get it back."

"But this is all I know. Ever since I was a child, seven or eight, I remember my grandfather telling me of my family, my ancestor, Vlad Dracul, vampire killer. He told me of the impaled vampires and the Nebuchadnezzars. He told me of the wars fought as they terrorized Europe. They came to unleash the Trinity, and Vlad stopped them. It made him mad. It made him a murderer of men, too. The evil he fought made him evil. My grandfather told me about the legend of Nimrod's wife, hidden somewhere in Romania after she'd killed Vlad. And he told me about Nimrod himself, creator of vampires. Kill him, you kill them all. All my life I have wished for this moment. But look at me. I am full of dread."

"That's a shame," said Aaliyah. "But I'm telling you, Goga, you'd better find your guts and tuck them back in your belly. You dragged me halfway across the world and promised me that if we killed this creature, I could be with Jake in a place without vampires. That's what you said. I've turned my back on my friends, and maybe lost Jake, too, just because I listened to you. So don't even think you're getting any sympathy from me. Now stand up straight and show some fucking backbone. We're going to this Irkalla place, if it exists, and we're going to kill this monster, if that exists."

CHAPTER 36.
MY BROTHER, THE PM.

"AND they voted for me," said George, his face glowing red on the computer screen. His was either drunk or elated. "They made me fucking Prime Minister. Do you believe that, Alfie?"

Alfred did believe it. He believed his brother could do anything. Even be Prime Minister. It was George's destiny to be in power. He had all the attributes of a ruler – he could lie, he could cheat, he could steal, he could kill. It was how you succeeded. It was how the Fuad brothers had always succeeded.

It was how they'd run their used-car business in the 1980s, and it was how they'd run F&H Wellbeing, the homeopathic business they'd launched with Afdal Haddad as a front for the experiments that finally yielded the drug Skarlet.

Poor Haddad, thought Alfred. George had killed the old man.

"He's no good to us anymore," George had told a shocked Alfred. "He lacked vision, he lacked ambition – he lacked balls."

Haddad had warned the brothers against resurrecting Nimrod.

"You cannot control him," he'd said.

But George was confident.

George could do anything.

Rule a country or master gods.

And Alfred knew that. So he stuck with his brother. He went along with all his decisions, even though something deep inside told him some of them were wrong. But that was doubt. That was fear. It was weakness. And it was good to ignore such feelings. They made you vulnerable. They made you lose out in life and in business. You'd be last in the race if you let things like that take control of you. You'd never fulfil your destiny.

And they were so close to fulfilling theirs.

Alfred could taste it. It was honey on his lips. He licked them. They were damp with moisture. He was sweating with excitement. He took another drink. The whisky burned its way down his throat.

"Don't drink too much," George told him over Skype.

"I'm only celebrating your victory."

"Yeah, whatever, Alfie. Just don't drink too much."

Alfred wanted to know what his brother thought of the work so far in Iraq. He expected praise. He wanted to be told, "Well done, Alfie."

He asked, "You liked the video I emailed? Filmed it in the tunnels. Did you see those pillars? The pillars of Irkalla? Stretched for miles. We've dug really deep, George. We're so close now. So close to Nimrod."

He drank again, emptying the glass. He wanted to get up and go to his cupboard to find another bottle. But his brother was scowling.

"Get closer," said George. "I'm getting bored. You've had months."

Alfred felt disheartened.

"I'm going to run the country," said George. "Next time we speak, I hope you'll have good news for me."

The screen went blank with Alfred's goodbye still lodged in his throat.

He felt rage build up in his chest.

George needed to treat him with more respect. They were virtually equals in this. He'd worked as hard as his brother to realize their success so far. But sometimes he felt George just didn't respect him. He was about to connect again to Skype when someone knocked on the door, and before Alfred could say, "Come in," Laxman swaggered into the office. The mercenary carried a sheet of paper. He slapped it down on Alfred's desk.

"What's this?"

"Look at it, Alfred."

Alfred looked. The sheet was a fax and showed an image from a closed-circuit television camera. It depicted two people, seen only in silhouette, lurking among the equipment trucks.

"Where's this?" he asked.

"Just outside the perimeter," Laxman answered.

"Well, we knew they were in Hillah."

"Been following us for a while."

"And now they've come to us," said Alfred. "Bring them to me alive – or dead."

CHAPTER 37. THE WELCOMING COMMITTEE.

AALIYAH thought the cold thing pressed against the back of her neck was an insect and she went to slap it away.

But it wasn't an insect.

And when her hand flapped against something hard, something steel, she wheeled around and found herself looking down the barrel of a gun.

The man holding it wore fatigues, and a shemagh hid the lower half of his face. Only his cruel brown eyes could be seen. A scar ran across his bronzed forehead.

The man said, "Tours don't start till nine in the morning."

Her mouth dropped open. She twitched, her instincts telling her to react. But she stayed still. And a second later, Goga shot out of the darkness.

The Romanian had left Aaliyah hiding between the trucks while he'd gone to the fence to see if they could get through. She thought they were safe in the shadows, but obviously Alfred Fuad's people had rigged some kind of security system that had spied Aaliyah and Goga.

Now the armed man shoved her out of the way. She staggered. Goga swung with his walking stick, shouting with fury. The armed man lunged, blocking Goga's strike, and at the same time struck the Romanian a blow under the chin with his open palm.

A Krav Maga move, thought Aaliyah. Blocking and striking at the same time. Lawton had shown her. He'd shown her a lot of self-defence stuff. None of it you'd learn in a class at a leisure centre. It mostly involved biting, gouging, scratching, and kicking your attacker – if he was a man, as he invariably was – very hard in the balls.

The armed man loomed over Goga.

Two men wearing black stumbled out of the dark.

"How did you let him get the better of you, dickheads?" said the armed man.

"He… he had a stick," said one of the men.

"Fucking idiots. Don't know where the fuck Fuad found you, but you'd've never made it past selection for my team. You, get the girl, and you, cuff this fucker," he said.

One of the men approached Aaliyah. She tensed, ready to fight back.

"You, bitch," said the armed man. "You come quietly, or I'll blow this fella's face off." He cocked the pistol and pointed it at Goga's face. Then he crouched, removed Goga's aviator sunglasses and popped them over his eyes. "Nice pair," he said, still looking in Aaliyah's direction as the black-clad man handcuffed her.

They were led into the compound.

Goga was struggling. He was unsteady on his feet. He had blood coming from his nose.

No one said anything as they strode in between the buildings and finally came to a halt at another tall fence marked with warnings to trespassers. Beyond the wire lay a huge hole, and above the hole loomed an enormous drill. The type, Aaliyah guessed, that oil companies would use. At the edge of the abyss stood a gatehouse through which you entered an elevator.

Aaliyah glanced at the armed man. He was strong and powerful. He looked like a solider. She wondered how he'd got the scar across his forehead.

The armed man took off Goga's sunglasses and narrowed his eyes. He pulled the shemagh away from his mouth.

"Keep moving," he said.

They kept shoving Goga and Aaliyah towards the gatehouse. They finally stopped at the edge of the pit, and Aaliyah and Goga stared down into it.

She gasped. It was endless. Striplights showed how deep it was. It kept going and going, down and down.

"They've been digging here for three months, day and night," said the scarred man.

"For Nimrod," said Goga.

The man laughed.

"You work for Alfred Fuad?" said Aaliyah.

"He pays me, yes," the man answered.

"And he'll kill you when this is done," said Goga.

Doubt flickered in the scarred man's eyes, but then he put Goga's aviator's back on.

"Lots of tougher men than Alfred Fuad have tried to kill me and fucked it up," he said.

"He will not," said Goga. "He'll give you to Nimrod – all of you."

"Shut up," said the scarred man.

"What's he talking about, Colonel?" said one of the black-clad men.

"Nothing," said the Colonel. "Shut up, right?"

But Goga continued. "If Nimrod is awakened, Fuad will not be able to control it. No one will."

"I will," said the Colonel.

"You will die," said Goga, "that's what you will do."

The Colonel put his gun to Goga's forehead. "Say another word, and I'll nudge you backwards a few steps and stand here ten minutes while you scream your way down into hell."

"Fuad is tricking you," said Aaliyah.

The Colonel whipped round and put the gun in her face. "I don't give a shit about the gender of my victims, darling. Once you're dead, you're dead. Now, I want the both of you to shut your fucking mouths and – "

She was lightning quick.

Her knee shot up and smashed the Colonel full in the balls. His eyes crossed. His cheeks puffed out. He bent double. And as he fell, Aaliyah used her other knee to crack him in the jaw.

She whirled round in time to see the other two men raise their guns.

She ran at them and barged into them, and they reeled, off balance. But she was unsteady, too, with her hands cuffed behind her back. She sat on the floor and quickly scooted her hands underneath her backside so at least they were in front of her.

"Come on, Goga," she said.

She leapt to her feet, turned to run, and walked directly into the Colonel's fist.

She saw stars, her head spinning.

He came at her at full pelt. She tried to defend herself. But she had no chance.

He grabbed her by the collar and lifted her and carried her towards the edge of the pit, and she kicked out at nothing as he prepared to hurl her down into hell.

CHAPTER 38.
BRITAIN IS BABYLON.

FORMER RELIGION NIGHTCLUB, SOHO, LONDON – 10.52PM (GMT), 19 MAY, 2011

"I KEEP in touch with my brother in Iraq," said George Fuad.

"Still alive then, is he?" said Murray.

"He's had lots of good news in recent days."

"Been diagnosed with cancer, has he?" said Murray.

"I'm just dying to share it with you, Christine."

"*You've* got cancer."

"You think you're funny, I don't, and when I have your tongue taken out no one will find you amusing."

Murray kept her mouth shut.

Fuad smiled. "I like it when someone's face goes that pale. That's what fear does, Christine. It's what power can do. Now, I have some news that'll maybe put a smile back on your face."

Murray doubted that.

"Your mate, Jake Lawton, has been caught by the Iraqis."

Murray's stomach lurched. She was elated for a moment. Jake was alive. But then her joy petered out, to be replaced by dread.

He'd been caught. He would fail in his mission. Without him, they didn't have a hope.

She looked around. The place was as drab as she'd remembered it. They were in the nightclub's top floor. All the rooms had been knocked into one. There was a long chamber now, with a big table in the middle. There was one chair at the head of the table, and that's where George Fuad sat. It was the only chair in the room. No one else could sit. Murray was standing near the window, two big Neb thugs either side of her. A few other Nebuchadnezzars were hanging around in the chamber as well, smirking at her, chatting among themselves, looking pleased. A huge photograph covered the far wall. It had been blown up from a newspaper shot of Fuad waving at supporters from the stage of his recent Hyde Park rally. More portraits of him hung throughout the room. Murray felt the desire to smash them, one by one.

A 50-inch flat-screen TV hung on the opposite wall. It showed Fuad's victory as presented by the BBC. Already the channel was starting to feel like a state broadcaster. Fuad was obviously choking any balance out of its battered old body. It had only taken him an hour from the polls closing to do this. What could he do in a day or a week? she wondered. What could he do in a year?

"You won't hold Jake Lawton for long," said Murray.

"I'm not holding him at all, darling," said Fuad. "It's the Iraqis, like I say. But if he does get out, we'll be waiting for him. He won't get far. It's all over."

"Are you proud of what you're doing?" Murray said.

"I will be. Once I clean up this country," he said, indicating the TV. A report showed people queuing up outside a soup kitchen. "The Jeremy Kyle bunch. Scum. Lowlifes. Criminals. They'll make good food, eh? That's how you deal with social ills, see. But no politician until now has had the guts to sort it out."

"You lied to those people, a lie that said vampires and humans can live together."

"Oh, but why can't we, Christine? Why can't we live together in harmony?" he said, and started humming the song "Ebony And Ivory" by Paul McCartney and Stevie Wonder. Then he stopped. And the fake smile left his face. A scowl creased his brow. "Oh, yeah, I know why we can't – 'cause they hunt us. They are our natural predator. Well, not us. With this mark." He flicked at the red tag on his lapel. He got up and strode towards Murray. She knew what was coming. "You won't be needing this anymore." He ripped the red mark from her jacket. "You shouldn't have ever worn it, anyway." He tossed it on the floor.

Murray felt suddenly vulnerable. She became queasy, as if someone had taken away a pill that protected her from disease.

She was now in serious danger. She would be a target for vampires.

"Are you going to kill me?" she said, almost hoping he would, so she could avoid the horror of being a vampire's victim.

Fuad grinned. "You know what? No. I've got something worse in mind for traitors like you." He strolled back to his chair and, sitting down, leaned back. "I hear your kid's out there. What's his name? David? And the rumour is, he's looking to kill me – a fucking assassin. Ain't that a laugh? A boy assassin."

Murray said nothing. The mention of David brought the pain flooding back. She had been a terrible mother. And now all she could do was be brave for her son. He was out there somewhere, a child not yet fourteen. A boy soldier fighting a desperate war. She would make up for all the years of rotten parenting by doing everything from now on to keep him safe and support him in his quest to kill Fuad. She knew she didn't have long to live, but every second she had would be lived for David – as it should have been from the start. Now she would do anything to see him one more time, see him and ask him to forgive her. She nearly cried, but fought back the tears. She did not want Fuad to see her weep.

Fuad went on, "So I'll let you live and see your kid again, if you make a public appearance, on TV, urging him to give himself up."

"Give himself up?"

"That's right. On TV. We're going to Parliament now. Stand outside the ruins. Remind people what Jake Lawton did to their democracy. Burned its heart out. And right there, you'll tell that kid of yours to hand himself over to me."

"Never," she said.

"Then I'll publicly execute you and do fucking awful things to you, and your son will see – he'll see everything wherever he is, and imagine his pain, then. Imagine how horrible that's going to be, to see his mother fucking stripped naked, raped, burned, just imagine that, Christine."

"You'll pay for this one day. You will."

"You believe in fate? Not sure I do. But if it does exist, you deal with it like you deal with everything else in life – you grab it by the balls and squeeze. I am the master of my destiny, Christine. But more than that, I am the master of yours, as well. Yours, your son's, Elizabeth Wilson's, even Jake Lawton's. I am the fucking king of my life and the king of yours. Vampires will walk the streets. Britain is Babylon. I've done what emperors have failed to do, what Jacqueline Burrows nearly did. I have taken control. Soon the whole fucking world will cower when they hear my name. I'll stop at fucking nothing, and I know that sounds over the top, but I mean it. I've tasted power, and it's fucking lovely."

"You're mad," said Murray.

"Who gives a shit."

CHAPTER 39. NOTHING BUT WAR.

DAVID watched his mother on TV, and his eyes filled with tears.

She was standing behind George Fuad while he addressed the nation in a press conference at the burned ruin of Parliament.

David felt love for her fill his heart, but he also felt anger boil in his blood.

He had been lied to and abandoned. He'd never had a childhood. All he could remember was fighting – first between his mum and dad, then between humans and vampires.

War was his life.

Now he felt more bitter than ever. His friend Kwan Mei had gone up north with Ediz Ün to fight vampires. Mei could muster some forces up there. Her rebellion in February had started in Manchester. She now planned another insurgency. But David had sulked. He wanted to kill George Fuad. He wanted to make a big statement. He wanted attention.

He wanted people to say, "That's David Murray – he assassinated George Fuad."

People wouldn't say things like that if you killed vampires, because lots of people killed vampires. It was nothing special. He wanted to do something special.

"You all right, son?" said Old Bill.

They were in a bedsit in Soho – a crummy, dirty flat that had needles and mouldy food on the floor. A shitty, smelly apartment that had rat poo and dead flies on the windowsills.

Bill said it used to be a brothel before the vampires came. A woman would stand outside and ask men if they wanted to meet a girl. If a man said yes, the woman would take him upstairs into this bedsit, where the men could have sex with one of two Russian girls.

The TV was old. One of those ancient ones with tubes. It sat on the sideboard. There was a damp old mattress in the corner. It was stained with something.

Old Bill sat on a creaky wooden chair.

David sat on the cold, hard floor.

"That's my mum, there," he said.

"Nice lady," said Bill. The old man rolled a fag and handed it to David. David used a match to light the ciggie. He'd been smoking since he was twelve. He was hooked. But at least he hadn't started drinking yet. Lots of kids his age were already alcoholics. There was nothing else to do in vampire Britain. Schools were only running part-time, three days a week at best. Nothing much for kids to do other than hang around on the streets. And it was probably the first time in history that young people actually listened to their parents' demands to be in before dark.

David looked at his mum on telly and had a yearning for her to tell him what to do.

Her face was pale. Fear glittered in her eyes. He could tell she didn't want to be there. It fuelled his hatred for Fuad.

Noises came from outside in the street – laughter, growling, screaming.

"Those vampires getting confident again," said Bill.

The old man was right. The undead sensed their prey was weaker now. And they had probably been unleashed by the Nebuchadnezzars.

Vampires had stalked humans for years. Mostly it had been done on a small scale. They didn't want to draw attention to themselves. They knew how clever and effective humans could be at fighting back. But now the vampires were confident. They had allies in power. Nothing to fear anymore. No one to challenge them.

The prey was weak. The hunters were strong.

Welcome to Britain, 2011. Vampire Nation.

David's blood was up. He listened to what George Fuad was saying on the television: "We can all look forward to a better Britain, a Britain where human and vampire live side by side."

Side by side, thought David, *with a wire fence between us – the humans penned inside, the vampires snarling and sneering, waiting to drink our blood.*

It would be like Nazi Germany. Concentration camps all over the UK. Humans farmed to produce food for vampires. Some people would be slaves, building the Babylon Fuad dreamed of creating.

Sweating and bleeding for the undead.

I'd rather die, thought David. *And I will, if I have to.*

He smoked his cigarette. Old Bill smoked too. The bedsit filled with the smell of fresh tobacco. The street outside filled with screams. It was 11.30pm. The time of the vampire. The time for death.

On TV, George Fuad laughed while David's mum wept.

And that triggered David's tears again. He loved his mum so much. He wanted her to be his mother again. Like she'd never really been. But that wasn't to be. Fortune wasn't going to smile on David and his mum. Fate would not give him a family.

Fuad was inviting David's mum to the microphone. David's nerves were on fire. He felt sick and dizzy.

"What's happening?" he said.

"Turn it up, son," said Old Bill.

David went to the TV set. The volume knob was missing. He had to twist a screw to increase the volume. He managed it just as his mum's shaky voice was saying, "And I would encourage anyone thinking of hurting our new government, or its leaders, to hand themselves in. There will be an amnesty for forty-eight hours. Prime Minister Fuad has pledged this. He is a man of his word."

"No way," cried David.

"She's being forced to say this," said Old Bill, "you can tell. Look, lad, she's crying. Crying while she's reading from that piece of paper. And her voice is shaking."

"I would particularly," said David's mum, "like to ask my own, dear son, David, to hand himself in. Prime Minister Fuad has told me, myself once an enemy of the state, that David and I can be together, as mother and son, and we can live safely under the care of the new government. This is true of all sons and mothers, fathers and daughters, who have been torn apart by the terrible war instigated by… by men like… "

David's mum fainted.

Black-clad thugs rushed forward to grab her.

David stood up and yelled out for his mother.

Fuad's face for a second showed fury, but then it softened, and he moved forward to the microphone.

"The poor woman's under a great deal of pressure," said Fuad as his thugs carried David's mum out of shot. Fuad looked directly into the camera. "This has been caused by you, David. Your mum loves you. I'm sure you love your mum, son. We all love our mums. She wants to see you again and be a proper mum to you.

Come on, son, give yourself up. All the rest of you, too. You want to see your mums and dads and sons and daughters again? You want to be families again? Give yourselves up and live at peace in my new England."

Fuad stepped away from the microphone. The camera wheeled to a news reporter, who started talking. But David wasn't listening. He was in a fury. He was gathering his stuff, getting ready to go to war.

"Calm down, son," said Old Bill.

"I can't calm down."

"You can't go with all that fire in your belly."

"I'm going to kill him, Bill."

"Best do that when you're cold, not when you're hot."

David tried to calm down. Old Bill was right. He had to be in control of his emotions. Jake always told him to do that – control yourself, then you can control other people.

Where was Jake now?

He could really do with Lawton's company.

"I wish Jake was here," he said.

"He's with you, son. In your head, in your heart."

"I hope he's not dead; I wouldn't know what to do without him."

"You'd know. In war, the young have to be old before their time, son. War makes men of boys like you. Fighting makes you hard and cruel. But you've got to fight when you're calm. Jake would tell you that. Give yourself an hour or two. Have a little plan. Even if you don't stick with it, it's worth it. Come on, let's have a drink and another fag."

David lay on the cold hard floor again.

He thought about killing Fuad.

The fire in him died. In its place came an icy determination.

CHAPTER 40. JOURNEY TO THE CENTRE OF THE EARTH.

HILLAH, IRAQ – 11.35PM (GMT + 3 HOURS), 19/20 MAY, 2011

"ENOUGH," said a man's voice as Aaliyah dangled over the pit. "Let her go, Laxman."

The scarred colonel called Laxman tossed her aside. She hit the ground hard.

"She kneed me in the balls," said Laxman.

"I'm paying you top whack, and you let a bird get the better of you?" said the newcomer. "I might have to cut your salary, Laxman. Bring them down."

The speaker, who was in his sixties and wore his dark hair in a ponytail, was Alfred Fuad. Aaliyah recognized him. She glared at Fuad, feeling the hate for him and his brother well up in her breast.

Fuad went to the elevator and opened the scissor-door.

Laxman pulled Aaliyah to her feet and shoved her towards the lift. The other two men ushered Goga into the elevator.

A clanking noise indicated the lift had fired up, and soon it started to descend. Aaliyah's legs were shaking. The elevator dropped quickly. No one said anything. Aaliyah looked at Goga. He seemed groggy. He was still bleeding. She was about to say something, but he caught her eye and shook his head.

After a few minutes, the elevator came to a stop, and they stepped out into a cavern.

Aaliyah craned her neck and stared upwards. They were a long way down.

Equipment filled the cavern. Drills. Spades. Trowels. A monitor perched on a table. It looked to Aaliyah like a radar machine, and it bleeped now and again. Computers lined the far wall, and staring at the screens were young Middle Eastern men. At the far end of the cavern was the entrance to a tunnel. A Jeep was parked there.

How did they get a Jeep down here? thought Aaliyah, and she looked up again.

She and Goga were shepherded towards the vehicle and told to get in. She sat in the back, between Laxman and Fuad. Goga got in the front, lodged between the two black-clad men, one of whom started the engine.

The tunnel was illuminated by the same neon strip lights attached to the sides of the pit.

Finally, Aaliyah asked, "What is this place?"

"First, introductions, darling," said Fuad.

"I know who you are," she said.

"I know you, too. But who's this fellow?" said Fuad, nudging Goga.

"I am Apostol Goga, ally of Jake Lawton and Aaliyah Sinclair," said the Romanian.

"The now-in-custody Jake Lawton," said Fuad.

Laxman laughed. "Your boyfriend's been taken by Iraqi security, is what we heard. They'll probably take him out into the desert, put a bullet in the back of his head."

Aaliyah nearly passed out. Her blood ran cold. *Keep it together*, she told herself. *They want you to faint or cry*.

"We're approaching the underworld city of Irkalla," said Fuad. "The city of Nimrod."

Had they found the vampire god? Aaliyah wondered. Had Fuad resurrected the monster? Were they too late? If this were true, and if Jake had also been captured, they really didn't have much hope.

"You are a fool to awaken Nimrod, Fuad," said Goga.

"You're a fool to stop me, Goga."

"I will stop you – or kill the beast."

Laxman laughed again. Aaliyah glanced at him. She wondered if Jake could deal with him. She'd seen Jake deal with bigger men. She'd seen him deal with monsters. But he wasn't here. He was holed up in a prison cell in Baghdad, if these men were to be believed. He'd been arrested. Her heart thundered. She sweated, fear coursing through her.

Goga said to Fuad, "You are mad to think you can control Nimrod. You and your crazy brother."

"Don't you fucking call my brother mad – George is a genius. Smack him, Laxman."

"He's had enough smacks," said Laxman.

"You fucking smack him," said Fuad.

The Colonel sighed, reached over, and swatted Goga across the back of his head. It wasn't hard. It was just a gesture to appease Fuad. But it didn't mollify him. It made him madder. He glared at Laxman, and Aaliyah thought he was going to berate the man with the scar on his forehead. But he didn't. Instead, he turned away and said, "My brother's going to lead Britain into a golden age."

"He will destroy it," said Goga. "And the world with it."

"The age of monsters is here, and to control them, we'll be monsters too," said Fuad.

"And there is no more vile a monster than your brother, that is quite clear," Goga said.

Fuad said nothing.

They drove on.

The route sloped downwards.

Journey to the centre of the earth, thought Aaliyah, remembering a film she'd seen as a child with one of her mother's boyfriends. He had loved monster movies. *He'd love this, then*, she thought. Real monsters. She wondered what had happened to him. Her memories spooled. They made her sad, and she felt tears well. She fended them off, not wanting to cry in Fuad's presence.

The Jeep stopped in a tunnel that was nearly thirty feet high and fifty across. It was lit with floodlights. Bulldozers and JCBs were parked up along the wall. Men with hardhats were checking plans. Tents had been erected. It was an underground camp.

Goga and Aaliyah were taken into one of the tents.

"Get back on duty up top," Laxman told the two black-shirts, "and if I hear of a man with a stick getting the better of you again, I'll fucking do you both."

"Fucking girl got the better of you, mate," said one of them and smirked. He was still smirking when Laxman slid a knife from his belt and sliced open the man's throat.

Blood spurted.

The smirk turned into a look of horror.

The man's legs buckled.

He hit the ground.

Blood was a fountain coming from his throat.

He twitched.

His back arched.

He gurgled.

He coughed blood.

He died.

Laxman wiped the knife on his sleeve.

He told the other man, who gawped in horror at his pal, "I'll do you as well, if you have anything to add."

The man shook his head.

Fuad told the bloke, "Take him to Malik and tell him to get rid of the body in a shaft."

For a moment, the man hesitated.

Fuad repeated the order in a louder voice.

The black-shirt dragged the body out of the tent.

Aaliyah gathered herself.

She'd seen death before. Lots of it. She'd seen how cruel men and women could be. But there was a brutal coolness, a vicious matter-of-factness, to the way Laxman had butchered the man. She caught his eye. He held her gaze for a second, a blank stare that said nothing, and then he put Goga's sunglasses on to hide his eyes.

Fuad spoke as if nothing had happened. "Come to the table; I want to show you something that'll cheer you up."

Aaliyah and Goga were made to stand at the desk while Laxman fired up a laptop. He clicked on a Windows Media icon, and a video player popped up.

And then the footage played.

Aaliyah nearly fainted.

The recording was grainy. It came from a security camera. It showed the white, sandstone steps of a building, and beyond it a street. People wearing Arab clothing walked by. A dark Range Rover came to a sharp stop at the bottom of the steps. Three men in suits leapt out of the vehicle. Big men. Moustaches and dark glasses. Guns at their belts.

They dragged someone out of the car.

The man was stripped to the waist.

He was pale. He was lean and strong. His black hair shoulder length. There was something wrong with his left eye. It seemed swollen, and his head was canted to the left.

His hands were tied behind his back, and the three men led him up the stone steps, and then he was gone from view.

Aaliyah couldn't stop herself from crying.

"What have you done to him?"

"I ain't done nothing to him, darling, more's the pity," said Fuad. "The Iraqis picked him up a few days ago. Somewhere in the north. They brought him to Baghdad for questioning, according to our sources. Any luck, they'll torture him."

"You bastard," said Aaliyah.

"I know, doll," said Fuad, "but having Lawton tortured is number one on my bucket list, see. Likely they won't do that, of course. Seems they're not into that kind of stuff anymore, at least with Westerners. They're a bit more civilized since Saddam and his Ba'ath thugs were ousted. He wanted to rebuild Babylon, you know. Saddam. The fella had vision. He knew about Nimrod, too. He tried to do what we're doing. If he'd got this far, if he'd found Nimrod and Irkalla, he might well have been running the Middle East by now. Destroyed the fucking Jews. Smashed the fucking oil states. Sadly, he got a bit carried away. Bit too arrogant. We'll just finish the job for him, eh?"

Aaliyah lunged at him, but Laxman slapped her across the face. She saw stars again and fell to the ground. Her cheek smarted.

Fuad kicked her in the leg, and the sharp pain made her wince. Goga leapt to her aid, but Laxman punched him, decking the Romanian.

Fuad said, "It's all over, Miss Sinclair. For Jake Lawton. For you, and Mr Goga, too. Your fates are sealed. Colonel Laxman here will travel to Baghdad to finish the job on Lawton. His death will symbolize the end of men and the rise of monsters. Tomorrow, you'll witness the resurrection of a god. You'll have front-row seats. And you'll also have the privilege of being its first sacrifice."

PART FIVE.

FAITH.

CHAPTER 41.
THE LAST RESORT AND OTHER OPTIONS.

BAGHDAD – 1.07AM (GMT + 3 HOURS), 20 MAY, 2011

LAWTON was in his cell. Thinking all the time.

Never stop thinking. Keep your brain fired up. Like an engine. If it stalls, you might not get it going again. Be aware all the time. Aware of everything. Of the hum of electricity. Of the insect on the windscreen. Of the beads of sweat on the driver's neck. Of the hint of a woman's perfume layered beneath the stench of BO in the all-male team of security officers. Try to work out an escape route. Even if there isn't one, make one up. Craft something. Anything. Look at every possibility.

Even suicide as a last resort.

That's what they taught you.

But Lawton wasn't at the last resort just yet.

When he was taken by the soldiers, they brought him to the town of Tel Isqof. His captors treated him decently enough. Gave him water, gave him food, didn't beat him. They made him take his shirt and his belt off. They didn't want a foreigner killing himself in their cells.

The last resort, he thought.

After a couple of hours left stewing in a grubby cell, they led him out and drove him to Mosul.

All the while, he was thinking.

Keep thinking.

Keep planning.

Keep surviving.

He had faith in his abilities. Faith in his strength. Faith in himself.

In Mosul, they swapped vehicles.

They got into a Range Rover. Four men with him. Three to watch him, one to drive. All in black suits. All wearing sunglasses. All scowling and silent.

They drove south. He guessed they were taking him to Baghdad. The capital. They'd know what to do with a foreigner found wandering in the desert. They could decide.

Lawton thinking.

Lawton planning.

Lawton surviving.

It was nearly 250 miles from Mosul to Baghdad. Plenty of time to guess what they had planned for him.

Anyone in his position would think the best-case scenario would be to be handed over to his country's representatives in Iraq. The British consul, in Lawton's case. But he thought that was the worst-case scenario. He would be on the next plane home. Flown straight into Fuad's hands.

Other options: He might be charged with illegally entering Iraq. That could mean a trial. Lots of publicity. Time in a Baghdad prison. For most people, that would be the *worst* thing that could happen. For Lawton, it was an opportunity to come up with an escape plan – and he would not be handed over to Fuad.

Staying in Iraq was the first plan. No vampires. No Nebuchadnezzars. Only Nimrod. And Nimrod had to die. He thought about Ereshkigal. He hoped they hadn't found her. They'd not mentioned anything about a woman. Or a vampire.

No one said a thing on the journey.

They had travelled through Kirkuk. Then they drove south through Tikrit. Saddam country. Then on to Samarra, and finally into Baghdad.

Long, wide highways hemmed in by skyscrapers and sandstone buildings welcomed them. They passed abandoned compounds, the fencing rusted, the walls scrawled with graffiti. They weaved around craters and passed ruins, evidence of Allied bombs.

They had come to a busy metropolitan area. Lots of bustle. Plenty of people. Men in suits and men in kurtas, the loose fitting shirts worn in Middle Eastern countries. Women in skirts and women in burkhas, the oppressive garment forced on females by the Taliban in Afghanistan.

Traffic raced through the streets. Horns blared. Drivers shouted at each other.

The Range Rover had stopped outside a white building, steps leading up to it. When he got out of the car, Lawton clocked the sign that said he'd been brought to the Ministry of the Interior.

They took him inside. Led him into the bowels on the building. Eyes watching him. No one saying a word. Along a corridor, his feet cold on the tiles.

Just before they shoved him through a door and locked it behind him, one of the men said, "You will tell us everything."

And at last…

In his cell.

Thinking.

Escape strategies.

There had been the threat of interrogation.

A noise outside in the corridor made him step out of his thoughts.

Footsteps. Someone approaching. The cell door being unlocked. He stiffened, waiting for whatever was to come. Expecting the worse.

He knew that in Saddam's day, he'd either be dead now, which would have been lucky, or he'd be being tortured.

The cell door opened. Two men in army fatigues entered. One was in his twenties. Clean shaven. Brown eyes that gawped at Lawton. He appeared to outrank the other man, who was short and squat and in his fifties.

The young man said, "You will come with us, now."

"Where to?" asked Lawton.

"You will come with us to answer questions."

"Ask me here," said Lawton, delaying as far as he could.

Thinking. Planning. Surviving.

The young man frowned. "Please do not make this a hard job for us."

Lawton got up off his bunk. The short guard handed him a kurta and nodded. Lawton put on the shirt and creased his brow, confused. He was sure he'd seen respect in the older man's expression.

Lawton was led along the corridor. His kept his breathing and his heartbeat under control. He was cool. He was calm. He was controlled. He was getting ready for what was to come. He was preparing for the worst.

CHAPTER 42.
THE STAIN.

SHE carried the spear made from her husband's bones. She carried the only weapon that could kill him.

The desert was cold at night. But she felt nothing of its icy fingers. Nothing apart from the burning need for blood.

Ereshkigal walked south. Strapped to her back was the sack the man Lawton had brought with him. It contained the spear of Abraham. Her husband's bones. Her husband's doom.

The men who had taken Lawton had not searched the truck. And she had remained huddled inside until night came. She knew that Lawton had protected her as any faithful servant would have done, as any Nebuchadnezzar would have done.

Only he wasn't a Nebuchadnezzar. He was their enemy. He was a vampire killer. And he was hunting her Lord Husband. He was going to kill the Great Hunter.

But still, he'd kept her safe when the soldiers came by day.

This played on her mind.

Her enemy protecting her.

It stayed with her while she buried herself under rocks during the day. It stayed with her when she crawled out at sunset to keep walking, keep moving. It tapped into something that she had once been.

Human.

There was no human left, of course. Nothing tangible. But maybe there was a stain of it. A trace left somewhere of what she had been.

She felt none of what a human felt. No love, no hate, no jealousy. She believed only in blood. Only hunger and the raw, brutal need to survive compelled her to go on. And survival meant being in Irkalla with Nimrod. It meant stalking Babylon at night and feeding off her citizens.

The desert became pasture.

Trees flourished. Rivers flowed. Cities passed.

She walked.

Did she know where she was going? Something told her she was headed in the right direction. Not for Irkalla. But for Lawton. She would go to him. It was that unquantifiable thing ticking inside her, insisting she go to him.

She dismissed any hints of emotion she felt.

It was impossible, anyway.

She only thought of Lawton as useful, that had to be it. He was human, and humans were always beneficial. Simeon had been valuable until his death as a ninety-seven year old. Vlad had been useful with his power, his greed, and his eventual madness and murderous lusts. King Richard of England, the one they called Lion-heart or Melek-Ric, had been a mighty lover and a cowering servant.

Like Vlad, he had come to fight the vampire plague. To crush the Nebuchadnezzars' plans. But her flesh had weakened their resolve. It had made them mad. They had fucked her cold dead body that felt so young and warm as they writhed with her. They hated themselves for loving her. But she was irresistible. She was their weakness. And because of it, she was able to destroy them both. Stop them from wiping out the vampire race.

Both Richard and Vlad had similar strategies in their wars against the undead and their human allies.

They were secret campaigns. They had both pretended to be fighting a religious enemy – the Saracens and the Ottomans.

But they were not fighting the Muslims. Neither conflict had been holy. They had been wars of survival. The survival of humans.

Now Lawton was fighting that battle.

And she would do the same to him. Take him into her bed. Become his lover. Destroy his campaign against the Nebuchadnezzars. It was what she did. It was her instinct.

But now that other feeling was rearing its head.

That stain that she couldn't wash away.

The trace of what she had been and how she was supposed to feel.

Headlights glowed in the distance. She smelled diesel on the air. An engine's growl grew louder. The car approached.

She stopped and waited. Her white dress fluttered on the breeze.

Her skin rippled with the excitement of a blood feast.

She licked her lips. She looked vulnerable on that lonely road in the night.

She was there to be ravished, surely.

The car slowed down.

It stopped in the middle of the road.

Three young men leapt out. They wore denim and white T-shirts. They had black hair. They were in their twenties, young, confident. One of them wore glasses.

They spoke in Arabic.

She smiled at them.

They gaped, excited at her response.

She smelled their lust. She smelled their blood.

They circled her.

She smiled wider, opening her lips.

Showing her fangs.

One of them saw, and fear flared in his eyes.

Another reached out to touch her, but before his fingers brushed her arm, he was dead, his jugular vein spouting blood.

In a split second, the second was dead.

Ereshkigal turned on the third. He was frozen to the spot. She glared at him. Then she kicked him hard in the belly, sending him crashing into the car.

Before the dead men's blood ran cold, she drank it from their open veins. After she was done, the third man was coming round. She picked him up and slammed him on the bonnet of the car. She bared her bloody fangs and hissed in his face: "*Yakhedney ala Beghedad.*"

CHAPTER 43.
ONE SOLDIER.

THEY took Lawton into an interview room. It was better than the cell. It had a carpet and a table and chairs. He sat and they gave him coffee – black and strong.

The younger man said, “An officer from the Department of Border Enforcement will be coming to ask you questions.”

“My favourite categories are films, sport, and travel.”

The young man furrowed his brow.

Lawton drank the coffee. He stared into the dark, thick liquid. The smell was overpowering. He started to think about Ereshkigal. He wondered if she’d got out of the vehicle. His own objective concerned him. His quest to kill Nimrod. Without the Spear of Abraham, he didn’t think it could be done. He hoped that somehow Ereshkigal had escaped the soldiers and taken the spear with her. He focused on her. He tried to dream her, like he had dreamed her before. His head had started to throb again. The false eye smarting. It had swollen on the journey from Mosul and was bruised. He could feel the tentacles of red flesh encased in the glass eye seeping out and coiling around his nerves. But he couldn’t pull the object out. It hurt too much, and he felt he would tear part of his brain out with it.

"I don't understand completely," said the young man.

"Don't worry, you understand mostly – and your English is good."

"I learn from the British soldiers. I was seventeen when they came. They saved us from Saddam."

Lawton looked at the man. *An ally*, he thought. Someone who thought the action in Iraq was worthwhile. Many of the young man's compatriots did think that. Or at least the ones Lawton had met. He had been thanked hundreds of times when he'd walked the streets of Basra with his squadron. But times had changed. He didn't know what Iraqis thought of it all now. So he would be grateful of any support he could find.

The young man said, "You had wounds on your body – bullet wounds."

"How do you know they were bullets?"

"My father has them. He was shot by Saddam's men in 2000. They shoot him through here," he said, pointing to the back of his knee.

"Kneecapping," said Lawton.

"Shooting," said the man.

"Yes, that's what they call it – shooting from behind the knee… kneecapping."

"Kneecapping," the man said, as if he were tasting the word.

"Why did they do that?" asked Lawton, feeling he was forging a relationship with the man.

"We are Shia. From the Tigris-Euphrates Marshlands originally. Marsh Arabs. My father was in the uprising of 1991. My people rose up after the Americans promised to help us defeat Saddam – but they left. The British, too. Everyone left. We were alone, and we had no chance. Many of my people were killed. The wetlands were drained. My family escaped. But they hunted down my father. Kneecapping."

"Where did you escape to?" asked Lawton.

He eyed the other man, the squat frog-like fellow. He'd been standing quietly in the corner of the room. He was watching Lawton, trying to follow the conversation. But maybe his English wasn't as good as his colleague's.

"Basra," the young man answered.

Lawton's spine tingled. He kept his eyes narrow. He kept his bearing cool.

"Do you know Basra?" asked the young man.

Lawton hesitated. Then he said, "I was there in 2003, with the British Army."

Big risk. But he'd evaluated the odds. He took a punt.

Although they had welcomed Western intervention, many Iraqis had become disillusioned, particularly when the insurgency began and foreign fighters flooded the country to cause carnage.

Basra had been relatively peaceful – relative in Iraqi terms. So there was a chance the young officer may not hold any grievances. However, it could have all been a ploy to get information out of Lawton. The man might be a former Saddam loyalist. There were many still in positions of authority. But that was part of the gamble Lawton took. He held the young man's eyes. They glittered.

"British soldier?" he said.

Lawton nodded.

"Will you tell me your name?" asked the Iraqi.

Lawton said nothing.

"You will have to," said the man.

"Maybe."

"No maybe. You will have to. And you are not an enemy here. We are not your enemy."

"Maybe."

"The British saved my life."

"I'm glad."

"I was going to worship."

Every nerve in Lawton's body tightened.

"Hundreds of us going to the mosque."

Memories flooded back.

"Al Qaeda bombers with explosives on their backs came, and they were going to kill us. Butcher us while we prayed. British soldiers killed them. They saved our lives. One soldier. One man."

Lawton's skin goose fleshed.

"I am Fadoul Khoury," said the young man. "Lieutenant Fadoul Khoury of the Federal Police."

Lawton nodded, knowing.

"I know your face," said Khoury. "I knew from when you walked in. I know the shape of your body. The way you move. I know your – your eye, the one you have left. Steel grey. I know you. One soldier."

Lawton said nothing.

"Allah has worked a miracle," said Khoury.

The man's lip trembled, and a tear ran down his face.

CHAPTER 44. PLAN OF ACTION.

"I WAS there that day in Basra," said Khoury. He looked at his watch and yawned.

Lawton glanced at the man's wrist and saw it was about 4.40am. *Stupidly early*, he thought. *Or stupidly late*.

They were trying to psyche him out, denying him sleep. But if anyone could go without sleep, it was Lawton.

Khoury had dismissed the short guard. Told him to get more coffee and something to eat for their guest. "I was a police cadet. Nineteen years old when it happened. I had joined the new police of the new Iraq. I was being trained by British police."

Lawton narrowed his eyes.

Was the man trying to dupe him?

"I have seen your face on the internet," said Khoury. He was sitting opposite Lawton, staring straight at him. "I have watched you in England, fighting your demon enemies, and I say to myself, 'I know who that man is.'"

He hesitated and stared at Lawton's face.

"You are Jake Lawton," said Khoury.

Lawton said nothing. He was considering the odds on another bet now. Playing it safe until he knew everything he could possibly know.

"Two men leapt from a VW," said Khoury. "I remember clearly. Two men with backpacks. Bombs on their bodies. I remember waiting to go into the mosque. Still in my cadet uniform. A soldier shot one of the insurgents."

Rabbit, thought Lawton. That's what they called him. A true comrade. A brother in arms.

Khoury continued.

"But the other one fled. Down an alley. I remember. And it was *you* who followed him, *you* who shot him dead. You saved our lives. Hundreds of lives."

"I did my job."

"You stopped evil."

Lawton said nothing.

"Why are you here?" said Khoury, his brow furrowed.

Now it starts, thought Lawton. Maybe this was all part of a psychological game. Maybe Khoury was nowhere near Basra that day. But whatever the case, he knew about Lawton's actions on that November 2004.

Khoury said, "There are no vampires in Iraq. Europe, I know, suffers, but we are not contaminated yet. Are we?" A look of fear crossed his face. "Tell me if this is the truth?"

"I don't know if you have vampires."

"Then why does a man known on the internet as a vampire killer come to Iraq illegally?"

"Are you interrogating me now?"

"Hardly," said Khoury. "But someone might, very soon. The men from the Department of Border Enforcement will come before Hassan is back with the tea. You have no authority to be here. You have no visa or a passport. Are you doing contract work?"

"What do you mean?"

"Are you working on a security mission, secret mission?"

Lawton said nothing.

"I am not asking you from interrogation," said Khoury, "I am asking you because I am interested in Jake Lawton – the man who saved my life."

"What's going to happen to me?"

"You will be questioned. You might be charged with entering the country illegally. You will be put on trial. You will be found guilty. You might be sent to jail, or you will be fined 10,000 dinar."

"How much is that?" said Lawton.

"Eight dollars."

"That'll break the bank."

Khoury looked confused.

Lawton said, "Forget it."

Khoury said, "You might be sent back to Britain, if you are lucky – expelled."

"No, that would not be lucky."

"Not be lucky?"

"They will kill me."

"But you are a hero. We read of you on the internet."

"I'm not a hero now. Britain has changed. There are powerful people who want me dead. And if I'm sent back, they will kill me."

"What can I do?"

"I don't know, what can you do?"

Khoury shook his head.

Lawton started thinking. Thinking hard. Planning. Strategizing.

Never stop thinking. Keep your brain fired up. Like an engine. If it stalls, you might not get it going again.

He had to get away. That was it. And for that to happen, he needed an opportunity. Just a second's hesitation by his guards. Just something to unsettle them, to make them lose concentration. And he had to be outside this building. Outside in the streets among the traffic and the crowds. Outside where you could easily lose yourself so that no one could find you.

"I need you to do something," he told Khoury.

The Iraqi looked worried.

Lawton told him what he needed him to do.

Khoury leapt to his feet, the chair flying across the room.

He said, "No, never! I am not a barbarian!"

CHAPTER 45.
THE ROAD TO BAGHDAD.

LAXMAN and two of his colleagues, Xavier and Ashton, took the same route as Lawton had taken to Baghdad. But their journey was more pleasant. They were stopped once at a checkpoint outside Tikrit, but their papers were in order.

Laxman chilled out in the back of the Toyota Land Cruiser, music on his iPod, the interior of the vehicle at a nice temperature. Xavier drove with Ashton riding shotgun.

He gazed out at the night. They drove through cities and towns and passed shacks on the roadside.

They passed compounds protected by barbed wire, with warning signs in Arabic hanging off the gates.

They saw the skeletons of tanks and Humvees. Ruins from the war. A war Laxman would have loved to have been part of. But he'd had to wait for it to be over before he could bring his White Light Ops team in.

They were hired in 2004 to protect American industrialists. The Yanks were in the country to make a profit in the aftermath. The insurgency had just kicked off. Al Qaeda nuts joined forces with Ba'athist thugs, and anyone they regarded as an enemy was murdered or kidnapped. There were videos posted online of fanatics sawing people's heads off with a butcher's knife. It was a crazy place at that time. A dangerous place. But it gave a military man like Laxman a permanent hard-on. His blood was up. Adrenaline was in constant supply. He just loved it. Loved the danger, the action. You had to be constantly on your guard against insurgents. But that was part of the fun for him.

He had a grudging respect for them. He hated what they stood for but liked their ruthlessness.

He didn't mind killing or torturing civilians, but he wouldn't do it for pleasure – and he thought from watching some of those decapitation videos that the psychos doing the sawing were in it for the blood and the shit.

They probably jacked off after slicing off a head.

Those guys were willing to kill anyone, at any time, for no reason.

However willing Laxman was to slaughter, he did like a fair fight. Especially if it improved his skills. Bad odds bored him. Sure, having an edge was important, just to make certain he came out on top. But you had to give your opponents a chance.

That's why he was looking forward to taking on Lawton.

His head told him to pop Lawton from a distance – bullet in the brain from 100 metres.

But his heart told him, "Go hand-to-hand with this fella."

Lawton had a serious reputation. He was a first-class soldier who was drummed out of the army because he'd done his job.

After his discharge, he'd acquired a reputation as a bareknuckle fighter. They said he was undefeated in illegal bouts all over England.

It was all part of the mythology that had built up around Lawton during the vampire plague.

He was the only one to fight the monsters up close and the only one who seemed to win.

People liked that.

Laxman liked that.

He admired Lawton's tough-guy approach to life.

But he also knew that Lawton was vulnerable. He was vulnerable because he would never sacrifice a mate so he could survive. He would never turn his back on a colleague. He would never let someone weaker than himself suffer.

And that's what exposed Jake Lawton.

That's why Laxman had the edge.

That's why he would win.

Laxman thought about Alfred Fuad. He wondered what the guy was up to. Laxman had been hired by Howard Vince. They'd known each other during the first Gulf War in '91. At the time, Vince was an officer on the frontline, but he later became Chief of the General Staff. The military big cheese in the UK.

Laxman and his firm were being paid well. More than a million pounds. And it was an easy million, as far as he was concerned. It was not as if White Light Ops had been forced to sweat for their wages. The only problems they'd encountered so far were that girl – Laxman's balls ached at the thought of her – and the foreign fella with the walking stick. Nothing else. Until now. Until Jake Lawton.

He'd guessed that the main reason he was here was to keep Lawton at bay.

He wasn't completely clear on what Fuad was up to. Digging for some ancient mummy. Something called Nimrod. Fuad and the others seemed to believe this creature might still be alive.

Laxman wasn't going to argue with that. He didn't care what people believed. He had his own faith – in weapons. Shooting a gun was like a religious experience to Laxman.

But then everyone had their superstitions.

Some of the Iraqi diggers on the site were jittery about vampires.

They spoke about witches and goblins. They spoke about the ghost of Nimrod's wife, still stalking the earth, still trying to find her way home.

And when she did, there would be trouble.

Always trouble when the wife comes home, thought Laxman, brushing the scar across his forehead. His missus had smashed him across the head with an iron after a domestic. *Bitch*, he thought, smiling. *Loved that girl.*

Laxman knew about vampires. The UK was plagued with them. He'd never believed in them before, but there was no doubting their existence now. But he wasn't bothered. Laxman had spent most of the past few years living in Switzerland and working in Africa and the Middle East – well out of the way of any vampires.

The dawn was starting to peek over the horizon, a white band cresting the skyline.

"How long?" he asked now.

Xavier, a Swiss national who'd worked with Laxman for ten years, said, "Thirty or forty minutes."

Ashton said, "What's the plan, boss?"

"I'm just thinking one up," said Laxman.

He shut his eyes and had a nap.

CHAPTER 46
SPYCATCHER.

KAMAL Najib, forty-seven in years and also around the waist, combed his moustache in the mirror of the gentlemen's toilet at the Ministry of the Interior.

The former Iraqi Army major, now senior investigator with the Department of Border Enforcement, coughed. He grimaced. His chest ached, and his throat was burning. It had to be an infection. His wife said, "Lay off the cigarettes." He smoked eighty a day. Some said Marlboros could kill you. But Najib reckoned it was just another lie the West told the Arabs.

He lit one now in the bathroom. Just to clear his throat. It hurt when he sucked in the smoke. But it would clear out any mucus trapped in his lungs.

He was getting ready to interrogate the British spy they'd found in the desert up north. He'd got the call an hour ago. Dragged out of bed at 4.00am.

"Can you come in?" a voice had said.

"It's four in the morning," he'd screamed.

And then the voice at the other end had told him why they wanted him in. He was happy to oblige. Anything to interrogate a spy.

Of course, it wasn't proven that the stranger was a spy just yet.

But Najib would find the proof.

He checked his watch – it was 5.15am now, so by 8.00am the Briton would have made a full confession.

Najib smiled at his reflection, proud that he was going to send some interfering Westerner to jail.

He hated them. They had invaded his country. They had killed his leader.

Najib was a Ba'athist. A Saddam loyalist. A true believer in the regime. He had met Saddam and had been honoured to follow an order once to kill another army officer who had been disloyal.

However, in his job as an assistant director of the Department of Border Enforcement, Najib had to keep secret his previous allegiances. He was expected to act within the laws of the new Iraq. The democratic Iraq. How could you get the truth out of a prisoner you weren't allowed to torture? Fear was the key to getting the facts. But these days, the regime was reluctant to sanction extreme techniques. They were scared of being told off by their new masters, the West.

Najib sneered.

He hated the US, the European Union, and Britain. It was time that his countrymen stopped regarding them as allies. They were colonists, usurpers, and infidels. They were imperialists intent on conquering Arab lands and corrupting the countries of the Middle East with democracy and human rights.

He farted. He smoked the cigarette before dropping the stump down the sink. He farted again. He walked out, leaving an odour of shit behind him, which made him smile.

He took the elevator to the basement, where the prisoner was being kept. Khoury, a western-loving young lieutenant with the Federal Police, had been keeping watching on the spy. Also on duty was Hassan, a fat lazy oaf. One of them would have made a mess of things, for sure. Najib would have to sort it all out. He'd show this spy, this criminal, this trespasser, that you can't just walk in and out of Iraq just because you claim to have liberated the country.

He exited the elevator and farted once again, just as the doors were shutting behind him He grinned, thinking about the odour that would waft out of the lift when the next passenger opened the doors.

A slim young woman wearing a tight skirt walked towards him along the corridor. She was beautiful. In her twenties. A secretary, probably. From the admin pool. One of the early shift. Najib was glad fanatical Islam had not infiltrated Iraq too deeply. It would be a shame to see women covered up. The wives, maybe, but not the secretaries. Not the students. Not the actresses. He liked looking at them – at legs, at breasts, at faces, at hair.

As the girl pressed herself against the wall to allow Najib to pass, he stroked her hair and said, "You are looking beautiful today. What is your name?"

She blushed and looked worried. But they always did. They loved the attention. He pressed his large belly against her, pushing her into the wall.

"Leyla," she said.

"You know me?" he said. He kept stroking her hair. It was so silky, and she must have liked it being stroked. She was flinching a little.

She nodded that she knew him and then said, "Please, I must… "

"Ah, no rush. You must visit me in my office to take some notes. Later today, perhaps."

"I am, I can't – "

"But it is an order – "

A door flew open. Khoury sprang out. He ran off down the corridor. Najib stepped away from the woman. She hurried away in the opposite direction to Khoury. But he wasn't about to chase her.

A gurney had burst out of the room Khoury had exited. Four medics shoved the stretcher down the passageway in Khoury's direction. An oxygen mask was clamped to the patient's face. Whoever he was, he was twitching on the gurney. And there was a lot of blood. The man wore a white kurta, but it was red now with blood.

They wheeled him down the corridor.

Najib shouted at Khoury.

The lieutenant stopped and turned. His face bleached when he saw Najib.

"What is happening, Lieutenant Khoury? Who is this man?"

"Sir, it is the prisoner."

Najib gawped. He couldn't speak. His chest suddenly became very tight, and he could hardly breathe.

"He attacked me, sir," said Khoury. "I had to shoot him."

CHAPTER 47.
ANOTHER BULLET.

IT was chaos. Just what Lawton wanted. Panic in the ministry as they wheeled him out. Oxygen mask clamped to his face. Lots of shouting. Khoury next to him, taking a big risk. Lawton's eyes were wide open. Taking everything in. Thinking. Strategizing. Plotting. Four medics, one a woman. He smelled cordite. He felt pain.

Khoury had shot him.

Six bullets in his body, now.

He'd taken a risk.

Ereshkigal had said, "The weapons of men will soon barely graze you."

She had told him he might have vampire DNA in him. He had rejected such a notion. But now it could save him. It took a huge leap of faith. He had to trust the words of a monster. But the situation he was in demanded quick action. It demanded a decision.

And he decided that he'd rather be shot than be sent back to Britain.

If Ereshkigal had told him the truth, a bullet would not mean death – but going back home certainly would.

As they wheeled him, they attended to his wound. It was in his side. Just under his ribs.

"Shoot me," he'd told Khoury.

Khoury had said, "No."

"Shoot me and get me out of here."

"I can't shoot you."

"Tell them I attacked you."

"Lawton you have not attacked – "

Jake had leapt across the desk. Pinned Khoury to the floor just as the lieutenant was going for his weapon. Grabbed Khoury's gun hand. Jammed the barrel into his side. Pressed Khoury's trigger finger. Ereshkigal's words in his mind as the pain blinded him.

It was agony. He'd experienced it before. First, it was like being punched in the side, hard. Second, the ache turned to fire. His insides boiling. Blood pulsing out. His body weak and cold.

Khoury was in a panic. He had called an ambulance.

Now they were outside, bouncing down the steps. Heat and chaos. Everyone shouting. The world spinning. Lawton dizzy and sick. Thinking, *Ereshkigal lied to me. I am dying.*

He cursed himself for being a fool. He got ready to embrace death. It was almost a comfort. He felt OK with it. He blinked. Everything became blurry. He blinked again. His left eye throbbed. Images swirled in his brain. His mind was reeling. He groaned and blinked again. The light in the sky was weak. Dawn coming. When vampires slept. *When Ereshkigal slept*, he thought. The noise was suddenly deafening. Screaming and shouting, a chorus of voices in his head.

They lifted him into an ambulance. The smell of disinfectant hit him. People speaking Arabic. People speaking English. Shouting at each other. Shouting at him. Khoury was there, looking down at Lawton. Then he was gone. The doors slammed shut. The vehicle was moving. Sirens screamed. The medics removed his mask.

"Are you OK, mister?" said a medic.

Lawton blinked.

The man pointed at his eye and said something to his colleague in Arabic.

Lawton blinked again.

The pain in his body faded.

A surge of power raced through him.

He'd wait until they came to a halt. Despite having the sirens on, the ambulance was sure to be trapped in traffic. This was Baghdad. Early morning rush hour. Driving here was crazy. Lawton would get a chance. He'd have to be quick. But he *felt* quick. He felt alive.

CHAPTER 48.
TRAFFIC PROBLEMS.

ASHTON ran back to the Toyota and got in the passenger seat.

"He's been taken to hospital," he said.

"What?" said Laxman.

"He was shot by a police officer."

"Shot?"

"Shot."

"Dead?"

"They said he was alive, but they didn't know how bad."

"Which hospital?" said Laxman.

"The Baghdad Medical City complex in Bab Al-Moatham."

"You know that, Xavier?" said Laxman.

The Swiss driver said, "I know where the complex is, but which hospital? It is a fucking massive place."

"I say the Surgical Specialities hospital," said Ashton. "It makes sense if you've got a bullet wound."

"Try that," said Laxman. "Get going."

Xavier fired up the Toyota. He swung it round and headed into traffic, causing drivers to stray out of the lane and press down on their horns. It was 6.00am, and the roads were quickly filling up.

And drivers were getting hot under the collar even at that time of morning.

It took all of Laxman's discipline not to leap out of the vehicle and start shooting at people. He glared out of the Toyota's window, clenching his jaw, praying to any god that would listen, "Keep Lawton alive so I can kill him, keep Lawton alive . . . "

Have faith, JJ, he told himself, *have faith*.

They had reached the Ministry of Interior ten minutes earlier. They had parked up across the street. Ashton had run in to see if "a colleague of theirs had been arrested."

They headed west now towards Medical City, a compound of training hospitals once called Saddam Medical City. The surgical hospital had been built in the 1980s. Saddam certainly spent on health for his mates, and to train doctors. But he didn't really care that most of the population was starving and disease-ridden. In the 1990s, some blamed sanctions for that. But food was being supplied. Equipment was coming in. Saddam and his cronies had decided to stock it all and use it themselves. He let his people starve and hoodwinked those foolish enough in the West to think he was a decent bloke.

No one, Laxman knew, was a decent bloke. He didn't believe in rubbish like that. He'd seen enough to have his faith in humanity wrecked. Now he only believed in one thing – himself.

The traffic was maddening. The noise deafening. The fumes overpowering. But it was like any other city. Busy and frantic.

He thanked the stars for air-con, because outside it was getting hot, even at this early hour.

Sirens blared.

Laxman became alert, looking out for the source of the noise.

There was a convoy up ahead – police cars and an ambulance.

They were headed in the direction of the medical complex. The vast, grey compound could be seen in the distance. Road signs directed drivers towards the hospitals.

"Up ahead, Xavier," said Laxman. "He's got to be in that ambulance, with all those police cars around it."

"Seen it, boss," said the Swiss mercenary.

"Maybe he's dead already, huh?" said Ashton. "We can pray, yeah?"

"I don't want him dead already," said Laxman.

"Save us the trouble, though, chief," Ashton said.

"I want the trouble."

The Toyota came to a halt. It was gridlock up ahead. Horns blared. The ambulance was skewed in traffic, as if it had been struck by something. It sat halfway across two lanes.

The ambulance's back doors burst open.

A man with shoulder-length black hair, his long, white shirt a bloody mess, leapt out and started striding across the roofs of the cars.

CHAPTER 49.
WE'LL BE BACK.

GOGA said, "No alliance has ever been struck between humans and Nimrod."

The Romanian was still badly hurt hours after the beating he'd got. Aaliyah was worried about him. But he said he'd be all right. His suffering was not important, he'd said. He was only bruised, just a few cuts. Nothing to what would happen if they didn't stop Alfred Fuad.

Aaliyah and Goga were "guests", Fuad had told them.

Guests who just couldn't leave.

They had been locked in a cell for a few hours. It was tiny, a crevice carved into the rock face, a hefty, oak door making sure there was no escape.

Aaliyah couldn't keep track of time. They had taken her watch and her phone. She couldn't measure it by sunlight or dark.

Goga had slept, but she couldn't. She'd been wired since they'd got caught. All kinds of worries raced through her head. Mostly they were to do with Jake. What was going to happen to him? Fuad said that even if the Iraqis didn't kill him, Laxman would. She felt very frustrated. Trapped here, unable to do anything. Unable to help. Unable to save Jake.

An hour ago, men with guns had come to take Aaliyah and Goga to Fuad's tent. She had asked what time it was, and they had told her, "Early."

Early or late, Fuad was drinking when they got to his tent. The smell of booze hung in the air. Howard Vince was there too. He had been scowling at Fuad when Aaliyah and Goga had been shoved inside. Aaliyah guessed they'd been arguing, maybe about Fuad's drinking, maybe about something else. But it gave her hope. She would try to take advantage of any rift between her enemies.

Goga went on now: "He does not need allies. He was a king. A god. A builder of cities, and their destroyer, too. He made Babylon, Fuad. He is the one who made the darkness dark."

"You don't half rattle on, Vladimir," said Fuad. "My brother would be bored to death of you."

"My name is not Vladimir," said Goga.

"You're Russian, ain't you?" said Fuad.

"Romanian, you fool."

Howard Vince was gritting his teeth.

"I don't care what you are," said Fuad. "It doesn't matter. From now on it only matters if you're Nebuchadnezzar or not Nebuchadnezzar."

"And for those who are not?" Goga said.

Fuad shrugged. "We've got plenty of non-Nebs who support us. My brother got elected on the back of votes from those who are not as lucky as me and General Vince here."

"Lucky?" said Goga.

"Lucky to be descended from a king."

"You are nothing but apes like the rest of us," said Goga. "And Nimrod will show you that. He will devour you and the world, if you free him. There will be nothing for you in this expedition."

Aaliyah noticed some concern on Vince's face. The general was obviously worried. He might not have been convinced by the Fuads' mission. Resurrecting Nimrod had never been the

Nebuchadnezzars' original plan. Their objective was simply to create a vampire nation in the UK. Recreate the Babylon of their ancestor, who had ruled the golden city with a vampire army behind him. Maybe some of the Nebs thought the Fuads were going too far.

"Nimrod will be weak when we dig him up," said Fuad. "He'll need allies. He'll need builders for his city. He'll need leaders for his nation. We are those builders and those leaders. Me and George. Me, George, General Vince here, people like us. London's going to be his new golden city. And from London, we'll spread across the world. We'll be rich and fat."

"Five thousand years ago," said Goga, "a mad prophet stopped Nimrod. Centuries later, the Great Hunter's children were defeated first by Alexander the Great, and later still by Jake Lawton. What will make it different this time, Fuad?"

Fuad smiled. He drank his whisky.

"It'll be different this time," he said, "because there's no mad prophet. There's no Alexander. And there's no Lawton."

Silence fell in the tent. In the distance, the great drill echoed through the caverns as it ploughed deeper into the earth. Aaliyah could feel the ground tremble.

"Greed will be your undoing," said Goga.

"It's not greed, mate," said Fuad. "It's belief. Belief that some of us have a right to rule. Belief that things would be better if we were allowed to be in charge. Belief that humankind is changing, that most of it is just scum and worthless in the great scheme of things. Such a belief drove every conqueror, Goga. Whatever god they worshipped, they believed firstly in themselves. And that's us. Me, George, the rest of the Nebuchadnezzars. We believe in ourselves. Nothing can shake that belief. That's why we'll win in the end, because we'll keep coming back. No matter how many times you knock us down, we'll be back, and back, and back. And this time, we're going to achieve our final victory."

Aaliyah's belly lurched.

She was in the presence of a madman.

Her hopes were dwindling.

Perhaps it was time to give up.

George Fuad controlled Britain. Alfred was excavating a monster in Iraq. Jake was a prisoner. She and Goga were captives too.

But I have to have faith, she told herself. *If Fuad and the Nebs do, then so can I.*

She had always believed in fate. She was convinced it had played a hand in her meeting Jake.

But he'd rejected such notions.

"Hundreds of people have died so we could meet?" he'd said. "No, babe. There's no such thing as fate or destiny or God. There's only anguish. And love. That's all there is."

Love. That was the meaning of everything for Aaliyah. That was her faith, her religion. The love she shared with Jake. The trust she had in him.

I have to believe, she said to herself. *I have to believe.*

Believe that he would never leave her. Believe that he would somehow get free and come to find her.

She fought off the gloom with that belief. Held it up like a shield to keep the misery at bay. Hacked at the darkness that was enveloping her.

He will come, she thought. *He will come, and we'll be an alliance again – me and Jake against the world, and when he comes, we will fight our way out of this.*

CHAPTER 50.
RUN FOR YOUR LIFE.

LAWTON had been running for an hour. The sirens told him the police were in pursuit. People stayed out of his way. Drivers stopped and stared, causing more traffic congestion. He was badly wounded, and the kurta he wore was soaked in blood. He was a white man and looked pretty wild with his long hair.

No wonder the city was gawping at him. No wonder it looked at him with dread.

He had to get off the streets. He had to find somewhere to hide.

He felt a dull ache in his side, where Khoury had shot him. The wound seeped. But it didn't hurt badly. Not like it should have done. It only throbbed now and again. Throbbed like his eye did. As if there was something living in there. Something that wasn't him but that was becoming part of him.

He stopped in an alley to catch his breath.

Khoury came to mind. He wondered if the young police officer was safe. If his superiors would believe the tall tale he'd tell them about Lawton's escape. He felt for the Iraqi officer. The guy had taken a big risk. Lawton had taken a big risk.

Lawton now felt guilty because he had had to physically threaten Khoury to shoot. He shook the feeling off. He had to focus on survival.

He started running down the alley. Rubbish was piled up down the sides of the passageway. Boxes and wrappers, the waste from food shops and restaurants.

He heard voices behind him.

He glanced over his shoulders.

He'd rested too long.

The cops had caught up with him.

Overhead, a helicopter swooped. It would appear any second, its passengers targeting Lawton.

He ran harder. The alley led him into the backstreets. Market traders were selling their wares. It was noisy and busy. He smelled meat and perfumes and spices. He saw fruit, vegetables, clothes. He heard the sizzle of someone frying something, the shouts of the traders, the bark of dogs, and the braying of sheep and goats.

He weaved along the busy thoroughfare. Some of the businesspeople reared away from him. Others tripped over, spilling the contents of baskets into the road.

Lawton glanced over his shoulder. The cops were still coming. A dozen of them. And overhead, the chopper had him in its sights. He wondered if either the cops or the helicopter team would start firing. It was a busy street, full of people. Years ago, the shooting would have started. In Saddam's day, the authorities didn't care about locals getting in the way of a manhunt. Lawton hoped their attitude was different these days.

He came to a junction and, without thinking, turned right.

Up ahead was a main street.

He burst out of the alley, stared right and left.

Traffic was busy. People everywhere.

"Over here, mate," said someone.

Lawton turned, not expecting to hear an English voice.

"Over here, come on," said a big guy in military fatigues.

He stood next to a Toyota Land Cruiser, the back door open.

Two other men sat in the vehicle's front seats. Both looked military.

Again the big man beckoned Lawton.

He looked behind him. The cops were coming, he could hear them. The helicopter pilot was pointing at him. Voices boomed from a loudspeaker, telling him to stay where he was and to get down on the floor.

"No time like the present," said the big guy standing next to the Toyota.

Lawton sprinted towards the vehicle. He had to take a chance. The big guy was a bear. Well over six feet. As wide as a doorway.

"We'll get you out of here," he told Lawton.

He leapt into the back of the Toyota. The big man joined him in the rear seat and shut the door.

"Go," he said.

The driver hammered the accelerator. Tyres screeched. Rubber burned. The Toyota barrelled its way through traffic in the wrong direction. Horns blared. Drivers veered out of the way, mounting the pavement. Lawton was thrown around in the back seat.

"I'm Laxman," said the big man. He had a scar across his forehead. His smile told Lawton, *Don't trust him*.

Lawton nodded.

The Toyota raced through Baghdad. The cops tailed it.

CHAPTER 51.
STREET FIGHT.

LAWTON had a lot of things on his mind, and he was trying to stop them from getting mixed up and confusing him.

First, there was Aaliyah. Where was she? Was she safe? She was in this country somewhere. Hillah, hopefully. At least he could find her if she was there.

Then, there was the Spear of Abraham. He felt lost without it. As if an appendage was missing. Had Ereshkigal taken it with her? He hoped it had not fallen into the hands of the authorities or bandits.

And then there was Ereshkigal herself. She was constantly on his mind now. He had come full circle, from despising vampires to having to trust one. But she had saved his life. And he had protected her. *Two species benefiting each other*, he thought. *Evolution, maybe.*

Finally, and most immediately pressing, were the three men in the Toyota.

Who were they? How had they just happened to be in the right place at the right time? Lawton didn't like coincidences. They suggested to him that there were darker forces at play.

He glanced at the guy called Laxman, the leader. He was big and strong. He was bronzed, which told Lawton the fellow travelled a lot. He had that scar right across his forehead. War wound, maybe.

The driver was blonde and had a dragon's head tattoo on his scalp. The passenger was dark-haired, shoulder muscles like boulders.

They all wore fatigues. Laxman was armed, a pistol strapped against his ribs. It was a Makarov, once popular with terrorists in the Middle East. Carlos the Jackal's gang had been armed with Makarovs when they'd raided the OPEC HQ in Vienna in 1975, Lawton remembered.

He couldn't see if the guys in the front seat were packing, but he assumed they would be. You had to. You always had to think the worst.

These men were mercenaries.

He could smell it on them.

"You guys working out here?" said Lawton.

"That's right," said Laxman. "Working."

"Security – or something else?"

"Some security, some 'something else', too."

"You still in the forces?"

"No, I run White Light Ops. Private security firm. Got an office in London, but mostly we work out of Geneva. Heard of us?"

Lawton hesitated. They hadn't asked him what he was doing yet. Had not asked him why he was running away from half of Baghdad's Federal Police. And why should he have heard of a private security firm? You'd assume that only military people had heard of such organizations.

His eye throbbed badly. As if it were signalling danger. A beacon warning him of peril ahead.

They were driving through a residential area. Tower blocks. Kids playing on the streets. Washing hanging out of windows.

Dust swirling. Vehicles lined the kerb. A mangy dog dragged its hind quarters along. It had something in its mouth.

"You plan to drop me off somewhere?" said Lawton.

"Where would you like to be dropped off, Lawton?" asked Laxman.

The hairs on Jake's nape stood on end.

They hurtled along narrow roads, weaving through residential Baghdad.

"Where are you taking me?" said Lawton

"To safety," said Laxman. "Away from those cops chasing you. Or you want to go back into town?"

"Here's fine."

The driver glanced at him in the rear-view mirror. Lawton held on to the door handle and tested it. Locked. He bent forward, groaning.

Laxman said, "What's the – "

But he wasn't allowed to finish his question.

Lawton's right elbow, with a 180 pounds of force behind it, swept upwards at high speed and smashed into Laxman's jaw. At the same time, Lawton's left fist smashed into the back of the front-seat passenger's skull. The guy jerked forward as Laxman slumped.

Lawton snatched the Makarov from Laxman's holster.

He shot out the windscreen.

It shattered. Glass sprayed. The driver screamed. The vehicle swerved.

Lawton fired again. This time into the rear driver's side window. His window. It exploded. Glass rained over him.

The driver spun the wheel. The Toyota hit something. It came to a halt. The passenger groaned. The driver swivelled, his face red with rage. Lawton shot him in the shoulder. The man screamed. Blood splashed. He writhed in agony. The smell of cordite was strong in the vehicle.

Lawton shook his head. His ears rang.

He threw himself out of his shattered window. Glass cut his skin. He didn't care. He was out. He hit the ground. Dust made his lacerations sting.

He groaned, the gunshot wound pulsing, the sixth bullet still lodged in his side.

He got to his feet, disorientated.

The driver was still screaming.

The passenger was coming round, reaching for a weapon.

Lawton scoped the area. Dozens of voices filled the air, all of them speaking Arabic. The world spun. Faces loomed out of high-rise windows. Screams erupted. People were shouting. His head ached badly. The smell of meat and spices made him salivate. He started to stagger away from the Toyota, which had ploughed into the side of a building. He stumbled away, his vision blurred, his ears ringing.

The police car screeched to a halt, blocking the junction ahead of him, its blue lights flashing.

Four cops spilled out. He turned and went back towards the Toyota.

"Shit," he said as another cop car sped down the road towards him.

It came to a stop. Four police officers poured out of that one, too, and they were all armed.

They shouted at him in Arabic, pointing their weapons.

He recognized Khoury. His eyes were wide. He was terrified. He trained his gun on Lawton.

He thought, *Can I take another bullet and live?*

The passenger had got out of the Toyota and started shouting in Arabic at the police officers.

Laxman also staggered out of the vehicle. He looked dazed. He glared at Lawton. He said something in Arabic. The driver was still shouting, and he crawled out, blood pulsing from his shoulder.

"You and me, you bastard," said Laxman, spit oozing from his mouth. "You and me, Lawton. How did you guess, huh?"

"You said my name, you fucking amateur."

Laxman grimaced. "You and me, man to man, one on one."

The mercenary tore off his jacket. He wore a white T-shirt. Under it he was heavy with muscle and fat. Tattoos covered his tree-trunk arms.

"You think these cops are going to let us fight?" said Lawton

"'Course they will, since I paid them," said Laxman.

The officers formed a circle. Khoury was there, his eyes telling Lawton that he was scared, that he had no choice.

A crowd had started to gather. Boys with a football. Men started to gamble. A woman in a burkha carrying a sack. More women, most of them covered.

"Let's give them a show," said Laxman.

He charged Lawton.

CHAPTER 52.
THE GLINT OF DEATH.

LAWTON dodged Laxman's charge.

The mercenary hurtled forward and stumbled, hitting the floor. The rough ground ripped skin off his hands, but it didn't stop him. He got up. His face burned with hatred.

"Come on, you fucking bastard," he said.

"You have anger issues, Laxman," said Lawton. "Ever thought of therapy?"

"My therapy would be to have your head on a plate."

Some of the policemen were shouting at them to stop, but they were silenced by the others – those in Laxman's pay, probably.

The passenger from the Toyota grabbed the woman in the burkha. She dropped her sack. Something clicked in Lawton's head, like a light switch. And for a second he saw something.

But then Laxman pummelled into him. The air was knocked out of him, and he flew across the street. He slammed into a wall and saw stars. Shaking himself down, he saw Laxman barrel towards him again. Laxman's buddy held the woman and pointed a gun at her head. Some of the police moved in, but the mercenary warned them to stay back.

Confusion reigned. No one knew what was going on. Some policemen wanted to stop the fight. Others were allowing it to go on. The helicopter roared overhead. All around, locals shouted and gambled.

It took Lawton back a few months, when he'd taken part in illegal, bareknuckle fights to raise cash. He'd been undefeated.

No point starting a losing streak, now, he thought.

He sprang to his feet to meet Laxman's charge.

The mercenary was powerful. He swung wild punches. Lawton fended them off, using the *pensador* defence pose from the Keysi Fighting Method – hands on his scalp, elbows up. This position protected his head and face from Laxman's blows, and by moving his body left and right, he could fend off the blows and create space for his own attack.

Which came in a flash.

With flying elbows, Lawton smashed open Laxman's weak defence. A right hook, followed by a straight left, forced Laxman backwards. His eyes rolled back in his head. His arms windmilled as he tried to keep his balance.

The crowd roared.

Lawton followed through with big punches to the mercenary's head – three powerful blows that decked the big man.

The crowd cheered.

Lawton pulsed with adrenaline. He felt immensely powerful. He sensed everything – every sound, every sensation. He almost welcomed the pain in his body. It felt necessary for his survival. The agony was what made him alive. He tightened every muscle, every nerve.

Laxman was trying to get up.

Lawton went straight for the passenger holding the woman hostage.

The driver said, "Let's get the fuck out of here, Ashton."

The police looked confused now. Some still trained their weapons on Ashton. Others aimed at Lawton. But he didn't care. He marched on. They could shoot if they wanted to. He felt now that nothing could kill him. He felt superhuman.

"In the car, Xavier," said Ashton, and then he said something to the cops in Arabic, and they all turned their weapons on Lawton.

Khoury said, "He will kill the woman if we don't kill you."

"Yeah, that's right," said Ashton. "Shoot him, you bastards, or I'll rip this bitch's burkha off and blow her head off."

"Let her go," said Lawton.

Laxman was groaning. He had blood on his face.

"You Ashton?" said Lawton. "Why don't you come fight me, man to man, like your boss?"

"I'm not stupid, mate. Easier ways to skin a cat. Kill him," he said, and then in Arabic, "*Qetlh*."

Lawton looked at the veil behind which the woman's eyes hid. He felt something. His eye pulsed. It was as if an electric current was delivered into his brain, and there it became a voice. It called his name.

Behind the woman's face-veil he sensed something. The glint of death. It was like a religious experience. His heart filled with joy. But he felt scared for her, because it was daylight. And the light would kill her. But she was covered head to foot. No flesh showed. Every inch hidden. Every horror concealed.

Lawton held his breath.

The woman whirled and snapped Ashton's neck. The cracking sound his death made caused Lawton to shy away, and it sent a gasp of terror through the spectators.

Before Lawton could take a breath, the woman leapt on Xavier and sliced open his throat.

Lawton looked at Khoury and said, "Get out of here, man."

Gunfire barked. Lawton threw himself down. Screams filled the air. The smell of blood lingered.

PART SIX.

JUDGMENT.

CHAPTER 53.
CUTS AND WOUNDS.

SOHO, LONDON – 2.15AM (GMT), 20 MAY, 2011

AT about the same time as Kamal Najib was pondering how he would torture the British spy captured in Iraq, George Fuad leaned forward on the desk in his new London headquarters and stared into the camera. He furrowed his brow, masking his true feelings with a look of sincerity.

"There is no need to fear," he said into the lens. "Stay in your homes. You'll be safe. Humans and vampires can live in peace, side by side. This is the beginning of a new age. Embrace it. Enjoy it. Live it. This'll be a time when no one is judged for what you are – vampire or human. Thank you. Sleep safely."

"That's it," said the director. "We'll edit it, and it'll be on the morning bulletin."

Fuad rose and loosened his tie. The grimace returned to his face. He stomped out of the room, followed by two members of his staff and a bodyguard.

It was very late. But he didn't feel like sleeping. There was work to do. He'd spent the past hour recording messages that would be broadcast on TV and radio, over the internet, and on big screens he planned to have erected in city centres. They would feed the people a daily dose of propaganda.

His blood was up. He was in charge now. King of the country. It was what he'd always wanted. So why was he so worried, so unnerved?

He felt so unsettled he wanted to kill someone. Nail someone to the wall and throttle them. Stab someone over and over, just to take his frustration out on a body.

He should be happy. He was in power. He was at Religion, the new base for the United Party, and the centre of government while the Palace of Westminster was being rebuilt.

He trudged along the corridor. It smelled musty in Religion. This building had also been damaged by fire once. You could still smell the charred wood, the burnt bricks.

He thought about halting the development in Westminster. Maybe he'd let the old parliament buildings smoulder, a reminder of what Jake Lawton had done to Britain.

At the end of the corridor, he fished out a set of keys from his pocket.

"Stay here," he told his companions.

He unlocked the door and threw it open.

Christine Murray nearly leapt out of her skin.

She had been sitting on the couch, watching him on the TV bracketed to the wall.

"Not asleep?" he said.

She stared at him.

He looked around the room. Bars covered the window. The paint on the ceiling peeled. Damp blackened the wallpaper. The carpet was dusty and old, and a rank smell saturated the air. There was a table with a lamp on it. Murray had a couch to sit on, and in the corner was a single bed, and next to it a door that led into the toilet. A tray sat on the floor with a half-eaten pizza, and an empty mug was perched on the arm of the sofa where Murray sat.

This was her cell.

Elizabeth Wilson was contained in a similar room down the corridor.

"Hope you're enjoying your stay," he said.

She said nothing.

"It won't be a long one, Christine."

He looked at her, watching out for any fear. But she showed none. She showed grit. And that's what made him wary. That's what made him nervous. His enemies weren't as scared as he wanted them to be. But he'd make them tremble. He was determined that they would be begging for mercy soon enough.

"Killing us all, George?" she said.

"These are days of judgment."

"You're kidnapping people from their homes. You're cramming people into trucks and taking them God knows where. You're putting innocent people in prison cells with killers and rapists."

"No one is innocent. They're enemies of the state. They're awaiting punishment. Death or slavery."

"You're mad, completely mad."

"It's subjective, madness. We've all got our own truth. Isn't that the new age way? Well, just happens that my truth is the right truth today. And it's going to stay that way. I am going to reign like a fucking emperor."

Now a glimmer of fear did show in Murray's eyes. That gave him a lift.

"You think you can get away with this?" she said.

"You think I can't?"

"What made you like this, George?" asked Murray.

He grinned. "My mother never cuddled me."

"Your mother would be ashamed of you, I'm sure."

His blood boiled. He tightened up and was close to pounding Murray to the ground. But he mastered his rage and forced another smile.

"What would you know about motherhood, bitch?"

She paled. He liked that. He'd struck a blow.

"You fancy another crack at motherhood, then?" he said.

Murray gawped.

"We could get wed, Chrissie," he said.

She said nothing.

"You'd make a nice first lady – or queen – or consort. Fatten you up a bit. Bit of slap. New clothes."

Her throat went up and down. She'd gone even paler.

He laughed.

"Maybe not, eh?" he said. "You couldn't keep up with me, I don't think, love. Here, let's have a look at the telly."

He turned the TV on. He found the BBC News Channel. The production looked cheap. Cardboard sets. Ropey old presenters. But that was the new BBC. The BBC that had suffered cuts like everyone else. *Cuts and wounds*, he thought.

The TV showed footage from Manchester, shot on a hand-held camera. The picture was grainy. The sound was shoddy. There was an army of black-clad Nebuchadnezzar thugs herding people into trucks. Any trouble, the Nebs had an order, from him, to shoot to kill. No law to worry about, now. No human rights.

"Manchester goes first," he said. "Then Birmingham. Liverpool. Fucking Scots up in Glasgow and Edinburgh, Aberdeen, Perth. Then the Taffy cunts in Cardiff, Swansea, Prestatyn, fucking Rhyl. Britain's being purged, darling. Fucking purged."

Murray was shaking. He was sure she'd start crying any second. He wanted that. He wanted her tears.

"You'll cheer up in the next few days. You can watch a few nice little executions with me."

She looked at him, her mouth open.

He said, "Elizabeth Wilson."

"No," she gasped.

"Then that little Chinky bitch when we find her."

"You bastard."

"And if he's got the guts to come and find me, your little boy. I'll have him killed for you, Christine. Baked alive, maybe. Burnt at the stake. And I'll feed you his cooked balls."

He expected that to make her cry. But she was fighting the tears. Biting her lip and looking him in the eye. He smiled, and shrugged at her. Then slapped her hard across the face, sending her reeling across the room. And when she lifted her head, he nodded to himself. She was finally crying.

CHAPTER 54.
BEING BRAVE.

MANCHESTER – 2.35AM (GMT), 20 MAY, 2011

"WHAT can we do now?" said Ediz Ün.

"Keep fighting," said Mei.

"For what?"

"For the people."

"They are not fighting."

"Some are. Some fight. There is still fight. We must."

Ediz shook his head.

"We can't give up," said Mei. "If we give up, we die."

Ediz was thinking. His forehead creased. He was scratching the wisps of hair on his chin that might one day become a beard.

"Maybe they'll treat us well," he said. "Maybe Fuad is telling the truth – that people and vampires can live together."

Mei raised her eyebrows.

"OK," said Ediz, "maybe not."

Mei had never met anyone from Turkey before she came to the UK. If you had asked her about Turks five years ago, she wouldn't know what to make of them. But now she'd met Ediz, and he'd become her friend. She'd met other nationalities, too. Iraqis and Afghans and Russians; Australians and Canadians and Moldovans; Ukrainians and Indonesians and many more. She had met them all when she raised an army of migrants to stand up for Britain. To fight the vampires.

They were holed up in a flat above a former Chinese bakery on Faulkner Street. It used to be the home of Liao Bo, the elderly woman who had saved Mei when she'd arrived in Manchester. Before the war the area was known as Chinatown. Now it was a Ghost Town. The takeaways, the restaurants, the stores had nearly all been boarded up. Business was dead. The vampires had conquered. Customers had gone.

Mei practiced some moves with her wakizashi swords. Outside, chaos reigned. The authorities had come in the middle of the night. They had vampires with them. Screaming and shouting filled the streets. Nebuchadnezzar thugs growled orders over loudspeakers as they filed Mancunians into trucks. Gunfire barked, and that triggered shrieks. Someone had obviously tried to run away. And they'd been mowed down. No mercy. No law and order. No rights. Everything Kwan Mei had dreamed about when she had first come to Britain had gone. But she was determined to get them back.

"Why don't the army do anything?" said Ediz.

"Army do what government tells it. Even if they hate to. And most soldiers have abandoned posts. They do not want to fight the people. The new army is Nebuchadnezzars."

"We are going to die," he said.

"Then we die fighting."

His brow furrowed.

"Ed," said Mei, "we can't wait here in this flat. They will come if we sit and do nothing. We go out, kill vampires. Fight back. Look, we are safe, we are protected."

She indicated the red ribbon clipped to her shirt, and the band looped around Ediz's wrist.

"We have killed vampires," she said. "We have killed Nebuchadnezzars too. We can be strong."

"Not enough of us, Mei. They've come to Manchester first because they know we're here. Our army is here. This is where we started out. Where you brought us together. So they come here first to crush us. They bring us their judgment, Mei. In the middle of the night like this. Drag us from our homes. Take us to their firing squads. They will destroy us."

"Then fight them."

She stood and clinked the blades of her swords together.

I go to fight for my friends and for David, she thought.

She missed David. They had been good friends. He was a boy but as brave as any man. He had the courage of a lion. It would be good to have him here now. He would make a good ally. But he had a different objective. He was driven by rage. His blood boiled. His eye was trained on a target.

George Fuad.

She nudged Ediz with her foot.

"Kill vampires with me, Ed."

She sheathed the swords and exited the flat. Reluctantly, Ediz followed. She glanced behind her. He was carrying a rucksack that was filled to the brim with wooden stakes.

He'd be OK once he was outside. He liked slaughtering the undead. He had a taste for it. Driving a stake into a vampire's heart, seeing its body start to char and smoulder, before it disintegrated, was enjoyable. It was like a drug in your veins. It gave you what Ediz called a kick.

He was brave and handsome. He had been a good fighter when the war broke out in February. He had been on the frontline with Mei all the way to London. From these streets, they had marched south. On the way, they had picked up new recruits, and they had killed vampires and Nebs. They were migrants, but the white people cheered them on. Even some white people who usually hated immigrants.

They walked down the stairwell, listening to the noise outside in the street. It scared Mei, but she steeled herself. She was ready to fight. She was ready to bring judgment down on these criminals who had stolen her new country.

Ediz and Mei opened the door at the bottom of the stairs, and the havoc spilled inside.

Vampires were attacking humans. Nebuchadnezzars were herding Mancunians into coaches and trucks. The vehicles were lined up, waiting for their reluctant passengers.

"Are you ready to fight?" said Mei.

She unsheathed the wakizashi.

"Always ready to fight," he said.

He armed himself with stakes.

They charged out into the street. The noise hit Mei. It was deafening. The sound of terror. Screams and shouts. Sirens blaring. Gunfire erupting.

For a second, Mei hesitated. She thought, *Where are the British police?*

But the cops were gone. Most had left their jobs. They were either fighting the vampires as part of a small resistance army somewhere, or they'd been killed or herded off to one of the Nebuchadnezzars' camps. Those officers who remained in uniform kept a low profile. Some probably joined the Nebs, just to survive. But they couldn't do anything to stop this takeover. That was down to people like Mei and Ediz.

Mei shook off her fears.

A vampire was pinning down a girl.

Mei leapt forward, kicked the creature in the head.

It rolled away, snarling.

It got ready to pounce on Mei, but baulked when it saw the red mark. It looked confused for a moment, the question haunting it: *Why has a Neb attacked me?*

Its dithering gave Mei a chance to attack.

She launched herself at the creature like a harpy, shrieking at the top of her voice.

She plunged a sword into the creature's chest, and its heart burst. A screech poured from its throat. Fire ran like a dynamite fuse along its body. And it fragmented. Erupted into dust. Its ashes washed away on the breeze.

Mei wheeled, ready for another kill.

She saw Ediz nail two vampires, one on his left, the other on his right.

"Over there," said Ediz, pointing.

Two vampires were clambering over a Fiat that contained a woman and two little children. The car had stalled. The kids were crying. The mum was screaming.

The vampires crawled all over the car, trying to dig their fingers into the door frame, trying to smash the windows.

Mei sprinted towards the scene. She leapt and landed on the boot of the car. One of the vampires turned to her and hissed. She drove a sword into its chest, and it wheeled away in agony, crumbling before it had gone ten feet.

The other vampire realized what was happening. It turned tail and fled, but ran straight into Ediz, who slayed it.

Mei encouraged the woman in the car to fire up the engine, which she managed to do. The car drove off, tires skidding.

Ediz and Mei scanned the streets.

"Too many of them," he said.

It did look hopeless. Vampires everywhere. Nebuchadnezzar thugs were separating families, putting women on a coach, children on another, and forcing men into trucks.

It tore at Mei's heart.

A vampire attacked them. Ediz turned to face it. The creature's eyes widened in terror. It saw the red mark around the youth's wrist.

"You're Nebuchadnezzar," said the vampire.

Ediz marched up to it.

"What if we are?" he said.

"You… you are killing vampires?" said the creature.

"You can't trust anyone these days," said Ediz, and he drove a stake into the vampire's chest.

Two-black clad Nebuchadnezzar soldiers raced forward.

They fronted up to Mei and Ediz, aiming their guns at them.

For a few moments, they were all silent – a stand-off.

Then one of the Nebs said, "What the fuck are you killing vampires for?"

Three other Nebs joined them, one carrying a clipboard.

He was looking at his clipboard, and then looking at Mei, and he did this a few times before a smile spread across his face.

He showed her the clipboard. A photo of her at the head of the army she'd led through England a few months before was pasted to a sheet of paper.

"It's her," said the Neb. "The foreign bitch with a price on her head."

The thugs moved in.

"Run, Ediz," she said.

"I'm not going anywhere without you."

The Neb with the clipboard said, "Unfortunately, guys, we need to take them alive. Mr Fuad wants to make an example of every rebel."

The Nebs charged.

They overpowered Ediz, pinning him to the ground and handcuffing him.

Mei shrieked, slashing with her wakizashi.

A Neb lunged. She twisted away, stabbing backwards. Her blade slid through a gap in the Neb's Kevlar vest. She felt it go into him, shredding arteries, scraping bone, slicing organs. He yelled out in pain. She yanked the sword out of his body, and blood spat from the wound. The man fell, writhing in agony on the road.

"Hey, Slanty Eyes," said the Neb with the clipboard.

"Racist bastard," said Mei. "I cut your tongue out."

"I'll blow his head off first."

The Neb held his gun to Ediz's head.

The Neb said, "Down on the floor, you tart. Hands behind your back. Or the Paki gets it."

"I'm Turkish," said Ediz.

"All the fucking same," said the Neb. "All fucking foreigners pissing on this country. Put the fucking weapon down, sweet and sour, and get down on the floor."

Ediz said, "Don't do it, Mei. Run. Let them kill me."

"I will fucking kill him, I promise you," said the Neb. "Come on, China doll. Give it up. It's judgment day."

CHAPTER 55. DANGER ON EVERY CORNER.

DAVID waited in line at the burger van. It was parked on a side street in Soho. About half a dozen others were with him, waiting for food.

The burger seller was fat, and grease stained his Metallica T-shirt. The cooking area didn't look hygenic, but people weren't concerned about environmental health. They were concerned about where the next meal was coming from. And since a lot of supermarkets had closed down, the burger vans were the only source of food for many people.

The smell of beef and fried onions made David salivate. His stomach rumbled. He'd not eaten since the previous afternoon. And it was now nearly 3.00am. A very dangerous time. The vampires were out. But people had nowhere to go. The shelters were full. You had to take your chances if you wanted to eat. If you wanted your kids to eat.

There was a portable TV sitting on a shelf in the burger van, and it showed footage from Manchester. People were being herded on to buses and trucks. They were being shot in the street. Fires raged across the city. It looked like the end of the world. *Maybe it* is *the end of the world*, thought David.

A man in a scruffy suit said, "He lied to us, that bastard Fuad – he lied to us."

The woman standing next to him had seen better days. Her hair was a mess and her make-up smeared. Her business suit was tattered and torn.

She said, "Maybe it'll be OK. Maybe he's just getting rid of criminals."

"They look like criminals to you?" asked the man, pointing at the TV screen. "Kids and old people? They look like criminals to you?"

The woman bowed her head and cried. "Don't shout at me. You're always shouting at me. It's not my fault."

Two children and two grown-ups – a man and a woman – were in the queue for burgers. David guessed they might be a family – dad, mum, two sons. It made him pine for his own family – dad, mum, two sons.

The kids leaned into their parents. They were trembling, and tears made their eyes red. They had suitcases, their lives packed into them. But they had nowhere to go.

David glanced up and down the dark street. It was quiet here. Only a few loners tucked away in doorways. Two or three groups like the one he was part of, staring into windows or huddled from the rain, queuing up for food.

The numbers of homeless had rocketed in the past few months. Human-on-human violence had also increased. *That's what happens when everyone is fighting over food and shelter*, David thought. Society was breaking down.

David could fight off vampires. He wasn't worried about them. He was protected. So to him, humans were more dangerous. Nebuchadnezzars, who roamed the streets with guns, or desperate people looking for something to eat or somewhere to hide.

Screaming and shouting came from Leicester Square, less than half a mile from where they were standing. A helicopter hovered overhead.

"Right," said the burger seller, "I'm packing up." He slapped a burger into the hand of the father waiting with his wife and kids, and then pulled the shutters down.

"No, you bastard, I'm fucking starving," said the man in the suit.

"The vampires are coming," David said. "You want to get to safety."

"We're hungry," said the woman in the suit.

"You should find somewhere safe," said David.

The man in the suit said, "And where's safe, eh?"

The woman said, "The kid's right, we should try to – "

"Tell me, son," said the man, "where's safe?"

"I don't know where's safe, mate," David said. "I'm just saying."

Now the dad stepped forward, looking mean and desperate. "You got food in that rucksack, lad?" he said. He had given the burger to his children, who had scoffed it immediately, and now they fought over the crumbs.

"No, I got nothing."

He had some stale bread and beef jerky, but he wasn't sharing. He started backing away. You had to look after yourself. Especially if you were on a mission like he was. If he saw someone starving or being attacked, he'd help. He always did. But Jake had told him, "Make sure you're OK first, then look after everyone else. It's like what they tell you on aeroplanes – put your own oxygen mask on first before helping the person next to you with theirs. You're useless dead."

The businesswoman tried to pull the man away. But he hit her, making her lip bleed.

She gasped in shock. "You hit me – you fucking hit me."

"He's got food," said the man. "This kid's got food."

"I got kids," said the father. "You can't let my kids starve."

"Give us the food," said the mum.

"I'm hungry," said one of the kids.

David panicked.

He remembered what Jake had said:

Keep your head, control your fear, and fix on a plan.

His plan was to escape.

He wheeled, ready to sprint down the road.

The businessman lunged at him and grabbed his sleeve. David punched the businessman in the face. The bloke staggered away. David started to run down the road.

And three vampires ran towards him. He stopped dead.

The creatures leapt over parked cars, and bounded off the sides of buildings.

The children screamed.

The mother said, "Oh my God, Alan."

The dad, Alan, said, "Christ almighty, give them the boy."

The businessman shoved David towards the vampires and ran the other way. But the vampires swung away from David, spotting the red ring he wore. They glanced at him and hissed, knowing they could not touch him. But to them it didn't matter. They had their sights on a food supply.

Those people were going to die. The kids. Their parents. The businessman and his wife.

They were screaming and running.

David shouted, "You bastards, treating me like that – you deserve what you get."

He cursed himself. For being weak. For being a child. For being a coward.

He took two stakes out of his rucksack. He chased the vampires.

CHAPTER 56. THE SCHOOL PHOTOGRAPH.

"SORRY about what we did," said the woman in the torn business suit. She was called Clare. Her lip was swollen. Her husband, Jeff, sat slumped in the alley. "We... we didn't know you were... you were a vampire killer."

"That's all right," said David.

There were only the three of them. The family had fled. The vampires were ashes. Nearby, the screams and shouts continued. But to David it seemed that he was in a tranquil place where nothing could get at him.

"You were very brave," said Clare. "A boy, but very brave."

She was staring right at him, her eyes glazed over. She glanced at her husband. He was out of it, trembling and whining in the alley. Then Clare lunged forward and kissed David on the cheek.

He froze. He felt weird. He looked at her. Her blonde hair was matted with grease and blood. Her face was dirty. But her eyes glittered.

"Can I have some food?" she asked. "I'm starving. I'll... I'll... oh, my God... do anything... "

He reached into his rucksack and gave her a piece of bread and some jerky. Glancing at her husband, the woman wolfed it down. Crumbs peppered her jacket and skirt. Spit oozed from her mouth. She ate like an animal. But David knew how she felt. Starvation did that to you. Made you go primal. He gave her his canteen and she started to drink, but then hesitated.

"Is it… is it clean?" she said. "Not vampire water? Not contaminated?"

He shook his head. She stared.

"You first," she said.

He took the canteen back and gulped down a mouthful, before handing it back to the woman.

She drank, just a couple of swigs. Then gave him back the canteen.

She said, "Thank you, thank you for not making me do something absolutely awful for a little bit of food. You're kind. I'm sick. I'm disgusting."

"It's OK."

"I – had a son your age. Fifteen?"

"Nearly fourteen."

"He – he – " her face creased up with emotion. "He was… yes… he was fifteen. His sister, she was – was twelve. They – they were taken, oh God, taken by vampires. Two months ago. Oh God, do you think they're dead?"

"No, they're undead," said David.

Clare looked at him.

"Do you have a mum, a dad?"

"Dad's dead. My brother too."

"Were they… "

He nodded.

"Your mum?"

David fought back the tears.

"You don't have to – "

"It's OK. She – she's with the government, I think."

"What?"

"I think they're holding her hostage."

"Your mum? Why?"

He told her who his mother was.

"Oh God, so you know Jake Lawton?"

He nodded.

The woman's face darkened.

"He caused this," she said.

"No he didn't."

"He caused it, that's what they say."

"That's a lie."

"Your his friend and you gave me food, you little shit."

"I'm not a shit," said David.

"You've probably poisoned that water."

"I drank it, you saw."

"Jake Lawton caused this," she said, getting to her feet. "He killed my kids."

Her eyes burned with hate. Her face was twisted into a mask of rage.

"If he hadn't killed all those vampires, they'd've left us alone," said Clare. "We'd be living peacefully with them."

"You're joking," said David, standing up, getting worried, retreating down the alley.

"You are one of them. Your mother is Christine Murray. Lawton's ally. Lawton's friend. They're probably doing it, too. You're a rebel, a traitor."

"Traitor?" said David.

Shit, he thought. *Trapped*.

He'd stupidly backed down the alley. Stupidly lost concentration. Stupidly let her cut off his escape route.

He wasn't sure about the rights and wrongs of attacking a woman. Jake had said, "If you're life is in danger, your responsibility is to protect it."

"That's right – traitor," said Clare, her face malevolent. Her eyes glittered in the darkness. Her hands curled into claws. David's rucksack was on the floor behind her. He had no weapons, just his fists. He was being forced back down the alley, towards where Clare's husband was sitting.

"Jeff," she shrieked. "Jeff, wake up, you bastard."

David heard shuffling behind him. He looked over his shoulder. Jeff was coming to. He got to his feet.

"What's – what's going on? Clare? What are you – "

"He's one of them," she said, pointing at David. "He's one of them traitors."

David was trapped between Clare and Jeff. He panted, his heart beating fast. Sweat soaking his clothes.

"His mum's that Murray woman, and he's friends with Jake Lawton. He's Jake Lawton's little buddy."

"That soldier bloke?" said Jeff.

"That's right, the one who caused all this," said Clare.

"He didn't cause it," said David. "George Fuad lied to you. You saw it on the TV. Everyone's being carried off to camps. The vampires are taking over."

"He's right, Clare," said Jeff.

"You can't believe the telly," she said. "Might be a plot by him, this kid, and that Lawton."

"You what?" said David. "I saved you from those vampires."

"He did save us, Clare."

"And I gave you food," said David.

"He gave you food?" said Jeff.

"He wanted sex off me," she said.

"You what?" said Jeff.

"He wanted to make me a pervert, make me fuck a little boy."

David gawped. Clare looked out of her mind. Jeff was angry.

"I didn't," said David. "She's lying. I gave it to her."

"Oh, you *gave* it to her, did you," said Jeff, striding up the alley towards David. "You *gave* it to my wife."

"No, the food, I gave her food."

Jeff ran full pelt towards David.

If your life is in danger, your responsibility is to protect it.

David charged at Clare.

She screamed in anger.

He barged her out of the way, ran over her.

He raced out into the street, scooped up his rucksack.

Clare and Jeff came shrieking after him.

She was shouting, "He's one of them, he's a traitor, he's a traitor."

David ran. Just anywhere. He cursed himself. Jake had always said, "Focus, focus."

He was knackered. Sweating and panting.

He raced along an alley and found himself in Chinatown. The road was closed at both ends. And blocking off his routes, east and west, were Nebuchadnezzar patrols. The restaurants were boarded up. Everything was dead. He thought about turning back, going down the alley again. But Clare and Jeff were still chasing him.

They came up the alley screaming, "Traitor, traitor."

The Nebs hadn't seen him, yet, hadn't heard Jeff and Clare.

But the couple were getting closer and getting louder, screaming at David, thundering along the alley.

He looked both ways, and both ways Nebs waited.

And out of the alley came Jeff and Clare.

David bolted right.

The couple raced after him, yelling.

The Neb militia up ahead noticed.

Four of them leapt to attention and aimed their guns towards David, Jeff, and Clare.

"Stay where you are," one of them called.

David slowed. Clare bumped into him. They fell. She pinned him down. He tried to push off her him, but she clawed at him and slapped him.

"He's one of them," she said. "He caused it – him and Jake Lawton. He's that bastard Lawton's friend."

The Nebuchadnezzars rushed over. They shoved Clare away. They grabbed David. He struggled, but they were strong. They tore the rucksack off his back and emptied its contents.

"He's got a mark," said one of them, grabbing his hand and seeing the ring. "You a Neb?"

"Yes, I'm a Neb," said David.

Another Nebuchadnezzar thug tipped out the rucksack. Stakes clattered to the ground.

"Not what you'd expect to find in a Neb's possession, son," said the most senior militia men.

"It's their rucksack," said David, gesturing at Jeff and Clare. She was going mental, screeching and spitting. Jeff tried to pull her away.

"Fuck off, kid," said the senior Neb. "You're a fucking rebel cunt. I know your ugly little mug. Gemmell, get me that file from the truck."

After a few moments, the Neb who'd been ordered to retrieve the file came back with it. A plastic folder fat with pages. The senior militia man creased his brow and flipped through it. Then he stopped at a page and smiled. David knew he was in trouble. The militia officer held up the file. The page showed a photograph of David. It was a school photo. He wore his uniform. In the photo, he was grinning. He looked young and innocent, and untainted by the world of vampires. Seeing it punched a hole in his heart.

"Ah, cute fella," said the senior Neb. "David fucking Murray."

The Neb slapped him across the face. The blow stung. David tasted blood in his mouth.

"It's the Murray kid," said the Neb.

"Traitor," screamed Clare.

"Chuck him in the back of the van," the Neb said. "You're under arrest, sunshine. Don't say anything, or I'll cut out your tongue.

Mr Fuad wants to see you personally. He's going to be your trial judge himself. And your jury. And your fucking executioner, kid."

They dragged him towards the truck. David fought as hard as he could, but strong hands gripped him.

He heard Clare say, "Is there a reward?"

The senior Neb said, "Reward? No. No reward. Only judgment, you stupid tart. Toss her and that bloke in the trucks. Put him in the food truck, and her in the farm truck. She'll be good for breeding."

Clare and Jeff screamed as they were separated and dragged away.

CHAPTER 57. DARK DAYS.

MURRAY gazed down from her room in Religion.

The streets were filled with carnage.

Cars were strewn everywhere. Vampires attacked humans. Nebs herded people into trucks and coaches. A lot of people had locked themselves away. But those with no homes – and there were many – were in the line of fire. People had thought they were relatively safe at night. But vampire attacks had increased immediately after Fuad's victory. The nights would be very dangerous from now on.

What's worse? she wondered. *To be killed by vampires now, or to be herded into those trucks and buses and taken to breeding facilities or food centres?*

Some of those innocent people would be crammed into prisons, where they'd have to share cells with rapists and murderers. Others would be dumped into the human breeding programme that would ensure humans were never an endangered species, that vampires had enough food stocks.

Those not fit to breed would be food themselves. They would go directly to warehouses or prisons where they would be stored, ready for feeding time.

It made Murray sick. She had to sit down or she was going to pass out if she had to think anymore about the state of Britain.

But her mind had been infected by Fuad's vision. His plans were imprinted on her brain. There was no getting away from the atrocities he was committing and would continue to commit. No human was safe unless he or she was a Nebuchadnezzar or had declared support for them. And even then, who knew what Fuad would do? He could turn on his friends as easily as he'd turned on his enemies. Like all dictators, he displayed evidence of paranoia. He had told Murray of terrible things, of the savagery he would inflict on Britain.

"But it's all for the best," he'd said. "Britain will suffer before it gets better."

He'd spoken of gladiatorial games, where the public would gather to watch vampires unleashed on humans.

He spoke of spreading his empire far and wide and told her how he'd conquer nations with his vampire army.

He spoke of bringing Nimrod from Iraq and how he would stand shoulder to shoulder with a god.

He was mad. But who would stop him? Lawton had been captured in Baghdad, according to Fuad. Her son was lost in London, but what could a boy his age do?

It was all over.

The days ahead were dark.

Every enemy of the state would face judgment.

She turned on the TV, but more of the same played out on the screen. Images from Manchester were showing. It had been the first city after London that Fuad targeted. He wanted to target Manchester because that's where February's rebellion had started, where Kwan Mei had raised her army, and where her march on the capital had begun.

But where was she, now? Captured? Dead? Hiding?

There was no one left – that was the terrible truth.

Murray felt alone.

She started to think about dying. Should she kill herself or allow a vampire to kill her? Or perhaps she should see out her life as a slave to Fuad. Maybe he'd let her live. Maybe that way, she'd see David again. Thinking of her son ignited hope in her heart.

She would fight, she decided in that moment.

And she would die doing it.

She looked at the clock on the TV news channel. Nearly 5.00am, another day soon to dawn.

She was so tired. She wanted to sleep. But the noise from the street had kept her awake, and now and again Fuad's milita men would stomp along the corridor, laughing loudly as they boasted about some cruelty inflicted on unfortunate victims.

In a while, one of Fuad's lackeys would bring her a cup of tea. It was a ruse to keep her awake, she thought. Deprive her of sleep. Be noisy during the night, and then rouse her at an ungodly hour. They liked keeping her on her toes.

Right on time, there was a knock on the door. Before she could say, "Come in," the door was unlocked and opened.

A man in a waiter's uniform came in. He was in his fifties. Green eyes. Tattoos on his big, thick hands. Rings on every sausage-fat finger. A handgun in a holster on his hip.

"Morning," he said. "Tea's up. Compliments of our new Prime Minister. Start the day as you mean to go on, and all that."

He placed a tray containing a cup and saucer, a teapot, milk jug, sugar bowl, and teaspoon, on the coffee table.

"Back in fifteen," he said before leaving and locking the door behind him.

She took the tray into the bathroom and emptied the teapot down the sink.

Back in the living room, she waited for a few minutes. She checked the time. Seven minutes before he would return. Three minutes. Two minutes. One. A knock on the door, the key turning.

She lay on the sofa, jug in her hand.

The waiter entered.

She heard him start locking the door.

She opened her eyes.

He had his back to her.

She sprang from the sofa.

He turned.

She smashed him across the temple with the teapot.

The porcelain shattered.

Blood sprayed.

The waiter teetered.

She cracked him another blow across the skull. The jagged edges cut him.

She hit him a third time. He keeled over, groaning. Blood pulsed from wounds in his scalp.

He fell forward on all fours. Murray saw red. She smashed him across the back of the head, once, twice, three times, until he hit the floor face first, blood everywhere.

Murray reeled away, crying, covered in the waiter's blood. He wasn't moving. She'd killed him. She felt scared, appalled by what she'd done.

But I had to, she thought. *I had to survive. I have to survive.*

Murray went to the waiter's body and rolled it over, retrieving his keys.

They were soaked in blood.

Then she looked at the gun.

CHAPTER 58.
ESCAPE.

CORLEY SERVICE AREA, M6 – 5.21AM (GMT), 20 MAY, 2011

"LEAVE her alone," said Ediz as a Neb tossed Mei roughly into the back of a police van.

"Shut your gob, Arab."

"I told you, brain-dead, I'm a Turk," said Ediz.

"Well fucking shut up then, doner meat. Get in the fucking back of the van, and no fucking monkey business."

"You fucking racist," said Ediz.

He got in and sat next to Mei on the bench. He put an arm around her, and she nodded to say she was OK.

The Neb laughed. "Racism's the least of your worries, son." He turned back to other Neb militia. They wore black. They sported black Kevlar vests. They carried automatic weapons. Pistols and knives were strapped to their utility belts.

They had travelled down from Manchester in the back of a cattle truck. Crammed in with dozens of other people, the journey had been terrible. They'd been tossed around. People were crying and screaming. Mums and dads were desperate to comfort their children, but how could they? People were asking, "Where are they taking us?" and "What's going on?"

Mei knew where they were going and what was going on, but she didn't have the heart to tell them.

After about two hours, Mei guessed, the truck pulled off the motorway. They came to a stop, and the rear doors were opened. They were in the car park of a motorway service area. It was quiet, no cars, no travellers taking a pit stop on the M6.

Milita men warned everyone to stay put in the truck, but some tried to make a run for it. They were either shot or shoved back inside.

A militia man had stepped forward and said, "Kwan Mei, who's Kwan Mei?"

"I'm Kwan Mei," said Ediz, standing up.

"Sit down, Spartacus, before I cut your balls off."

Ediz stayed standing.

The Nebuchadnezzar militia man glared at him.

Mei pulled Ediz down.

"Don't get killed," she said.

"I don't care."

"I care. I need you with me."

"Get out," the Neb had said. "Come on, China girl."

Mei hadn't moved. And that's when two black-shirts bounded into the truck and grabbed her, dragging her out.

Ediz lunged at them.

"Right," said the milita officer, "if he's so in love with her, he can come too."

Mei went quietly. Ediz had ranted and railed against the black-shirts.

But the Nebs finally shoved them in the back of the police van.

The officer shut the door.

"They're taking us to London?" said Ediz

“If one of us get chance, we got to escape,” she said.

“You thinking of trying to get out of here?”

“I try to get out of every trouble, Ed.”

Mei leaned her head against the side of the van to listen. It was quiet. Maybe the Nebs were dealing with the other prisoners.

She said to Ediz, “Don’t stop for nothing, OK. I don’t stop, you don’t stop. Just keep running. We got to get our brothers and sisters together again. Got to march on the city like before. OK?”

Ediz nodded.

The back door opened.

Ediz kicked it.

The milita men reeled.

Mei had no idea how many of them were outside, but she and Ediz had to take a chance.

They leapt out of the van and started running.

“Run, Ed, run fast,” she said as the Neb black-shirts realized what had happened and started chasing them.

“Stop or we’ll shoot,” came the warning. “Stop or we’ll shoot. Stop – ”

Ediz ran ahead of her across the car park. She sprinted after him.

“Stop, I said,” came the warning, and then: “Shoot to kill!”

Mei flung herself down when the gunfire started.

CHAPTER 59.
POSITION OF POWER.

SOHO – 6AM (GMT), 20 MAY, 2011

GEORGE Fuad put the phone down. Some good news, some bad. *You can't have it all*, he thought. But it was going to be his first full day of power, and that was reason to celebrate. He'd not slept much. Far too excited. And he liked to be around at night, when the vampires hunted. He enjoyed seeing them kill and feed.

One of his officials was waiting to talk to him, and the bloke had that rabbit-caught-in-the-headlights look. He was shifting from foot to foot. Sweat trickled from his ginger hair down his brow.

"Go ahead," said George.

"Yes, sir," said the ginger. "In parts of London, Kent, South Wales, Scotland, and Leeds, we have incidents of the Armed Forces fighting back – "

"Fighting back?" said George. "Tell me again, with details."

The official reported. More bad news.

"And what are our forces doing?" he asked now.

"They've been able to quell the incidents, Prime Minister. But it is taking a lot of manpower. Although the Armed Forces are not well armed anymore, they are, of course, still trained military personnel and are providing us with a few casualties."

"Said like a civil servant," said George. "Are we using vampires?"

"Yes, sir, the vampires are being deployed."

"That's good."

He sat back in his chair. He concentrated for a moment, thinking about things. It was quiet now. The calm before the storm. Builders were coming in later to start the refurbishment. They were building him a castle in Soho, on the site of the old Religion nightclub. A castle for a king. A seat of government. It would protect him from any enemy. It would be guarded by Neb militia in daylight and vampires in darkness.

He tipped his chair back, eyes scanning the room.

Portraits hung on the walls. They were mostly of his family – father, mother, even his brother. But taking pride of place was a black-and-white photo of his grandfather, who had first told George about his bloodline. Grandfather Fuad stood alongside a short young man with black hair and a moustache: Afdal Haddad, the man who'd brought the Nebuchadnezzars together in recent years, the man whom George had tipped out of a window in Westminster.

Afdal had no vision. He couldn't see beyond Britain. He rejected the idea of resurrecting Nimrod. Said it was too dangerous. Said it was impossible.

But to George, nothing was impossible. If things were impossible, he would not be in power.

"I want the insurgents caught alive, if possible," he said. "I want them brought to London, where they'll be put on trial for treason. Every fucking one of them."

"Yes, sir," said the official.

"Bring our guest in and fuck off."

The official scuttled out of the room.

George thought about Alfred and wondered if his brother was any closer to digging up Nimrod. He felt a shudder go through him. A moment of doubt shaking his confidence. *It'll be all right*, he told himself. *Everything will be all right. What can go wrong, now?*

Elizabeth Wilson entered with two Nebuchadnezzar guards.

"So what do you think of my first few days in power?" George asked.

"I think if this were still a democracy, you'd be trounced at the next election," she said.

He laughed. "Lucky it isn't, then. You look like shit, if you don't mind me saying. When was the last time you had your hair done, Liz? And you never wear make-up these days. You should. You used to be a relatively tasty old bird; now you're just a weather-beaten old slapper."

She said nothing.

"Anyway, too late for all that," he said. "After tonight, no more hair-dos, no more make-up. Judgment day for you, Lizzie. The day you pay for your treason."

She trembled, and George thought she might fall over.

"You're destroying this country," she said.

"I'm rebuilding it."

"The nation dies and you… you fiddle."

He laughed. "Oh, fuck off."

"You're killing people."

"I'm culling them, Liz. The population is being put to good use. No more fucking welfare. No more free rides. Everyone does their bit. You are either breeder or food or worker. It's easy. This is a perfect political system. It's a model that'll spread worldwide, I'm telling you."

She said nothing, just stared in horror at George.

"Britain will be a trading culture," he said. "People will have to produce to survive. If they can't, they die – or they think of another way to serve the ruling class. Democracy has failed. It's produced a dependency culture. We are returning to the days of absolute monarchy, of feudalism. I'm king. The rest of my Nebuchadnezzars are the ruling classes. The wealth stays with us. It's for the best, because we know how to use it. We'll make decisions. We'll run the show. Britain will be fucking great again. It'll be built on the bones of the underclass."

"And on vampires."

"Yeah, what an army, eh. Nothing'll stop 'em. And when we have Nimrod, we'll have a god to go with our army. Religion and military might combined – now that's unbeatable."

"This won't last, Fuad."

"It will. For-fucking-ever."

"The people will turn against you."

"The fucking people can't turn in their graves."

"Maybe the vampires, then. Why would they need a human leader?"

Something stirred in his belly.

He stood up and went to the door.

"Take her back to her room," he said. "Give her a decent last meal and all that. Execution day today, need to plump her up a bit."

He grinned at her and then opened the door, but when he turned to leave the room he found himself staring down the barrel of a gun.

CHAPTER 60. THE "SOME GOOD NEWS, SOME BAD".

"CHRISTINE," said George when he saw who was holding the gun. "I think you're outnumbered, darling."

Her eyes stayed on him. Big, bright eyes full of fear, glinting with desperation.

The kind of desperation that makes someone pull a trigger.

He had to play it cool.

Out of the corner of his eye, he saw that the two Neb guards had their weapons trained on Murray. Liz Wilson had been shoved into a corner, where she was cowering.

"All I got to do," he said, "is give them the word, and you're smeared all over that corridor."

"You'll be smeared with me, Fuad," said Christine Murray.

How the fuck has she got out? he thought. Whoever fucked up would face judgment tonight with her, Wilson, and the rest of them.

Murray stood in the door. She was shaking. Sweat beaded on her brow. Her hair was matted. She was there for the taking. But she had a gun. And it was pointed directly at George's face.

His bowels were icy with dread. But he tried not to show that he was scared.

"So what'll it be, Christine?" he said.

"I can kill you right now," she said.

She meant it. Or sounded like she did.

He wondered what the two bodyguards were doing behind him. If they had a clear shot, Murray should have been dead. Perhaps if he shuffled to the right or to the left, they'd be able to nail her. But if he did, she might just shoot him.

His fear diminished. Having a gun pointed at your face made you jittery. But when you pulled yourself together and realized you had the upper hand after all, the fright faded.

George played his trump card.

"Do you want to see your son again?"

Some good news, some bad, he thought. The phone call he'd received before he'd spoken to his rabbit-caught-in-the-headlights advisor was a message from the frontline, where the Neb militia were bravely butchering and kidnapping the waste-of-space chavs and the fat-cat bankers.

"We've got that kid, David Murray," the Nebuchadnezzar officer had told him.

Very good news.

Added to the very good news of Lawton's incarceration in Iraq. Added to the very good news of Kwan Mei's arrest in Manchester. The bad news was the escape of Mei's fellow prisoner. He'd legged it while they were being transferred from vehicle to vehicle. George wasn't going to worry too much about it. The kid would go into hiding. No one would probably see him again. It was a glitch, that was all.

Everything was coming together.

Hearing about her son made Murray flinch. A little twitch. A sign of weakness. A bolthole into her brain. And once he was inside her head, George could wreak havoc.

He'd always been good at that. Finding a flaw in people. And once he'd done it, he was like cancer, eating away at their confidence, their hopes.

He'd done it with his own brother.

Alfred's weakness was that he loved George so much. And that love had the potential to make him weak. But George enjoyed the adulation, so he allowed it. He let the weak spot grow.

"Well, do you?" said George now. "Do you want to see your kid? If you kill me, you never will."

"You don't know where David is," she said, panic in her voice.

"Why shouldn't I know where he is?"

"You don't know."

"Christine, my darling, I know everything. I am the man. The man in the know. The man in charge. I know."

The doubts made her brittle.

"You know," he said, "that we picked up your little Chinky friend in Manchester? She's on her way down here."

"You're lying," she said. Her hands shook, the gun getting heavy. Her heart like lead, he imagined. Thinking about her son. Missing him. Broken up about not seeing him. George knew a mother's love could be strong, but it could also make a woman vulnerable.

He showed his hand and played his cards: "I have your son, Christine."

She made a funny noise, like an animal in distress.

"You can see him soon, if you like," he said. "Or not. Up to you. I'm sure he's missing his mum, ain't he. Young fellow. Not seen you in an age. Crying his heart out, no doubt."

She had no cards left.

She burst out in tears.

Her gun hand sagged.

George lunged forward, followed by the two bodyguards.

He slapped Murray in the face and snatched the gun out of her hand.

The guards went for her, but he stopped them.

He watched her roll up into a ball on the corridor floor. She was shaking and crying and looking up at him.

"You bastard," she was saying, "you fucking, monstrous bastard."

"Thanks," he said. His phone rang. "Oh, Avon calling." He answered it and listened and said, "See you in a second." He put the phone back in his pocket. "What's that Paul Simon song? 'Mother And Child Reunion', that's it."

The door at the far end of the corridor flew open. Two Nebuchadnezzar militia men shoved a young boy into the passageway. He was dirty, his hair matted. His clothes torn. His shoes too big.

Murray screamed her son's name and was up on her feet in a flash.

The boy yelled for his mum and stumbled down the corridor towards her.

They fell into each other's arms and cried and howled, while George laughed at them and thought how nice it was of him to let a mum and her kid face his wrath together.

PART SEVEN.

RESURRECTION.

CHAPTER 61.
SPILLING THE BEANS.

AL-ASKANDARIYAH, IRAQ – 5PM (GMT + 3HOURS), 20 MAY, 2011

HER eyes burned red, her fangs brushed Laxman's throat, and he said, "OK, OK, I'll fucking tell you, just get this fucking witch off me."

After the street fight with Laxman, and in the chaos that ensued, Lawton had handcuffed the mercenary and tossed him in the Toyota's boot.

Ereshkigal, protected against the sun by the burkha, had terrified the crowd by killing Ashton.

The panic had given Lawton the chance to get the Land Cruiser started. Ereshkigal, encased head to toe in the black garment, leapt in next to him. She had said nothing. They had looked at each other for a second. Although her eyes were hidden behind the face-veil, Lawton felt her gaze on him.

Then, he'd sped off.

With the authorities at sixes and sevens, they'd fled the city and driven through Al-Mahmudiyah, the southern district known as "The Gateway to Baghdad". That morning it was the gateway out of Baghdad.

Lawton's plan was to hit Highway 8, south, and head for Hillah. But they would be hunted. And in daylight, so soon after the incident in Baghdad, they would be sitting ducks.

He left the main highway and made his way along dirt tracks. He even doubled back a few times. He was trying to out-think the authorities, trying to stay one, or even two, steps ahead of them.

At Al-Askandariyah, an ancient city named after Alexander the Great, they stopped. They had only driven twenty-five miles out of Baghdad but had spent most of the day doing it.

They needed a break, and he needed the truth.

Laxman had been in the boot for a while. They had made sure he had water, passing it through a compartment in the back seat. While they did so, Laxman swore at them and threatened them, before finally trying to bribe them with treasure "from this dig I'm protecting".

Lawton, wearing Ashton's jacket over his bloody kurta, had gone looking for food and fuel. He was confident he'd given the authorities the runaround. He knew how to make himself invisible.

When he got back to the Toyota, it was dark, and Ereshkigal took off her burkha. She was still in her white dress. Her hair looked blacker than ever, her skin paler. But her red eyes burned. Lawton was transfixed for a moment. But then he said, "I need you to scare the shit out of our friend in the boot."

She had nodded.

"I'll fucking tell you, I'll fucking tell you," said Laxman. "Just get this thing off me."

Lawton sat in the driver's seat, smoking a roll-up. Ereshkigal was terrorizing Laxman in the back seat.

Jake looked around. They were parked in an alleyway. It was quiet and dark.

"Go ahead, Laxman," he said.

Laxman started. He'd been hired by Howard Vince, former Chief of the General Staff and now head of Armed Forces for the Nebuchadnezzars, apparently. "He's just gone back to the UK," said Laxman. "Or I'd hand him my resignation. He said nothing about fucking witches."

Ereshkigal hissed at him, and he flinched.

He went on:

"White Light Ops was employed to handle security at an archaeological dig in Hillah. Run by this guy called Fuad. Arab name, but he's English through and through. Typical Bulldog Brit."

Lawton nodded. Alfred Fuad was in Iraq. He'd guessed that much.

"Fuck knows what they're digging for," Laxman said. "He's been vague. But there are rumours. Artefacts connected to some god, some Nimrod, a mummy."

Ereshkigal made a yearning noise.

Laxman cringed. "What the fuck?"

Ereshkigal lunged at the mercenary. "I will kill him."

"No, wait," said Lawton. "We need him."

"Yeah, you fucking need me," said Laxman.

"For what?" Ereshkigal said.

"To get to where you want to go," Lawton told her.

Ereshkigal sat back down.

Lawton relaxed a little. His head hurt badly, the false eye now burning in his skull. The material encased in the glass had seeped out and merged itself with his nerves. He could do nothing about it. At least not now. Later perhaps. When all this was done. When he'd achieved his objectives. After everyone was safe, he'd finish this. He'd sort this pain. He'd never let anything alien or undead take over his body. If he was being re-born as something that wasn't fully Jake Lawton, he'd abort it.

He touched his side, where Khoury had shot him.

The wound was healing. It throbbed but didn't hurt. He should be dead or sick. But he felt more alive than ever. Was the vampire DNA he despised so much keeping him alive?

He thought about Khoury. He hoped the young police officer was OK. He'd seen him flee while Ereshkigal killed Laxman's men.

He looked at her. She had crossed the country to come to him. Forced a young man to drive her to Baghdad and then killed him. She was cruel, and it appalled Lawton. But she was devoted, too. She had brought him the spear. Kept it safe and returned it. He just wasn't sure about her motives, but for now she was a very useful ally.

He glanced at Laxman and said, "You're going to take us to the dig."

"You what?"

"Wasn't that the plan?"

"The plan was, Lawton, you fuck, to make sure you didn't leave Baghdad alive."

"You screwed up. I *am* leaving Baghdad alive, and I'm leaving with you as my hostage."

Laxman shrugged. "Gladly, pal. My men are there."

"We'll introduce them to Ereshkigal. She'll like that."

Lawton started the Toyota and drove south.

CHAPTER 62.
HIGHWAY 8.

"FUAD told me they were looking for buried artefacts, Babylonian gold," Laxman said.

They were back on Highway 8. Lawton wanted to make it to Hillah before dawn. Before Ereshkigal had to go into hiding.

It was about 8.15pm. The road was busy, traffic filtering in and out of Baghdad. He kept glancing in the rear-view mirror for army or police vehicles. But Lawton's tactics of doubling back, taking a longer route, and generally doing the opposite of what someone running away would do, had given the authorities the slip.

He wasn't resting on his laurels, though. He knew the search for him would intensify. He had to be on alert.

Taking the decision he did to delay his progress to Hillah in order to avoid the authorities had already put Aaliyah at further risk. It was likely that she was in the area already. But if he had raced down to Hillah, using Highway 8 all the way in broad daylight, he would have been caught. And what use would he be to her then?

"So what *is* he digging up over there?" said Laxman.

"Hell," said Lawton.

Ereshkigal growled.

Her started to think what would happen when they got to Hillah. He and Ereshkigal had some kind of pact. But would that last? He wasn't stupid enough to think it would. The knots that bound their allegiance were already fraying.

Their objectives were at odds with each other. He wanted to kill Nimrod. She wanted to be reunited with him. A clash was inevitable.

Lawton kept an eye on Laxman. The mercenary stared out of the window at passing traffic. His brow was furrowed. He was thinking. Thinking about how Fuad and Vince had misled him, hopefully.

Lawton decided to stir.

"He's lied to you."

"And cost me good men."

"Fuad wants to release Nimrod on the world."

"That's his call."

"You've been keeping well away from the vampire plague, Laxman."

"I sure have, mate." He glanced at Ereshkigal. "Bit too close to one, now, I can tell you."

"When Nimrod comes, there'll be nowhere to hide. If Fuad and his brother have their way, the world will be infected."

"Then I'll have to fight."

"You think you can fight them? This woman overpowered you. Imagine what an army of them would do."

Laxman fell silent for a few seconds.

After a while he said, "So if this vampire here – "

"I have a name," said Ereshkigal.

"All right," he said. "If… this one is Nimrod's wife, as she says, how come she's not killing you if you're planning to kill her husband?"

"We have an allegiance," said Ereshkigal.

"She needs me, and I find her quite useful," said Lawton.

"Needs you?"

"To get back to Hillah," said Lawton.

"And what happens when she does get back?" Laxman asked. "One of you will have to kill the other."

I know all that, thought Lawton. *I don't need reminding of it.* But he said nothing.

But Ereshkigal spoke. "Maybe we will kill you instead," she said.

"Vampires," said the mercenary. "Who'd have believed in them ten years ago? And here we are: the bloody world's crawling with them – and I'm sharing a ride with one of the bastard things."

They drove in silence for a few minutes before Lawton said, "Did you notice Fuad and Vince and some of the others wearing red rags, scraps of material?"

"So what?"

"Alfred's got a ponytail, and it's tied with a red rag, isn't it?" said Lawton.

"Your point?"

Lawton stopped the Toyota on the side of the Highway and turned to look at Laxman in the back seat. He showed him his eye.

"See this? Made of the same stuff."

Laxman wrinkled his nose.

"You know what it is?" said Lawton. "This stuff in my eye?"

Laxman shook his head.

Lawton told him what it was.

Laxman curled his lip.

Lawton noticed a pair of aviator sunglasses poking out of Laxman's breast pocket. He leaned over and took them out. He slid them into the breast pocket of his kurta. *Useful to hide the damaged eye*, he thought. He said, "Believe it or not, it keeps vampires at bay – it protects people from them."

Lawton caught Ereshkigal looking at him. She was going to say, *It doesn't protect you from me*. But she stayed quiet. And he silently thanked her for it.

"You haven't got one, Laxman. Fuad didn't worry about keeping you safe, then. You and your men are expendable."

Laxman still looked perplexed.

Lawton started up the Land Cruiser again and accelerated into traffic. He said, "My guess, he was going to let you die if it came to it. Your money'd be no good then, Laxman. Your Swiss bank account."

Lawton allowed Laxman to digest the information.

In the distance, the lights of Hillah flickered. It was home to nearly 400,000 people. A modern conurbation so close to an ancient metropolis.

"Anyone else we need to know about at Fuad's compound?" said Lawton.

Laxman's eyes flashed as if he'd remembered something: "We had a couple of prisoners come in, trespassers."

Lawton's stomach lurched. His eye suddenly ached, and he slowed the vehicle down.

"Who were they?" he asked.

"Some foreign geezer with a walking stick, and some bird. A real fox. Dark skinned. Black hair. Tall. Fucking Amazon. Looked a bit like that Beyoncé bird."

Lawton gripped the steering wheel tight, his knuckles going white.

CHAPTER 63.
THIS IS OUR TOMB.

HILLAH – 5.38PM (GMT + 3 HOURS), 20 MAY, 2011

AALIYAH peered through the keyhole.

"We got to get out of here," she said.

"It is too late for getting out," said Goga.

He was slumped in the corner of the cell, his forehead pressed against the handle of his walking stick.

He looked old and broken.

When Aaliyah and Jake had met him a few months earlier, Apostol Goga had been tall and strong, a man in his fifties capable of looking after himself. He had been a member of the GSPI, the Romanian counter-terrorist and interior protection organization. He had a reputation for being tough and strong, and Aaliyah had guessed at the time that he had a ruthless streak.

But all that had seeped out of him now. Leached away in the last couple of days. All his life he had imagined coming to the ancient city of Babylon and destroying Nimrod. But now that he was here, he looked as if he'd struggle to squish a bug.

Their cell measured about six foot by six foot. A rotting wooden bench was attached to one wall. It was where Goga sat, demoralized.

The walls of the chamber were damp, and moss and weeds grew freely. The cell seemed to have been dug into the wall of the tunnel. It was just a crevice, really. But someone had attached the hefty wooden door across the opening. The lockup smelled old, and Aaliyah was convinced she could whiff the odour of death.

"We've got to get out," she said again.

"We won't. We're dead. I am the last of my line. The last Dracul. The last Vlad. After today, we die, and with me dies the hope of destroying this evil. Only evil is immortal. Not goodness. I know that, now. We are… fucked."

"Stop being so pathetic and melodramatic. Jake's still out there."

"The Iraqis have arrested him. And if he is released, Laxman has been sent to dispose of him."

"You think he can dispose of Jake, do you?"

"I don't know."

"Jake won't leave us here, Goga. He won't abandon us. If he knows we're here, he'll come. He'd never leave anyone behind. Not if he can do something about it. Jake would come back from the dead to rescue his friends. You're not even dead yet and you're giving up."

A drill started rumbling in the distance.

"They are getting closer to the end of the world," said Goga.

"It's not the end till Jake – "

"Jake will not come."

"He will, you watch. This is why I came to this fucking place, why you persuaded me – to kill this monster, end the vampire plague, so me and Jake can be together. So I'm not giving up on that, I'm not."

"You should."

"You brought me here, you bastard."

He shut his eyes tight and groaned.

"Get up and sort yourself out," said Aaliyah.

He leapt to his feet. Colour flooded his cheeks. She thought her words might have done the trick and was surprised at how easy it had been.

But then he said, "Nothing to do, can't you see? Nothing to do. We are trapped here in this box-room of rock. Fuad will let us die here. Starve to death. Buried alive here. This is our tomb. This is our end."

"He won't do something as clean and as simple as that. Fuad will want to put on a show. He said something about us being Nimrod's first sacrifice. Well, that's an opportunity for us to escape."

Goga slumped back on the bench, and it creaked under his weight.

"Aaliyah," he said, "I am injured. I have broken ribs. I have other wounds. How can I fight?"

"The only wound you have is cowardice."

"I am not a coward."

"What would your ancestors say?"

"They are dead."

"They died fighting. They didn't die crying."

"Vlad the Impaler died mad, an arrow through his heart from one of his own men, a vampire queen in his arms. He was poisoned by his hatred for the undead, and he was killed for it. I have been poisoned too, and I'll pay the same price."

A key turned in the door and it swung open. A guard stood in the doorway.

"Out," he said.

"Where are you taking us?" said Aaliyah.

"Fucking spa, where do you think?"

CHAPTER 64. ISLANDS.

THE closer they got to Hillah, the more Lawton's nerves jangled.

His head was still hurting, and his eye pulsed. He was hearing voices, and they were calling to him.

"One of us, one of us," they whispered, barely audible.

He desperately fought with his demons over the last remnants of what was human in him.

It was nearly 9.00pm. Laxman dozed in the back seat, dried blood on his face, his eye swelling.

Ereshkigal sat in the front next to Lawton and stared ahead.

She'd hardly spoken. He didn't mind that. But there were questions bugging him.

"Why did you come back for me?" he said

"I came for the Great Hunter."

"You brought me the spear."

"I am returning it to Nimrod."

"And so am I."

Make him one with himself, thought Lawton. He was starting to think he knew what that meant. He was starting to see how to kill Nimrod.

"This woman that Laxman spoke of," said Ereshkigal, "this, how did he say, 'fox'? Is she your woman?"

"She was."

"You have lost her?"

"She left to come to Hillah with a man who promised her things."

"What did he promise her?"

"He promised her me," he said, and told her.

"My husband's death would give you to this woman?" said Ereshkigal.

"Nimrod's death would mean an end to all vampires – and then Aaliyah and me could be together, safely. That's why she came here."

"She loves you very much."

He said nothing.

"Do you love her?"

His skin goosefleshed.

How would he and Aaliyah cope after this conflict was over?

It was violence and war that had brought them together, and it was violence and war that had kept them together.

Perhaps they could never be a couple under normal circumstances.

No threat, no danger, so maybe no passion.

Nothing but humdrum.

And humdrum scared him.

He hadn't been the best at relationships in the past. He had tried. But he'd never had good role models – his dad had abandoned his mum before he was born, and his mum was a drunk. And sometimes Jake just panicked at the thought of being with someone for a long time. Although part of him craved it. The stability. The security. The sharing.

He and Aaliyah could make it work – he was sure of it.

But whatever happened, he would not let her die.

He would save her.

He would kill everything that threatened her.

He would destroy whatever Fuad dug out of that earth, and he would wipe out the vampire race.

Then Aaliyah could have peace. With him or without him. He was determined that she would have that. She would have that harmony, that tranquillity. It would be his gift to her.

As a child, he'd seen pictures of Scottish islands. The isolation had appealed to him. The silence sounded wonderful.

He must have been eleven or twelve when he'd seen them, and he'd probably forgotten about them as he got older.

Then he'd joined the Army. He'd found a family. He'd found mates. He'd found a purpose.

But they'd taken all that away from him when they'd kicked him out.

Recently, he had been thinking about those islands again recently. He remembered again how he felt as a boy, seeing those photographs. He could see the islands, and he could hear them. The rough landscapes of greens and browns and grey. The wild seas, lashing the rocks. The sheep dotted about. A sheepdog barking. The wind whistling. An old cottage, isolated, in need of care and attention. A home for them in the wilderness. A beautiful desolation they could share.

But for now it was a distant dream

A dream that might not come true.

But it was a goal at least. A gift to give Aaliyah. An island. A haven. A home.

It resurrected a determination in him to get this job done.

Kill this fucking monster; hand Aaliyah its head on a plate.

"Yes," he told Ereshkigal, answering her question. "I do love her."

CHAPTER 65. ENEMIES AND ALLIES.

LAXMAN farted and groaned.

"Lovely," said Lawton.

"The man makes a terrible smell," said Ereshkigal.

"Where are we?" said Laxman.

"Twenty miles to the outskirts of Al Hillah," said Lawton.

"Ah, home," said Laxman.

Home, thought Lawton. He looked at the clock on the Land Cruiser's dashboard. It was around 9.20pm. *Three hours ahead of London*, he thought. Three hours before it would be dark. Three hours before the city would be crawling with vampires. But maybe he could stop them.

"Where's the dig?" he said.

"South of the city," said Laxman. "Runs alongside the Euphrates river."

Lawton glanced at the man in the rear-view mirror.

"How long did you serve, Laxman?"

"Serve? Twenty years. Left in 2001, just before 9/11."

"What regiment?"

"Royal Engineers," he said. "And special services. You?"

"King's."

"The old Manchester regiment," said Laxman.

Lawton's old friend Tom Wilson had been in the Manchesters. Wilson had fought at Hillah in 1920. While seeing action in the region, Wilson had learned about the vampire trinity, about the Spear of Abraham. He'd looted the weapon, along with the remains of Kea, Kakash, and Kasdeja. Kept them in his loft for years to make sure the Nebuchadnezzars never got hold of them. But led by the old chemist, Afdal Haddad, the Nebs had tracked Wilson down. They'd stolen the jars containing the remains of the three vampires, resurrected them, and dragged Lawton, Aaliyah, Christine Murray, Tom Wilson, Fraser Lithgow, and everyone else into this cauldron.

Tom had been murdered by the Nebuchadnezzars. He was over a hundred years old. He'd seen wars and survived them. But he'd been butchered in his flat by thugs.

And they'd sent Lawton his head in a box.

"I'd heard of you," said Laxman. "You had a name."

"Bad one, I guess."

"Yeah, shitty. But I never thought you'd murdered an innocent man in Basra. Guessed you'd have a good reason for doing it. You did the right thing."

"I'm filling up," said Lawton.

"Soldiers always get blamed first."

"Like Fuad will blame you, if things go wrong."

Laxman sighed. He realized Jake was trying to play mind games.

"What are you going to do with this vampire at the end of all this?" said the mercenary. "You're not going to let her live are you?"

Playing some of his own, now, thought Lawton, but he said nothing.

Ereshkigal stared ahead.

"I mean, you can't let her live, can you?" said Laxman.

Ereshkigal was as still as a statue.

Perhaps when the time came, he should leave it to Aaliyah.

He glanced at Ereshkigal. She had once been a beautiful woman, but now only the shell of what she'd been remained. Human emotions had been stripped away. Only an instinct to kill was left.

But she was still beguiling.

Desire simmered in his blood, a poisonous need, and those voices echoing in his head were getting louder.

What's happening to me? he thought, his head throbbing, the pain in his eye getting worse.

He braced himself for whatever was to come and drove towards the tower blocks and sandstone buildings and street lights and traffic of Hillah.

It was a modern Middle Eastern city.

But lurking beneath this modern chaos was an ancient bedlam, a place that could drive men mad.

CHAPTER 66.
THE GATES OF IRKALLA.

THEY were deep underground. Deeper than ever. Deeper than Aaliyah had thought possible. It was stifling. It was hard to breathe. Her chest was tight, and she had to gasp for air. It was like being close to hell – hot and terrifying.

It felt as if the tunnel went on and on endlessly.

Neon torches were attached to the walls and they hummed like bees. They showed the way and gave her a glimpse of the darkness.

As they walked, their footsteps echoed.

Alfred Fuad led the way. Behind him came Aaliyah and then Goga, looking worse for wear. He was hobbling and coughing, and Aaliyah had to help him along. The Romanian had aged so quickly. After the beating, he'd gone downhill. But the damage wasn't just physical. He'd realized that his lifetime's crusade was going to end in failure.

Behind them came three guards, all armed.

All around them, workers troweled in the dirt. They were like ghosts, coated in dust and debris. They watched as Aaliyah and the others passed, their eyes glittering as if they'd not seen other humans in a long, long time.

Maybe they haven't, thought Aaliyah. Maybe Fuad had been using them as slaves, imprisoning them down here for months, forcing them to dig and dig and dig.

Fuad stopped. "This'll do," he said.

Some two hundred yards down the tunnel, a huge drill was tilted on its axle, its bit pointing upwards. It was like a monster at rest. Around it, people smoked and drank from Styrofoam cups. They leaned on the drill, and they sat against the walls of the tunnel. They looked exhausted.

"That's it," said Fuad. "The gates of Irkalla. City of Nimrod. Beyond that opening we've just made is a gatehouse, which then slopes downwards towards the city itself. You'll have the honour of being among the first humans to enter Irkalla for about 5,000 years. How's that sound?"

"Sounds crazy, Fuad," said Aaliyah.

"You and your mad brother will pay for this," said Goga. "You all will." He looked at the guards. Their eyes strayed from him. He said, "Do you hear me? This man is taking you to your doom."

His warning echoed down the tunnel.

"Shut up, Goga," said Fuad. "I'm resurrecting him. He'll be grateful. He'll recognize me as an ally."

"He will recognize you as a slave – if you are lucky – or he may recognize you as food."

"He's already got a meal planned," Fuad said.

Aaliyah glanced at the guards. They looked worried. And some of the workers were talking among themselves.

"Do you realize that Babylon was a slave nation?" the Romanian said. "Nimrod built the Tower of Babel using slaves, and the city was fuelled by slaves."

"That's how we'll run London," said Fuad. "We'll run it with slaves. The world will be feudal again. It's the best system. The best when it's run properly, by a group of select humans, supported by vampires. That's the way forward. That's the way to save England, mate. Save the world. Democracy has failed."

"Democracy has given my country hope, Fuad," said Goga.

He buckled. Aaliyah held his arm to brace him.

"My country is now healthy and thriving because of democracy," he said.

"It'll soon be dead and decaying, like the rest of Europe," said Fuad. "Come and see what's going to kill it, Goga. You too, darling, come and see your fucking god."

Goga and Aaliyah were herded down the tunnel. The place smelled of diesel and blood. Fumes rose from the drill. It was huge. They had to squeeze past it into the opening, and when Aaliyah slipped through the gap between the drill and the wall and stared ahead, she stopped dead.

Her mouth fell open, such was the awe-inspiring sight.

A huge gateway, three-storeys high, towered above them. It was in the form of an arc. Gargoyles and demons had been carved into the stone. The walls into which it was built were long gone, fallen to dust, crushed by time.

Aaliyah craned her neck and gazed beyond the gateway.

Pillars of sandstone extended into the darkness above them. *Where did they end?* she thought. There had to be a roof, surely. But it seemed the pillars were never-ending, as if reaching to heaven. Not only did their height seem impossible, they also stretched away as far as the eye could see. It was a forest of pillars, spreading out into the dark distance.

An endless distance.

Many of the columns had collapsed into piles of masonry. Some that stood teetered precariously.

Aaliyah scanned her surroundings. She was trying to take it all in, trying to understand how this place – its dimensions – could be real.

Dread filled her. The thought that in this vast, underground, unchartered frontier, something horrific lurked. Something ancient and powerful. Something more frightening than she'd ever known.

"Welcome to the Gates of Irkalla," said Fuad.

Aaliyah's astonishment suddenly dwindled, and she came to her senses. The smell wafting out of the distance struck her. It was putrid. Like death.

And then, from mountains of rubble up ahead, figures crawled. They reared up, the masonry falling off them like water, and they lumbered out of the gloom.

Aaliyah froze.

CHAPTER 67.
THE FAR, FAR DISTANCE.

ALFRED laughed at the Sinclair woman.

"You're frightened of my workers, darling," he said.

The guards chuckled.

"Thought you were supposed to be some kind of Amazon warrior queen," said Alfred. "You wait till you meet Nimrod."

"I'm so excited," said Sinclair.

She was a mouthy bitch. Alfred couldn't wait to see her scream at the sight of Nimrod.

"There is nothing but dust and rubble here, Fuad," said Goga. "Nothing but dead history."

The workers skulked from among the rubble. They were covered in dirt. Their eyes gleamed, but their faces and clothes were soiled.

They do look like ghosts at first sight, thought Alfred, *stumbling from the rubble*.

Among them was a middle-aged man. He wore glasses, which he took off now and wiped on the hem of his shirt. He clicked his fingers, and a girl handed him a wallet-sized item that was filmed in dirt. The man wiped the item clean on his shirt. It was an infrared detector. It looked for movement. It looked for life. Alfred licked his lips, wondering what secrets the detector held.

"Dr Meyer," he said, "did you find anything?"

Roland Meyer was a Nebuchadnezzar and an archaeologist. Alfred and George had proposed to him the possibility of going after Nimrod the previous year.

Such a quest was heresy among the Nebs. It was like Christians trying to find the face of God. It was dangerous and foolish.

But his academic inquisitiveness had finally got the better of Meyer, and he'd left his post at the Eberhard Karls University in Tübingen, Germany, the previous September, and had started to prepare for this expedition.

One of his university's former students was Manfred Korfmann, the archaeologist who had continued Heinrich Schliemann's work at the site of Troy. Now Meyer felt he would be mentioned in the same breath as Korfmann and Schliemann. He was about to uncover a truly mythical city, and, along with it, a god.

"We have found a city, Mr Fuad," said Meyer.

"Yes, but any life in that city?"

"Just ourselves."

A ripple of panic ran through Alfred. What would George say if there were nothing here? Nothing to resurrect? Nothing to worship? Alfred might as well stay underground if he had nothing to give his brother.

Goga laughed. Alfred backhanded him across the face. The Romanian fell. He dropped his walking stick. The Sinclair woman went to his aid.

Alfred fumed. "If he laughs again," he said to one of the guards, "just fucking shoot him."

He turned to Meyer.

"Doctor," he said, shaking inside. "We're in Irkalla. You understand Irkalla?"

"I understand Irkalla, Mr Fuad."

"Irkalla. The underworld. Hell. The dwelling place of Nimrod."

"According to myth."

"Then where is he?"

"I said, sir, according to *myth*."

Alfred's head hurt. He thought it would explode. He ground his teeth together until his jaw ached.

He was thinking, *What would George say? What would George do?*

Should he have Meyer shot? He knew that killing a Nebuchadnezzar was unlawful. No Neb could purposefully harm another, although a few months earlier, George had thrown old Afdal Haddad out of a window. But he supposed the law didn't apply to George. Not if he *made* the law. Maybe it wouldn't apply to him, either, as George's brother. He thought of reaching for a pistol and blowing Meyer's fucking clever brains out of his fucking clever head.

But he stopped himself.

Christ, what am I going to do if this fucking Nimrod's not real? he thought.

Maybe nothing was real. Everything was a myth. The dream of a new Babylon. The vampires. Being down here in this stifling, airless hell-hole.

It was all just something he'd dreamt.

All the glory that they'd planned for, all the blood that had been spilled, nothing but ten minutes in his sub-conscious.

He had to make the dream reality. He had no choice. He had to make it live again.

The lust for power was too much. The fear of letting down his brother was unbearable.

No, Nimrod definitely existed. The trinity had existed, and legend said they'd been ripped from the Great Hunter's chest. They were his three beating hearts, born as monsters.

"Give me my fucking laptop," he barked at one of the guards.

The guard took the computer out of its case and handed it to Alfred, who flipped it open and logged on.

He fired off an email to George:

"Drop everything. We have a problem. Need to talk – now!"

After logging off, he handed the laptop back to the guard.

"Meyer," he said, "how long have you been down here?"

"We have been at this level for three days, Mr Fuad, myself and my team."

Alfred scanned the faces. They looked thin and grey. They looked like earthquake survivors, dug out after days. They were mostly students, eager to work for Roland Meyer. They all looked like they could do with a square meal.

Meyer continued:

"We have not seen the sun in days."

Alfred thought. He supposed that since most, if not all of the students, would never see sunlight again, they deserved a break. These weren't Nebuchadnezzars, so they would be slaves or food under the new regime. None, except Meyer, wore the red mark. For a moment, Alfred pitied them.

"Let your team get some food," he said. "The canteen is one level up. Take them up there, Dr Meyer, and eat as much as you want. I'll give you ninety minutes. Then, back to work at" – he checked his watch – "eleven thirty at the latest, right?"

The doctor nodded, and he trudged away with his team.

"Take this pair back to the cell," said Alfred.

"You fucker," the Sinclair woman said.

The guards marched them away. Alfred was left alone. He stared at the rubble.

It so was quiet. The ruins of Irkalla stood before him. Empty. Void. Useless.

He walked through the gate. Goose pimples raked his body, and he shivered.

The silence was piercing.

He stared up into the endless darkness and wondered how such heights were possible under the earth. It seemed as if the apex was higher than the first and second tiers of the dig, which were between 200 and 500 feet below ground.

It didn't make sense.

But after all, it had been built by a god. Maybe this wasn't earth. Maybe it was a place for gods. An imaginary city, outside natural law.

It might explain the Tower of Babel story, he thought.

The Bible said Nimrod had built the tower so he could reach God, so he could be God.

Had he succeeded?

Craning his neck, Alfred truly thought so.

He wondered if it were true that Abraham had come down here to the deep and did battle with Nimrod. Most archaeologists, theologians, and historians dismissed such things as myth, fables. But they did not have vision. They did not have ambition. They were not the Fuad brothers. And they had not seen the depictions on the cave walls.

Alfred scrambled up a pile of rubble. He nearly slipped a couple of times, debris streaming down behind him. But he made it. Stood on top of the little hill of masonry like a king surveying a conquered land. Stood proud. Stood tall.

Where are you? he thought.

And then he shouted, "Where are you?"

His voice echoed through the caverns and raced away into the far, far distance, and it scared Alfred to think of his call hurtling back in time through the darkness.

Where had his voice reached? Who heard that call? What unnamed, unchartered places had his words reached?

Maybe somewhere beyond Irkalla. Maybe the deepest part of hell.

He waited until the echo died.

He waited for something to come back.

But nothing came. No answer.

Just silence and darkness.

He shook his head gloomily, trying to think how George would take this.

He turned and trudged down the mound of rubble and started to make his way towards the gate. He needed a drink. He needed lots of drinks.

Behind him, where he'd stood moments before atop the masonry, there was a disturbance. Only a slight one. A dribble of rocks and pebbles rolling down the slope. Alfred saw nothing of it. He was gone. But had he been standing there, he would have heard a rumbling noise, similar to a growl produced by a very large animal. The noise came from the heart of the deepest darkness. The far, far distance.

And had Alfred heard it, he would have known, then, that something lived in the abyss.

CHAPTER 68.
HURT FROM SOUL TO SKIN.

"IF you do anything stupid," said Lawton, "I'll have her rip your throat out."

Laxman shrugged.

Lawton emptied bullets from the Makarov he'd snatched from Laxman.

"I'm walking in front of you," he said. "You hold the gun on me, say I'm your prisoner."

Laxman shrugged again.

He took the gun.

He seemed to weigh it in his hand. *Making sure I've not left any ammo in it,* thought Lawton. Laxman curled his lip when he realized Jake hadn't accidentally left a bullet in the gun.

"You think I'm stupid, Laxman?"

The mercenary smiled. "I got to hope."

"You stay there for a second," said Lawton.

He got out of the Toyota. They were parked on a narrow street about half a mile away from Alfred Fuad's base.

He looked towards the compound, through a pair of binoculars he'd found in the Land Cruiser. He surveyed the scene. High-wire fencing hemmed in quick-build units. Floodlights illuminated the entire complex. Trucks were lined up outside the perimeter and inside, too. Mostly 4x4s. All black. Right in the middle of the facility, poking out above the single-storey buildings, was scaffolding, and clamped within it a huge drill unit.

He smelled something – sweet decay.

She was right next to him.

"Do you trust this man?" she asked.

He looked into her red eyes and said, "As much as I trust you."

"Not much, then."

"Very little."

"You think I would kill him for you?"

"I think you'd kill him for yourself."

"I might kill the both of you."

He dropped the binoculars from his eyes and looked at her. "I'm not sure if you can kill me."

She glared and curled her lip slightly, showing a fang. But Lawton held her stare. He felt he could. The sense that he was something beyond mortal was strong.

And he was starting to embrace it.

He'd been shot in the side, and the bullet had had no effect. The wound was virtually healed. And it was all to do with the vampire DNA spooling around his own; he was convinced of it. They were merging, human and vampire genes, to create something completely different to either species. They were merging to create him.

And, looking deeply into his one good eye, Ereshkigal said, "You are not like other humans. You are the one with wounds. This is what I believe. You were foretold as the killer of my Lord Nimrod."

"Wasn't that Abraham?"

"He had no wounds – you are hurt from soul to skin. You are the one with wounds. You are the one who shall kill my husband. You must fulfil your destiny, while I must fulfil mine."

"And what's yours?"

"To protect him from you."

They looked at each other, and Lawton felt himself drawn to her, this ancient dead thing. He was leaning towards her – but he stopped himself, rearing back.

She laughed.

"You go as red as my eyes," she said. "You shouldn't be ashamed of your feelings. I was a bride-to-be, full of hope, full of desire. In many ways, I still am. A girl in love with her betrothed. A girl who wants to be loved."

"You are a vampire," he said. "I know vampires. Every shred of what you were has been stripped away. All that's left is your black heart."

She grabbed his hand and held it to her breast. He tried to pull away, but once it was pressed on her flesh, he kept his hand where it was, and his skin was on fire.

Her heart pulsed under his palm. Her breast was firm in his fingers. Fire filled his blood, and he sensed the same heat course through Ereshkigal.

"Could I grab a feel, too?"

Lawton yanked his hand away.

Laxman had poked his head out of the Toyota's window. He was smiling, waggling the empty gun.

"Fondling geriatrics these days, Lawton?" he said. "Necrophilia's got to be illegal, yeah?"

Lawton glowered at him.

"Get out of the car before I let this geriatric cut open your veins."

CHAPTER 69.
INTO THE COMPOUND.

THEY drove into the compound and parked next to another 4x4. Lawton switched off the lights. They sat in darkness and in silence for a few moments. Lawton listened to his heartbeat and to the voices in his head, calling from somewhere deep inside him. Calling from somewhere ancient.

He clocked a CCTV camera. Their arrival had probably been noted. It didn't matter.

He waited a few more seconds. His eye smarted. It watered. He wondered if it might be tears.

"Right," he said, "let's go."

Laxman got behind him and poked the gun in his back. Lawton cupped his hands on the back of his head. The rucksack was slung over his shoulder. Behind them, Ereshkigal lurked. Lawton hoped he could trust her. If Laxman tried anything, Jake was depending on the vampire to protect him. But once they were inside the compound, he wasn't sure what she would do.

At the main gate, Laxman acknowledged a couple of guards and flashed his ID.

As the barrier was raised, one of the men asked Laxman, "When are we getting out of here boss? When are we getting paid? There's some weird stuff going on."

"We'll be out, soon, Mo," Laxman said. "And the cash'll be in your account, ready for you to lose it all at the tables again, mate."

The man and his mate laughed. They eyed up Ereshkigal as she, Laxman, and Jake entered the compound.

"Why did you show your ID?" Lawton said. "They'd forgotten your pretty face already?"

"Good practice, Jakey boy."

Further on, they faced another pair of guards, who welcomed Laxman's return and said, "You got him, chief."

"I got him," said Laxman, once again badging the guard.

Again, they gawped at Ereshkigal.

Lawton was tense. He sweated profusely. His headache was almost unbearable.

He was now also convinced that he was seeing through his false eye, that he could make out shapes and movements.

Once inside the compound, Lawton scoped the area. Lights came from tents and mobile units. Armed mercenaries smoked. Groups of Middle Eastern students lazed around. They were covered in dust and dirt. They looked exhausted.

He saw movement from the corner of his good eye.

Laxman trying it on, raising the gun to pistol whip Lawton across the back of the skull.

Jake wheeled, too quick for the mercenary.

He kicked Laxman in the ribs. The big man grunted and hit the ground, dropping the gun.

Lawton scooped up the weapon.

Laxman groaned. "You're fucking lucky I'm injured, Lawton, or I would have had you."

Ereshkigal flashed her teeth.

"Where's Fuad?" said Lawton.

"Get me up."

"Get up yourself. Where is he?"

Laxman groaned again. He had injuries to his face and a cracked rib or two, for sure. Lawton took the clip out of his pocket and slid it back into the Makarov.

"He spends most of his time underground now," said the mercenary, "but his office is down there, on the right."

Lawton gestured for Laxman to lead the way.

They walked between the pre-fab structures until Laxman pointed at one of the buildings.

They entered.

Maps of modern Hillah, and one of ancient Babylon, were pinned to the wall. Scraps of paper covered in notes, diagrams, and mathematical formulas were strewn across a desk. A photo of George Fuad stood on the shelf amid Bibles, Korans, and other religious texts. The place smelled of booze.

Lawton noticed that Ereshkigal was hissing and spitting.

He looked her in the eye.

He knew what she wanted.

"I'll give you a head start," he said.

She glared at him. Hate poured from her eyes. She sensed Nimrod, or maybe thought she did. It would be dangerous to make her hang around.

"Go," said Lawton. "Go and find him, before I do."

She shot out of the door.

"Lovely gesture," said Laxman.

Lawton rifled through a drawer. He found a BlackBerry. He listened to the messages. He glanced at Laxman.

"You might like to hear this."

As Laxman took the phone, the ground shook. The quake sent files and books tumbling; it made the desk jerk, and chairs fell over.

A growling sound filled the air, like an animal.

Then an alarm blared.

Lawton bolted out of the door.

CHAPTER 70.
AN IMPOSSIBLE ANGEL.

AALIYAH had been battering at the door of the cell for ages. Dust rained from the ceiling of their cramped little chamber. Everything was shaking, and the earth rumbled menacingly.

Goga said, "Fuad has found Nimrod, and the earth is rebelling."

Aaliyah steadied herself against the wall. But the stone crumbled when she touched it. And cracks started appearing in the rock. The place was disintegrating. It was going to cave in on top of them.

She pressed her face against the door and screamed for someone to let them out, but no one was listening.

Goga sat on the ground and did nothing. His black clothes and his black hair were coated in dust. He leaned his forehead on the cane. He had given up.

Aaliyah's blood boiled.

"We've got to get out of here," she said.

The noise of destruction had grown louder. At first, it had been a grumble, but during the past hour, it had increased in volume. And now it was a roar.

Aaliyah grabbed Goga and shook him. He looked up at her. His eyes were filled with despair.

"Apostol," she said, using his first name for the first time she could remember. "Apostol, we have to get out of here, or we'll be buried alive."

"That is our fate."

She slapped him across the face. "It's not my fate," she yelled. "My fate is to be with Jake."

Huge eruptions shook the cell. Aaliyah cowered. She lost her footing and fell. The explosions kept coming. Aaliyah was trying to get to her feet. Goga rocked back and forth as the cell quaked.

Screams came from outside their prison. And then gunfire. Automatic gunfire. The crack of a pistol.

Jake, she thought, *please don't abandon me. Please don't let me die here*.

She started to cry.

The thunder claps continued. The room kept shaking and was slowly falling to pieces. The ceiling was caving in. The walls were cracking. Debris fell, chunks of it.

"What *is* that noise?" said Aaliyah, needing to shout now to make herself heard.

"It's the devil," said Goga. "It's the Lord of Irkalla. He's awake, I tell you. Fuad has resurrected the beast. If he has, we are doomed. Everything is finished."

The door buckled. The wood creaked. And then it split down the middle, the oak snapping as if it were balsa wood. Part of the wall next to it collapsed.

Aaliyah was covered in rubble, and she screamed. More gunfire erupted from beyond the shattered door. The smell of cordite filled the air. Dust from falling debris billowed into the cell. Shouting and screaming came from outside. And the continued *rat-tat-tat* of shooting.

Was someone firing at the guards?

They certainly wouldn't shoot at each other.

Or maybe they were firing at Nimrod.

The ground lurched.

Aaliyah gasped.

A crack appeared in the floor near where she lay, and it then spread from one corner of the room to the other, wrenching the cell apart.

She tried to get up.

Another one of those huge blasts shook her.

It threw Goga across the cell. He landed near the door.

Aaliyah struggled to get to her feet.

The crack in the floor widened. The earth opened up.

Terror turned Aaliyah's insides into ice.

She stared down into the crevice. It was pitch black and endless. A rotten smell laced the atmosphere. Heat scorched her face.

She rolled away from the cleaved earth, but as she did so, one side of the crack rose up, making a horrible grinding noise.

The ground tipped upwards, and Aaliyah felt herself slide. She clawed at the stony ground. She stared, horrified, at Goga. He looked back, wide eyed and open mouthed.

She shouted at him for help.

But Goga was gripping the remains of the door, trying to stop himself from sliding back into the cell and towards the fissure.

Aaliyah kept slipping back.

And she couldn't stop herself.

She kicked against the earth. Her nails tore as she tried to claw the stony ground for purchase.

But nothing stopped her sliding.

Gravity was powerful.

She yelled out as her legs went over the edge of the abyss, and the darkness below started to pull at her.

Her blood froze as the lower half of her body dangled over the chasm. But she managed to dig her bloodied fingers into the ground, preventing herself from falling.

She cried out in pain but held on for dear life.

The ground tilted again, groaning as it did so. Aaliyah lurched a little deeper into the hole. Her arms ached. Her fingers were shredded. She couldn't hold on much longer.

Everything juddered violently. She shut her eyes and steeled herself, desperately trying to muster a few last ounces of strength.

But she couldn't. She was done for. Nothing left to give.

She opened her eyes and screamed.

The door split in two. Goga nearly lost his grip on the doorframe.

The room titled again. Aaliyah slid further into the gorge.

A dark figure materialized from the clouds of dust swirling outside the cell.

And someone called her name, the voice filling her with hope.

She cried out his name.

"Jake!"

But then her mind said, *No, it's a dream, Jake's a prisoner in Baghdad – or dead.*

"Aaliyah," he called again.

"Jake! Oh, God, Jake!"

He stepped from the debris, an impossible angel.

"Aaliyah, hold on," he said and threw himself on the ground, reaching out to her.

She smiled and cried and said his name over and over.

He reached for her. She reached for him. Desperate to feel his skin on her skin, his hand in hers. And their fingers were so close, so close.

Her heart lifted at the inevitability of his touch.

But his touch did not come. Horror came.

Her other hand was too weak to bear her weight.

The darkness wrenched at her. The emptiness pulled her down.

And she plunged into the rift.

Jake's horrified face shrank above her, a dwindling vision in an ever decreasing circle of light.

But still she thought he would come for her. Still she thought he would be her saviour and rescue her.

As she fell, a voice from the cell, a heavily accented voice, said, “Forget her, you must kill Nimrod.”

She tried to shout at him not to forget her.

But the voice – Goga’s – came again:

“Forget the woman, save the world, forget her, for – ”

But the words died in the darkness that engulfed her, and she fell.

CHAPTER 71.
MEETING A GOD.

LAXMAN was going to kill Alfred Fuad.

He stormed through the tunnel as dust and debris rained on him. He ignored it. He ignored his men and the Iraqi workers and students as they fled the other way. He had one thing on his mind, and nothing was going to stand in his way.

Slaughter that fucker.

He'd heard the message on the mobile phone. George Fuad telling his brother to kill Laxman and his men. Telling him to use them as bait to draw Nimrod out of his hole. Telling him to sacrifice them.

"Go on, then," Lawton had said. "I'll leave you be, if you leave me be."

Laxman agreed. He didn't really want to be bothering with Jake Lawton. Not unless he was being paid to sort him out. And since Fuad had no intention of compensating White Light Ops for their work, any obligation Laxman had to protect his lying, cheating employer had been cancelled. And it would be further cancelled when he stuck the barrel of the Heckler & Koch MP5 submachine gun he'd nabbed off the body of a dead soldier up Fuad's arse and pulled the trigger.

Lawton had been right. You couldn't trust Alfred Fuad. You couldn't trust either of the Fuads, or their allies.

Laxman fumed. He was angry with himself for having been stupid. But he'd feel better once he'd skinned Fuad alive.

The earth was shaking. The walls were giving way. The tunnels were falling in on themselves. The ground was tearing and tilting.

As they fled, students and workers fell into the fissures. Their shrieks echoed through the underworld.

Some slipped down a cleft in the ground and held on, screaming for Laxman to help them as he hurtled past. But he ignored them, and eventually they lost their grip. Or the earth's plates shifted and pressed together, crushing the victims to a pulp, leaving nothing but a hand poking out of the ground.

Laxman was in pain. Lawton had beaten him up pretty well. But he was determined. He wanted revenge. He and his men had been betrayed, and he would never let that pass.

It was a long way down. It took him a while to make his way into the tunnels. He'd lost track of time.

The passageway behind him was quickly filling with rubble. But he'd made a decision that killing Fuad was more important than living. He would think about survival after completing his mission.

Adrenaline had kept him going, but now his leg started to ache.

He hobbled through the raining rubble. It was all falling apart. The noise was thunderous.

Keep going, he told himself.

He was reaching the base of a slope, now. It was where the tunnel had previously come to a dead end. But they'd been drilling through it over the past few days. Beyond the rubble left by the drill, Laxman saw pillars. Tall, gigantic pillars. A forest of them, spreading out for miles, disappearing into the gloom.

He clambered through the gap in the wall and then froze.

Piles of masonry filled the chamber. And more continued to fall. The pillars shook. A roaring sound deafened Laxman, and his ears hurt. He scanned the vast room of columns, the piles of rubble – and then his eyes locked on a figure.

Crouching next to a mound of masonry, from which spouted a tube of smoke, was Alfred Fuad.

Rage erupted in Laxman.

He bounded towards Fuad.

With Laxman only yards away from his target, he skidded to a halt.

Fuad wheeled to face him. The man's face was red and wet with sweat. He had been working on a computer, typing away, sending a message, Laxman guessed.

Then a tinny voice came from the laptop.

"Alfred! Alfred, show me again!"

"What the fuck's going on?" said Laxman.

"He's here," said Alfred Fuad. "George, he's here."

He was speaking to his brother. "I fucking *am* here," said Laxman. "You tell your fucking brother that after I torture you to death, I'm coming for him."

"He's here," said Alfred again.

"I told you, I am – "

Fuad turned to glare at Laxman, his face creased with rage.

"Not you, you shit," he screamed, "not you," and then he laughed hysterically.

The pile of rubble spewed fire now – fire and smoke.

Laxman gazed up.

And then in the smoke a figure formed. At first it was vague, just a shape. But it slowly gathered density.

Laxman retreated a few steps.

Fuad shrieked with laughter.

The figure was huge, about fifteen feet tall. It stepped from the fire and the smoke. It flexed its powerful body.

Laxman tried to say something, but no words came from his throat.

And Nimrod glared at him through his red, fiery eyes and saw not a tough, battle-hardened soldier, but a flea in need of crushing.

CHAPTER 72. INFECTED.

LAWTON watched her plummet into the darkness. He shouted her name, but she was gone.

The cell rocked back and forth. The ground rolled under his feet. He was sliding towards the abyss into which Aaliyah had fallen. For a moment he thought he'd let himself fall. Then he tried to grab onto something. But there was nothing. He was slipping towards the gorge.

"Hold this," came a voice through the clamour.

Goga was reaching for him with his cane.

Lawton grabbed it.

He braced himself.

Goga curled his lips as he strained.

Lawton managed to get a foothold in the earth. He started to pull himself away from the fissure. Once he was clear, he sprang to his feet and pushed Goga out of the cell.

Lawton followed him out into the tunnel. Behind him, the cell caved in. The floor had given way. Goga had saved his life. But Lawton was still angry with him.

"You let her fall, you bastard," he said.

Goga tried to get to his feet. All around them, debris fell. People were running. Some got crushed. Others got away.

"You let her fall and did nothing," said Lawton.

He pulled Goga to his feet by his lapels. The Romanian's face contorted in pain, and he tried to defend his actions: "We have to get Nimrod; he is the most important thing."

"Not to me he's not," said Lawton.

"He should be. The world will end if he survives. We must kill him. Make him one with himself again. That's what the legend says."

"I don't care what any legend says."

"Forget her, Lawton. She is just one sacrifice to save millions."

Lawton slapped him across the face. Dust came off Goga's cheeks. He staggered away.

Lawton said, "Maybe I should sacrifice you as well."

"You can if you wish. It will not matter. Our lives and our deaths are meaningless. What matters is that Nimrod dies. He has been resurrected, Lawton. You hear that noise? The roaring of the monster? You see this destruction? His power tears down the walls. And soon he will tear down the cities of the earth. We must stop him."

Lawton said nothing.

"You must forget her," said Goga.

"Like you told me to forget Britain?"

Goga nodded. "Those are my sunglasses," he said.

Lawton took them off.

Goga's jaw dropped. "Your eye, Lawton, what have you done?"

Lawton told him.

"You fool," said the Romanian. "You allowed the flesh of the undead to *enter* your body?"

"It didn't say I shouldn't in the instruction manual."

Goga didn't get Lawton's black humour. "You are infected, now," the Romanian said. "You are already poisoned. The skin will knit with yours. You will be like them. If I had a gun, I would shoot you."

"I'm not sure it'd make any difference if you did. Tell me where Fuad is. Where did you see him last?"

"He's down there, deep. That's where he stays, now. That's where they all are. That's where Nimrod is."

Lawton marched down the tunnel as the place caved in around him. If he were going to die, at least he would die trying. He spotted a pistol lying on the ground, covered in rubble. He picked it up and put it in his waistband. On his back he carried the rucksack containing the Spear of Abraham. He wasn't sure if he'd need it. The weapon was meant to kill the vampire trinity. It was made from the horns of Nimrod, according to legends. Even if it were useless, at least Lawton could return it to its rightful owner and maybe drive the ivory horns into Nimrod's ugly face.

Lawton stopped and thought about something.

His eyes widened as he realized he might have answered a difficult question. A new hope fired up in his breast.

He carried on walking, thinking now that he might hold the secret to killing Nimrod. And if Aaliyah were dead, that would be his main priority.

As he made his way deeper into the underworld, he began to lose any desire he had for life. He would welcome death. His lack of self-preservation would make him more dangerous. He would not worry about his own well-being. And if what Ereshkigal had said was true, that he was virtually unkillable, then nothing would stand in his way. Nothing but himself.

I'm the one with wounds, he thought. *The one destined to kill the monster.*

His body pulsed. His head throbbed. Voices called out to him. Echoes from the past.

He was infected.

He was resurrected.

A new being.

A murderous creation.

A creature with nothing to live for.

He came to the edge of a pit.

He stared down into it.

Darkness stared back.

The elevator that had ferried Fuad's workers down into the hole was hanging off its scaffold. It had been wrecked in the tremors.

There was nothing for it.

Lawton started to climb down the scaffold. It was shaky. It creaked and rocked. But he kept going, oblivious to the danger.

Halfway down, darkness below him, darkness above him, he stopped.

Through the cacophony of destruction, he heard a sound.

A scream.

And the scream becoming a word.

"Nooooooooooooooo!"

Resonating from the depths.

And following the scream, a roar.

The roar of an animal Lawton could not identify. A monster that had no name. A beast from the pit, unseen by human eyes in thousands of years.

It was a roar filled with fury, a roar filled with anger, a roar filled with hunger.

CHAPTER 73. DISCIPLE OR SACRIFICE?

LAXMAN screamed again:

"Noooooooooooooo!"

"Look at him, look at him," Alfred said. He lifted the laptop. He'd been speaking to his brother through Skype. And now he was showing him what had risen from the rubble.

While George could witness what was going on thousands of miles away, Alfred was also recording the event on the computer's camera.

"Look what I've done for you, George, look."

George's face on the computer screen changed. His eyes widened, and his mouth opened.

"You love it, Georgie, don't you?" said Alfred.

Nimrod rose high above the debris. The god was trying to tear himself from the rubble. He'd been trapped there for thousands of years. It was a lot of grave to dig himself out of.

Alfred gawped at the Great Hunter.

Nimrod's brown, leathery body was powerful, like a steroid-enhanced bodybuilder. Dark fluid had caked on his face. Great wounds scoured his head where Abraham had ripped the horns from his scalp. His hands were the size of wheelbarrows, and his talons were like machetes. Something pulsed against his chest, inside the iron cage of his ribs. He had terrible scars across his breast where he had ripped out his own hearts thousands of years ago to give birth to Kea, Kakash and Kasdeja.

He was a remarkable sight, and Alfred stood in awe.

The monster towered over Laxman. The mercenary had come back from Baghdad, where he was supposed to make sure Jake Lawton was dead. But the soldier-for-hire had come back not with Lawton's head but with a murderous fury – directed at Alfred.

"What the hell is it?" Laxman said.

"What do you think it is?"

"You promised me treasure."

"I lied."

"Why are you filming?"

"So England can see you being torn to pieces, mate. So they can see what's coming. Look at him, Laxman, look at that fucking god." He then addressed his brother: "Look at him, George. Look at what I got for you. I did this for you."

Laxman faced the Great Hunter again. He aimed his petty little submachine gun at Nimrod. He fired. The bullets smacked into Nimrod's pectoral muscle. The bullets did nothing. Just pinpricks.

Laxman screamed once more.

Alfred laughed.

The monster was still pinned in the rubble from the waist down. Alfred was a little glad. He still wasn't sure how Nimrod would react, whether he'd recognize Alfred as a disciple or a sacrifice.

"Let me speak, let me speak," shouted George over the Skype connection.

Alfred raised the laptop towards Nimrod.

The god looked down at him. Its red eyes bore into him.

This was a physical presence like Alfred had never seen. Fifteen feet tall, it would lead the Fuads' vampire army across the world. No one would stand in their way. It made Alfred fizz with excitement, though at that moment, with Nimrod glaring down at him, he felt as if his balls were shrivelling.

"Lord Nimrod," said George. "Lord Nimrod can you hear me and understand?"

Nimrod canted his head. He growled gently.

"Don't go near it, Fuad," said Laxman.

But Alfred wasn't listening. He stepped closer, holding up the computer. If anyone could persuade Nimrod, George could.

"We're your loyal servants," said George. "We've come to save you from your grave, and we bring you the world as a gift. We've prepared the way for your return, and London will be your new capital."

Something slid down a mountain of rubble behind Laxman. It was a body, and it rolled down the slope.

Finally, it hit the ground and came to a stop near Nimrod.

It was the woman.

It was Aaliyah Sinclair.

"Who the hell's that?" said Laxman.

"Your salvation," said Alfred. "He can have her instead of you."

Laxman turned the submachine gun on him. Alfred felt a cold chill run down his spine.

But then the woman screamed.

Laxman wheeled away and ran towards her.

Idiot, thought Alfred. *Not so heartless after all, Laxman. Running off to save a woman.*

He scurried around a corner to hide, peering to see what was happening. He didn't want to miss anything.

"What the fuck's going on, Alfie?" said George.

He told him about the woman.

The whole of Irkalla suddenly rocked.

Laxman was bounding up the mountain of rubble.

He fired straight into Nimrod's face, a stream of bullets from the automatic weapon.

They churned the Great Hunter's flesh but made no real difference. Lead couldn't kill it. Steel couldn't kill it.

Nothing can kill it, thought Alfred.

Nimrod scooped up the Sinclair woman in his huge hand.

She screamed and punched and kicked.

Again it had no effect.

Nimrod opened his mouth.

His fangs were like swords.

Laxman kept shooting.

Shooting until his gun fell silent.

He'd run out of ammunition.

Alfred laughed.

Nimrod roared.

He hauled himself free of the stones.

The rubble avalanched.

He was loose, his tree-trunk legs kicking away the masonry.

He still held the struggling woman.

Laxman was caught in the landslide.

Nimrod stepped free of his grave.

Alfred nearly pissed himself with excitement.

"Oh fuck, he's so beautiful," said George.

Nimrod tossed the woman aside.

He went after Laxman.

The mercenary tried to fight.

But he had no chance.

The god scooped him up.

Laxman screamed.

Nimrod grabbed him in both hands, as if he were about to pull apart a cracker.

And that's what he did.

He wrenched and snapped Laxman in two at the waist.

Even cut in half, the mercenary managed to shriek.

Alfred felt faint.

George laughed.

Laxman carried on screeching.

He stared in horror as his legs dangled too far away from his torso for him to survive much longer.

His intestines snaked out.

His organs slopped on the ground.

The smell of meat filled the air.

Nimrod lifted Laxman's still living torso to his mouth, bit off the mercenary's head and spat it out, and then tipped him like a bottle and drank the blood that poured from the man's neck.

And then he flung Laxman aside.

Nimrod roared again. Stronger, this time. More powerful. More alive. He had tasted blood. It had rejuvenated him. He shuffled forward, still unsteady on his legs after thousands of years trapped under tonnes of masonry.

He saw Alfred, who wetted himself.

The smell of piss filled his nostrils.

"Not me," he begged, "not me, Lord Nimrod."

"Sacrifice yourself if you have to," said George.

"What are you saying?" Alfred said.

"You'd be a martyr, Alfred. The first martyr. Die for me, mate. Die for your brother and your faith."

Nimrod came forward.

"The woman," cried Alfred, "take the woman."

Nimrod bared his teeth.

They were terrifying. Stained still with Laxman's blood, pieces of his brain and skull wedged between them.

Nimrod reached for Alfred, who screamed.

But then the Great Hunter hesitated.

He turned, as if listening.

A cowering Alfred then heard what had drawn Nimrod's attention.

A voice. A woman's voice. Piercing the din of destruction. It was sweet and chilling. It was old and young. Like something that had been resurrected after years, unchanged under the earth.

And she appeared from the darkness, a vision in white – pale skinned, black haired.

Nimrod looked at her, and his eyes lit up.

PART EIGHT.

SACRIFICE.

CHAPTER 74. WELCOME TO THE NEW ORDER.

WEMBLEY STADIUM, LONDON – 8.37PM (GMT), 20 MAY, 2011

AS Jake Lawton had neared the caves where Nimrod was buried, 4000km away, George Fuad scanned England's famous old football ground.

The stadium was full. The floodlights were on. Seven poles stood in the centre circle. The stakes were ten feet tall, positioned in a semi-circle. A cage wrapped around the poles. Leading from the cage, across the pitch, straight into the players' tunnel, a metal walkway stood six feet off the ground on stilts.

George stood in the Royal Box. Other senior Neb officials surrounded him. Howard Vince, recently back from Iraq, was there. They had been watching the footage from Hillah. Watching Nimrod's resurrection. They were all, apart from George, pale and wide-eyed. He was excited and focused.

His image was being projected onto the big screen. The crowd, 70,000 of them, applauded. Most were ordinary members of the public who had made the sensible decision to support the new regime. Despite their backing, to George they were traitors. Cowards who had turned their backs on their country and their friends, probably, just to live. He hated them. They had sacrificed their principles just to survive. But their collaboration was useful for now. And as long as they behaved, they would be relatively safe.

Neb militia men mingled with the crowd. Just to listen out for any anti-government comments, or plots against the regime, and to make sure everyone applauded. They were in the stands generally to intimidate people. And so far they were doing a good job.

"Fellow Britons," he said into the microphone. His voice boomed around the stadium. "Welcome to the new order."

Cheers rang around the stands.

It was spine-tingling. What he'd seen on the computer only minutes ago had put him on cloud nine. And now the crowd was cheering him. It couldn't be better.

He carried on talking:

"Tonight will teach us that to be a criminal in New Britain is a dangerous pursuit. Tonight will teach us that justice is swift and brutal in New Britain. We'll not shirk from cruelty when it comes to the law breakers. We will not be soft on crime."

More applause.

I like this politician lark, he thought.

He went on:

"Seven face execution today for treason – the vilest crime."

A murmur of appreciation rippled through the crowd.

"Treason not only threatens the state, it threatens every citizen of that state. It is an attack on every single one of you and every single member of your family. That's why the judgment is lethal."

He waited for the applause to die down, and then:

"Seven cowards will die here tonight, but they'll die for your entertainment. This is reality TV in New Britain, friends. These cowards won't infect you or your families with their poison. They will die as the judgment of the people demands. *You*, the people."

He was rousing. But the applause from some was muted. They didn't like this public murder business. *Tough*, he thought. They had to love it. Or die.

This spectacle would scare people. It would scare a lot of the Nebuchadnezzars, too. They'd been wishing for a New Babylon for years. Now it was here, they had to learn to live with it. They had to get accustomed to its new laws and traditions. Some of them might not like the cruelty, the near-fascism of George's government. But they had little choice. Anyone who stood in his way – civilian or Neb – would suffer.

Soon, Nimrod would be shipped to Britain. He would be a god for the people to worship. George had seen the monster already, glimpses of it on his computer. The images had excited him.

Some had warned him not to trifle with Nimrod. It was too dangerous, they said. He was a god who had never sought an allegiance with humans.

But George feared nothing. This was his destiny. He would sacrifice virtually everything – including his brother – to hold on to this power he had won.

"When you go back to your cities, your towns, your villages," he said, "tell your neighbours what you saw. Tell them about justice and power. Tell them about New Britain. And tell them what happens to her enemies."

Applause rang out.

"Bring out the traitors," he said.

CHAPTER 75.
BLOOD FOR THE BEASTS.

THE walkway stretched before them, ending in the distance at the cage in the centre circle. They were seated on a bench that lined the wall of the players' tunnel. Armed militia stood guard. Nebuchadnezzar officials spoke into radio mikes, choreographing the whole event. The crowd roared and stamped their feet. George Fuad's voice boomed over the loudspeaker system.

Fear raced through Christine Murray.

Fear for David, for herself, for the country.

She looked at each of the other captives, starting with David. Then Kwan Mei. Then Elizabeth Wilson. Then three she didn't recognize – two men and a woman.

Until ten minutes ago, they had been locked in one of the Wembley dressing rooms. David had said it used to be the England dressing room. But no footballers had been using it for ages. In fact, no one had been inside for a long time. It was smelly and dirty. Blood stains smeared the walls. The odour of urine and shit laced the air. There was no water, because the supply had been poisoned, and Fuad had made no effort to address the issue, no more than Elizabeth Wilson had when she was in government.

Wilson looked dreadful. A few years ago she had been an ambitious politician, full of hope. Now she was just a scapegoat, a sacrifice on the altar of a New Britain. Blood for the beasts who were going to rule the country.

Murray felt tears well. She shuffled closer to David.

"Are you all right?" she said.

"I was going to kill him," he said. "But I was rubbish. I got caught."

"You weren't rubbish, darling, don't say that. You were brave. You *have* been brave. You *are* brave. The bravest boy in the world."

"Yeah, but it's not doing me much good, now."

She didn't know what to say.

"You are brave."

Murray glanced across at Kwan Mei.

The Chinese girl carried on talking:

"Very brave. He is brave. I fight vampires with him, and he has courage of lion. More courage than men like this." She kicked out at a Neb militia man. He raised the butt of his gun, threatening to hit her with it. But she didn't flinch. "Weak, stupid, coward," she said to the militia man, mustering her limited English to form the best insult she could.

"I wish we could go back to how it was," said David.

"I wish I could tell you we can," said Murray.

"Mum?"

"Yes?"

"Do you think Jake is dead?"

"I don't know, David."

"He can change the world. He can make it go back to how it was… well, nearly how it was."

She knew what he meant – no dad, no Michael. But no vampires either. No Nebuchadnezzar. No slavery. No tyranny.

"I'm sure he'll do it," she said.

"He won't, Mum, the Iraqis caught him."

"If anyone can get out of a hole, it's Jake."

David shook his head. The hope had seeped out of him. She felt devastated, her son's despair tearing her apart.

"There's no point without Jake," he said.

"Don't say that; there's always hope."

"Mum, don't treat me like a baby. I'm not a baby."

"I know… I know, you're not."

A commotion nearby attracted Murray's attention.

Mei was on her feet, berating a militia man.

"You fat man, you shut up," she said.

"Sit back down, chinky bitch," the militia man said.

"You don't call me 'chink', you fuck face."

"Sit the fuck back down, chicken cully and lice," he said, mocking Mei's Chinese accent. His colleagues laughed.

Murray started to stand up so she could make Mei sit down.

But someone rushed past her, bumping her.

She gasped.

It was David, off towards the militia man like a greyhound out of the traps.

He blazed across the room with his head down and slammed into the man's belly.

The black shirt's face turned red, and all the air was knocked out of him.

He flew backwards, crashing into his colleagues.

David's attack triggered Mei.

She karate kicked the guards, catching one or two with decent blows.

David had floored a Neb in a suit and was biting the man's throat. The fellow screamed. Blood was pouring down the front of his white shirt.

Murray screamed. This was going to end badly. The courage shown by Mei and David would be for nothing. She knew that.

And seconds later a dozen black shirts poured into the tunnel. They wielded batons.

Murray was still screaming.

She watched with horror as the militia men threw David and Mei to the floor and started beating them with the batons.

With their hands tied behind their backs, David and Mei had no means to defend themselves.

The beating was relentless and savage, blood pouring from many wounds. Blood pooling on the concrete floor. Blood splashing over the black uniforms of the attackers.

Murray screamed still, and continued to scream after someone had shouted, "That's enough," and the black shirts had stopped thrashing her son and the Chinese girl.

Murray wanted to rush to David's aid, but she was held back by a militia man.

She heard him groan. She saw him writhe. She thanked whatever god might exist that her boy was at least still alive. Mei sat up. Blood matted her hair. It poured down her face. But her expression was determined. Her eyes were filled with hate. Her mouth twisted in a gritty frown.

The newcomer spoke again:

"Stop this nonsense. You can't kill them before they're put to death, you morons. Or you'll have to replace them out there. We'll rip your bloody marks off and let the vampires go at you. Right, show's about to start. My wife, son, and my two grand-daughters are out there, and my name is on the programme as having part-organized this circus. I want everything to go smooth, is that clear?"

"Yes, General Vince," a few of the men mumbled.

"I've just come down from the Royal Box, and Prime Minister Fuad is very insistent that everything runs smoothly. If there are cock-ups, boys, your arses are on the line, I'm telling you. All right?"

"Yes, sir."

"Prime Minister Fuad is about to show an interesting film, recently received from Iraq – lovely place. I had a delightful time there."

A few of the black shirts chuckled.

"So," said Vince, "let's get this sorted. Let's be military about this. Let's be disciplined. Without discipline, we are nothing but barbarians, is that clear?"

"Yes, sir."

"Excellent. Take those bloody traitors outside, and get them ready for the show. They can watch the footage while they ponder what is to come for New Britain – a New Britain they'll never see."

He sneered at the seven prisoners, lastly staring at Murray and laughing in her face.

CHAPTER 76.
REJOICE! REJOICE! REJOICE!

THE footage filmed by Alfred was being broadcast on the stadium's big screens. Wembley was silent. A few gasps, one or two shrieks, broke the hush. But most of the 70,000 spectators stared with awe at the pictures.

George Fuad, on his feet in the Royal Box, watched the video transmission.

The quality was poor, and for that he could have roasted Alfred. But you could make things out if you looked hard enough.

You could make out Nimrod.

The crowd held its breath.

George held his, too.

All the sacrifices had been worth it. All the sweat, all the tears, all the blood had been justified.

George was elated.

He was transfixed by the footage.

Now, Nimrod, through the static and interference, could be seen listening for something – cocking his huge head to the right.

The monster had already killed Laxman. Torn the mercenary in two. It terrified the crowd when George had replayed the clip. And fear was a good thing.

Let them see what could become of them if they piss me off, thought George.

Better even than Laxman's death was the apparent demise of Aaliyah Sinclair. Nimrod had tossed her around, and George presumed the impact would have injured her badly, at the very least.

He was impatient to get Nimrod back to Britain. With the Great Hunter at his side, there would be no chance of a rebellion, no hope for insurgents. The people would fear. They would worship. They would behave.

He wondered how Alfred would transport the god. He'd better have a plan. George would have no qualms about sacrificing his brother for this cause if he had to.

No one was safe. No one except him.

The other Nebuchadnezzars had warned him not to try and resurrect Nimrod. Their pledge, they said, was to the trinity. It was to re-establish Babylon. Build a golden city of slaves and vampires. That was their ancient oath. It had nothing to do with digging up the deadly creator of the undead. That was playing with fire, they'd told him.

"And you'll get burnt, George," they had warned.

He laughed to himself.

He glanced behind him at the Nebs in attendance. They were pale with shock. Some were obviously horrified by what they were seeing on the big screen. They were all mouth and no bollocks. They talked the talk, but most refused to walk the walk. They were like those armchair executioners George hated – they demanded the re-introduction of capital punishment, but ask them to flick the switch, pull the trigger, or empty the syringe, and they would baulk.

Cowards, he thought. *Gutless, spineless, cowards.*

Fuck them, he said to himself.

There was more crying and shrieking in the crowd. Maybe some of the kids were frightened. But that was a good thing. Instil fear in them at a young age, and they wouldn't rebel when they got older.

George bit his lip. He felt a nervous twinge in his belly. The cries of terror spread.

What's the matter with them? he thought.

It was time for some motivation.

He grabbed the microphone: "Rejoice! Rejoice! Rejoice! Our enemies are dead. The path is clear. We won't be stopped. Rust is gone from this city. Rust and decay. They're gone. Only gold and diamonds, now. They'll pave the streets, people. I promise you, Britain will be resurrected."

He still sensed nervousness in the crowd. He wanted them to fear. He wanted them to dread. But he didn't want them to be disgusted by what they saw. They had to appreciate the terror. Be in awe of it but not be appalled by it.

He put his hand over the mike and said to a nearby Nebuchadnezzar militia man, "Get on the line to General Vince and tell him to get the fucking prisoners out – we need some light entertainment."

The militia man left the Royal Box.

A voice behind him said, "Can we control this creature?" The man was a former Liberal Democrat MP and a peer of the realm, who was one of George's political advisors.

"Of course we can," he answered.

"We know nothing of this *thing*," said Zella Shaw, a well-known actress who George fancied. Or had fancied until she started to complain. "It seems uncontrollable."

"Everything can be controlled, darling," George told her.

He looked up at the screen. Through the debris of transmission, Nimrod's size and might could be seen. He had a huge, powerful body. Bulging muscles strained against the leathery skin. The claws were like daggers. The fangs were like a dinosaur's. The creature looked unstoppable. Doubt crept into George's mind for a moment.

Maybe this thing can't *be restrained*, he thought. *Maybe I'm wrong. Maybe Alfred should sacrifice himself right now, blow the whole place up and bury the bastard thing for another five thousand years*.

The crowd started booing.

George looked down towards the pitch.

Black-shirts led the traitors along the walkway.

The doubts George had were momentarily put on hold.

Christine Murray headed the line of traitors, followed by her son. Then came Liz Wilson, the Chinese girl, and three Nebuchadnezzars who had led an attempted coup against George soon after his victory in yesterday's election. It had been nipped in the bud quickly. He had moles everywhere. Spies who would betray their own families if it meant not being excommunicated. That was the threat issued to any Neb thinking of turning against George:

"We'll remove your mark, take the red away from you, and then you'll be nothing but vampire meat."

He was creating a republic of fear, where mother would grass on son, daughter on father. Kids would be asked by teachers if their parents said bad things about Britain around the dinner table. Citizens would put their country first, their families second. Just like all good religions. Just like Jesus demanded of his disciples.

It was coming up to 9.00pm. The sun was going down.

Nearly feeding time.

George spoke into the microphone:

"Here comes the entertainment, ladies and gents. These are the traitors who wanted to destroy your future. They wanted to create hatred and war between vampires and humans, between citizens and Nebuchadnezzars. But we won't let them poison New Britain."

A huge cheer went around the stadium.

That's better, he thought.

Off mike, he turned to his guests in the Royal Box and said, "Now you lot sit down and stop complaining, or I'll rip off your marks, and you can join that bunch in the cage."

Down on the pitch, militia men tied the prisoners to the seven poles.

George looked up at the screen. There was no more footage. He tutted. He'd have to get back in touch with Alfred, tell him to upload some more video.

He sat back in his seat and flipped open the laptop that stood on a small table next to him.

The link to Hillah was down.

His phone rang.

He answered it.

"What the fuck's the matter with you?" he said when he heard Alfred whimpering.

His brother said, "Georgie, I have to get out of here."

"Stay where you are."

"We can't control this creature."

"Tell him who you are."

"I don't think he speaks English, George."

"Make him understand."

"I can't make – "

"Make him understand, Alfred, or don't bother coming home. We need Nimrod."

"We don't need him. We have power without him."

George fumed. “Don’t you fucking contradict me, son. This is our plan. You’ve wanted this as much as I have. So now you’re turning yellow?”

“George, I might die.”

“Then fucking die, but do not let me down.”

He cut off the call. He shuddered with rage. Down on the pitch, the prisoners were ready. He tried to focus on what was going to happen. But it was hard to control his fury. Hard to stop those doubts from creeping into his head again.

CHAPTER 77.
WAITING FOR UNDEATH.

WHEN they tied his hands to the pole, David had flexed his wrists. Tightened his fists, just to expand the muscles and the ligaments a little bit. After they'd bound him and attached the rope to the pole, he relaxed the tension.

And there was just the tiniest bit of give in the rope.

The crowd was jeering. People were throwing things. Cans and bottles, food. Some were even ripping seats out and tossing them towards the centre circle. They clattered off the cage. But the wire wasn't going to hold for long. It buckled and bent as the missiles smashed into it. The militia men were panicking. They were being pelted too, and they didn't like it.

They fired shots into the air. A voice over the loudspeaker system asked the crowd to quieten down.

It did the trick, although the booing continued.

David started to ease his right wrist out of the rope. There was hardly any give. Hardly any, but enough. Millimetres, probably. He squeezed slowly, rotating his wrist. The rope chafed. His skin burned. But he ignored the pain. He had to get free. He had to try and save his mum.

He glanced at her. She looked terrified.

"It'll be OK, I promise," he called out to her.

She looked him in the eye and said she loved him.

Tears welled. His eyes burned.

He kept twisting his hand in the rope, easing it out. His wrist really hurt now. Blood trickled down the twine.

The crowd bayed. The night closed in. Panic suddenly filled him, making his guts icy cold. Would this be his last sunset? Would this be his last darkness? He started to breathe deeply, trying to master his fear, thinking, *What would Jake do, what would Jake do?*

Jake would keep trying.

So David did the same.

He was nearly up to his knuckle now. The bones ached. The skin of his hands had been torn away. They were raw. They were bloody.

He looked towards Kwan Mei. She stared at him. She'd seen what he was doing, and her eyes urged him on. Next to Mei was Liz Wilson. She was humming to herself, staring up at the sky. Tears poured down her cheeks. She'd given up and was waiting for death. He wondered if he could save her, too. Save them all. He tried to come up with a plan – how to get out of here once he was free. He sweated and ached. No plan came. But his hand was coming free. It was really close, now.

The sun was nearly completely gone.

The vampires would soon be released.

They would pour along the walkway and into the cage, and they would slaughter David, his mum, Mei, and the others. *We won't stand a chance*, he thought. Death would be painful.

Death followed by undeath.

It panicked him, and he worked his hand harder, nearly cracking the knuckles as he wrenched them through the rope. He gritted his teeth against the searing pain.

He had to keep going.

He had to be like Jake.

If he died, so be it. As long as he'd done his best. As long as he'd been brave and had tried to save his mum.

His wrist came loose.

He gasped.

His hand was numb.

The sun fell.

He didn't have much time, but worse, he didn't know what to do now.

CHAPTER 78.
QUEEN AND COUNTRY.

EDIZ Ün was parked on Rutherford Way, next to what had once been the busy Wembley Retail Park. It was a few hundred yards away from the stadium. All the shops that used to be there – Halfords, Carpetright, Comet – were gone. They weren't of any use in a vampire nation. No one had any money anymore. Everyone was focused on just one thing – trying to survive.

The stadium was lit up. Floodlights drowned it in a powerful glow. Ediz could hear the rumble of the crowd and the crack of gunfire.

He and the half-dozen men with him in the van had followed the stream of spectators earlier. He had asked someone what was happening, and the man, accompanied by two smiling children, had looked at Ediz and said, "They're executing those traitors, you know? Those friends of Jake Lawton. That bastard who started all this. You should come. You really should."

Now, as darkness crept over the city, Ediz sat in the driver's seat, waiting. He was tired. He hadn't slept. He'd spent the whole day hitch-hiking to London and then had gathered the remnants of Mei's army together. He'd managed to contact seven lads, all of them from London.

Ediz stared at the stadium.

"What's the plan, man?" said a young Pakistani called Ab Khan. "The seven of us going to rush Wembley, overpower all the Neb guards, and save the princess?"

Ediz shrugged. "Maybe." He looked at Ab. "You still ready to fight?"

Ab nodded.

"You too?" Ediz asked the guys in the back of the van.

They nodded, or murmured, that they were ready.

"You know," said Ediz, eyes back on the stadium, "we're the only ones standing up for this country now. All the people who called us names, who spat at us, told us to go home – "

"Even though we was born here, man," said Ab.

"Yeah," said Ediz, "even though some of us were born here. All of them people, they're gone now. Gone, or given up. We can save this country, make it better. We can make it *ours*, man."

"And we can kill vampires," said another guy in the back.

"Sure, we can kill vampires," said Ediz.

He had fought vampires before. He had been with Kwan Mei at Parliament Square when humans had gone to war against vampires. He had stood with her, and she had stood with him. They had held the front line. Thousands of them. Men and women like the seven of them in the van. Men and women considered foreign by most of the population. Men and women gathered by Mei.

Different people from different countries. Different religions. Different colours. Different languages.

They'd all stuck together against a common enemy.

Mei had learned how to lead them. How to bring them together under a common cause. She could wave any flag and they would follow her, even though her language was different to theirs.

She would be his inspiration now.

She would be *their* inspiration.

"So you got a plan?" said Ab.

"We have to fight again, like before."

"Sure, but they have guns. As well as vampires."

"I don't care, Ab. We have to find a way. I'm not giving up."

They lapsed into silence.

"You know the British Army are still fighting in some places?" said one man in the back. "I mean, I used to hate the army, but I guess now they're on our side."

Another said, "They will not fight with foreigners."

"They might, for Britain," said Ediz. "That's what they do – for Queen and country."

"Will they listen to us?" said Ab.

"I don't know." He thought for a while. "But I think I know who they might listen to."

"Who?" said Ab.

He started the van, and headed towards Central London. He reckoned if the roads were clear, and if he drove like crazy, he could make it in twenty minutes.

But he didn't know if he had twenty minutes.

CHAPTER 79.
DESPERATE MEASURES.

GEORGE was getting worried. The crowd bayed for blood. But it was becoming uncertain as to whose blood they were baying for. The spectators had been clearly angry at the traitors when they had been marched out. But now the mob had turned its fury towards the militia, who'd started firing in the air in an effort to regain control.

He felt the heat of panic prickle his nape.

It was up to him to regain some control.

"Get that screen working again," he told a lackey.

The lackey scurried away.

George opened the laptop and clicked on the Skype icon.

On his mobile phone, he texted Alfred, telling him to sign on so they could talk.

It took a couple of minutes, in which George nearly chewed his fingernails down to the quick, for Alfred's mug to appear on screen.

Without even addressing his brother, George said, "Stick your camera on Nimrod again; I want the crowd to see him."

"He's gone."

"Gone? What do you mean gone?"

"Just gone. Stormed off into the darkness down there somewhere."

"Well, go after him, you idiot."

"But, George, there… there was this woman… a… a ghost… she spoke to him, and he followed – "

"I don't give a shit – go after him or don't bother coming home."

He slammed the laptop shut again. His blood was boiling. The MP asked him what was happening.

"Are we going to execute these traitors or not, George?"

He said nothing.

Zella Shaw said, "George, the crowd will flood the pitch soon, then you'll have dead traitors on your hands anyway – but they'll think you weak. They'll see that mob rule can overcome us. Get is sorted."

His temples throbbed. He was hot and sweaty, his belly grinding. He felt sick.

He picked up his phone and dialled General Howard Vince, who was down in the players' tunnel, supposedly organizing this fiasco.

Vince answered.

"Shoot into the crowd," said George.

"What?" said Vince.

"Fire into the fucking crowd, Howard. Teach them a lesson."

"I think that's unwise, George."

"Don't fucking *George* me, you fat cunt – follow orders, or I'll find someone who will."

"George – Mr Fuad – Prime Minister – if you shoot civilians in a situation like this, when we haven't yet truly established ourselves, you are risking a rebellion."

"Then I'll crush it. Do as I say, Vince, or I'll have you demoted to private quicker than you can say 'cunt', is that clear? Cunt?"

Seconds later, the shooting started.

Zella said, "What are you doing?"

He wheeled to face her and the other Nebs in the Royal Box.

"This is my country," he said, "and my game. I made this. I acheived it. None of you. I've sacrificed loads for this. You've done fuck all. So don't any of you say a fucking word, or I'll have you excommunicated – and you fucking know what that means."

The sound of gunfire filled the stadium.

Adrenaline coursed through George.

Behind him, down on the pitch, it sounded like chaos.

"Sir," a militia man whispered in his ear.

"What?" he said.

The militia man gestured towards the pitch.

George wanted to scream but managed to stop himself.

The crowd had already started spilling on to the pitch.

Some militia men were running away.

And the seven poles where the seven traitors had been tied moments ago were now empty.

CHAPTER 80.
THE WOMAN.

HILLAH, IRAQ – 9.11PM (GMT + 3 HOURS), 20/21 MAY, 2011

ALFRED crawled through the dust and falling debris. Deeper into Irkalla. Deeper into hell. Obeying his brother's command. Willing to sacrifice himself for George. Scared, but ready to die for the better Fuad.

I have to do as he says, he thought. *George knows best.*

So he crawled on hands and knees through the rubble, through the falling masonry. He crawled past Laxman's lower body. Blood and gore spilled from the stump of the mercenary's waist. His guts were on the ground. His pelvic bone jutted out from the twisted remains.

Alfred curled his lip and fought the nausea. He grabbed Laxman's submachine gun and then fished through the mercenary's pockets. He found some ammo. He managed to load the gun, despite his trembling hands.

He moved past the body. He was shaking. He was sweating. He felt sick and weak and wanted to put his head down and sleep this nightmare off.

It wasn't meant to happen like this, he thought. He must have fallen asleep because he and George had everything planned, and it was supposed to go smoothly.

He got to his feet and staggered onwards. He clambered over mounds of rubble. He fell and got up again, fell and got up. His chest hurt. His hands and knees bled. Sweat poured down his face. His breath was short, his mouth dry.

He groaned in desperation.

He wanted to get to Nimrod and tell the Lord of Irkalla that the Fuads were his allies – his servants, his disciples.

But that beautiful, pale-skinned woman in the billowing white dress had appeared. She had spoken to the Great Hunter in a language Alfred didn't recognize. It wasn't Arabic, which he knew, and it wasn't Persian, which he could understand. But whatever it was, her words had sent Nimrod off. She had then curled her lip menacingly at Alfred before sweeping after Nimrod.

He panted as he scrabbled over another pile of rubble. The quake had subsided now. At least it didn't seem he would be crushed under falling debris. But that was small comfort. Ahead of him lay darkness. The towering pillars stretched for miles. He was seeing the ruins of buildings, of a town. Empty windows stared down at him. Towers leaned precariously. Doorways invited him in.

He kept going, weaving through what had once been streets, scaling walls and dunes of stone.

"Where are you?" Alfred shouted. "Where are you, Lord Nimrod?"

His voice was lost in the darkness.

He stumbled through a gateway and stopped dead, staring in awe.

It appeared that he had entered some sort of arena. A huge area the size of two football pitches lay before him. It was covered in debris. The field was hemmed in by banks of seating that had been chiselled into the rock. At the far end of the area lay an opening – a dark mouth that drew Alfred. He stumbled through the wreckage, and then, in the very centre of the arena, came to a halt.

He held his breath.

He sensed something.

She emerged from the dark mouth. A vision in white. She shimmered, as if light came from within her. She stepped into the arena and came towards him, gliding over the debris.

Her pitch-black hair fanned out. Her eyes burned red. As she came closer, Alfred weakened. He knew he was in the presence of a devastating power. A sexual energy that could destroy him in an instant.

About ten steps away, she stopped.

"I am Ereshkigal, bride of Nimrod," she said. "Who are you, and what do you want with my Lord?"

"Why… why did you… send him away?"

"To protect him."

"But… but he's… he's in no danger, look," said Alfred, and he yanked the red band from his hair. "Look, I'm… I'm a Nebuchadnezzar."

"What's that to the Great Hunter?"

He fell to his knees.

"I… I am his servant. Your servant. My brother… my brother… we've stolen a country for your… your Lord… slaves for him… a throne… and together… together we can… can rule the whole world."

"Why would my Lord wish to rule the world with you?"

"Because… because… "

He stuttered. He had no answer. Why would a god want to share power? George had never really thought about that.

Ereshkigal was waiting for an answer.

Alfred whimpered.

A low growl came from the doorway at the far end of the area. The sound chilled Alfred's insides. All the strength had left his body now.

Nimrod appeared. He was monstrous. Part-dragon, part-human, part-bull. He dragged his huge, tree-trunk legs through the rubble, scattering piles of masonry as if they were pebbles.

The monster stood behind the woman, and it growled in her ear.

Ereshkigal translated the Great Hunter's words.

"My Lord wishes to know what use he can make of you, other than sacrifice?"

"I… we… my brother and me… we can get you out of here, give you a city, give you blood," he said. "You can't do this yourself, my Lord. Not in the light. Not in the day. We can be your servants. Your disciples. We can ferry you from nation to nation, watch you lay them to waste. And then, then you can return to your capital, to London, to England, and you can rest there, and reign."

Ereshkigal turned and whispered in Nimrod's ear.

Nimrod growled.

"I have been to your country," said the woman. "I travelled there with Richard Cœur de Lion. Melek-Ric."

"Richard… the Lionheart?" Alfred said.

"He was my enemy," she said.

"Was he?"

"And my lover."

"R-r-right… "

"My enemies are often my lovers."

"Well, I ain't an enemy, and I – "

"Weak enemies die, strong enemies bed me."

"Oh – "

"Vlad was strong. I bedded him and I slayed him. Richard was strong. I bedded him and I slayed him. His friend Saladin, also. He lay with me and died at my hands. And Jake Lawton – "

"Jake Lawton?"

"He will be my lover when this is done."

"Lawton?" said Alfred. "No. Lawton has to die. He… he wants to kill your… this… Lord Nimrod. That's why he's here."

"Jake Lawton led me to Irkalla. He guided me home. I owe him some gratitude. He is an honourable man. But he will not kill my Great Hunter," she said. "He will join him in my bed. He has ancient blood in him. He has been knitted from the heart of Nimrod."

"What… what the fuck do you mean?"

"He has the skin of my husband's children in him, woven into his fabric, into his being."

Alfred gawped. He didn't understand what was going on or why this woman was saying this stuff. He held up the red mark.

"This," he said, "this… this is the skin of Kea, Kakash, and Kasdeja. The trinity. Born of… of Nimrod's body. Torn from him. Look. This skin. I told you. It's my protection. It marks me as a Nebuchadnezzar. A servant… servant of the… the trinity."

"Lawton does not *wear* this – it is *part* of him."

Everything was going wrong. He had a moment of clarity – it was time to cut his losses. Nimrod wasn't going to join forces with him and George. It was more likely that he was going to join forces with Lawton. Alfred had to get out of here. Or he'd be sacrificed. The thought of suffering in the same way Laxman had horrified him. He managed to get to his feet and retreated a few steps.

He was about to say something when a scream pierced the air, and a figure shot from behind a shattered pillar.

It was a woman.

It was Aaliyah Sinclair.

She wielded a spear, six feet long and rusted, an artefact she'd obviously discovered in the ruins.

Nimrod wheeled.

Ereshkigal hissed.

Alfred stumbled backwards.

Sinclair was covered in blood. Her clothes were torn. She looked wild. She was shrieking.

She drove the spear into Nimrod's thigh.

The god howled.

Irkalla trembled.

Sinclair yanked the spear free of Nimrod's leg.

She prepared to drive it into his body again.

The god swatted her away.

But she sprang to her feet, screeching once more.

She launched another attack.

She is fearless, thought Alfred. *She is foolish.*

Ereshkigal showed her teeth and got ready to counter. But Nimrod shoved her out of the way. He growled something at her. The woman in white retreated and faded into the gloom.

Nimrod met Sinclair head on, hacking away the spear and grabbing her around the waist.

He shook her violently, and she yowled.

Alfred started to sneak away.

Nimrod tossed Sinclair.

She slammed into stones and bones cracked.

She struggled to her feet, moaning. Her right arm hung limp. Her left knee was twisted awkwardly.

Nimrod prowled towards her, growling.

Sinclair shouted a name:

"Jake!"

And then again:

"Jake, don't leave me here to die! Jake, I love – "

Nimrod swept her up and roared, bringing her up to his open mouth and his knife-like fangs.

CHAPTER 81. LEAVE NO ONE BEHIND.

LAWTON clawed at the earth.

The cave-in had blocked off the tunnels. It was full of soil and stone.

Lawton's hands were bloody. He was hurting all over. Those voices in his head were a chorus, now. They seemed to chant his name. They were calling to him... *One of us... one of us...* but he tried to ignore them. It was hard – they were persistent.

He looked over his shoulder.

Goga stood there, leaning on his cane.

"Thanks for all your help," said Lawton.

Goga said nothing.

"I abandoned her," said Lawton, more to himself than to Goga.

But he was still angry with the Romanian over Aaliyah. Lawton wanted to hit him. Hit him hard, so he wouldn't get up. But instead he put his energy into digging. He felt exhausted. His head hurt like hell. His eye socket throbbed. He was convinced he could see through it now. Through an eye that wasn't there.

How could that be?

Ereshkigal had said he had vampire blood in him. The DNA of the undead. The genetics of an immortal.

But he didn't want to live forever. He wanted to grow old. He wanted to stumble about and tuck himself up under shawls with Aaliyah. He wanted to curl up with her in front of a fire and drink soup. He wanted to hold her hand as he died peacefully in his sleep when he was a hundred years old. He wanted Aaliyah to kiss him goodbye as he slipped away. Aaliyah, whom he'd abandoned.

Leave no one behind – that's what he'd learned in the army. You got your mates out whether they were dead or alive. That was the pledge.

He'd promised Aaliyah he'd never let her down. Never leave her. But he'd broken his promise. And he felt less of a man because of it.

He kept digging. The earth smelled stale.

Although the quakes had diminished now, there were still some aftershocks.

He wondered how much damage had been done to the city of Hillah. The disaster would have brought the Iraqi army into the area. Perhaps they'd grow suspicious of what was going on down here and send a few squadrons underground. They might come in useful if he had to take Nimrod on.

As he clawed away at the soil and stone, he thought of home. He wondered about Murray and David and Mei and the others.

Maybe I'll never see them again, he thought. *But the least I can do is make sure they have a future.*

No – he *would* make it out.

He *would* find Aaliyah, and they *would* escape.

This would be his destiny – *their* destiny.

Write your own future, he told himself.

He clawed at the earth.

CHAPTER 82. CHAOS.

London – 9.17pm (GMT), 20 May, 2011

"WHERE are you going?" said his mother.

"I'm going to kill Fuad," said David.

"No, we have to get out of here"

"You go, Mum. I'm going after him."

They had fled into the stands. The crowd was panicking. The militia was firing. Hand-to-hand fighting had erupted, civilians tussling with black-shirts who had been mingling with the spectators in the stands. There were dozens already dead.

In the chaos, David and his mum had managed to release the other five, and Kwan Mei had gone racing off to arm herself. She wanted a fight, so she'd gone looking for one. Liz Wilson sat in the stands.

"We have to get out of here," said his mum again.

"You go, get Mrs Wilson out of here."

"David, you listen to me – "

"Mum, don't order me about. I love you, but you can't tell me what to do. I have been on my own for years. I've had to survive.

I've had to make decisions. And I am making one now. Take Mrs Wilson out of here, and I'll find you."

His mum started to protest, but Wilson said, "I'd listen to your son, Christine. He seems to know what he's doing."

David kissed and hugged his mum. It felt good, and for a moment he was a small boy again, safe in his mother's arms. Every dark thing dwindled. The world was full of light and peace.

He slipped out of her embrace, and the darkness returned. The noise of the mob hinted at violence. The shooting continued, although the militia men's aim was now lower than it was – and soon they'd be firing directly into the crowd.

David ran off, weaving through the mob as he made his way out of the exit tunnel.

The walkway was full of people. They were fleeing the arena. Families with young children getting away from the trouble brewing inside Wembley.

David went to a door marked No Entrance. Doors marked No Entrance were always a good sign. They got you places you wanted to go. The places other people didn't want you to find. He wrenched it open and raced up the narrow stairwell.

At the top of the stairs, he looked out of the window. Across from him was the Royal Box, where George Fuad had been lording it over the mob. David had to get to him.

He crashed through a door and into a corridor lined with red carpet, the walls decorated with photographs of England football games.

David ran down the corridor.

CHAPTER 83. DEATH AND ROSES.

HILLAH, IRAQ – 9.29PM (GMT + 3 HOURS), 20/21 MAY, 2011

"IRKALLA," said Goga, hobbling past Lawton.

"Looks like a shithole to me."

"This is the capital of the underworld, home to Nimrod."

"Hope he's happy here."

Lawton was exhausted. His hands were red raw. His bones ached. But he had no time to rest. He got moving, following Goga into the darkness.

Rubble was piled high everywhere. Pillars teetered, and some had collapsed entirely. But hundreds were still standing. Lawton stared up. He furrowed his brow, not comprehending the scale of this underworld city.

"How can we be so deep underground?" he said. "Surely we've not come that far?"

Goga's voice echoed back:

"This is a place of nightmares, Lawton. What you see may not be real. Men have been driven mad here. Abraham was a maniac after he came out. A lunatic prophet who nearly killed his own son because he claimed to hear voices."

Lawton knelt and took the Spear of Abraham out of his rucksack. He detached the weapon and brandished it as two swords.

He followed Goga into the cavern, calling out to the Romanian – but Jake got no answer.

Shit, he thought, tightening his grip on the swords.

He moved carefully around a tower of rubble and then stopped dead.

Laxman, he said to himself, seeing the torso lying in the dust. The mercenary's head lay a few yards away. The eyes were wide open, as if his death had come as a great shock to him. It must have been traumatic – he'd been cut in half. Lawton scanned the area and spotted Laxman's legs. He thought for a moment. He should get going. He fought an urge. But he couldn't defeat it. Finally, he succumbed.

He retrieved Laxman's lower half, and put the mercenary's body back together as best he could. It still looked as if the man had been torn in half, but Lawton hoped he'd brought him some dignity in death. He knelt and shut Laxman's eyes before continuing his journey.

Up ahead, he could see the arena.

He gazed with awe.

What did they do here? he thought.

A scream came from the ruins.

Lawton recognized the voice.

He'd know it anywhere.

She was alive.

He bolted towards the colosseum.

As he approached the entrance, he saw figures inside the arena.

And one of them was huge and monstrous.

He kept going.

He was about to race through to the arena when a flash of white shot out of the darkness and crashed into him. He was sent sprawling. He hit the ground hard. She straddled him. Her smell was strong – death and roses. She pinned his arms to the ground, but he kept hold of the swords. He'd not let them go for anyone. They'd have to kill him first.

"Maybe I will," said Ereshkigal.

He gasped.

How had she known?

"You are, bone and blood, a hybrid creature, Jake Lawton. My husband's spirit crawls through you. You shall be my best lover."

She opened her mouth and bent towards his throat.

CHAPTER 84
KILL THEM ALL.

WEMBLEY STADIUM, LONDON – 9.33PM (GMT), 20 MAY, 2011

DAVID lurked at the bottom of the stairs leading up to the Royal Box. It was situated in the middle of the North Stand. Normally you would have had dozens of security guards strutting around, and the public would never have gotten access into the box.

But these days were different.

These days there was chaos.

No real security, no real strategy.

The Nebuchadnezzars gave the impression that they were in charge, that they were organized, but in reality they were in disarray.

They were leading Britain into anarchy. No order would exist, just savagery.

Shouts and screams filtered from the stadium. A stampede hurtled through the walkways and the corridors. The whole arena shook and rumbled as 70,000 people made their escape.

David looked for a weapon and found a clump of masonry.

Silhouettes filled the stairwell above him.

George Fuad and some of his companions came down the stairs.

David skulked in the shadows.

He heard Fuad speak. The man was raging. His voice got louder. David heard "fuck" quite a lot. Fuad got to the bottom of the stairs, appearing right next to David, who pounced.

But Fuad saw him coming.

He lifted his arm to protect himself.

David struck him on the shoulder.

Fuad grunted.

Neb militia rushed in.

They mobbed David, forcing him to the ground. They were rough, shoving his face into the concrete, pulling his hair, punching him in the ribs, swearing at him. He was already hurting from the attack in the players' tunnel. His body was wracked in pain, and the further thrashing made it much worse. He wanted to scream but didn't – there was no way he was screaming for Fuad.

"Get the little cunt to his feet," said Fuad.

They picked him up.

"Fucking shit," said Fuad. "You could've broken my arm."

A militia man pulled a gun. He cocked it. He put the barrel to David's temple. The boy got ready to die.

"Don't shoot him," said Fuad. "Too quick. Where's your mum, you little cunt?"

"Fuck you," said David.

"Hit him," said Fuad. "Very hard."

The gunman pistol-whipped him. Right across the scalp. It hurt like hell and brought tears to David's eyes. Blood poured from the head wound.

They threw him on the ground and someone kicked him in the ribs. He grunted, the air knocked out of him. The pain was awful. But he was determined not to cry. He bit his lip.

Fuad was smiling down at him.

Someone said, “We have to go, Mr Fuad. The situation here is not good.”

“You go,” said Fuad. “Leave me with the kid.”

“George,” said a white-haired man in a pin-striped suit, “George, we have to – ”

“Fuck off, the lot of you,” Fuad shouted. “Me and this kid, we got things to discuss.”

The others drifted away. One or two militia men hung around, but Fuad told them to back off.

“He’s just a stupid little kid. Just a boy who cries for his mummy.”

“Shut up, you bastard,” said David.

“I should cut out your tongue – and feed it to your mumsey. Fellas, give me a knife, then fuck off.”

One of the militia guys handed Fuad a knife.

“Sir,” said the black-shirt, “are you sure you’re – ”

“Fuck off, I said. Go get my car. Tell the commanders to shoot the rioters. Shoot everyone. Kill them all. I’ll sort this kid out. Send some vampires here – six or seven. Tell ’em it’s dinner time.”

The Nebs left.

The roar of the crowd was loud. The stadium trembled as they fled.

“It’s over for you, Fuad,” said David. “The people hate you. You’ll have civil war on your hands.”

Fuad kicked him in the ribs. A white light flashed before David’s eyes as the pain surged through him. He thought he would pass out, but he managed to stay conscious.

Suddenly his scalp felt as if it were on fire.

Fuad had grabbed his hair and was dragging him around. He straddled David and got in his face. The man smelled of sweat. His breath was fetid. Spit oozed from his mouth. He pressed the knife to David’s cheek.

“Right, you little shit, let’s cut your tongue out.”

Fuad pried David's mouth open.

David writhed, trying to fight. But Fuad was strong. Panic coursed through the boy. He was in pain. Every inch of his body, it seemed, screamed in agony. He felt like throwing up. He had no strength to fight Fuad off. And now he was plucking David's tongue out, preparing to slice it off.

David tried to struggle, but Fuad had his knee on his chest, keeping him down.

Fuad laughed and put the cold steel against David's tongue.

David tried to scream.

Then Fuad lurched forward, his grip on David loosening. He fell sideways. The knife spun from his grasp. Blood splashed across David's cheek, and for a second he thought it was his own.

But then he saw the wound on Fuad's skull.

And he looked up. Standing over him, a rock in her hands, was his mum.

He mouthed the word:

"Mum... "

She smiled at him and then launched herself at Fuad.

She shrieked with rage and pummelled the man with the rock. Fuad defended himself, taking vicious blows to his arms. And then he kicked out desperately – and took his attacker's legs out from under her.

David's mum hit the ground.

Fuad staggered to his feet.

"Help me," he called, "help – "

David lunged for the knife. He scuttled over to Fuad. He drove the knife into Fuad's chest.

"You fucking bastard," cried Fuad.

He was trying to pull the knife out of his chest.

"You fucking little cunty bastard."

David's mum pulled him away from Fuad.

"Oh, that fucking hurts," cried Fuad, yanking the blade out of his chest.

There was blood everywhere. David could smell it, the coppery odour making him dizzy. And if he could smell it, he knew that something else could also smell it.

He stiffened.

"Mum, we've got to get out of here – "

"Too late," she said.

Seven vampires loomed from the shadows and circled them.

CHAPTER 85. THE BROADCAST.

LEICESTER SQUARE, LONDON – 9.42PM (GMT), 20 MAY, 2011

"I AIN'T worn a suit in years," said Old Bill. "Do I need to wear one, you reckon?"

Ediz said, "You look very smart, Bill."

"Smart or not, mate, I don't know why I need to wear one."

"Are we ready?" said Ab Khan. He trained the camera on Old Bill. Ediz adjusted the old man's tie.

They were in an abandoned underground station near Soho. They had found Bill near Leicester Square, where he usually hung out. He'd survived the vampire attacks thanks to the red mark David had given him. Ediz and his crew also wore marks. Lots of Mei's army had them. They always had spares. They were spoils of war, stolen from the bodies of dead Nebs.

Ediz had heard a lot about Bill and had met him a few months ago for the first time. The old soldier was David's friend. The tramp also knew Jake Lawton, and he seemed to have a lot of contacts in the military.

"What am I doing again?" said Bill.

"You are going to speak into that camera there," said Ediz, "and the footage will go out over the internet, and hopefully the British soldiers who are fighting the vampires will hear you, and they won't just fight individually, or in small groups – they'll come out and fight as an army again. That's what you're doing, Bill."

Although TV and radio had been limited since the vampire plague had broken out, the internet had proved vibrant. Some rebels had kept in touch through Facebook and Twitter and BlackBerry Messenger. Fuad's government had yet to shut the social networking sites down. It proved to Ediz how useless the Neb regime really was. He was confident they could be beaten, now.

"Why should they listen to me?" Bill said.

"You are one of them," said Ediz.

"They'd listen to you better – you and your pals have fought for this country. You died for it on the streets," Ab said.

"We're not one of them, though," said Ediz.

Bill nodded. He licked his hand and slicked down his unruly hair. He coughed. He stared at the camera. His image appeared on the computer screen.

"This is feeding live," said Ediz.

"Let's hope people are watching," said Ab.

"Go ahead, Bill," said Ediz.

Bill spoke into the lens:

"Hello. This is a message to all the military guys and gals out there. Those of you who've been left without a regiment because of this anarchy. My name is Bill Goodwin. I'm an old soldier. I served in Northern Ireland, Cyprus, a few other places people don't know about. But since I left the forces, I've fallen on hard times. My country didn't do much to look after me. But still, I took an oath to protect it. Yes, it treated me badly. But that was mostly the politicians' fault. Not the country. Not the name of it and its history. Not the people. I am asking you all – and you don't have to listen to me, an old man on the scrapheap – but I am asking you to lift arms and fight this enemy within that's menacing our country. I know lots of you are fighting. A lot of you, I know, are keeping your heads down. And that's OK. But you know from your experience that if you join forces, nothing can stand in your way. We're the best army in the world. Look, I'm just an old soldier calling out into the darkness and hoping some of my comrades can hear. This new-fangled internet thing, I don't know much about it, but they say it can bring people together. Well, I hope it brings my words to you. I hope you hear it. If you're in London, head for Wembley – there's a ruck going on. If you are in Manchester, or Glasgow, or Cardiff, or wherever, then pull together. Form units. Organize. Take the bastards on. Give 'em no quarter. Lay waste to them. Fight for your mates, like you always do. Then for your Queen. Then your country. Thanks for listening to me."

Ab put the camera down and said, "Brilliant."

"Will it do any good?" said Bill, taking off his tie.

"Hope it will," said Ediz.

"Get me my clothes," he said.

Ediz picked up the pile of smelly old clothes and handed them to Bill.

"You want to wear these again?" he said.

"It's my home," said Bill. "My home. Right, where am I going to get a gun?"

"Gun?" said Ediz.

"You think I'm missing out on the fun?"

CHAPTER 86.
"DIE SLOWLY".

HILLAH, IRAQ – 9.52PM (GMT + 3 HOURS), 20/21 MAY, 2011

ALFRED was terrified. He stayed out of sight behind a boulder as Nimrod sank his teeth into Aaliyah Sinclair's throat.

She screamed and threw her fists at the monster. But it made no difference. Sinclair slumped as the monster bit her on the clavicle.

Nimrod drank a little from her, then let her fall to the ground.

The woman groaned.

She was still alive.

Alfred was wondering what to do – stand up and try to communicate with Nimrod again or just get out of there?

But before he could make a decision, he heard someone approaching from behind.

It was Apostol Goga, hobbling along, using his cane.

Alfred stood up and faced Goga. He pointed the submachine gun at the Romanian.

"Where d'you reckon you're going, Long John?"

Goga kept coming.

Alfred hesitated.

"Ain't you seen my gun, Goga?"

"I have seen."

Alfred backed up, still pointing the weapon at Goga.

"I'll fucking shoot."

"And you will miss," said Goga.

Alfred nervously glanced behind him. Nimrod was just standing there, waiting. But waiting for what? Now and again, the monster nudged Sinclair, but mostly he loitered. Maybe he was disorientated after his resurrection. Maybe he was waiting for orders from that woman in white.

Alfred checked on Goga again.

The Romanian limped towards him.

"You don't think I'll shoot?" said Alfred.

"I said, you may shoot, sir, but you will miss."

Alfred fired. The submachine gun barked. He jerked backwards and saw stars. Pain shot up his arm.

Goga laughed at him.

"You cannot shoot straight," said the Romanian. "Throw me the gun, and I will show you."

Alfred gathered himself. He took two steps forward, still aiming the gun at his target. He was still a little woozy but was determined to blow the Romanian to bits.

And Goga's eyes widened.

Alfred said, "Now you're scared, you fucking – "

Goga turned and started to limp away.

At first, Alfred wanted to laugh at the man and call him a coward.

But then Goga said, "He is coming for you."

Alfred heard the thunder of feet.

He felt the fear race through him.

He whirled round.

Nimrod had shaken off whatever lethargy had taken hold and was coming straight for Alfred.

He seemed to be speaking in that low, guttural voice – words Alfred failed to understand.

He shrieked and begged. His legs felt weak, and the terror had sapped his strength.

He collapsed and crawled away behind some ruins, waiting for Nimrod to dig him out and tear him to pieces.

But then Goga was moving forward again – shuffling towards the advancing Nimrod. He yanked the gold ferrule from his walking stick to reveal a blade.

He thrust, stabbing Nimrod in the leg.

It had little effect.

Then Alfred thought of something. He aimed at Goga and fired. The bullets raked the ground and sliced into Goga's right leg.

The man screamed and his knees buckled. He dropped his cane and hit the ground, groaning. Blood pulsed from his shattered leg.

Alfred buzzed with excitement. He smelled the cordite. It was like a drug. He leapt from his hiding place, ready to take the credit from Nimrod for protecting him.

But the monster didn't seem interested in gratitude. His red eyes fixed on Alfred, and his shoulders hunched as if the monster were ready to attack.

"No… " said Alfred.

She came from nowhere, and Alfred couldn't understand where she got the energy from. Initially, he thought she was dead. Blood poured from her throat. But Aaliyah Sinclair had found the strength to launch another attack on the monster. She struck Nimrod with the spear with which she had stabbed the Great Hunter earlier. Her offense had less potency now. She could not break the beast's skin with the spear. She just didn't have the power to drive it home.

Alfred fired at her.

He missed.

Goga was trying to get up.

Nimrod fended off the woman, shoving her to the ground. She definitely had broken bones and a terrible injury to her neck, where Nimrod had bitten her – but she still had some fight in her. Alfred, for a second, admired Sinclair. But that respect quickly petered out when Nimrod fixed on him again. Alfred shrieked and made a run for a crevice in a wall, stuffing himself in tightly.

Goga laughed at him, calling him a coward.

"You'll die in this hell, Fuad," he said. "Die like the – "

Nimrod stamped on Goga. The huge foot slammed down on the Romanian. It crushed Goga's lower body into the ground. The crack of bones breaking echoed through the caverns, and Goga's squeal of pain made Alfred flinch.

Goga lay in the rubble. He was twisted and broken. Blood spurted from his legs. Bones protruded like branches. He twitched, only just alive. He stared in horror at his ruin of a body.

And then he began to shriek again.

Alfred laughed at him.

He checked that Nimrod's attention had been averted and scuttled out of his hiding place.

He stood over Goga.

The Romanian's eyes were wild, glazed over with madness and pain. He made a terrible, animal noise.

"You can die slowly, you fuck," said Alfred, "I got no bullets left."

Nimrod loomed over Sinclair.

Finish her, thought Alfred. *Finish the bitch.*

It was as if Nimrod had read his mind.

CHAPTER 87.
BAD DECISIONS.

"I CANNOT let him die," said Ereshkigal.

"I cannot let him live," said Lawton.

She had clawed him. Blood ran down his arms and from his cheek.

"Let me drink it better, Jake Lawton," she said.

"No more drinking."

"Let me bite you – then you will be vampire."

"You've got to be joking."

"You're almost vampire already."

"I'd rather die."

"I can do that."

He had heard gunshots. He'd tried to run towards them. He was desperate to save Aaliyah and get her out of there.

But Ereshkigal had him cornered.

"You are the one with wounds," she said. "The one they said would come to kill my Lord husband."

"Don't believe what they say; they just talk bollocks."

"Words spoken thousands of years ago, coming to pass."

"Old news."

"I can't let you fulfil your destiny."

He hesitated. No more jokes: "You can't stop it."

He sprang at her, and she pounced on him. They came together, limbs twisting together, flesh on flesh. He tried to stab at her with the swords, but she avoided the blows, spinning, ducking, bending, batting away his thrusts. She slipped inside his guard. Her jaw snapped shut inches from his throat.

He pushed her head back by forcing his left forearm under her chin, baring her throat, and he lifted the bone sword in his right hand to strike her.

But he hesitated, looking into her eyes – the eyes of a woman.

How could he beat a woman?

She's not a woman, he told himself.

She's an incubus.

A vampire.

A witch who murdered children.

He'd had no difficulties killing female vampires before – even his own former girlfriends – but for some reason, Ereshkigal was different. She had a strange hold over him.

Ereshkigal took advantage of his indecision and kicked him in the leg. He lost his grip and she was loose. She attacked again. He was forced to retreat. He hacked at her with the swords. She parried the blows, driving him backwards.

They wheeled violently, Lawton trying to repel her, Ereshkigal trying to tear at him.

"Fuck me or kill me," she said.

"I bet you say that to all the boys."

"I said it to Vlad. I said it the Lionheart. I said it to Saladin. And do you know which it was they did?"

Finding strength, he pried her hands off his throat and threw her aside. She rolled like a cat and was up on her feet again.

"I don't fuck dead things," he said.

She smiled. "But you are nearly dead yourself, my darling."

"Feels like it."

"You are nearly *undead*."

He'd fucked up – fucked up badly. It was the worst decision he'd made in a life of making bad decisions. But when he'd had the eye made in Rotterdam many weeks ago, he thought it would make him invincible against vampires. He wouldn't have to have the red mark pinned to his clothing, where he could lose it in a tussle. He'd have it implanted in his body. He'd lost an eye, so why not make an artificial one using the scarlet skin of the vampire trinity? Encase it in a glass eyeball, pop it in – protected for life.

But no.

The fool that he was had not taken into consideration that the flesh was still living. It had desires, wants, needs. It craved to exist again. It wanted to be part of a living thing. And he was that living thing. He had been infected.

"I'll never be what you are," he said. "I'd rather die."

"I offer you that."

"Won't take you up on it just now, thanks."

"You are slowly changing, Jake," she said. "You will become the dead. Let me hurry it along, now. Let me drink from you. Like I did in that cell. Do you remember? My touch? My teeth in you? Inside you? Your veins pulsing out blood, your life, into my mouth, and I swallowed you. Do you remember when you grew hard against me? I will make you grow hard again, and you will have my dead flesh as I make yours dead, too."

"I'll kill you first."

"I'm already dead."

"I'll kill you again."

"You are being ripped apart. You are at war with yourself. Do you hear the voices of the dead calling you?"

He did. He shook his head, trying to get rid of them. But they sang there now, a song of his doom.

“Jake, are you human or are you not? Soon, there will be an answer, and it will not be the one you wish for.”

He tensed, his hands gripping the handles of the swords. He’d have to finish this before that decision was taken out of his hands – before he’d lost all sense of who he was.

He was ready to launch himself at her when a cry echoed from the coliseum.

He recognized her voice.

“Aaliyah,” he said.

He took his eye off Ereshkigal.

He knew immediately he’d made a mistake.

Another bad decision.

And as he was turning to look at the vampire again, she was on him – a flash of white blazing through the black to crash into him and drive him backwards.

He hit a wall, and the impact winded him. For a second, he was defenceless. And it was a second too long. The next thing he knew, her teeth were pressed against his jugular vein.

CHAPTER 88.
TOO MANY DOUGHNUTS, NOT ENOUGH PORRIDGE

WEMBLEY STADIUM, LONDON – 9.55PM (GMT), 20 MAY, 2011

THE militia man was called Tony Drake. He was thirty-five years old. Before the war, he'd been a milkman, and he'd stacked shelves at a supermarket. Being given a gun and told he could kill with it had made him feel like a man.

He waited near Fuad's Daimler in the private car park. Already the prime minister's friends had been ferried off in a convoy of 4x4s.

Drake's mate, who'd been with him when Fuad had told them all to fuck off, was chatting to the driver of the vehicle taking Zella Shaw home. It was about to leave the car park. He glimpsed the blonde actress in the back of the 4x4. She was hot. He thought maybe now that he was a member of the elite, he could shag her. But that was a no go. There were always firsts, even among equals.

Drake had joined the Neb militia just after the vampire war three months ago. George Fuad had started making speeches about why Britain was in such a mess. It was because people were attacking vampires, he'd said, and because of those attacks, vampires were naturally going to defend themselves.

"So, we have violence," Fuad had said on TV one day.

It sounded so convincing. Drake had signed up at his kids' school, which had been shut down because Jake Lawton had inflicted this plague on England.

"You can't join the militia," his wife had said. "Too many doughnuts, Tony, and not enough porridge. Join the library corps or something. Or people who file things."

She had laughed at him. But he'd joined up. And they gave him a uniform. Not a milkman's uniform. Not a shelf stacker's uniform. A cool, black uniform that an elite soldier would wear. They also gave him a small red clip. It was a piece of leathery cloth with a safety pin attached. The tag was clipped to his collar.

"Never take it off," they'd said to the new recruits. "And never let anyone take it off you, either."

They also gave him a Kevlar vest, a helmet, Doc Marten boots, a utility belt ("Makes you look like Batman, Dad," said his son), pepper spray, a knife – which he'd given to Fuad to cut out the boy's tongue – a baton, and, of course, the gun.

A Smith & Wesson .38.

And they'd even shown him, and the others, how to shoot it. Just an afternoon of training, that was all. It didn't feel like enough time. And it proved to be the case a few times – some recruits had either accidentally shot themselves or a colleague. Drake heard rumours that some guys had been killed in shooting accidents, but they were told that the rumours were false.

"Lies spread by the anti-vamps," their commander had said.

The vehicle carrying the actress left the stadium perimeter. People were still spilling out of the arena. Drake kept well out of the way. The Daimler waited in the private car park, behind a set of iron gates. He felt safe behind those gates. Safer than he'd feel out on the streets tonight.

There was a bad feeling going round.

His mate started to wander off.

"Where are you going?" said Drake.

"Fag."

"Shut the effing gate, then."

But the bloke had wandered off.

Drake looked towards the entrance to the VIP lounges. He expected to see Fuad come out any minute. He really wanted to get going. There was a lot of trouble on the streets. Just beyond the gates, people were fighting. Gunfire erupted. Screams filled the night. He shuddered, suddenly worried about vampires. He touched the red tag.

I'm safe, he told himself, *I'm safe*.

He didn't really like vampires. They were terrifying. They scared his wife and his kids. And if he could have got rid of them all, he would have done so. But these days if you weren't a Neb or a Neb sympathizer, you were in trouble.

And you didn't get one of the little red tags to keep you safe from vampire attacks.

He wondered how the tag worked. He had no idea. But it didn't matter. He had no idea how antibiotics had cured his daughter's infection the year before. He didn't need to know. Only that they worked.

Drake shivered. The crowds were dwindling. Fighting continued, but it had spread further from the stadium now.

Come on, George, where are you? he said to himself, *I want to go home*.

Things had really gone pear-shaped tonight. Fuad was going to go mental. He'd throw a hissy fit like no other. Drake just didn't want to be around. He'd drive the man back to his Soho headquarters, then go home to his wife and kids.

He wondered about the boy who was now probably having his tongue cut out. Was it necessary to do such a thing? The lad had been a traitor, one of Lawton's allies. But surely they could just have sent him to a borstal or given him community service. Drake found the sacrifice business earlier on very worrying. He hated seeing those people tied to the stakes. It wasn't right. But he wouldn't say anything. Or he'd be tied up with them. And the wife wouldn't want that.

Across from the stadium, where the Wembley Retail Park had once stood, vehicles were lining up. They faced the arena. Their headlights glared. It was quite a convoy.

Drake started to worry.

It didn't feel right.

He jogged to the gate to see if he could get a better look.

A chill ran through him.

Is that a tank?

"Yes, it fucking is a tank," he said out loud.

Among the vehicles, he saw figures. Dozens of them. They wore army fatigues.

Reinforcements?

He saw other figures too – men and women, black, Asian, white.

Something was wrong.

Badly wrong.

He grabbed his walkie-talkie and tuned in to the military channel.

"Th-this is Drake at the gates, has anyone seen what's going around the retail park? Fuck – "

The vehicles, including the tank, were moving towards the stadium. And so were the figures. Men and women. Armed with guns and baseball bats and spades and…

"Oh, fuck," he said.

He dropped the walkie-talkie.

I'm not trained for this, he thought.

"Drake, get out here," said a voice.

It was his unit sergeant.

"Sarge, what the – "

"Drake, we need you," said Sarge.

Six militia men, including the Sarge, faced the oncoming army.

And it was an army. It had soldiers in it. Real ones. Not play ones like Drake and his mates.

The new force moved quickly towards the stadium.

"Right," said the Sarge. "Run!" He dropped his weapon and scarpered. So did the others. Drake was too slow. Too many doughnuts, not enough porridge.

He tried to flee, but the new force was on him quickly. He turned and saw it was being led by a Chinese girl who was armed with two short swords.

His last thought as they mowed him down was, *It's not true they all look alike*, because he'd recognized her.

She was the girl who'd been tied to a pole in the stadium less than an hour ago.

And now she led an army.

And her army marched over him.

PART NINE.

IMMORTALITY.

CHAPTER 89.
INTO DARKNESS.

HILLAH, IRAQ – 10.03PM (GMT + 3 HOURS), 20/21 MAY, 2011

ALFRED stumbled out of the coliseum in pursuit of Nimrod. The Great Hunter walked down a flight of steps. It was as wide as the arena, made of stone, carved into the earth. Thousands of years ago, Alfred imagined, the spectators would flood down the steps after witnessing blood games in the amphitheatre.

Nimrod bounded down, dragging Sinclair behind him. She yelled out in pain as she bounced along. She left a trail of blood behind her. *She isn't long for this life*, thought Alfred. But after being bitten by a vampire god, she was bound for another life. A long one. *Immortality*, he thought.

He hurried after Nimrod.

If I can bring him back to London, I'll be immortal, too, he thought. Not the undead kind. Eventually he would die. An old man. A rich old man. But his name would live on. His legacy would survive. The man who had brought a god back to London. Now *that* was real immortality.

"Wait," he cried, his voice echoing.

Nimrod appeared to be descending into darkness. Alfred didn't want to go any further if he didn't need to. He had to work out a way of getting this creature back to the UK. First, he had to gain its trust.

"Wait, please!"

Nimrod stopped and turned slowly.

Alfred stood frozen to the spot. He smelled of piss and sweat by now. He was terrified, but the thought of being remembered encouraged him on. The thought of pleasing his brother was also an incentive.

"We… my brother and me… we brought this woman for you, my Lord Nimrod," he said.

Nimrod growled quietly. Alfred wished that the woman in white had still been around. She understood this monster's language.

Nimrod glared at him with fiery red eyes. His leathery skin rippled. A mist wafted around the creature. *Steam*, thought Alfred, *rising from its burning heart*. Wounds peppered The Great Hunter's body. Blades and bullets had penetrated the flesh. But none seemed to affect him. Insects crawled all over him, feeding on his injuries, scuttling in an out of the pores.

"She's your enemy, Lord Nimrod," said Alfred. "She and her friends have been killing your children. Murdering them. For years. Destroying your offspring."

"I hope you choke on your balls," said Sinclair. She was badly hurt, and her voice was raspy. Her arm appeared to be broken, and her leg was twisted at the knee. Blood poured from the two wounds in her neck where Nimrod had bitten her.

"He's going to rip you to pieces, bitch," Alfred told her.

"Jake'll find you, Fuad. He'll find you and crush you."

"Your Jake's a dead man, whore. That bitch witch has killed him. She was going to shag him first, then kill him. Like that, eh? Him shagging that bird? He don't fancy you no more, you being all broken."

Nimrod started going down the steps again.

Shit, thought Alfred. *Kill her up here, for fuck's sake. Don't make me follow you down there – it's fucking scary.*

But he had to.

Sinclair screamed. Her cries echoed. Nimrod dragged her deeper and deeper.

Alfred followed.

CHAPTER 90.
HALF-THING.

"LOVE me, Jake," Ereshkigal said, her breath dank and old. It made him sick and it turned him on.

They tussled – a dance of death amid the ruins.

They wheeled around, slamming into walls. She clawed at him, tearing his flesh.

Her teeth had broken his skin at the throat, but he'd managed to force her away before they sank into his jugular. But her bite was hot on him. He could feel where her lips had kissed him.

She rammed him against a wall. The jutting rocks cut him.

He grimaced.

Pain on pain on pain.

She forced her thigh between his legs, pressing.

One arm locked around his waist, the other hand on his face, her fingers in his mouth.

His arms were wedged, one holding a bone sword inches from her throat, the other, pressing the second weapon into her belly, crushed between their bodies.

Lawton was dizzy. He felt sick. Voices sang in his head. That song of doom. His doom. The end of him as a human.

He fought against the change in him. Rejected his own evolution.

But you can't stop change. You can't stop nature, however twisted it is.

He groaned, fighting against everything – her, nature, himself.

He grew hard against her leg. His stomach lurched. His skin burned. His skull ached.

He saw swirling patterns through his dead eye. She curled back her lips. Her fangs were white. Her eyes blazed red. Her skin smelled of flowers and decay.

"I will make you mine forever," she said. "We'll never be parted. We'll be lovers for eternity. Be immortal with me."

"I… I thought this fucking eye of mine had done that… already… so why bother… "

"You are not unkillable, Jake; you are only more difficult to kill. There is still human in you. Ugly, horrible, worthless human. Let me suck out the poison. Let me drink it from you and make you vampire. Not a mongrel. Not a half-thing. Let me make you perfect."

She was strong. She had him virtually locked in her grasp. Her teeth pressed against his throat again. He felt them make indents once more.

Another second, he would be bitten.

And there was no escaping her this time.

His veins would be open to her.

He shifted a little, using the tiny amount of give he'd sensed between their bodies.

It was enough.

The skin broke.

They both gasped.

The flesh tore.

The blood was hot.

They gasped again.

His head swam.

He was weak, light-headed.

He heard the blood pulse. He felt it flow.

Arteries cut.

Another gasp.

Blood gushing.

Lawton gritted his teeth.

Ereshkigal threw her head back, her crow-black hair fanning around her chalk-white face. Her eyes were on fire.

She shrieked.

Her body stiffening.

He drove the bone sword deeper into her chest.

Her blood had stained him, and he felt it like lava on his skin – burning, scorching, charring.

He forced her away from him, her hands on his shoulders. He rammed the bone sword up again, to the hilt, into her solar plexus, through her heart.

And she screeched, an animal cry that rattled his bones.

Blood fountained from her chest, spraying Lawton.

She trembled in his arms and cried out his name:

"Jake! Jake! Jake!"

Her leg was locked between his thighs. Her death made him harder. His desire for her stronger than ever.

No, he told himself.

"NO!"

And he went hilt-deep into her body, and blood gushed, and its odour was strong and metallic.

She writhed and screamed, and she looked at his face, and he looked her straight in the eye.

Her skin withered. Fiery arteries raced along her flesh. The smell of burning meat filled Lawton's nostrils. Her body became increasingly hotter. But he held her. He wouldn't let go.

They looked into each other, and he felt something deep for her – he felt her peace approach.

"I give you silence, Ereshkigal," he said. "I give you sleep."

"I would have loved you more than any of them," she said.

And then she aged in his arms. Her beauty fading. Her skin creasing and charring, the fire eating her flesh. And all the while she made a keening noise, like an animal, and it went deeply into him, scoring his heart.

Her dying hurt him physically.

She was on fire.

But he took the pain, like he had taken all the pain in his past.

He suffered with her. Suffered until she became a blackened skeleton with his sword inside her ribcage. Suffered until the bones became dust.

And all that was left was him, the dance done.

CHAPTER 91.
PROTECTED.

WEMBLEY STADIUM, LONDON – 10.11PM (GMT), 20 MAY, 2011

DAVID and his mum curled up and waited for the vampires to devour them. The creatures circled.

George Fuad said, "Go on, feed on the fuckers, feed on them."

The creatures hesitated. They looked at Fuad. He was bleeding badly. Blood on his chest, where David had stabbed him, and blood coming from his mouth.

And the vampires were drawn to it.

They sniffed it.

They wanted to drink it.

But Fuad was protected – the red mark in the form of a band around his wrist.

He growled at the vampires:

"Kill 'em, go on, kill 'em – fucking rip their throats out – tear the cunts to shreds – "

One or two of the vampires looked back at David and his mum. They were trying to make a decision – which was the easiest kill.

But the fact that blood was flowing made it difficult. All their instincts told them to go for the wounded prey. But they couldn't. The bleeder was protected.

"Go on, don't look at me, you bastards," said Fuad, spitting blood. It sprayed on the ground. The vampires hissed and licked their lips. He showed them the mark. "I'm a fucking Neb, you disgusting filth. You can't touch me. But you can fucking do those two."

David thought quickly.

He saw the knife.

He went on all fours.

His mum tried to stop him.

But he was away.

Scuttling across the ground.

Eyes on the knife.

Vampires all around him.

Fuad screaming at them to kill David.

He grabbed the knife, dived at Fuad, clutched his wrist, sliced off the mark.

Fuad screamed.

David, without looking, scuttled back towards his mother.

He showed the vampires the mark:

"We're protected, we're protected."

Fuad screamed again.

The vampires growled.

His blood made them frenzied.

He was unprotected.

Not a Neb to them anymore.

Just food to them.

They went at him.

He screamed:

"You can't touch me, you can't fucking touch me!"

But they did. They piled on him. They tore at him. He shrieked. Only his twitching feet could be seen under a press of vampires, all of them trying to get at his wounds to drink his blood and make new wounds to empty his veins.

"Let's go," said David.

He started to drag his mum away.

But more vampires poured up the steps into the walkway. And now some of those who'd been feeding on Fuad rose to their feet, looking for more nourishment. Finding it right there in David and his mum.

The vampires prowled.

David had the mark.

"We're protected," he shouted, holding his mum close.

"Only one of you," hissed a vampire. The creature charged in and lunged at David's mum's leg. Grabbed it and tried to pull her away. She cried out. David yelled, "Mum"! He rammed the red mark into the vampire's face. It reeled, hissing, desperately rubbing its mouth and cheeks.

Another rushed forward, trying the same thing. David leapt up and stood in its way, brandishing the mark.

But behind his back, two more bolted towards his mum, making a grab at her.

She screamed, and David fended them off.

"We're protected," he said, crying.

"Just you, kiddo," said a vampire.

He pinned the mark on his mum.

"No, David," she said.

"Now her," he said.

"No, David."

The vampires snarled.

Gunfire erupted. Shouts came from nearby. A gang of people, some dressed in army fatigues, others in civilian clothing, rushed up the steps.

And David saw who was leading them.

"Mei!" he called out.

She was leading another army – just like she'd done months ago. And this time it was made up of soldiers. Real ones. They ploughed into the vampires. They pinned them down. They staked them. Mei was lethal. She wielded her wakizashi swords. The blades were bloody.

She embraced him.

Her army swept into the stadium.

"How did you do this?" asked David.

"Ediz found your friend Old Bill. He made internet message. Just a few soldiers heard it. Only a few, but enough to help us here. But more come. More come from all over England and Scotland and Wales."

David and Mei helped his mum to her feet.

"Still many vampires," she said. She looked at the body of George Fuad. It was covered in blood. There were bite marks on it – neck, face, arms, legs. He had a look of horror on his face. He had died in agony.

Good, thought David.

"Human leader dead," said Mei. "But they don't care. Vampires just feed. Vampires will kill anyway."

"Can I borrow one of your swords, Mei?" he said.

She handed him the blade. David drove it into Fuad's chest until steel hit concrete. He watched every second of Fuad's decay and didn't move until the last speck of dust had swirled away on the breeze.

As David stood up and handed Mei her sword, a voice on a loudspeaker said, "This is General Howard Vince. I am recently back from Iraq. I urge citizens to fight against this insurgent army that is invading the stadium. These are the friends of the traitor Jake Lawton. They are here to ruin Britain. The vampires will join you. Fight for England. In Iraq, we have discovered a great power that will make this country great again. A god for us to worship. A mighty warrior to lead us to victory. Fight back against the rebels. Fight back against the terrorists."

The noise inside the stadium grew.

Everyone was fighting everyone else.

And vampires were in the mix, killing anyone they could.

"What are we going to do?" said David's mum.

"Too many vampires," said Mei.

"Jake must have failed," said David. He couldn't believe what he was saying. "The Iraqis got him. He didn't get away. If this Nimrod thing is awake, and he survives, we're done. We've got no chance. We're lost."

A sea of people burst down the stairs from the Royal Box. The hurtled into the tunnel. Some fell and were crushed by the stampede. The mob roared towards David, his mum, and Mei.

"Run," he said. "RUN!"

CHAPTER 92.
THE HUNDRED BRIDES.

HILLAH, IRAQ – 10.15PM (GMT + 3 HOURS), 20/21 MAY, 2011

AALIYAH was crying. She was in pain. But that wasn't the worst of it. The worst of it was that her heart had been broken.

Her dream of being with Jake was over. The dream that had brought her to Irkalla. The dream that had taken her away from him in the first place.

But no, they didn't have a future.

It was going to die in this underworld.

Die with her.

Nimrod had dragged her down the flight of steps, and every yard hurt.

It felt like a long time before they finally came to a halt.

Aaliyah wiped tears from her eyes to take a look. They were in a clearing.

Behind them, the steps that led up to the coliseum.

Before them, a rock face that climbed as far as the eye could see. There was a cave in the rocks, and its entrance was framed by a gateway of red clay. It appeared to be the doorway to a temple. The gateway was warped and broken, but once, thousands of years ago, it must have been spectacular. Evidence of carved figures could be seen, although the surface of the artefact was now cracked and shattered completely in places. Ages ago, it must have given the impression of great wealth, of a bright future. Of something that would live forever.

But everything died.

Everything, thought Aaliyah.

She spluttered, tears relentlessly streaming down her face. Her body hurt. She'd broken her arm, for sure, and her leg throbbed painfully. She was bleeding a lot, particularly from the injury to the side of her neck where the monster had bitten her. He'd sucked some blood out of her. Not enough to make her dead, then alive again. But enough to weaken her.

Nimrod began dragging her towards the cave.

"Where are you taking me, you bastard?" she said.

He was silent.

Inside, the cave's floor slanted upwards. Nimrod dragged Aaliyah up the slope. It was dark, but she could make out skeletal arms poking out of the walls. Clamped into the bony hands were torches.

The floor levelled, and they went down a corridor, the walls decorated with murals depicting some kind of battle. A horned monster – *Nimrod*, thought Aaliyah – was at the head of an army that had savaged what appeared to be hundreds, maybe thousands, of people – men, women, and children. Torn bodies lay strewn across fields, in towns, floating in lakes. Blood was plentiful. The mural could well have been painted in it.

At last they entered a chapel-sized room. It triggered flashbacks to her childhood – going to church with her mother, singing hymns, praising God.

But later, she'd turned her back on all that. She wanted adventure. She had been drawn to flashy men – drug dealers and gangsters.

Nimrod flung her across the tiled floor. She came to a stop and sat up, dizzy, facing the altar. It was made of clay and stained with something. A dark liquid dried up.

Blood, she thought.

Next to the altar was a pool. The stagnant water smelled. Nimrod knelt at the water's edge. He reached into the pool and drew water, splashing it over his face and his scalp.

Aaliyah stared around the room. Portraits had been painted on the walls. The figures of women dressed in white. They were pale-skinned and dark-haired, their eyes red. They encircled the room, twenty-five on each wall. One hundred of them. The hundred brides of Nimrod. Just as Goga had said. She remembered the one with Nimrod in the arena. She had said something about Jake. About being lovers.

Her stomach felt gripey.

Nimrod groaned quietly to himself as he stared into the pool. Aaliyah took her chance. She started to crawl towards the door. Blood seeped from a gouge on her thigh, and her arm felt as if it were on fire. She could put no pressure on it. Her neck pulsed, and she felt faint.

But she had to try.

For Jake, she thought. Who'd let her fall – but it wasn't his fault. Who'd let Nimrod assault her – but Jake couldn't have done anything. Who'd abandoned her to death – but he would save her if he could.

Or maybe he was the white witch's lover?

She let out a cry.

Crawling, leaving a trail of blood behind her, she was nearly at the door.

She broke into a smile. She could survive this. She could make it out. She had to have hope. She had to –

Nimrod grabbed her leg.

She screamed as he pulled her back into the altar-room. She clawed at the tiles, but her hands slithered through the blood she'd left behind.

She screamed for Jake.

Her eyes were fixed on the door as she waited for him to surely burst through it any second and rescue her.

But he didn't.

And when Nimrod lifted her and slammed her on the altar, and then loomed over her, she knew she'd been deserted.

Because there was no one else to do it, she cried for her unfulfilled life just as the monster mounted the altar and pinned her down.

CHAPTER 93.
MONSTER.

IT was a terrible sight. One Alfred had hoped he'd never see again. But it was here. He'd come back from the dead. And he looked even more terrifying than Nimrod.

He was covered in blood and dust from head to toe.

In his right hand, he wielded the conjoined Spear of Abraham, and in the other, an ebony cane with a blade on the end. There was a pistol tucked into his belt, and Alfred was momentarily relieved that he wasn't going to get shot. But that relief soon faded when Lawton came closer.

One side of his face was bruised, and his eyeball seemed to be completely red, as if filled with blood.

Alfred wanted to scream. He nearly pissed himself for a second time. He pointed the submachine gun at the spectre.

"Can't you just fucking die?" he said.

"Not very easily, it seems," said Jake Lawton.

He strode towards Alfred, whose knees buckled. Lawton was a tough guy. He'd always been a tough guy. He was menacing and carried an air of "don't mess with me" about him. But now, he was a hundred times scarier than he'd ever been before. He'd become a monster. An angel of death.

And Alfred knew he was in trouble.

"You think you're passing?" he said, the gun trained on Lawton.

"I know I'm passing, Alfred."

He kept coming.

"I'll shoot."

"I've been shot before. Six bullets in me already. Few more won't make a difference. Do your worst."

"You might not be afraid of bullets, Lawton, but you come any closer and I'll have Nimrod rip your bitch to pieces, you hear me? He's in there now with her. I can tell him to stop. He listens to me. I'm a Nebuchadnezzar. I'm his… his master and his servant, Lawton. You hear?"

Lawton was hesitating. He'd stopped. Alfred felt strong all of a sudden. His grip on the gun tightened.

"See?" he said. "See who's boss around here?"

Lawton appeared to be thinking. He looked back over his shoulder. His eyes – or at least his one good eye – narrowed.

And then he curled his lip and charged.

Alfred panicked.

He fired, but the bullets went astray because his aim was affected by nerves and the fact he was shitting himself.

Lawton wasn't stopping. He was coming straight for him. Alfred's head screamed at him to run. But terror had frozen him to the spot.

He fired again. The shot grazed Lawton's shoulder, tearing a groove in the flesh. But it didn't stop him.

Alfred screamed and threw the gun at Lawton, who just batted the weapon aside.

"Bye, Alfred," Lawton said, and Alfred saw the cane jabbing at his chest and felt it break his skin and sink into him, and it was still in him long after Lawton had walked by. And then Alfred saw everything swim before him, his hearing dulled, he grew cold, and he thought, "Is this how I'm going to die?"

And darkness enveloped him.

CHAPTER 94
LIKE THEM.

LAWTON ran up the slope, then into the corridor. He stopped for a second to get his bearings, checking out the fresco. Then he was off again, pulling the Spear of Abraham apart as he ran, taking both ends in either hand as swords once more.

He bolted through an opening, and the smell of blood hit him.

He stopped dead.

It was an altar-room. The walls were decked in images of women wearing white. They were faded but he could make them out. And they all looked like Ereshkigal.

Up ahead, the altar stood bloody.

His heart pounded, and his skin crawled.

"Aaliyah," he said. "Aaliyah, are you here?"

Something loomed from the shadows behind the altar. Something large and lethal. It took shape as it moved out of the darkness and into the light, and Lawton saw it. He saw the leathery skin, the powerful limbs, the sharp teeth, the vicious talons, and he saw the wounds on the creature's scalp.

Lawton glanced at his swords, which he'd carried with him for years.

Now they'd come home.

Nimrod stepped over the altar.

It said something, a word that sounded like a growl at first:

"Avram… "

Lawton held his ground. He steeled himself for a battle with this monster. He was tense all over, his hands sweating on the swords, his skin tingling. The voices still sang in his skull, and the pain was such that he had now embraced it – he did not think he could survive without it, without the adrenaline it released in his body.

"Aaliyah, where are you?" he said again. "Where is she, you fucker?"

Nimrod said something again, and once more it sounded more like a growl. He pointed at the bone swords in Lawton's hands.

"I brought them home," said Lawton. "You want them?"

He remembered Goga's words:

Make Nimrod one with himself again.

The only way to kill him.

He knew what that meant now. It had come to him. It made sense. He would make the monster whole again. And if these tusks could kill every other vampire, why wouldn't they kill the father of vampires?

The god approached.

Lawton slowly kneeled.

He rested one sword on the ground and scooped up a handful of dust.

Nimrod growled.

Lawton lunged, tossing the dust into the creature's face. The monster reeled. Lawton grabbed the sword. Armed with both, he launched himself at the Great Hunter. The beast saw him coming and swatted him away.

Lawton went spinning. The world wheeled. He fell hard, hitting his head against the stone floor. He saw stars.

The ground shook. He wondered why. Then he realized and he got his bearings.

Nimrod was running towards him.

Lawton scrabbled to his feet, dizzy, unsteady.

The god loomed. His shadow fell across Lawton. Jake slashed wildly with his swords. Ivory sliced flesh. Blood sprayed. Nimrod howled.

Lawton stumbled backwards, and came to a halt against the wall. He pulled himself together, fixed on his opponent.

Nimrod snarled. Blood dripped from a wound in the Great Hunter's hand.

Is that all I did to him? thought Lawton.

"What have you done with Aaliyah?" he said.

He felt rage and pain. In his heart, he knew she was dead – or something worse.

But if she were, he would not leave her in this underworld.

You leave no one behind.

You take everyone home, dead or alive.

He cried out in fury as suddenly a world without Aaliyah became apparent.

He leapt at Nimrod.

The Great Hunter swatted again, but this time he missed, and his wayward attempt left his chest open for attack.

Lawton drove the bone-sword into the creature's breast.

The huge pectoral muscle sliced open.

Meat showed pink. Blood ran red. Bone gleamed white.

The god screamed.

Lawton rolled away.

He's killable, he thought. *He's flesh and bone. He bleeds. And these weapons can hurt him.*

Immortality wasn't final, he realized.

Death could get at anyone under the right circumstances.

The god trembled.

Lawton attacked.

But Nimrod was faking. He swung round to face Lawton and grabbed him around the waist, lifting him above his head.

Lawton looked down and saw the wounds on the creature's scalp where the horns had been ripped out.

They festered and crawled with insects.

Lawton hacked at Nimrod's arm, cutting into the flesh.

The monster let him go, and he fell to the ground.

He was up straight away, ignoring the pain, ignoring the dizziness. He leapt up on the altar. Blood was thick on the stone. He looked behind him, steadying himself – and there she was. She lay in a pool of blood. Her clothes were torn. He shouted her name and leapt down behind the altar.

"Aaliyah! No!"

Her eyes opened.

He cried with joy and cradled her, but she groaned in pain.

Blood came from her mouth, and from a terrible wound on her throat, and there was also blood between her legs – lots of it.

Her eyes glittered.

"Why did you leave me?" she whispered.

"No," screamed Lawton, "No, I never left you, I never – "

"Don't let me be like them," she said.

"No, Aaliyah, don't make me – "

Before he could finish, he felt himself being picked up by the leg, the world turning upside down, Aaliyah going further and further away.

Nimrod started to swing him round violently.

Lawton could hardly take a breath.

Aaliyah's face was branded into his mind. The pain it caused him made all his other agonies pale into insignificance. Her face represented all his failings –as a soldier, as a man, as a human.

Nimrod slammed him to the ground, and for a second he couldn't breathe.

He thought he'd let himself be killed, be fed on, because if Aaliyah was going to be undead…

Don't let me be like them

… then he would be too.

He would not be the half-thing he'd become. He would be vampire. He would be what he hated most. But for Aaliyah, he would do anything.

CHAPTER 95.
SANCTUARY.

LONDON – 10.23PM (GMT), 20 MAY, 2011

"TOO many vampires," said Mei. Her small force wasn't strong enough to take on the undead and the Neb militia. They were retreating – Mei, David, and Murray, along with some of her troops.

They had fled up Wembley Hill Road. The streets were laden with panic-stricken people, confused Neb militia men, and hungry vampires.

The group found refuge in a church, St Augustine's, a red brick building at the end of Wembley Hill Road.

At the far end of the room that they'd entered, Jesus hung on his cross over the altar. David looked at the Christ. He looked at him for hope, for salvation. Maybe now, at the end, there would be some kind of holy intervention.

But none came.

They armed themselves with plastic chairs and waited for the vampires.

"Mum, are you OK?" he said.

His mother hugged him. "I'm so proud of you."

"I love you," he said.

"Hey, don't cry – we're not dead yet."

She smiled at him, but there were tears in her eyes too.

She knew they were as good as dead. He could tell.

The doors buckled. The vampires, assisted by militia men with military vehicles, were breaking into the church.

"We die here," said Mei. "Good place to die, with Jesus."

She slashed the air with her swords.

Mei was so brave. David looked at her in awe. She had always fought against the odds, ever since he'd known her.

"We lose here, but we win in the end," she said.

Outside, a voice on a loudspeaker boomed:

"We are regaining control of the streets. The insurgents are being rounded up. Good people of Britain, please return to your homes. There is an immediate curfew… "

"That's Howard Vince," said David's mum. "He didn't waste any time grabbing power."

Vince's bellowing voice continued:

"Point us to the traitors, the foreign gangsters, the Lawtonite rebels. Offer them no sanctuary, or punishment will be brutal. We must have law and order. I will execute anyone who breaks the law. The law is your friend. The traitors are the enemies of the law."

The church doors shattered.

The vampires swarmed inside.

David told his companions to retreat towards the altar, and he stood in the vampires' way, brandishing the tiny piece of cloth he'd torn from George Fuad's wrist. He felt naked with it against dozens of the undead. But they baulked, hissing at him.

"Get out and leave us alone," he said.

A few of the vampires laughed at him. They skirted the walls, keeping well away from David.

"No," he cried out, "no, leave them – "

But the vampires were closing in on David's mum, Mei, and the others as they huddled under Jesus on his cross.

CHAPTER 96.
THE LAST BATTLE.

HILLAH – 10.25PM (GMT + 3 HOURS), 20/21 MAY, 2011

NIMROD swung Lawton round. The room whirled. Lawton felt sick. He wanted to puke. And just as he was about to, the monster let him go. He clattered into the altar, banging the back of his skull.

Nimrod charged.

Lawton lunged.

He drove one of his swords into the wound on the Great Hunter's leg, and then forward-rolled out of the way.

The god bellowed.

Lawton tried to get up, but his legs buckled. He was so weak now. But he had to keep going. He had to get to Aaliyah. He gritted his teeth and dug deep.

He hobbled towards the altar, but Nimrod cut him off.

The monster roared, plumes of smoke coming from his nostrils. His eyes burned with rage. He slashed and hacked at Lawton, forcing Jake to duck and dive and back away from where he knew Aaliyah was dying.

I have to get to her, he thought. *I can't let her down again*.

He faced Nimrod and thrust with his swords. He sliced into the monster's flesh. The creature seemed unconcerned by most of the blows. But now and again, Lawton's weapons sank deep into the Great Hunter's limbs, and his cries told Jake that the beast was hurting.

And if you could hurt something, you could kill it.

Lawton grew in confidence. His constant thrusts forced Nimrod back. The creature snarled, bearing its vicious teeth.

Lawton thought he saw movement from behind the altar.

Aaliyah.

He glanced out of the corner of his eye. Nothing there. Shadows, that was all. And blood –

The blow struck him in the belly. He sailed across the altar-room. As he hung in the air, he saw Nimrod bound after him. The tiles shattered under the monster's powerful feet. Shards of clay spattered across the floor.

Lawton hit the ground.

Nimrod was on him.

Lawton rolled just in time to avoid the monster's foot as it stamped down hard on the tiles.

Lawton rolled again as once more Nimrod tried to crush him.

He rolled a third time as Nimrod again tried to stamp on him.

Lawton came to a halt against the altar. The monster towered over him, Lawton strewn between the creature's legs.

The god reached down.

Lawton rammed one of his swords into the Great Hunter's crotch.

Blood sprayed out of the creature's groin, and he shrieked.

The god writhed.

Lawton rolled away and clambered up on the altar.

"Aaliyah," he said, reaching for her.

But she was gone.

A trail of blood led into the darkness beyond the altar.

"Aaliyah!"

Fury laced his blood. He turned in time to see an equally enraged Nimrod striding towards him. Blood ran down the creature's inner thighs. Ribbons of skin flapped where his scrotum had been. But the injury wasn't hindering the Great Hunter. He barrelled towards the altar.

Lawton launched himself.

He sailed towards Nimrod. He landed on the monster's shoulders. He scissored his legs around the creature's neck.

Nimrod clawed at him, ripping his flesh.

But Lawton ignored the pain.

He was the one with wounds.

He had to embrace agony. He had to invite it.

Nimrod whirled around, trying to dislodge Lawton. But Jake wasn't going anywhere. He looked down into the wounds on the Great Hunter's scalp. They were putrid. Gaping holes of rotting flesh. Torn skin and dried blood.

Lawton raised one of the swords, and rammed it down into the first wound.

Nimrod shrieked.

He wheeled violently.

Lawton held on with his legs.

The god wailed.

The cry of pain shattered the walls.

Lawton raised the second sword.

He roared, unleashing years of rage and frustration, unleashing the anguish of losing friends and lovers, unleashing the pain of a shattered future.

CHAPTER 97.
ASHES.

LONDON – 10.28PM (GMT), 20 MAY, 2011

THE vampires charged.

David screamed.

His mother, Mei, and the others were sitting ducks. They would be overwhelmed. David, dreading the thought of living without them, tossed the red mark aside.

"Take me too, you bastards," he said.

A vampire, sensing the boy was no longer protected, veered towards him.

The creature bared its fangs, a hateful smile on its face.

David prepared for death – and undeath.

The vampire's expression changed. A look of confusion crossed its face.

The smell of burning flesh filled the church.

David stared at the vampire.

Fiery threads ran along its body. Its skin turned black. Its eyes bulged, and its mouth gawped. The fangs faded to yellow and crumpled. The creature's legs gave way as the skin melted and the bones crumbled, and by the time it hit the ground, a yard from David, it looked like dried fruit.

And seconds later it was ashes.

It happened quickly, barely a second.

But David took in every moment. Every vampire's death for him took place in slow motion.

Their faces twisted in horror.

Their skin creasing and drying out.

Their limbs flailing.

Their skins burning.

Their bodies wilting.

All around him in the church, they wheeled violently, smoke coming off their boiling bodies. The odour of death in the air. Their decaying corpses decomposing, becoming ashes.

Every single one of them.

Every vampire.

All the dead, gone.

David heard his mother's voice:

"He did it," she was shouting, "Jake did it."

David thought, *He's killed Nimrod.*

He hoped it had been Jake. It meant he was still alive. And David honestly could not think of anyone else capable of killing such a monster.

Mei was surveying the layer of ashes on the floor. She shouted to her followers. They reacted quickly, piling into the shocked Nebuchadnezzar militia men.

Adrenaline coursed through David. The battlefield was now level. The Nebs no longer had the advantage of the undead.

It was human against human.

"Mum," he said. They ran into each other's arms. They were crying and laughing.

"We're going to win," he said. "You've got to take charge, Mum. You've got to start getting things in order."

She gawped at him.

"Come on, mum," he said.

They ran out of the church. The streets were crammed with people. They knew what had happened and were now turning on the Nebs. Some of the black-shirts had thrown down their weapons and were surrendering. Others tried to fight but were overwhelmed.

David and his mother embraced again. A car drew up. Liz Wilson peered out of the black window.

"Get in, Christine," she said. "Time to pull up our socks. Your boys did it." She smiled. *She's got her sanity back*, David thought. *She's got her hope back.* David's mum got in the car, and she threw her son a kiss before the vehicle drove away.

Someone tapped him on the shoulder.

It was Mei, a big smile on her face.

She had blood trickling down her forehead. Her face was sweaty. Ediz was with her.

They all hugged and laughed, and they praised Jake.

But David said, "We don't know if it was Jake. He might be dead."

"Who else kill monsters?" said Mei.

David shrugged.

"Come to fight," she told him.

David entered the fray. He piled in to a group of Nebs. They were disorganized now.

With former professional soldiers fighting alongside them, David, Mei, Ediz and the others had a distinct advantage over the militia men.

David made his way back towards the stadium. He'd disposed of one Nebuchadnezzar overlord; now his thoughts were fixed on another.

Howard Vince.

Cut off the head, and the body will die, thought David. He wanted to wipe out the Nebuchadnezzars for good. He'd hunt them down, every single one.

At the stadium, he asked a soldier if he'd seen Vince.

"He's legged it, probably. Who gives a shit about him. We've got messages coming in from all over Britain. The vampires just died, and without vampires, those fucking Nebs are nothing. We'll have them all, soon. Vince as well."

David ran into the stadium. It was still crammed with people. They were organizing themselves. They were corralling groups of Nebs, forcing them on their knees. It could have easily become a massacre, but people were restrained. They were waiting for whoever was in charge to come along and arrest the Nebs. The people wanted justice. They didn't want vengeance. They wanted this done properly. They were sick of the savagery, and it filled David with hope.

He made his way along the corridors that led to the executive boxes.

The walkways were empty.

Striding along the red carpet, looking at the old photographs of England matches, you would have thought that nothing had changed in Britain. You would not think that there had been a civil war, a plague, devastation.

Here, it was normal.

Normal, apart from Howard Vince standing at the corridor's junction up ahead with his hands in the air.

He was looking to the left. Someone had a gun pointed at him.

David made his way slowly down the corridor.

The muffled sounds of triumph came from outside. Car horns blared. Crowds cheered. Gunfire barked.

Vince turned to look at David.

Now, whoever had Vince trapped was wondering who the general was looking at.

"Get down on your knees, Vince," said David. "You are under arrest."

Vince's brow furrowed. He looked back at whoever had him covered and said, "My men are just around this corner."

A figure suddenly appeared in the junction.

David froze.

The man wore the clothes of a tramp, but he held a flame thrower.

"Bill!" said David.

"David, lad. Ain't this a hoot," said Bill.

Vince took his chance. He bolted. He was a heavy man, so wasn't making much headway when David and Bill went after him.

"Hey, Vince," said Bill.

The general turned.

Bill pressed the trigger.

David held his breath.

A tongue of flame shot from the tube of the thrower. The impact threw Bill backwards. David screamed, "No!" He didn't want Vince dead. He wanted him alive so he could face justice.

But the corridor was suddenly engulfed in fire. The flames swallowed Vince.

David threw himself to the floor.

He felt the heat and smelled the burning of carpet and plaster and skin.

After the flames died, he got up and first went to check on Old Bill.

"Hey, they listened to me, David, lad," said the tramp. "The boys listened to an old soldier like me. I told 'em over the internet, mate. Me on the internet, eh?"

"Well done, Bill."

"Here, you don't mind me killing that Vince bastard, do you?"

"No, not really."

"Go check see what's left of him."
David got up and turned, but the sight stopped him in his tracks.
The burned corridor was empty.
Vince had gone.

CHAPTER 98.
KISSED BY HIM.

HILLAH – 10.33PM (GMT + 3 HOURS), 20/21 MAY, 2011

LAWTON tried to get up, but he couldn't. Not straight away. He rested against the altar.

A few yards away, Nimrod's skeletal remains decayed. The horns were jammed into his skull.

The only way to kill him – make him one with himself.

"Good on you, Goga," said Lawton.

The pain in his body seemed worse. His eye hurt, and it felt grainy. He rubbed his cheek and checked his fingers. They were covered in a black liquid. He poked his eyeball. It was empty. No glass, no skin of old vampires.

Burnt, he said. *Burnt when Nimrod died*. It gave him renewed hope. Perhaps his actions in Irkalla had had an effect elsewhere. Perhaps he'd made vampires extinct.

After taking a few deep breaths, he got to his feet. He had only one thing on his mind.

Aaliyah.

He called her name.

The echo of it came back to him.

He suddenly had the sense that he was alone. Nothing in Irkalla alive but him.

A shiver ran through him.

Everything here was dead. It had always been dead.

He called her name again.

He stumbled past the altar. Before him stretched a tunnel. It was an endless shaft, with no light at all to be seen.

He looked at the floor. A trail of blood ran into the passageway.

He was about to step into the tunnel when he became aware of the voices calling to him.

He wheeled, trying to fix on the whereabouts of the voice. He couldn't. He faced the tunnel again. Was it coming from down there?

"Jake… Jake… " it called, echoing from somewhere. And it was a voice he knew. A voice he'd known. He remembered the nightmares he'd had after putting that poisonous skin in his body. They had drawn him to Tălmaciu, where Ereshkigal waited, and had waited for five hundred years.

Would he now suffer the same nightmares? Would another of Nimrod's brides call out to him?

Ereshkigal had said the red mark did not scare her and that killing Nimrod would not destroy her. She was the bride of a god. She was a separate being. Not torn from him, but kissed by him.

Kissed.

Like Aaliyah. A deadly kiss. A kiss that tore open her veins. A kiss that drained her of blood.

He called her name again, and only his voice came back, empty and hopeless.

He walked into the darkness, shouting "Aaliyah" as he went. He would keep shouting. He would keep going. And eventually he'd escape from this underworld, like he'd escaped from every underworld.

As he walked, he remembered fleeing from the belly of Religion, the nightclub in London where the plague had started years before.

There, in the pit of the club, he had destroyed the first of the trinity.

Lawton and the monster had fallen into a fiery cavern. Before they'd hit the ground, the vampire had decayed. Lawton had been trapped thousands of feet underground, everything collapsing around him.

But he wasn't the kind to give up. Not back then. He'd found a way out through natural tunnels eroded by ancient springs under the city of London. They had led him into the sewers and eventually into the Tube system.

There, in a tunnel not dissimilar to the one he was now stumbling in, he had met an old soldier called Bill Goodwin.

Bill knew everything about him.

Bill was like an old prophet.

He wondered if the old man were still alive. He hoped so. Maybe he could see him again. It was something to think about while he searched for Aaliyah.

Lawton no longer had the strength of the half-thing he had become. The vampire in him had died with Nimrod. He was glad of that. Glad to be a weak man again. Glad to be frail. Glad to be killable.

He walked into the darkness to look for Aaliyah. He knew, when he found her, that there was only one thing he could do.

CHAPTER 99. BETTER DAYS.

LONDON – 11.02AM (GMT), DECEMBER 20, 2011

SIX months after the civil war ended, Britain was slowly rebuilding.

It was nearly Christmas, and from his room at the Park Lane Hotel, David stared out at Hyde Park. The Christmas market was in full swing. Through his open window, he smelled mulled wine and sausages. It wasn't as busy as it had been in years past, but at least it was being held this year. Everything was slowly getting back to normal.

He shut the window and went to sit down. He and his mum lived in the hotel, now. It was nice. She was the Prime Minister of Britain. He was so proud of her, and in the past six months, they had healed their relationship.

He put his feet up on the glass coffee table and rolled a cigarette. He was only fourteen, and his mum had begged him to stop. But it was a habit he'd picked up during the vampire wars. It was hard to break, but he would.

After the vampires had died, it had taken a day to defeat all the Neb militia. Neb officials were put under house arrest. A lot of them got rid of their red marks in the hope of not being identified. But there were so many photos and so much footage that it was easy to track them down.

Some got away, but most were rounded up. Trials had started. Again, it was a nightmare of red tape and administration. The courts couldn't cope. Most of the Nebs had been cleared and released.

After the victory, meetings were held. Everyone got stuck in, rebuilding the country. One of the most important things to get up and running again was the London water supply, which had been infected by the Nebuchadnezzars. It was him mum's first priority, and it made her even more popular.

She then tackled the transport infrastructure The Tube in London would become fully operational again in early 2012. But trains ran. And there were bus services in the capital and the rest of Britain.

And more importantly, there was a sense of unity.

Kwan Mei was now leader of a youth movement that carried out voluntary work. She was a star. Everyone looked up to her. She and her friend Ediz Ün were role models.

David had also been invited to spearhead the movement, but he didn't want to. He wanted to go back to school. He wanted to be the boy he'd never been.

Being fourteen, it was a time when most teenagers thought they were grown-ups.

But David wanted to be a kid again. He wanted the youth he'd missed out on.

So he went to a school in Kensington.

He learned all over again, and more importantly he made friends.

He found himself a gorgeous girlfriend called Tamarat. She was Muslim. She had big brown eyes and wore a silk scarf to cover her black hair.

Perhaps before the war, her family would have scorned their relationship. After all, he was a Western boy.

But Tamarat's dad and older brother had been killed in the vampire plague.

Her mother and younger brother loved David, and they were happy for the girl to see him.

So everything was great – on the surface.

Hatred still simmered. Crime still blighted areas of Britain. People were desperate. They would steal to eat; they would kill to survive.

But Britain was getting better.

He smiled. That was his mum's slogan.

Britain is getting better.

She had promised an election a year after the end of the Neb regime, and it was coming up in a few months.

Two other political parties were contesting the vote, but they weren't putting up much of a fight. Christine Murray was a hero. Everyone wanted her to lead the New Britain. Her old friend Liz Wilson led the Tories, and she was eager for David's mum to be leader. It was the right thing to do this time round. Perhaps next time, the old politics would return.

Outside, bells rang. He went to the window. Snow was starting to fall. Father Christmas trundled along the street in a horse-drawn cart. The horses were dressed up as reindeer.

It was odd not seeing much traffic on Hyde Park Corner. Years ago, it had been jam-packed with buses and cars and trucks.

But Britain was a nearly a Third World nation. Unemployment and poverty were rife. Most people couldn't afford cars. Most didn't have enough to eat. Thousands were still homeless.

But at least now the aid was coming in. After the vampire plague had ended, the UN started sending in supplies. The Red Cross soon entered Britain, as did Save The Children and other major charities.

Everyone came.

Everyone except Jake Lawton.

David buried his face in his arms.

Jake had never reappeared after the war. Nor had Aaliyah or Apostol Goga.

Someone – one of them, for sure – had killed Nimrod.

If that hadn't happened, the vampires would still be prowling the streets, and the Nebuchadnezzars would still be in charge.

So Nimrod was dead. And David felt certain that, of the three, it was Jake who had killed the monster.

It had to be Jake.

When he'd watched the vampires disintegrate around him at St Augustine's, he couldn't imagine that at that moment, all around the world, every undead creature was becoming extinct.

Incidents of vampire deaths were reported as far afield as China and the United States. It showed how far the plague had spread, and it could have turned the earth into a vampire planet, had Nimrod not been killed.

Jake *had* saved the world.

And he had probably died doing it. He and Aaliyah.

The Iraqi government had been furious when news broke of what had happened. They jailed a number of officials who had been involved with Alfred Fuad's archaeological dig.

The city of Hillah had been devastated by an earthquake, and the whole area had been quarantined. Even UN officials weren't allowed in. Rumours suggested that whatever the Iraqis had found, they wanted it kept secret.

No news of Jake or Aaliyah or Goga was heard. Again, there were rumours that Jake had been arrested by security forces, but he'd escaped.

I hope he got out, thought David.

In his heart, he didn't think he'd ever see Jake Lawton or Aaliyah Sinclair again. And that made him sad. It was the one dark thing in his life now.

His mum's government had honoured Jake and Aaliyah with statues on Parliament Square. They were bronze and stood like warriors, protecting the new parliament building.

David would often visit and stare up at the statues and speak to them, asking Jake if he were OK.

He never answered.

There was a knock on the door.

It was Tamarat.

"Hello," she said.

Every time he saw her, more light came into his life, forcing the darkness into hiding.

She smiled her bright, white smile. Her eyes glittered.

"Are we going to the market?" she said.

He embraced her. She smelled of flowers.

"Are you OK?" she said.

"I am now," he said. "Let's go and have some chestnuts."

PART TEN.

REUNION.

CHAPTER 100.
THE CROFTER.

OUTER HEBRIDES, SCOTLAND – 11.51PM (GMT), NOVEMBER 28, 2016

HE knew the shepherd was Howard Vince. The burned face couldn't hide those mean eyes. And that fake Scottish accent did nothing to cover the former Chief of Staff's plummy tones.

The Nebs have found me, Jake thought.

He knew it would happen.

Although Britain had improved and rebuilt itself over the past few years, old hatreds had returned. Newspapers were cynical and grew more powerful. Politicians were corrupt. People were greedy, just like the old days.

It was as if humans had learned nothing.

Christine Murray remained as Prime Minister, but because of unemployment and poverty, her leadership was under scrutiny.

Her old friend Liz Wilson was now a political enemy, and polls conducted for the forthcoming election had them neck and neck and at each other's throats.

The Nebs, too, had resurfaced. They denied their old alliance with vampires. Just like modern days fascists denied any links they'd had with Nazism.

But they were back. They had regrouped under a new leader. A former actress named Zella Shaw. She was blonde and attractive, and knew how to put on a show for the cameras. She appeared to have no links with the old Neb regime. But he knew different. He'd seen her. He'd seen her at Religion nearly ten years before. She was there, among the leaders of the movement. She was old Neb dressed up as new.

And when Vince had turned up pretending to be a shepherd, he knew they were on to him.

And their resurgence was down to one thing.

They had a vampire in their midst.

The Nebuchadnezzars' objective was to build a new Babylon. Nothing else mattered. It was their secret manifesto. The tradition that gelled them as a movement. They were humans who had an ancient coalition with the undead, and there was no way they'd be back in the limelight, bold and arrogant, unless they had a vampire – and a powerful one.

The croft filled with the smell of meat. He went to the stove and lifted the lid off the pan. The casserole bubbled, and he salivated at the aroma. He gave it a taste. It was perfect and would be ready soon.

Good, he thought, *I'm starving.*

He only ate once a day now. A mountain of a meal at night. He lived like a warrior, seeking out food during the day, gathering fruit, killing prey, eating nuts or berries. Then at home at night, he would cook what he'd killed and have a feast. And after eating he would do something he had not done in years. He would sleep. Every night.

He scratched his beard and wondered about his meeting with Vince earlier that day.

Were they sending a human assassin to kill him? It surely wouldn't be Vince. He was an ex-solider, a former general, but he wasn't strong enough anymore.

More probably they were carrying out reconnaissance on him before a vampire attack.

His heart beat hard. The old fears rose up inside him. He was suddenly not so hungry any more. He put the lid back on the pan and turned off the heat. He would let the food stew, and if he were hungry later, he'd eat.

But for now, he would sit and wait.

The croft was just one room. He slept under furs and blankets. He cooked at the stove. He warmed himself at the fire, reading and thinking. His life was this one room and the island on which it stood. He'd rebuilt the croft five years before, on his own. The villagers would drop by now and again, say hello. But he mostly kept himself to himself. And they left him alone.

Just as he liked it.

He kept abreast of what was happening through his radio. He had no TV, and even if he had one, most stations were only just coming back on air full-time after the vampire wars. It was really only the BBC and Sky who operated now, and it was still a limited service.

He missed his friends, Murray, who was running the country, her son, David, Kwan Mei, all his other allies.

He couldn't make contact with them, because it might put them in danger.

Because ever since Jake Lawton had crawled out of the earth, three months after he'd first entered Irkalla, he knew something was hunting him.

Something that wasn't human.

Something that wasn't dead or alive.

Many would argue he was merely suffering some form of post-traumatic stress. But he knew his fears were real. And that was why, partly, he chose to live in isolation on the Scottish islands.

But he feared now that whatever had come out of Irkalla after him had found him.

That's why the Nebs had turned up.

"They've got a fucking vampire," he told himself.

And it was the creature that had slithered out of the underworld in pursuit of him.

It must have been a powerful vampire. A vampire born of Nimrod. An original sin of the monster. Something unkillable by the Great Hunter's death.

It was a bride.

It was Aaliyah.

He sat by the fire, Apostol Goga's cane leaning against his armchair.

At midnight, something scratched at the door.

Dread filled Lawton. He had to brace himself. He removed the gold ferrule from the cane to reveal the blade.

He opened the door to her, keeping the cane behind his back, and he nearly died of horror.

She wore a white dress that billowed on the breeze. Death had paled her dark skin, but her eyes blazed red. Her mane of pitch-black hair fanned out in the wind.

She was beautiful, and the horror saturated his veins.

But he kept himself steady.

"Your eye looks terrible," she said, her voice like silk. "Are you blind?"

"I can see OK."

She sucked in the air, making a hissing noise. It chilled his blood.

"Why did you leave me, Jake?" she said.

"I looked for you. For months I stayed there, under the earth. I ate rats and insects. I crawled through caves so narrow I nearly suffocated, and I swam great underworld seas. Three months, Aaliyah. But you weren't there. You'd gone. You have gone."

He gripped the cane tightly behind his back. He wondered if he would be able to kill her.

"You sent Vince?" he asked.

"The Nebuchadnezzars have been looking for a queen, and I've given them one. I rewarded Vince for his valour. A touch of my flesh. He died happily. He was weak. Much too weak to be a lover to me. But you're not weak, Jake. You were my lover in life. Will you be mine in death, too?"

She moved towards him.

He swelled his chest.

"You can't come into my home, Aaliyah."

"Why not, babe?"

"Because if you do, I'll kill you."

"My enemy, my lover," she said. "Did you become Ereshkigal's lover before you killed her?"

He said nothing.

"Let me in, Jake."

He stayed quiet.

"Let me in so that you can love me just one last time."

He didn't move.

Her eyes flashed.

"Let me in," she hissed.

He stepped out of her way. She breezed into the croft. He shut the door. He shivered. She'd brought the cold in with her. His grip on the cane tightened.

THE END.

ABOUT THE AUTHOR

Thomas Emson has published eight horror novels, including Maneater, Pariah, and The Vampire Trinity trilogy. He was born and raised in Wales but now lives in England with his wife, the writer Marnie Summerfield Smith, two rabbits, and a rather old, doddery dog named Mac.

ACKNOWLEDGMENTS.

It's done. The Vampire Trinity has been completed. I hope you have enjoyed it. Thank you so much for buying it, for borrowing it, for reading it, and for enjoying it – well, I think that applies to most of you. In fact, thank you for buying, borrowing, reading, enjoying all my books – without you, the readers, it would be pointless. I write to be read; it's as simple as that. So there's the first thank you: my readers. THANK YOU!

Also, everyone at Snowbooks, who have been excited about all my books and supported them. I'm grateful to you, Emma, Anna, and Rob, for the opportunity to be published.

Because of my books, I found myself an agent, Mariam Keen of the Whispering Buffalo Literary Agency, and I thank her for fighting my corner and for her continued faith in me.

Thank you to my mum and dad, who I don't think have read any of these books – and to be honest, I don't think they should. Also my brothers, Rhys Edwards and Dr Llifon Edwards, and their families. They've always supported me, even when I wasn't Thomas Emson, and I'm sure they'll support me when I am no longer Thomas Emson, as well.

Thanks must also go to my brother-in-law Greg Smith and

my remarkable mother-in-law, Maureen Smith MBE, who is astonishingly supportive.

And also to friends: Katie and Kevin Clifford, Lisa Devlin and Chris Found, Graham Bickley and Peggy Riley, Jo Roberts and Richard Corrall, Wojtek Godzisz and Michelle Kreussel, Sue McMackin, Holly Kirwan-Newman (proof-reader extraordinaire) and Greg Lawrence, who have read my books and said nice things about them.

Gratitude also goes to my fellow writers on Twitter, who are fun and informative to follow.

Finally, the biggest thanks of all goes to my utterly wonderful, gorgeous wife Marnie Summerfield Smith, who has been unflinching in her support. Never, ever has she even hinted that I should get a proper, full-time job to pay the bills. She has more faith in me than I do. Her love fuels me, and she is an inspiration.

Thomas Emson
February 2012

ALSO FROM THOMAS EMSON AND SNOWBOOKS:

PARIAH

CHAPTER 1. THE FIFTH.

WHITECHAPEL, LONDON – 12.07AM, MARCH 1, 2011

IT was going to be bloody, she knew that. The knife-man would cut her throat and disembowel her – he'd have to, if he wanted what was inside.

He loomed over her. His green eyes glittered through the holes in the terrifying, asylum-style hood he wore, and his breathing hissed.

In a whisper he said, "You scared of me?"

She said nothing, just stared at the blade gripped tightly in the killer's hand.

Again he said, "You scared of me like your sister was?"

She struggled but couldn't get loose. They'd tied her on a rusty bed frame. The room was tiny. It was filled with shadows. It smelled old, very old – because it was. She knew that. More than a hundred years old and lost in time.

This room had also seen murder. It had tasted blood in the past. For decades it lay hidden, buried in time. But now it was about to become a slaughterhouse again.

Death would come full circle.

The woman ached all over. She felt doomed. Steeling herself, she prepared to die. It was difficult. Death wasn't so terrifying, but dying was.

"Do it, you bastard," she told him. "If you're going to do it, do it now."

She tried to stop her voice from quivering. Her guts churned with dread.

But she wouldn't show it. Not to him. Not to the other two figures in the room, both lurking in the shadows, waiting for her to die.

The knife-man came closer and kneeled next to her and pressed the knife to her throat.

He said, "You'll show me you're scared."

She cried out, and he laughed.

"See?" he said. "See? I was right."

She spat in his face. He recoiled. The blade went from her throat. She struggled again, and the rope around her wrists and ankles cut into her skin.

She screamed, more in frustration than fear.

The knife-man wheeled to face her again, and fury burned in his eyes.

"Cow," he said. "You cow – you show me some respect. You show me awe."

"Fuck you," she said.

"Bitch."

He raised the knife, ready to plunge it into her.

She screamed for help. But help wouldn't come. Anyone who could save her was either dead or disappeared. She'd been abandoned to the fate of her ancestors.

The blade arced down. It sliced through the darkness heading straight for her throat.

She braced herself.

A voice boomed:

"Stop it there!"

The knife-man froze. The blade stopped two inches from her jugular vein.

"Stop it there," said the voice again, quieter this time. It sent a chill through her. The atmosphere grew colder. The shadows thickened.

The knife-man stumbled away. "I was… was going to open her up for you," he said.

The shadows in the room moved, and out of them stepped the knife-man's master. The one who'd controlled him. The one who'd been in his head all these years. The one who had called the knife-man to prepare the way for his return.

The master said, "We've got trespassers."

"What?" said the knife-man.

"A seer and… something else. The seer – it's this one's child again." He gestured at the woman, and she screamed. Her daughter was here. She yelled out the child's name and urged her to run.

The master told the knife-man, "Go get them," and the knife-man went to the door and opened it. Lying on the bed, her mind reeling, the woman thought she heard the sound of wind beating against sails. Or perhaps wings flapping, although they sounded too large for any bird. Maybe it was just her sanity dissolving, and all the noises of the earth were filling her head.

The master said, "You go too, eunuch."

The eunuch shambled out of the shadows.

"You bastard," the woman shouted at the neutered man.

He looked at her and whispered, "I'll look after your girl when you're gone, don't you worry," and he gave her a sneer, spit dribbling down his chin.

The woman stiffened with fear, and a scream locked in her throat.

The eunuch followed the knife-man out into the darkness.

The master loomed over the woman.

His chalk-white face was framed with long, black, greasy hair. His blue lips spread out in a smile, revealing rotting teeth, and his black eyes sparkled. A tuft of hair grew from his chin.

He looked dead.

He was dead.

But he'd never really been alive.

"Now, you be quiet," he said, right in her face. "Or I'll have them cut up your kid in front of you, just for show. You saved her the last time, but not again. This time she'll die. But if you behave, I'll have you killed first, so you won't have to watch. You understand?"

She whimpered.

The master laughed. It was a chilling sound.

She thought of the hope she'd found in this horror – the man who'd already saved her and her daughter once. Where was he now? Had he died too? Had everyone she loved now died? Everyone apart from her child, who was also facing death.

She screamed in desperation.

The chalk-faced monster laughed at her, and his breath stank of sewers. She retched.

He said, "You be sick, whore. Puke all over yourself. Choke on it. Make it easier to cut you open and pull it out of you. You're the fifth. Once you're done, I'll be free. Free of this place. Free of these streets. Then London'll be mine. I'll make it a slaughterhouse. Blood will colour her grey concrete towers. Gore will garland her thoroughfares."

A noise erupted outside the room.

The master's eyes suddenly showed concern. He straightened. There was shrieking and that sound of wind on sails again.

The woman felt drowsy, but she tried to focus.

She said, "Death's coming for you."

The master scowled at her.

Then from outside, a voice shouted, "I've got her."

Now the master smiled again, bearing his yellow teeth. "Now we have two seers to kill. Mother and child."

The woman thrashed about, trying to get loose. But there was no hope. No hope for her or her daughter. Her body slackened, and she slumped into the bed frame. She started to cry. The master laughed at her. But through her tears and his hysterics, she could hear that sound again.

And she knew it wasn't wind on sails.

It was wings. Vast wings that were powerful enough to carry something much larger than a bird. Something like a man. Or maybe an angel.

CHAPTER 2. SWEET VIOLETS.

WHITECHAPEL, LONDON – 12.59AM, NOVEMBER 9, 1888

"SWEET violets... "

She sang to keep the fear at bay.

"...sweeter than the roses... "

It made her feel better, but only a little.

"...covered all over from head to toe... "

It wasn't going to heal things. It wasn't going to wash away the dread.

"...covered all over with sweet violets."

But it was a nice tune, one her father used to sing to her when she was a kid.

She cried, thinking about her dad. It had been years since she'd seen him. He was working at an iron foundry in North Wales, the last she'd heard. He wasn't happy with what she was doing, being a whore in the East End of London.

But she wasn't either. What kind of life was it? But what choice did she have? She had to eat. She had to survive.

Despite having had terrible experiences with men, Mary still dreamed of the perfect one coming along and rescuing her. A prince to whisk her away. A farmer, maybe, like the one in Sweet Violets. Although he wasn't that nice, taking a girl into a barn. But any man would do. Any decent man.

But Mary was getting on a bit. Most twenty-four year olds she knew were married and had kids. Not her. She was an old maid. But not for long. Soon, her misery would be over. Soon, Mary would be dead.

She sat on her bed, humming and looking around the room. This was the sum of her life, what her twenty-four years amounted to – this grubby hole with a table and two chairs, a bed, and two small windows.

The room cost four shillings a week. It was in a three-storey house off Dorset Street, a narrow, 400-foot-long thoroughfare off Commercial Street. It was a rough part of Whitechapel, and that was saying something. Some said it was the worst street in England.

Common lodging-houses crammed the avenue. Slum landlords ran things and controlled most of the activities, much of them illegal. Whores roamed and thugs prowled. Drunkenness and violence were rife. Illegal prize-fighting left blood and body parts in the dirt. Stolen goods were fenced. Anyone stupid enough to get lost down here was beaten and robbed.

There was grease and there was grime. There was piss and shit. There were rats, there were dogs, and there were humans, all packed together. The air carried a putrid smell. It was the odour of thousands of unfortunates who'd lived and died there over the years.

Mary's skin would layer the ground before morning. Her bones would powder the walls. Her blood would fill the drains.

They would rip her like they'd ripped the others. Tear her open and plough around inside her for the treasure, the thing that gave *him* strength.

Him.

The ghost that stalked Whitechapel. The most terrifying killer in history. The one they called Jack.

And he was hunting her. She shivered. There was not much she could do. Nowhere to hide, nowhere to run. She knew he was coming, because she could see him. She had gifts. She had foresight. She could see the future.

And her future was death.

"Sweet violets, sweeter than the roses ... "

Such a funny song. Jokey and naughty.

Mary tried to smile while thinking about the lyrics. But it was a struggle to make her mouth curve up into a grin. Her lips quivered. Her eyes welled. Tears were easier. Her fear was strong.

Outside, someone screamed. A woman. Mary didn't flinch. It was normal. Silence, not noise, made you alert in Dorset Street.

A man cursed, saying, "Fucking tart."

The woman screamed again, begging to be left alone.

Another man said, "Cut her fucking nose off, Charlie."

Mary shut her eyes and laced her fingers together. Would a prayer do any good? It hadn't helped the others. Not Mary Ann, who'd been butchered in Bucks' Row on August 31. Throat cut, guts opened. A policeman had found her lying in a pool of blood. She'd put up a fight. Her teeth had been knocked out, punched after she'd punched first, probably.

That was Mary Ann – five-foot-two and hard as nails.

But being tough hadn't saved her.

Two days later, the man came from Austria. He came to look for Mary and found her in the Ten Bells, drinking. He said, "You have to come with me," and he gathered them all at an inn – Mary, Annie Chapman, Catherine Eddowes, Elizabeth Stride. They'd never met. But they were all prostitutes in Whitechapel. And according to the man, they all had a special gift.

A gift that would make their lives even more dangerous than they already were. A gift that could kill them.

He told them everything, and not all of them believed. Mary wasn't sure. Hearing what he said made her feel special. She'd always wanted to be special. But not so special that she might die.

Annie had refused to accept what the man had said, and she left in a huff.

But a week after Mary Ann's death, she was dead too, just like the man had warned.

Mary looked out of the small window. It was dark. But it was always dark there. Very little light found its way down Dorset Street. It was as if the day kept its distance. The night owned this part of the East End. The night and the darkness.

And a short walk from where Mary sat now, it had swallowed up Annie.

She had left her common-lodging house at 35 Dorset Street at 2.00am on September 8. She'd been drunk and needed money for a bed. Annie was happy to fuck for it. "Means nothing to me," she'd say. "And means nothing to them, after it's done."

She'd walked up Little Paternoster Row, and was heading towards Christ Church, Spitalfields.

But they got her in the darkness. They got her and cut her throat. They got her and ripped her open, taking her womb and parts of her cunny and bladder. They got her and stole her soul, just like the man had said.

Two down.

"Another three must be ripped."

Ever since Annie's death, that had been the whisper wending its way through the streets.

"Another three must be ripped."

Mary heard it wherever she went. She'd wheel round in a panic, expecting to see his terrible face.

But he was never there. Only his voice.

"Another three must be ripped."

And Mary knew one of those three would be her. She knew it the moment the man had met her at the Ten Bells and told her who she really was, told her she had a gift – a gift for hunting evil.

There was a fight going on outside. Shouts and curses filled the night. Mary heard a struggle. Men kicked and punched. Flesh and bone being smashed. Mary winced with every blow. But it comforted her. A fight attracting a crowd meant her killers would not be able to skulk to her door unseen.

Glass smashed. A crowd bellowed. Voices said, "Smash him, Bill," and, "Glass him, cut him up."

Women screamed.

"Break his face!"

"Cut his balls off!"

"Fucking Jew!"

"Christ killer!"

Jew, thought Mary. The East End was full of them, Spitalfields especially. But they stayed away from Dorset Street. But plenty of Irish. Plenty of Frenchies and Italians. Scots and Welsh, too. The place was a melting pot.

Outside, the noise grew. Insults were hurled. More Jew abuse.

They didn't usually come round here. They rarely caused trouble. But every race had its thugs. And maybe a few young Jew bulls had swaggered down here to booze at the Ringers pub on the corner of Dorset Street, where Mary sometimes drank.

She listened now. The fight went on. But now there was more than one tussle. She could make out a few. Gangs going at each other. Blades and bottles drawn.

A whistle pierced the cacophony.

Mary jerked, sitting up.

The whistle came again.

"Coppers," someone shouted.

Another whistle speared through the noise.

The fighters and the spectators scarpered. Mary heard their feet pound the pavement, their dark shapes shooting past her window.

And then came silence.

Cold, deadly silence.

The silence you should fear on Dorset Street.

She froze, her skin crawling.

A dark shape moved past her door. She saw it in the gap at the bottom – the two-inch space where the cold and the rain and the fog came in, and through which evil could seep.

Dread turned her heart to stone.

And it cracked into a thousand pieces when a pale, white hand slipped under the door, the fingers scuttling like spiders' legs.